THE
QUEEN'S
LADY

Joanna spent twenty-five years at the BBC writing and presenting for radio and television. Gripped by Shakespeare's history plays, Joanna originally began researching King Henry V's 'fair Kate' as a schoolgirl, and the story of Catherine de Valois and the birth of the Tudor dynasty went on to become her first historical novel, *The Agincourt Bride*. Joanna is now an internationally bestselling novelist with a legion of fans around the globe. *The Queen's Lady* is her seventh novel. She is married and lives in Wiltshire, England.

f /Joanna Hickson
🐦 @joannahickson

THE
QUEEN'S
LADY

JOANNA
HICKSON

HarperCollins*Publishers*

HarperCollins*Publishers* Ltd
1 London Bridge Street,
London SE1 9GF

www.harpercollins.co.uk

HarperCollins*Publishers*
1st Floor, Watermarque Building, Ringsend Road
Dublin 4, Ireland

First published by HarperCollins*Publishers* 2022
This edition published 2023
1

A catalogue record for this book is available from the British Library

ISBN (PB): 978-0-00-830565-9

Set in Adobe Caslon by
Palimpsest Book Production Limited, Falkirk, Stirlingshire

Printed and bound in the UK using 100% Renewable Electricity
by CPI Group (UK) Ltd

This book is produced from independently certified FSC™ paper
to ensure responsible forest management.

For more information visit: www.harpercollins.co.uk/green

For English book-clubbers Sophie and Katie, and Deborah and Lucinda who spread the word in Australia. Keep on reading!

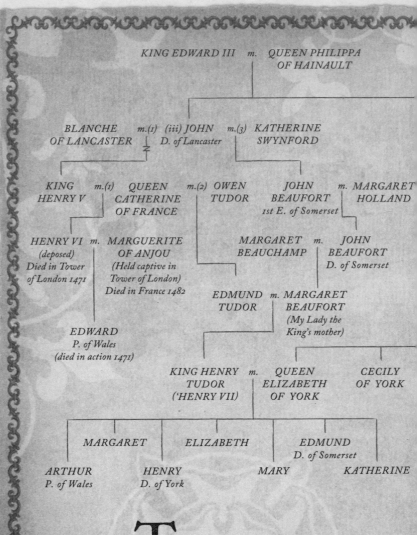

KING EDWARD III m. QUEEN PHILIPPA
OF HAINAULT

BLANCHE m.(1) (iii) JOHN m.(3) KATHERINE
OF LANCASTER D. of Lancaster SWYNFORD

KING m.(1) QUEEN m.(2) OWEN JOHN m. MARGARET
HENRY V CATHERINE TUDOR BEAUFORT HOLLAND
OF FRANCE 1st E. of Somerset

HENRY VI m. MARGUERITE MARGARET m. JOHN
(deposed) OF ANJOU BEAUCHAMP BEAUFORT
Died in Tower (Held captive in D. of Somerset
of London 1471 Tower of London)
Died in France 1482

EDMUND m. MARGARET
TUDOR BEAUFORT
(My Lady the
King's mother)

EDWARD
P. of Wales
(died in action 1471)

KING HENRY m. QUEEN CECILY
TUDOR ELIZABETH OF YORK
('HENRY VII') OF YORK

MARGARET ELIZABETH EDMUND
D. of Somerset

ARTHUR HENRY MARY KATHERINE
P. of Wales D. of York

TUDOR ANCESTRY

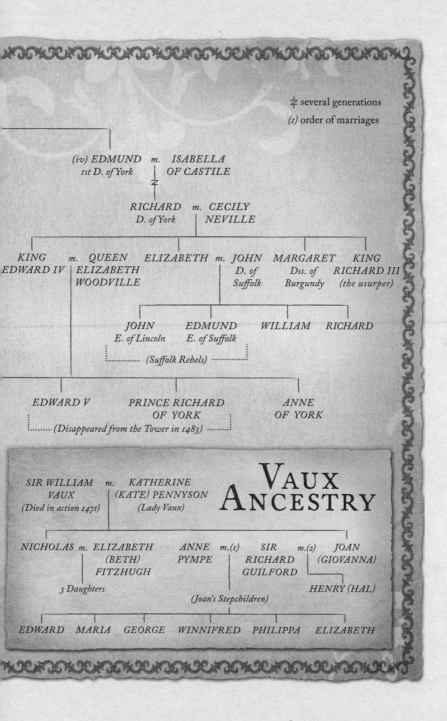

several generations

(1) order of marriages

(iv) EDMUND   m.   ISABELLA
1st D. of York   OF CASTILE

RICHARD   m.   CECILY
D. of York   NEVILLE

KING   m.   QUEEN   ELIZABETH   m.   JOHN   MARGARET   KING
EDWARD IV   ELIZABETH   D. of   Dss. of   RICHARD III
                  WOODVILLE   Suffolk   Burgundy   (the usurper)

JOHN   EDMUND   WILLIAM   RICHARD
E. of Lincoln   E. of Suffolk
.... (Suffolk Rebels) ....

EDWARD V   PRINCE RICHARD   ANNE
                        OF YORK   OF YORK
.... (Disappeared from the Tower in 1483) ....

SIR WILLIAM   m.   KATHERINE
VAUX   (KATE) PENNYSON
(Died in action 1471)   (Lady Vaux)

VAUX ANCESTRY

NICHOLAS m. ELIZABETH   ANNE   m.(1)   SIR   m.(2)   JOAN
                  (BETH)   PYMPE   RICHARD   (GIOVANNA)
                  FITZHUGH   GUILFORD

3 Daughters   HENRY (HAL)

                          (Joan's Stepchildren)

EDWARD   MARIA   GEORGE   WINNIFRED   PHILIPPA   ELIZABETH

DRAMATIS PERSONAE

The Tudor Court:

Henry VII – *in 1485, as Henry Tudor, Earl of Richmond, was victorious over Richard III at the Battle of Bosworth*

Elizabeth of York – *Queen Elizabeth, wife of King Henry VII*

Lady Margaret Beaufort, Countess of Richmond & Derby – *official title, 'My Lady the King's Mother'*

Princess Margaret – *eldest daughter of the King and Queen*

Princess Mary – *second surviving daughter of the King and Queen*

Sir Richard Guildford – *Royal Master of Ordnance & Weaponry, Comptroller of King's Chamber*

Joan, Lady Guildford – *lady-in-waiting to Queen Elizabeth; Lady Governess to the younger royal children; Guildford children; Edward, Maria, George, Pippa, Winifred, Lizzie; by Joan: Henry (Hal) (cf)*

Henry (Hal) Guildford – *Joan's son and page/squire to Prince Henry/Harry*

Katherine (Kate), Lady Vaux – *Joan's mother; friend and lady-in-waiting to Lady Margaret Beaufort (cf)*

Sir Henry Wyatt – *Master of the King's Jewels & Comptroller of the Mint*

Sir Thomas Brandon – *Privy Councillor & Master of the King's Horse*

Charles Brandon – *his nephew & squire/knight to Prince Henry*

Richard, Earl of Suffolk – *York claimant to the English throne; in exile*

Scottish Court:

James IV, King of Scots

Alexander Hume, Lord of Fast Castle

Earl of Morton, Lord of Dalkeith Castle

Poyntz Family:

Sir Robert Poyntz – *Anthony's father & Chancellor to Katherine of Aragon*

Lady Meg Poyntz – *Anthony's mother*

Anthony Poyntz – *Lawyer & former squire to Sir Richard Guildford*

Elizabeth Poyntz – *Anthony's wife*

Francis Poyntz – *Anthony's brother*

Margaret, Nicholas & Mary – *surviving Poyntz children*

Miscellaneous characters:

Martin – *steward in Guildford household*

Hugh – *servant at the Tower House*

Jake – *cook at the Tower House*

Hetty, Mildy & Rose – *Joan's personal maids*

Sim – *servant to the Guildfords*

John Whitby – *Prior of Gisburn – a monk*

Master John Grice – *Queen Elizabeth's apothecary*

PART ONE

I

The Tower of London

April 1502

I STOOD STOCK STILL under the alder trees, staring up into a tracery of branches budding with spring growth and dotted with the silhouettes of hunched ravens, their hooked beaks buried in chest feathers fluffed up for warmth. The clouds above the River Thames hung silver-grey, tinged with the blush of a hidden, sinking sun. Not a breath of wind stirred. It was an eerily still dusk that set off alarm bells in my head, while the noises of the city gradually subsided around the Tower of London.

My sigh alerted the girl beside me. 'What is it, Mother Joan?' she whispered. 'There's such a strange atmosphere.' It was my youngest stepdaughter, fourteen years old and apparently as affected as I was by the sense of anomaly.

'Yes, there is, Lizzie.' My voice emerged soft and low to match hers. 'When the ravens come in to roost they are normally vocal, reassuring each other as darkness falls, exchanging goodnight blessings before rest. But this evening they're silent, as if awaiting some event.'

'A sad event?' The girl's voice shook a little as she spoke.

'I hope not.' I put a consoling arm around her. I didn't

want her to be frightened but there was a reason why ravens were considered birds of ill omen. They could sense death. After all they mostly fed on carrion. It was part of their nature.

A sudden burst of sound sprayed down from the treetops as the roosting birds unanimously fluttered their wings and emitted a chaotic series of 'kaarks', like trumpeters tuning their instruments or a town crier loudly ringing his bell before making a public announcement. Perhaps it was an acknowledgement of some wind-borne message, for afterwards the big black birds fell silent once more and shuffled closer together, finally settling for sleep. Deep shadows began to creep up the White Tower and the sprawling fortress lapsed into its nightly routine. Footsteps died away on the cobbled lanes between the double curtain walls and torches began to flicker on the battlements, to light the guards as they stamped out their patrols.

I took Lizzie's hand and we made our way through the arch that led from the tree-lined Green, heading for the Water Gate to cross the moat to our home on the Thames quayside. 'A false alarm,' I said reassuringly, but her frown and pursed lips indicated that she was not convinced.

The year was moving on. The excitement and pageantry surrounding the wedding of Arthur, Prince of Wales, to Princess Katherine of Aragon and the Christmas and New Year celebrations that followed were now a dim memory. The royal newlyweds had made the long journey from London to Ludlow Castle on the Welsh border, where Prince Arthur was learning the art of ruling by presiding over the Council of the Marches. Although I had been seconded to Katherine's retinue during the wedding celebrations, I had not gone with them but gladly returned to my regular post as one of Queen Elizabeth's ladies-in-waiting. Now, as Easter approached, King Henry had summoned his court to Greenwich Palace to celebrate with all the usual processions and lavish feasting that marked the end of Lent. Afterwards, leaving my husband, Sir Richard Guildford, King Henry's Comptroller of the Household and Master of Ordnance, to join his fellow Privy Councillors at their traditional Easter meeting, I had taken a ferry upriver to our Tower of London home where I had been reunited with a delighted Lizzie, fretful and bored with the company of her governess. As the dusk gathered that evening we had made our way to the juvenile ravens' roost in the trees on Tower Green.

When we returned to the house and entered the hall where the trestle was laid for supper, unexpectedly we found Sir Richard waiting for us, pacing the room impatiently. 'You've stayed out very late, Joan,' he complained. 'I presume you've been with those damned birds.'

Chilled by the sharp wind blowing off the river I hurried to warm myself at the fire and it was Lizzie who responded. 'They seem very restless, Father. Mother Joan says something untoward has disturbed them.'

'Oh?' My husband raised a sceptical eyebrow. 'Is ravenish the latest of your many languages, Joan?'

Being accustomed to his ambivalence towards my raven obsession, I summoned a smile and dodged the question. 'You're supposed to be at the palace, sir. Was the Privy Council meeting cut short?'

With a grunt of irritation, he took his seat at the centre

of the cloth-covered trestle, while a servant placed a dish of fragrant-smelling shellfish on the board. 'No, it was cancelled,' he said, removing his eating knife from its belt-scabbard and placing it on the cloth, ready to partake of the meal. 'The king has given out that he is unwell but actually he is angry with the queen. They have fallen out over something.'

Lizzie and I removed our cloaks and handed them to a hovering maidservant. 'Everything seemed as usual when I left the queen this morning. What is this something?'

'I'm hungry. Let us give thanks and I'll tell you.' Richard threw his linen napkin over his shoulder.

When we had taken our places he swiftly muttered a grace and began cutting into a fresh manchet loaf, offering us portions from the end of his knife.

'King Henry has been obliged to take action after his agents uncovered a fresh Yorkist plot against the throne,' he began.

I nodded and frowned. 'Yes, when we arrived at the Tower today I was extremely surprised to hear that Lord Courtenay has been confined here.' Lord William Courtenay, heir to the Earl of Devon, was married to Queen Elizabeth's younger sister, Catherine of York. 'That must have upset Elizabeth.'

'But that's not all,' Richard continued. 'His properties have been searched and confiscated and his wife and children evicted.' His appetite did not seem affected by this extreme penalty, as he ladled a hearty portion onto his trencher.

'Then I fully understand why the queen is upset,' I said, trying to control my anger at this development. 'Her sister and her young children left homeless and penniless by order of her husband! That is surely a situation hard for her to bear?'

Silence fell between us as Richard lifted another meaty morsel to his mouth and wiped his fingers on the napkin. His voice acquired a tone of forbearing. 'Actually, they are neither homeless nor penniless, because they are living just up the river at Baynard's Castle – by the queen's invitation. That is what has infuriated the king. He did not grant her use of the castle in order to aid the relatives of a suspected traitor.'

'Surely he can't expect the queen not to come to the aid of her sister? Especially when there are young children involved.'

'You don't appreciate how much stress he is under, Joan. He had thought his kingdom safe once Prince Arthur's marriage secured England's alliance with Spain. But now this new conspiracy shows that there is still a strong Yorkist element at large, plotting against him. Also he is worried about Arthur's health.'

Lizzie had been quietly eating and listening to our conversation but now she ventured a question. 'What is wrong with Prince Arthur?'

She and the prince were much of an age, which explained her interest, but I could see that Richard was suddenly wishing he hadn't mentioned him. 'Nothing serious, Lizzie; it's just that King Henry thinks he is too thin and prone to agues.'

'King Henry was the one who insisted the marriage go ahead, despite his son's youth,' I pointed out. Arthur had been just fifteen, his bride a year older. 'And it was he who sent him off, back to the wind and wilds of the Welsh border. The queen told me they'd had word from Ludlow that Arthur was sick. She's praying for the boy's return to health but she made no mention of a quarrel with the king.'

Lizzie couldn't hold back a smirk. 'I can't imagine George having been married at fifteen. He still thought girls were stupid and he wouldn't have known what to do in bed!'

I smothered a smile. Her brother George had been married three years ago at the age of twenty. He was now a father and running his wife's estates in Essex.

Richard didn't find her remarks amusing. 'What would you know about it?' he snapped. 'You're too young to have any opinions on marriage.'

His daughter dropped her head, feigning contrition. But Richard was wrong; Lizzie was well informed about what to expect from marriage. I had seen to that. Not that I approved of girls being married before sixteen. I had managed to avoid it myself until my mid-twenties but even so I had suffered a traumatic childbirth. The thought of a girl barely out of childhood having a similar experience, or even dying from it, wrenched at my heart.

Richard continued to express his support for the king's actions. 'Henry is angry that the kingdom is obviously still at risk of treachery, even from those closest to the throne.'

My eyes grew wide and round. 'Are you suggesting that the queen herself is under suspicion, Richard? Should she fear arrest also?'

Lizzie's head jerked up in astonishment when I asked this and Richard's face suffused. 'Of course not! Do not even dare to suggest that, Joan – and Lizzie, you did not hear it! You misinterpret me. The royal marriage is on as firm a foundation as Westminster Abbey, where it was solemnised. Now I suggest we discuss the matter no further.'

Later, when we had retired, there was some urgent hammering on the door of our bedchamber and the voice of our long-serving steward, Martin. 'Sir Richard – my lady! A royal messenger is here, demanding to speak with you.'

We both sat bolt upright, any thought of sleep vanishing.

'I'll go,' said Richard, throwing back the covers. In the darkness I heard him swear as some part of his anatomy connected with a solid object.

I swung my legs over the side of the bed. 'Not without me! There must be bad news. The ravens are never wrong.'

I just had time to wrap myself in my chamber robe before Richard wrenched the door open and a handheld lantern threw light into the room. 'What's this all about, Martin?' he demanded.

'He refused to say, sir.' The steward sounded offended. 'He has a sealed letter and insisted it be handed personally to you or Lady Guildford. I'm sorry I had to disturb you.'

'You had no choice.' Richard clapped the steward on the shoulder reassuringly and I followed them down the stairs, the stones cold on my bare feet.

A single torch, hurriedly lit and thrust into a bracket, revealed a liveried messenger pacing the hall, his letter pouch hanging open. 'From Sir Richard Pole, sir,' the man said, handing the missive over.

A large seal bore the three ostrich feathers of the Prince of Wales. Dread swept through me like a tidal surge. Any message delivered at this hour would not bear good news.

In tense silence, Richard frowned deeply over the letter

and then handed it to me. 'Prince Arthur has died,' he said. 'Two nights ago.'

I made the sign of the cross as my eyes scanned the page. The official announcement had clearly been written by a scribe, doubtless one of several copies, which fast couriers must have galloped to deliver to members of the Privy Council. Before he signed this one, the prince's chamberlain, Sir Richard Pole, had added a personal note.

The exact cause of death is not yet clear. The princess has also been ill but is now expected to recover. You will need to arrange a mourning fusillade from the Tower to alert London. And if she is not with her, my wife suggests that Lady Guildford should rush to Queen Elizabeth's side, to give support in her grief.

Sir Richard Pole's wife was Queen Elizabeth's cousin, Margaret of Clarence, the only surviving child of King Edward the Fourth's treasonous brother George and now serving as chief lady-in-waiting to the Princess of Wales. Lady Pole knew very well of my intimate friendship with the queen, who may very likely, even at this late hour, be on her knees at Greenwich, praying for her precious eldest son's return to health. If I hurried I could break the terrible news to her; surely much better than being woken from sleep to receive a soulless message written by a scribe.

'I must go to her immediately, Richard,' I said, passing the letter back. 'Martin, please send for a ferryboat to take me to Greenwich.'

2

Greenwich Palace

April 1502

THE RIVER THAMES WAS an ever-changeable waterway. In daylight it bustled with activity, rippling around bend after bend like a sinuous length of brown silk, bearing craft of every description. Busy ferryboats bustled from bank to bank, dodging sturdy sail-driven wherries laden with fresh produce from upstream farms, their crews skilfully using wind and tide to tack around the galley barges of the rich and powerful being rowed to Greenwich.

At night however the river fell quiet. Occasionally, light flickered over the water's surface from a lantern on a passing ferryboat but in the small hours these were rare and the soft splash of the blades was broken only by the occasional thud, as an unseen obstacle glanced off the side of the ferry. I spent the journey listening to the creak of the oars and wondering how I should break the disastrous news to an already emotionally distressed queen.

As I had predicted she was not sleeping in her velvet-hung bedstead but praying in her private oratory off the bedchamber. Pushing the door open I heard the softly whispered stream of her prayers and smelled the fragrance of beeswax from the altar. Her fur-lined chamber robe fell in soft piles around her kneeling figure and her red-gold hair, already streaked with silver, strayed down her back and reflected the candlelight like dying embers.

'Forgive me, your grace,' I murmured. 'May I speak with you?'

She turned, her brow creased in a fierce frown, but it cleared a little when she saw it was me and rose stiffly, gathering the folds of her robe around her. 'Lady Guildford – Joan – what are you doing here?' Then her cheeks, which had flushed with irritation at the interruption, suddenly drained of colour and she reached to steady herself on my outstretched arm. I felt her nails dig into my skin and suppressed a cry of pain as she read my face. 'Oh no, you bring bad news!'

I gave a nod and a sigh. 'Come, sit, your grace.' A carved bench was set against the wall of the small sanctuary and I led her to it. She sat and I knelt before her, taking her trembling hands in mine. 'I am so sorry to have to tell you that your beloved son, the Prince of Wales, has died in Ludlow.'

Her pale face grew sheet-white. 'Oh dear God, I knew it would happen. I prayed and prayed but the Lord has turned his back.' Her eyes latched onto mine and an unspoken flood of utter despair swirled between us. 'Oh, my beautiful son, Joan! My stainless firstborn prince!'

I nodded solemnly. 'Yes, he was beautiful and a prince of great promise. Heaven has received a treasure.'

'Who will tell the king?' moaned Elizabeth, her voice cracking. 'His prized son and heir is dead. These dreadful tidings could break his heart.'

'The letter from Sir Richard Pole is addressed to the members of his Privy Council, your grace,' I told her gently. 'Most of them are still here at Greenwich and they will have decided who should break the news when the king awakes.'

By now tears were pouring down her cheeks. 'My lord will need me when he hears. God has ignored my prayers and our dynasty is threadbare.'

I had taken the precaution of bringing a supply of linen kerchiefs from the Tower and rummaged in my belt-purse for one, shaking my head as I handed it to her. 'Do not say so, your grace! You have three more healthy children.'

The queen sat back, making full use of the kerchief, which seemed to rally her forces. 'You are right, Joan. I need to arm myself with just such encouraging words if I am to comfort the king. Princess Margaret is here in my household but you can fetch Prince Henry and Princess Mary here from Eltham Palace and we will all mourn together. Henry must see that there is still a future for the Tudor throne.' There was a long pause and I was struggling to summon more words of consolation when Elizabeth suddenly sat up straight. 'Besides, we can have more children. I am not too old. Another child would ease my lord's despair.'

My heart skipped a beat. I had served the queen on and off for sixteen years and followed every detail of her valiant efforts to provide England with the dynasty she knew was essential to establish peace and unity in what had been a war-ridden realm. Between the six babes she had borne successfully there had been several heart-breaking miscarriages and the misery of Princess Elizabeth's death at the age of three. Then more recently, after she had birthed a third son, Edmund, suffering intense leg pain and other post-natal problems, barely a year later came the agony of the little boy's demise. Lately also her monthly bleeds had been erratic and profuse and in February, as her thirty-sixth birthday approached, she had confided to me that she hoped God would spare her from conceiving further children so that she might continue to serve the kingdom in other ways and look to Arthur and Katherine to provide the next generation of Tudors. So this change of heart was certainly courageous. However, although I did not say so, I could not believe it was wise.

With a deep breath the queen pressed the kerchief back into my hands and stood up. 'I know you will find the right words to tell Harry and Mary of their brother's death, Joan,' she said. 'Take them to the chapel to pray for Arthur's soul and then, when they are strong enough, please bring them here to Greenwich to comfort me and the king.'

Someone had woken the queen's chief lady-in-waiting, Lady Stafford, who now appeared in the queen's chamber and I was able to make my departure for Eltham. I was directed to a smaller vessel for this journey, one that could navigate the River Quaggy, a tributary much shallower than the Thames. There was a hooded shelter in the stern but it had an open front and although the sun was beginning to rise, the spring air was still cold and I huddled under the furs provided. Had it been warmer I might have managed to doze during the long pull the rowers had against the current but as it was I spent the time shivering and pondering how I might break the sad tidings to the two royal children.

I assumed it would be the princess who would be most distressed by Prince Arthur's death. When only four, Princess

Mary had greatly mourned the passing of her baby brother Edmund, whereas Prince Harry had shown only limited sorrow. However, when I found the two children together, breaking their fast, and told them as gently as I could of their brother Arthur's passing, it was the ten-year-old prince who immediately broke down.

'It cannot be! I saw him married!' he moaned, tears pouring down his cheeks. 'I escorted his bride down the aisle at St Paul's only a few months ago! He was fine then, well and happy; how can he be dead?'

'The cause is not yet known,' I said, hesitating to put a comforting arm around him as I might have done in the past. Approaching his eleventh birthday, he was becoming very aware of his status and I feared that familiarity of that kind, if offered, might invite rejection. 'I suggest we go to the chapel now. He will need your prayers to speed his soul to heaven.'

'It will be too late!' the prince declared, angrily swiping unwanted tears from his cheeks with the palms of his hands. 'Anyway, Arthur will not need help to get to heaven. His soul was spotless and now he has left me to rule England alone.'

I was surprised that he had so swiftly analysed his own radically altered position. Six-year-old Mary stamped her foot. 'Stop weeping, Harry! Mother Guildford is right, we should go the chapel and you can't go red-eyed.'

'Mother Guildford' was the name the princesses had given me, when I became their governess. My son had been nine when he came with me to Eltham Palace to serve as one of Prince Harry's pages and because Hal called me 'lady mother', the royal children used a similar form of address.

Now the prince turned his moist and frowning gaze on me, as if he had only just registered who it was. 'Hal should come to the chapel, too, Mother Guildford. Arthur liked him when they met at court. He is still in my chamber.'

I nodded. 'I will fetch him for you.' Without comment I handed him another of my clean kerchiefs, which he tucked up the sleeve of his chemise.

When the two royal children were settled before the altar with one of the chaplains I went to the prince's bedchamber and found Hal helping a chamberlain strip the bedclothes. At one time the two young Henrys had shared the four-poster but a wheeled truckle pulled from beneath it showed me that although Hal might still be held in high favour, he now slept nearer the floor.

The shutters were open, illuminating his surprise at seeing me. 'I thought you were Prince Harry, lady mother,' he said, abandoning his task to bend his knee and rise to brush his lips on my cheek. 'Where is he?'

'Be calm, Hal,' I said, returning his kiss. 'Your friend has received some bad news and is in the royal chapel seeking solace. He requires your presence there.'

'What bad news?' he asked in alarm. 'Is someone ill?'

'I will tell you as we walk but you will need a jacket and shoes, my son.' I gestured at his shirt and hose, the only garb he wore as he worked.

He hauled on his tawny livery and cast wildly about for his shoes. I had to catch his arm and point to a pair, stowed neatly under a chair. 'There they are. What I have to tell you has affected the prince greatly. It will be your task to comfort him, not appear before him distraught and dishevelled.' Although older than the prince, Hal was still only twelve and death to boys of their age was surely a grim subject. I crossed to a table where a set of bone combs lay before a mirror. 'Here, let me tidy your hair. Then we must go.'

As we walked down the cloister I revealed the demise of Prince Arthur and Hal was predictably shocked. 'This is terrible news, Mother! We hardly knew Arthur well but Harry worshipped his brother from afar. He must be very distressed.'

'Yes, he is. It will be up to you to keep him calm. Think of some words of comfort but not so maudlin as to make him cry again. He won't want to appear red-eyed before the servants.'

Hal gave me a long-suffering look, as if I was stating the obvious. 'I know how to turn his mind from grim reality. That is why he likes me.'

'His court jester, Hal?' I suggested with a faint smile.

He frowned and shook his head. 'No, but I have learned that wit and good humour are essential qualities in a courtier!'

3

Greenwich Palace

T HE QUEEN RETURNED FROM the king's apartments pale
and shivering, her hands tearing ineffectively at her headdress. 'You must remove this!' she cried desperately. 'The frontlet
is too tight and the hood too heavy. My head is bursting!'

I hastened to unpin the heavy lappet hood and swept it
away, while one of the maids of honour tackled the offending
jewelled frontlet. It had left a red line along the edge of
Elizabeth's forehead and I made a mental note to chastise
whoever had tied it.

When their solemn prayers were completed several small
ferryboats had brought the young prince and princess and
a number of their attendants to Greenwich Palace. There I
left them in their apartments and hurried to the queen's
chamber. If all was well it had been my intention to summon
the children but one look at their desperate mother told me
this was not the right time.

We stripped off her robe and kirtle and drew back the
bedcovers and when she was safely propped up on the pillows,
I poured a good measure of apple spirit and held it to her
lips. She took several gulps and for a moment her sobbing
ceased and she drew a deep breath. 'Oh, that is what I needed,
Joan. You always know the right treatment.'

'Prince Harry and Princess Mary are here but I think you should rest before seeing them. You have had no sleep and a terrible shock.'

Elizabeth closed her eyes with a slight nod of the head. 'Yes, you are right. Thank you for bringing them. I would not want to upset them by fainting.'

'Did you manage to bring any comfort to the king, your grace? He will be grieving terribly, I am sure. Prince Arthur was his pride and joy – and yours, too, of course.'

Deep lines creased her brow and her next remarks troubled me. 'It is true that Henry treasured his firstborn but when I look back I'm not sure that I ever really got to know Arthur. I provided the realm with the necessary heir but I never came to feel motherly towards him. Not like the younger children.' Her voice grew hoarse. 'You saw him taken from me as a tiny baby, Joan, and left with strange nurses and then Henry sent him away to Ludlow as soon as he was in hosen.' Her face crumpled and she cried out loud, 'Dear God, what did we do to him? Poor boy – he must have thought his mother did not love him, but I did – I did!'

She began to sob once more, loudly and inconsolably, hands tearing at her hair, tears flowing like the Thames at floodtide. Then her whole body began to shake. She made a violent turn and collapsed into the pillows, beating them with her fists so hard that the seams split and feathers began to fly. I managed to grab one hand and held it, expecting the storm to subside. But I although the hands soon grew quiet, the sobs did not diminish. Eventually, I crept from the chamber and instructed her usher to go and beg the Lord Chamberlain to tell the king that his wife was prostrate with grief and badly needed him.

Even if his attendants managed to convey the message to him I was far from certain that King Henry would be in a fit state to answer such a summons, and so I was caught unawares when he suddenly appeared at the door of the bedchamber, the sound of his arrival obscured by the dreadful moaning still emanating from his overwrought queen, lying face down among the tear-stained pillows.

Some backwards jerks of the king's hand signalled me from the room and although I caught his curt instruction to 'Leave us until I call!', I lingered on the threshold just long enough to witness him throw himself onto the bed beside his wife, crooning, 'I am here, Bessie. Calm yourself, my dearest.'

I had never heard words of such earnest intimacy uttered by the king to his queen and I craved to hear more but discretion and the presence of a small group of ladies hovering in the anteroom obliged me to move through the doorway and the dreadful sound of sustained sobbing faded behind the carved oak panels.

With no inkling as to how long the king would stay, I decided to visit the royal children again and try to explain the absence of their parents. I found Prince Harry in his schoolroom with Hal and several other young members of his household busy pursuing a variety of pastimes: reading, plucking at stringed instruments, writing poetry and playing chess. The prince's tutor was wandering among them, peering over shoulders, offering advice on rhythm and rhyme and keeping an eye on the chess battle between the prince and Hal.

With tactful diplomacy I attempted to brief the tutor about the absence of the king and queen but our murmured conversation evidently did not take place far enough from the prince's sharp ears, for while Hal was considering his next move, Prince Harry turned in our direction, his eyes wide and his brow creased.

'I think it may be some time before my royal father truly believes that his best-loved son is no longer with us, Mother Guildford.' His words cut like flint. It was the moment I became aware that Prince Harry was acutely conscious of being something of an also-ran in the king's eyes. 'I am half minded to go back to Eltham, because now that Easter is past we could be out on the chase and my favourite hunting steed is in the stables there.'

Hal completed his move and looked up. 'But it's raining, Harry. Even in Eltham Park we'd have dull hunting in the rain. It spoils the scent.'

Scarcely waiting for the chess piece to be placed, the prince had swooped on his opponent's rook with his knight. 'Checkmate, Hal!' he crowed. 'You were too busy ear-wigging! Anyway, these April showers are of no consequence.' He leapt to his feet, sending the chessmen sprawling. 'But let's just have a game of bowls in the privy garden. Who'll take us on?'

The tutor and I exchanged glances. 'At least we'll know where they are when the king calls,' he muttered, as we watched the other attendants abandon their books and instruments and follow the chess victor from the room. Judging by their cheerful quips, they were well used to the sudden whims of their young leader, and tipping the rolled brim of his cap, Hal shot me a sly wink in passing. He took pride in his skill at chess. I wondered how often he contrived to lose a game at such a carefully chosen moment.

21

Leaving them to their sport, I wended my way to Princess Mary's apartment, which offered blurred views of the Thames through rain-spattered windows. Her seamstress-attendant watched as, with unsteady stitches, her charge attempted to follow a pattern inked on a strip of linen. Although she persevered, embroidery was not really Mary's metier and I could see that she had already pricked her finger, for a streak of blood was smeared on the fabric. 'Mother Guildford,' she said, a look of relief replacing the frown on her pretty face as she lowered her handiwork. 'How is our mother? Has she sent for us?'

I hated to disappoint her. 'She is still with the king,' I told her. 'But they know you are here. I'm sure it won't be long before they summon you.'

'I suppose Margaret is already there?' With a jealous sniff, Mary tossed her handiwork onto the floor and leapt to her feet. 'It's not fair! I can't just sit here waiting. What is Harry doing?'

'The prince has gone to the privy garden to play bowls with his friends. It is drizzling with rain but if you put on your cloak you could go and watch them. I'm sure they won't mind.'

Nodding, she asked the attendant to fetch her cloak, then turned back to me. 'Is Charlie Brandon playing?'

I cast my mind back to Prince Harry's companions. 'Yes, I believe he is. Why, do you ask?'

Mary flounced past me to wait impatiently by the door for the maid to return with the cloak. 'He always stares at me. I don't like it.'

I heard the seamstress murmur as she passed me, 'She secretly does like it, m'lady.' I gave a barely visible nod of acknowledgement, resolving to have a word with young Brandon.

Back at the queen's antechamber I noticed that Princess Margaret had put in an appearance and was receiving the condolences of her fellow maids of honour. She looked surprisingly calm and had even acquired a veil of royal mourning blue to cover her thick brown hair, although I thought it incongruous with her gown of bright green wool and hoped she would soon be provided with more sober apparel.

As soon as she saw me she ducked away from her friends and I curtsied as she approached. 'I am so very sorry for your loss, Princess,' I said. 'Your brother's death must have come as a terrible shock to you.'

'Thank you, Mother Guildford; yes, it did.' She blinked away impromptu tears. 'I promised myself I wouldn't cry but I keep remembering the dance Arthur and I did at his wedding banquet. It was only while we were practising for it that I truly got to know him. He was so earnest and amusing and he did so love to dance.'

This confidence made me smile sympathetically. 'I'm so glad that at least you had that opportunity. I recall the dance vividly. You performed it beautifully together.'

She managed to return my smile. 'Yes, I think we did. Thank you. At least I have that to remember him by. How are my little brother and sister? I hear you went to break the news to them. That was good of you.'

'Prince Harry was extremely upset, Princess Mary less so – but then she barely knew her older brother. She's in the privy garden now watching the prince playing a game of bowls with his companions.'

'If I know Mary, she's probably persuaded the boys to let her join in.'

'You may be right. But tell me, apart from the terrible news of Arthur's death, are you happy here at court now?'

It was more than a year since Margaret had left Eltham Palace to live in her mother's household and in that time it seemed to me that she had matured considerably. On first arrival at court, aged only eleven, she had appeared silent and withdrawn, awkward among a group of lively teenage maids of honour, and it had been my fear that she might never grow used to being one of a crowd.

After a few seconds' thought, she gave an emphatic nod. 'Yes, I am, Mother Guildford. I have become friends with quite a few girls and some of them even say they'd like to come to Scotland with me, when I go to marry King James.'

'How lovely! So are you more resigned to that prospect now?' When I was her governess, Margaret had admitted that she wished with all her heart that she did not have to marry the Scottish king, who was a complete stranger and three times her age. The union had been negotiated to seal a peace treaty between Scotland and England.

Margaret's eyes rolled expressively. 'My mother and grandmother are trying to delay the marriage but the king thinks the treaty may collapse if it does not take place next year.'

I did a quick mental calculation. 'Before you are fourteen?' I tried to keep my instinctive disapproval hidden but evidently failed.

A cloud crossed the girl's face. 'My grandmother was married at twelve. She adored her first husband and has said she wishes to be buried with him.'

It was not a time to remind her that My Lady the King's Mother had given birth at thirteen and barely survived the experience.

'I haven't seen my mother yet,' the princess went on to complain. 'I wasn't here when she came back from seeing the king the first time. The ladies say she was very distressed?'

'Yes, she was. That is why we sent for him again. But she was also very concerned that you and Prince Harry and Princess Mary should learn of your brother's death before it was publicly announced.'

Margaret shrugged and tears sprang once more to her eyes. 'Lady Stafford told me in the end. But why should I not go in now? I might be of comfort to them both, Mother Guildford.'

It was hard to deny her. 'The king has asked for privacy. I am sure it will not be for long,' was all I could say.

4

Greenwich Palace

April 1502

WHEN THE KING LEFT he swept through the anteroom without stopping to speak to anyone, even his daughter. Perhaps he did not notice her but the chamberlain approached me to whisper that the queen had specifically asked for Lady Guildford to return. As I was swiftly ushered in I tried to avoid the affronted gazes of the other attendants, particularly that of Princess Margaret.

The queen was standing in her chamber robe at the end of the rumpled bed and raised a shaking hand to acknowledge my arrival. Her famous beauty had completely vanished behind the mask of her misery. 'I feel so guilty, Joan,' she said, her voice hoarse and cracked. 'I gave way to an ugly display of selfish despair, for which I fear God may never forgive me.'

It was clear that she was still fighting tears and the urge to console such abject misery was irresistible. I wrapped my arms around her like a mother enveloping her crying child. At first her body went rigid, as if she intended to reject me, but gradually I felt her relax. The chamber was furnished with a daybed and she allowed me to steer her gently towards it. When she sat, I dropped to my knees at her side.

To use her given name without reference to her rank went against protocol but formal address in such circumstances seemed insensitive, when I wished above all to give reassurance. 'You have lost three living children, Elizabeth, and several that never lived outside the womb. It is no sin to grieve.'

A low moan escaped her. 'Half my children, Joan! I have lost *half* my precious children – and two of them boys. I have failed in my duty as queen and the Tudor throne is quaking!'

Shocked, I asked, 'Did the king say that?'

She responded with a vehement shake of the head. 'No, no! He kept saying it is God's will. But I told him that we could – we must – have another child and I shall visit every shrine between here and Arthur's grave to pray for it to be a son.'

I bowed my head over my clasped hands, so tightly joined that my knuckles turned white. 'No, Elizabeth! I beg you not to do that. Remember how ill you were after Edmund's birth. God has blessed you with a fine son in Prince Henry and he is healthy and strong. I'm certain he will make a magnificent king in good time.'

'But a dynasty needs more than one son, Joan. The monarchs of Europe will not consider England safe under Tudor rule if it has only one heir. The king will never feel secure on such an unstable throne.'

'You have two healthy girls. Why should they or their children not inherit, as Princess Katherine's mother did? Queen Isabella of Castile has proved a strong and mighty ruler. You must not endanger your health by embarking on another pregnancy – I beg you, my dear Elizabeth!'

All of a sudden the woman I had thought my friend became my queen. Her body stiffened and her expression became angry, her voice icy. 'When, Lady Guildford, did I give you permission to address me as "my dear Elizabeth"? You have the honour of being a lady-in-waiting to your queen. It is your duty to serve me without question. Do not dare to tell me what I must and must not do!'

Inwardly, I berated myself. With the best of intentions, I had overstepped the mark. 'Forgive me, your grace,' I said, trying to retreat awkwardly on my knees. 'If I have offended you it was entirely out of concern for your health.'

She pushed me away with unexpected vigour so that I sprawled sideways. 'I have physicians to advise me on my health. A queen's attendants are required merely to fulfil her wishes. I have promised my lord that I will bear him another son and that has brought him much comfort. I will not renege on that promise and you will not beg me to do so ever again!' She stood up and walked stiffly to the mirrored space where she was dressed and coiffed, often twice daily. 'Now you may help me recover my countenance and demeanour and escort me to visit my children. Then you may return to London and order another batch from the apothecary of that very effective potion that soothes my headaches. You have neglected to keep me supplied. After that you are dismissed from my service.'

I gave an audible gasp of shock, unable to believe what I heard, but I managed to scramble to my feet and an ominous silence persisted between us as I smoothed an unguent onto the queen's ravaged cheeks, helped her into a clean kirtle and sober-coloured gown and pinned a royal blue bereavement veil over a white linen coif, remembering where it had been stored since the death of Prince Edmund. I could find no mourning jewellery in her coffer so I threaded a black ribbon through the ring of her gold cross and tied it around her neck. Then I escorted this ice-cold Mother Superior figure to the royal children's quarters, relieved to find that Prince Harry and Princess Mary had returned from the game of bowls and been joined by Princess Margaret. The servants and the prince's companions were dismissed while the queen commiserated privately with her three remaining offspring and so I was able to have some quiet minutes with Hal. I did not mention the queen's abrupt and out-of-character dismissal to him because I could not truly believe it myself.

For the first time in my court career, I had not been offered transport on a royal barge but fortunately mine was a familiar face to the royal oarsmen, one of whom agreed to row me to the public dock, where I hired a ferry to take me back to the Tower Quay.

When or even whether the queen would restore me to favour I could not be certain. However, the following day I did as she had requested and made a visit to her appointed apothecary, who had premises in the Blackfriars enclosure on the other side of the city. Instead of hiring a ferry, I chose to make the long walk there from the Tower through streets already hung with black banners and pondered sadly on the circumstances of my dismissal. I found myself harbouring a simmering sense of injustice. Apart from occasional absences for family reasons, I had served Elizabeth and her children for sixteen years and until now she had consistently shown me friendship and favour. I hoped in my heart that her sudden change of attitude was due to her anguish at her son's death and that when she recalled the history between us she would reconsider.

But days went by with no recall. To discuss the funeral arrangements for Prince Arthur the king called a meeting of the core members of the Privy Council at Greenwich Palace and Richard returned to the Tower with unexpected news. 'Arthur is to be buried in Worcester Cathedral,' he revealed. 'There has been constant rainfall in the Welsh March and the state of the roads is judged too hazardous for a royal funeral cortège to travel all the way to Westminster.'

'Does that mean the king and queen will not attend?' I asked in surprise.

'Yes. As the cause of death is not clear there is a need for haste and the king has decided that it would be appropriate for the Prince of Wales to be interred in the Welsh March, where he spent most of his life.'

'So he will not attend his precious son's funeral?' I could not hide my disapproval. 'It is as if he is angry with him for dying!'

'That's a bit harsh, Joan.' Richard's brow furrowed. 'Henry is very distressed but he is also deeply concerned about this new threat from the Yorkist conspiracy. Don't forget that there are prisoners here in the Tower and the king wishes the trial to be soon.'

I took a deep draught from my wine cup. 'There is also a York princess who has been evicted from her home and three Courtenay children who are without the protection of their father.'

Richard's face suffused. 'Which they hardly need when their aunt shelters them in regal comfort at Baynard's Castle,' he protested. 'By the way, Lady Stafford asked me when you were returning to the queen's service.'

'I hope you told her to ask the queen that question.'

My husband gave me a stern look. 'Have you written to the queen? She won't invite you back just for the sight of your face, you know, Joan. You'll have to do some serious apologising.'

As Comptroller of the King's Household, he was understandably eager to remain in favour with the royal couple but I had not chosen to tell him precisely why Elizabeth had suddenly turned on me. I considered her offer of comforting the king by trying for another child to be private between them and not something that should be discussed by the members of the Council. 'I'm not sure I want to go back just yet, Richard. Would it trouble you if I went to Frensham for a while?' Situated close to the Guildford estates in Kent, Frensham was the manor he had given me as a wedding present.

A rare look of concern flickered across his face. 'Why, are you ailing, Joan?'

'No, I'm just tired and in need of some country air. I can take Lizzie with me. She is bored here and what with the royal wedding and serving the queen and the poor Princess of Wales, I haven't been near Frensham since last summer. I need to check with the reeve and see how the spring sowing is proceeding. And Hetty has been tutoring her younger sister in the art of being a lady's maid. If the queen does want me back I could bring her up to London with me when I return.'

As my personal maid for several years, Hetty had enjoyed travelling around the royal palaces and castles with me but now she was married and back in Kent and I had been searching for a replacement. If the little sister turned out to be anything like her she would be a great asset.

Richard gave a heavy sigh of resignation. 'Well, perhaps it might be a good opportunity for you to pay a visit to Frensham. You could also check on things at Halden. But I still wish you to write to the queen.'

I tossed my head. 'I will; just not yet.'

Meanwhile, I would spend some time relaxing in the calm security of my own manor and perhaps she would find solace in her surviving children and realise that there was no need to risk her life providing the Tudor dynasty with a spare heir.

5

Frensham Manor

April 1502

AT SUNSET, WHEN I returned from fulfilling Richard's errands at Halden Hall, I was grateful to find my new maid waiting for me with a supper of cold meats and wine.

'Thank you, Mildy, this is thoughtful of you. I hadn't meant to be away so long but there was more to do at Halden than I expected. And I must admit that I'm hungry.' I lifted a cut of roasted cony onto some bread and watched her pour wine into a cup. She was sixteen and as bright and capable as her sister Hetty had been when she'd joined us at the same age. 'Has Lizzie had supper?'

'Yes, madam. She went out to visit her hawk. I think she was doing some training with it today.' Lizzie and I had ridden down to Frensham Manor two days ago, escorted by a couple of Richard's men at arms. 'A courier brought that for you this afternoon,' she added, indicating a letter lying off the cloth on the bare polished end of the long hall table. 'Is that not Sir Richard's coat of arms?'

I reached out for it, turning it over in my hands. It felt more bulky than the usual one-page note from my husband, who was not a prolific letter-writer, and I must have looked concerned for Mildy added, 'I hope it's not bad news, m'lady.'

Resolutely I put the packet down again. 'Well, whatever it is, it can wait until I have supped. I'm impressed that you recognised the seal though. Well done.'

Her cheeks flushed. 'Hetty made sure to show me the plaque in the church. It's a pretty design.'

I swallowed my mouthful and smiled. 'I think so too. And did she tell you the heraldic description?' At the shake of her head I added, 'It is *Or, a saltire between four martlets sable*. In other words – a gold shield with four black martlets between the arms of a black saltire cross.'

'I love the little martlets,' Mildy said. 'Every year they make nests under the eaves of our home and I watch the fledglings tumble about in the sky while they learn to use their wings. Then within minutes, it seems, they're expert fliers. It's amazing.'

'Isn't it? If I'm here long enough I must take you to see the ravens, which nest in the woods at Halden. They're very amusing when they fledge.'

'Are you not staying long then?' There was disappointment in her voice.

'That depends on what is in the letter. I'll know when I've read it. But when I leave, sooner or later, would you like to come with me, Mildy? I may return to serve the queen and I will need a good personal maid. Would you like to travel with me around the royal palaces like Hetty did?' As I asked this I crossed my fingers under the table because I had no idea what might be in the letter, even supposing it was from the queen.

However, I was pleased at the way her face lit up. 'Oh yes, m'lady. That is what Hetty trained me for.'

Satisfied, I turned my full attention to satisfying my hunger. When I had eaten my fill she gathered the dishes and without my having to ask, poured me a second cup of wine before leaving the room. Whatever happened I certainly didn't want to lose Mildy!

Taking a deep breath, I steeled myself to tackle the letter. I broke the Guildford seal and unfolded Richard's note, setting aside a second sealed missive concealed within his. My husband's message was brief and written by a scribe:

I thought I should send this letter on immediately. Let me know what it says and whether it changes your immediate plans. The queen's chamberlain has informed the Constable that she will be visiting the Tower for several days at the end of the month.

His scrawled cypher below it was in stark contrast to the precise calligraphy on the other letter, which was addressed in her own clear hand and displayed the queen's personal seal on the back. My heart skipped a beat. This was a truly private communication, for my eyes only.

I hesitated, waiting for my heartbeat to slow and staring at the precise lettering of the address, remembering how Elizabeth had taken such pride in teaching her precocious son Henry to write when he was only three, and how he had been so eager to gain her approval of his early success. Would I be as delighted by the contents of this letter, I wondered, or would it be the knife-slash that severed the ties between me and the queen once and for all?

Taking a deep breath I gingerly broke the seal.

To Lady Joan Guildford, greetings.

How should I excuse my extraordinary action in dismissing you, except by claiming a temporary loss of mind caused by the death of my dearly beloved son? I have faith that in the circumstances you will forgive me and once more lend me your company and invaluable service as my wisest adviser and friend. In short, I cannot do without you, dear Joan, and thank you earnestly for remembering to arrange for the apothecary to send me the remedies I so urgently needed, despite my regrettable action in sending you away. I will be staying at the Tower of London at the end of April and pray that you will be available to assist me in the burdensome task I must undertake there. For reasons of security I will not divulge any details but assure you that I would be deeply grateful for your help and advice at that time.

I await your reply in anxious anticipation of a favourable response.

Elizabeth, your sorely beset queen

For a few minutes I mused over the letter. Then I read it again. Elizabeth was beset by a 'burdensome task'. Of course I would go to her.

I knew I must send my answer straight away because Richard's courier would be staying at Halden Hall and would have been told to wait for my reply. There was a writing table in the corner of my chamber. I took paper from the shelf, drew up a stool and opened the inkpot, hoping Mildy had filled it. She had and had also placed a set of sharpened quills alongside. I was appreciating the girl's unexpected skills more and more. She definitely had a future as my personal maid.

I did some rapid calendar calculations and worked out that I could stay at least another week at Frensham before I would need to return to London. I wrote to Richard with this plan, suggesting that he arrange for Lizzie to go and stay with Pippa, her recently married sister who now lived in Surrey and was expecting a baby. I could deliver her there on my way.

My letter to Elizabeth took more time to compose. I expressed my heartfelt gratitude that she still considered me a friend but added that I needed to stay a little longer at Frensham. However I promised to be at the Tower in time for her arrival.

6

The Tower of London

April 1502

RICHARD GREETED MY RETURN to the Tower with relief. 'I thank God you're here, Joan. The queen arrives in three days and King Henry hinted to me that she is in particular need of you.'

I had been later getting to the Tower than I had anticipated because I'd been delayed in Surrey. The arrangement for Lizzie to go to Pippa had been agreed but when we got there we found her crippled with morning sickness. There was a good selection of herbs in her garden and so I stayed a couple of nights to make her a concoction of mint and balm in order to soothe the horrible condition. It was something my midwife had showed me when I was carrying Hal. I also taught Lizzie how to make more doses when mine ran out.

'Have you any inkling as to why the queen might be so much in need of me?' I asked Richard. 'She called it a burdensome task.'

He shook his head. 'No, I haven't spoken to her in person and I have no idea why she is coming. I thought the king would come alone. All I know is that arrangements are underway for the trial of the Yorkist conspirators to take place at the Guildhall early next week and the Constable of the Tower has been told to prepare for King Henry to visit the prisoners. There was no mention of the queen accompanying him.'

'Perhaps she wishes to visit Lord Courtenay,' I suggested. 'Her sister may have asked her to.'

'That may be so, but he is not on the list of those arraigned for trial.'

I raised my eyebrows. 'Really? Who are the accused then?'

'Sir James Tyrrell is chief among them. You won't know the rest. They're small fry.'

'Tyrrell has turned his coat more than once already, hasn't he? I thought he'd been pardoned.'

'Indeed – but this seems to be yet another turn and judging by King Henry's present mood if his guilt is proven there'll be no chance of a pardon this time.'

My brow furrowed. 'None of this gives me any idea why the queen should need me to be here now, when only a few weeks ago she sent me packing.'

Richard made a frustrated gesture. 'Well, I suppose you'll soon find out.'

'True. Meanwhile are there any ravens present?'

My husband's frown grew deeper. 'How should I know? I haven't noticed. That's your department, isn't it?'

'Well, if you haven't noticed them the chances are they've left and if that is so, the king really has a problem. I'll go now and search. The Tower walls may already be crumbling.'

'That's not funny, Joan!'

'It wasn't meant to be funny, sir,' I said solemnly.

* * *

There was no sign of the ravens but I noticed that the number of archers on the Tower walls had been doubled. Either this had scared the birds away or they'd all been shot. I hoped fervently it was not the latter. The old adage that the walls of the Tower would crumble if the ravens left included a warning that the kingdom would also fall. I took Mildy to the kitchen to make her acquaintance with Jake, our resident cook, and used the opportunity to remind him to keep some meat scraps aside, something he was accustomed to do when I was in residence at the house we occupied on the Tower Quay. That evening I placed these on Tower Green and waited while the sun set. No ravens flew in to roost in the alder trees.

Two days later they still had not come when I stood with Lady Digby, wife of the Tower's Lieutenant Constable, while he and Richard waited to greet the king and queen at the quayside. As the royal barge docked a parade of yeomen in their ceremonial Tudor green and white liveries formed a guard of honour and the guns on the river bastion sounded a deafening salute. Rising from my curtsy to Queen Elizabeth as she passed me, I marked the pallor of her cheeks and the dullness of her expression. She did not speak, merely acknowledged me with a brief nod and passed on in the king's wake. I wondered whether Richard had been mistaken when he said that she was eager to see me, for she certainly gave no sign of it. On the contrary, to my consternation I thought she resembled a condemned prisoner going to the scaffold.

However, early in the evening when all the ceremonial had concluded, a page came to the house to ask me to attend the queen. Like other ancient royal castles with their considerable defences, the Tower of London was both fortress and palace and there had been alterations and improvements to the queen's apartments since the last time I had been there. So I was grateful to follow the page through the labyrinth of gates, towers and stairs that took us over the moat and through the old palace passages to the new queen's lodging. Lady Stafford, the chief lady-in-waiting, met me at the door of a candlelit solar, where Queen Elizabeth was seated alone in an oriel window.

'She is not happy to be here,' Lady Stafford whispered before moving into the room. 'I hope you'll forgive her if she is somewhat distracted.'

The queen stood up. 'There's no need to whisper, Beth. Lady Guildford knows I am here under sufferance.' She moved forward to greet me. 'I am so glad to see you, Joan. Please, come and sit down. We have wine and sweetmeats and Lady Stafford will be leaving us alone.'

With a toss of her head the chief lady made a brief curtsy, cast an exasperated glance in my direction and closed the door behind her. I made my own curtsy and was pleased to see the queen smile and take my hand to lead me to the window where two chairs were placed beside a table.

'You pour the wine, Joan,' she suggested. 'This room is new and I like this oriel. There is still enough daylight for a view of the privy garden, which is fresh with spring growth and I cannot see any of the towers where prisoners are kept and interrogated.'

'Is that what you dislike about coming to the Tower, your grace?' I asked gently. 'The thought of prisoners being interrogated?'

She was giving careful consideration to the choice of

sweetmeats on the platter and did not reply until she'd made her selection. Then she gave me a rueful look. 'Yes, but I also fear meeting the ghosts of my brothers. That is another reason I like this lodging, because they could never have been in this new part of the palace.'

I could have kicked myself for not realising this. It was nearly twenty years since the two princes, the uncrowned king, Edward the Fifth, and Richard, Duke of York, had disappeared while being housed in the Tower during the chaotic months following the death of their father, King Edward the Fourth. It was for allegedly supporting the claim to the throne of their York cousin-in-exile, Edmund de la Pole, Earl of Suffolk, that Sir James Tyrrell was confined in one of the Tower cells, awaiting trial in a few days' time.

'Why did you agree to come then?' I asked. 'Could you not have refused?'

'Yes, I could, but the king told me Tyrrell claims he has something to say about my brothers' deaths that he would only reveal to me alone.' I saw tears well suddenly in her eyes. 'I don't want to be here and I don't want to see him, Joan! But for my brothers' sakes I feel that I must.' She had her own kerchief this time and paused to dab at her eyes.

'So how may I help you, your grace?' I asked, resisting the temptation to simply tell her she shouldn't feel beholden to her brothers' ghosts.

'Tyrrell's sister is a nun at the convent of St Clare, up behind Tower Hill here. She has agreed to see me and I have ordered a litter to take me there tomorrow morning. I would be extremely grateful if you would come with me, Joan, because I trust your judgement of people. I don't know what she will have to say and despite her calling she might

42

still tell me a pack of lies but before I see the man himself I want to ask her what she knows of Tyrrell's movements at the time of the disappearance.'

It was raining when we made our way in the curtained litter across the moat and around Tower Hill to St Clare's Abbey, a place of refuge where elderly widows went to see out their days and women stricken with incurable disease were cared for until the end of theirs. Eleanor Tyrrell had taken the veil by choice and was one of the nuns who devoted themselves to caring for these lay members. She was close to Tyrrell and claimed that her brother could not have been involved in the death of the two princes because he was in Cornwall and Calais during the reign of Richard the Third.

'I would have known if he'd come to London during that time because he always came to visit me whenever he was here and he didn't come at all during Richard's reign,' she said earnestly, her hands busy with the beads of her rosary. 'Besides, I'm sure he would not have been involved in anything untoward that concerned children. He had four young ones of his own.'

'But he was one of Richard's loyal lieutenants, was he not?' the queen asked. 'I know this because my uncle told me.'

'He was very fond of you, your uncle, wasn't he?' Eleanor's tone was sharp and it obviously rankled with the queen, who stood up.

'We will leave now. I have heard enough.'

'But you haven't given me any sign of which way the trial might go,' the nun complained as the queen walked quickly to the door. 'I pray God that James will not have been tortured into making any false confessions.'

Back in the shelter of the litter Elizabeth sighed and frowned. 'Well, what did you think, Joan? Was she telling the truth?'

I paused before giving her my answer because I was trying to judge the queen's own impressions of the meeting. Mine were ambivalent. 'I'm not sure, your grace,' I confessed. 'She is probably telling the truth about not seeing her brother during the usurper's reign but that doesn't necessarily mean that Tyrrell didn't make a trip to London. He may just not have visited his sister. And her claim that he would not have harmed children because he was the father of four is neither here nor there, because he could still have appointed subordinates to actually perform the dreadful task. To be honest, your grace, I don't think the interview was of any help to you. Your only hope of discovering the truth is to hope that Tyrrell's confession includes a guide to where two young bodies are buried.'

The queen nodded and sighed. 'You are right, Joan, I do need to know where their bodies are, or I will never truly believe they are dead. I am hoping that when he sees and understands the need, Tyrrell will tell me where they are. But you seem doubtful.'

She was clearly expecting further response and I racked my brain for something appropriate, while the queen kept her eyes on me, full of hope. I wrestled with my conscience, wondering whether to prevaricate or give her my candid opinion.

I heaved a sigh. 'I cannot believe he will reveal that, your grace; perhaps because the usurper arranged for other people to attend to the gruesome task of giving them burial. Or perhaps simply because Tyrrell is an evil conspirator who

44

wants the world to keep wondering whether one or both of the princes might still be alive. My only earnest advice would be to suggest that when you see him, no matter what he says, you don't give him the satisfaction of seeing you discomforted. I could not bear him to go to the scaffold thinking that he had achieved some sort of callous Yorkist triumph over Tudor.'

For several seconds, Queen Elizabeth looked as if she was going to send me packing again and I steeled myself to receive a tongue-lashing. But then her expression changed and her rigid shoulders slumped. 'Sometimes, Joan, I believe you know me too well. And since you do, you know that when I have to I can hide my true feelings for long stretches of time and I promise that I will do so if Tyrell does not reveal the resting place of my brothers. Nonetheless, I still hold out hope that he will.'

For the first time since my return we exchanged genuine smiles. 'I very much hope that I am proved wrong, your grace,' I said with some warmth. 'And that tomorrow's meeting provides you with the reassurance you desire and deserve.'

7

Woodstock Palace

June–July 1502

THE QUEEN DID NOT get what she most desired. Tyrell did confess to her that on the orders of her uncle Richard, he had 'arranged' the deaths of her two brothers, along with two of his retainers. However he professed not to know where the bodies had been buried. In fact, he claimed that later they had been moved from their original grave 'on King Richard's orders' and he therefore had no knowledge of their whereabouts.

As soon as the confession had been made, King Henry ordered a proclamation to be issued to that effect, determined to reinforce the claim to the throne of his new heir, Prince Henry. At the trial, Sir James Tyrell was found guilty of high treason and beheaded on Tower Hill four days later.

I took a break from the queen's service at the beginning of June to attend the wedding of Richard's eldest daughter Maria to the young heir of one of Kent's foremost families but towards the end of the month I was called to Woodstock Palace, where the royal family were taking a summer break at King Henry's favourite hunting palace north of Oxford. It was a long journey from Kent and although Elizabeth had written that the courier who had brought her letter would escort me and my maid, Richard had insisted on accompanying us, along with a small retinue.

On our arrival I was disturbed to find the queen confined to her bed. She greeted me propped up on pillows and looking alarmingly pale. Even her voice was weak, a worrying sign in the speech of someone who was usually clear and purposeful in her delivery. 'I'm sorry to greet you like this, Joan,' she said faintly, as I leaned closer to hear her. 'I simply have not the energy to rise at present.'

Ignoring protocol I pulled up a stool beside the bed and sat down. 'What ails your grace? What does your physician say?'

A sigh accompanied Elizabeth's weak smile. 'Please do not scold me, Joan – for I am pregnant. And the condition is draining my strength – as it has done before at this early stage.' Her words came in brief bursts, interspersed by short intakes of breath, and I hope I hid the alarm I felt at hearing this news. 'I expect to feel better soon – especially if you have brought me some more tonic.'

'Of course I have. I will send some to your chamber as soon as my baggage is unpacked. Master Grice the apothecary says he has slightly changed the formula. I did not know of your pregnancy but he said it has more blood-strengthening qualities now.'

She nodded. 'I am grateful to him. I did write that I was *enceinte* and asked him not to reveal that to anyone. It has not yet been made public.'

'Then you can be sure that he obliged you, since he did

not tell me. Let us hope that his new recipe is both potent and palatable.'

'The taste is never wonderful,' she admitted with a slight grimace. 'But I usually have some honey added.'

A slight expression of guilt accompanied this admission, prompting me to smile. 'I think you may be forgiven for that, your grace.' Observing that she had already found our conversation tiring, I stood up. 'With your permission I'll leave you now and send the potion to you directly. I look forward to seeing you dancing about the court very soon.'

The queen frowned. 'For the time being I think I will leave dancing to my daughters. But come again tomorrow, Joan.'

I made my curtsy and left and only then did I realise that I had not congratulated her on the new pregnancy, nor did I feel inclined to do so.

When I entered the apartment allotted to us I found an exuberant Richard, who had been received by King Henry in his private chamber. 'He told me straight away and in confidence that the queen is pregnant, as you have no doubt discovered. Henry is delighted but he seems anxious about her condition. How does she seem to you?'

'Not well. Not well at all. I must get the apothecary's tonic to her as soon as possible. Where is Mildy? I thought she'd be here.'

'I sent her for refreshments,' Richard said. 'We have missed dinner and I'm starving. She won't be long.'

'We can't rely on that. She's never been to Woodstock and the palace is a warren. She's bound to get lost. Couldn't you have sent your squire?' My anxiety about the queen was making me short-tempered.

'My horse picked up a stone in his hoof and I needed him to deal with it. I must leave tomorrow and I can't risk a lame mount. Why are you so tetchy?'

I crossed to where my travelling chest had been stowed and removed the key from my purse. 'I'll have to find the potion and take it to the queen's apartments myself then. If I'm tetchy it's because of the royal pregnancy. I warned Elizabeth against it because I feared for her life.'

Richard moved to help me lift the heavy lid of the chest. 'If they are still an active married couple I don't see how she could prevent it. Is that why she dismissed you? You never told me that.'

'I thought the matter private.' I sank to my knees and began to search anxiously among the contents of the chest. 'I wrapped the flasks in skins and Mildy packed them among my clothes to protect them during the journey. I hope they haven't broken— aha!' My fingers connected with a hard object under my smocks and I pulled out one of the wrapped flasks. 'Why are you leaving so soon, Richard? Is your business with the king all concluded?'

'All settled,' he crowed. 'I'm free to ride to Eaton Bray tomorrow.'

'Oh, I see. There should be several more bottles, but this will do for now.' I stood up and began unwrapping the potion carefully. 'I hope your visit to Sir Reginald doesn't involve another loan.' Sir Reginald Bray was the king's chief minister and in my opinion unforgivably rich.

'Only a short-term arrangement,' Richard admitted. 'I'll soon pay it back but I need hard coin to pay Maria's dowry. Funds are tight because of Pippa's marriage at the New Year.'

'Yes, it's been an expensive six months.' I tucked the flask into my purse and turned for the door. 'I'll take this to the queen's chamber myself. And when Mildy does come back, please leave some refreshments for me.'

He grinned. 'Perhaps a few crusts.'

The tonic took nearly two weeks to work a cure but early in July Queen Elizabeth at last felt well enough to venture out of her chamber and take short walks around the palace gardens. While resting in the perfumed shade of a rose arbour she confided to me that she intended to make a solo progress around the shrines of West England and the Welsh March. 'I wish to pray at the many shrines along the way and make offerings to the saints for the successful birth of a male child to assure the Tudor succession. And I hope you will keep me company, Joan.'

I was surprised. 'Will the king not be coming with you, your grace? After all, it is for his sake you are bearing his child.' In the past the royal couple had always made their summer progress together, using the warmer months to visit the country homes of noble friends and relations, primarily for hunting and entertainment but also in order to show themselves to their rural subjects along the way.

A stubborn expression spread over the queen's face. 'No, he has business in the other direction and wants to return to London. I cannot abide the city in summer, particularly in my present state, so I've decided to go alone. But of course I won't be alone. Beth Stafford has agreed to come too and will arrange other young ladies and Sir Roger, my Master of Horse, has arranged the itinerary and made a map of my route. We can study it together when we return to my lodging.'

'I assume you do not intend to ride all the way, your grace. It would not be wise in your present condition.' I failed to keep a tone of disapproval from my voice and she heard it.

'I'm afraid you are becoming a bit of a nag, Joan. I hope you won't continue in this vein for our entire journey. But in order to allay your misgivings I will tell you that Sir Roger has had my chariot reupholstered and recruited two strong porters to carry it whenever I feel the need to use it. He has also installed a hood to keep off the rain.' She rose stiffly from her seat beside me. 'It is painted a very royal shade of purple. We can return to the palace via the stable block and I will show it to you.'

8

The Queen's Progress

August 1502

AT THE START OF the queen's progress the weather was kind to us and, having always been a keen horsewoman, she rarely used the hooded chariot unless we were caught in a summer shower. We rode at the centre of the royal procession, Queen Elizabeth between me and her chief lady-in-waiting, Beth Stafford. Ahead and behind rode members of her escort of knights and squires, their cuirasses gleaming in the sunshine, while at the rear of the cavalcade came the wagons and servants, some mounted, some walking and others balanced among the loaded baggage and furnishings needed to ensure the queen's comfort during her overnight stays. The most colourful wagon was that of her minstrels and mummers, brightly painted, fluttering with ribbons, alive with song and peopled by an ever-changing cast of characters hired along the way to bring music and entertainment to the queen's picnics and evening meals.

I had been unofficially allocated the position of Mistress of the Stool for the duration of the progress. It not only placed me in ideal circumstances to monitor the queen's health in her pregnancy but, rather less enthusiastically, to inspect and deal with the contents of her grace's close-stool. Our conversations during these intimate sessions mostly concerned her obsessive desire to provide the king with another son to replace the essentially irreplaceable Prince Arthur.

'After all, God granted St Ann the birth of the Virgin Mary at a considerable age and then her daughter meekly accepted the visitation of the Angel Gabriel without hesitation, even before he promised her a boy, the Son of God. I am not looking to bring forth a Messiah but the birth of a son is so important to the king and if I entreat as many saints as possible to further my cause I should succeed, don't you think?' Of course I could only encourage her, however sceptical my secret thoughts and at least the local shrines were enriched by the gold coins she offered.

The length of the summer evenings meant that once I had dosed her up with the prescribed measures of tonics and tisanes and she had restored herself with an hour or two's slumber, there was still time for refreshment, music and merriment before dark. Invariably this also involved cards and dice and further raiding of the royal purse. Because Queen Elizabeth loved to gamble. Usually her hosts were called on to provide opposition, be it by playing themselves or nominating suitable members of their household, and the queen would pursue her losses well into the evening, after the sun had set and candles had been lit. Of course it was an honour to play with the queen but also it was a rare night when Elizabeth emerged the winner and her losses were often enough to cover the entire cost of her stay.

One stop I had been particularly looking forward to was the manor of Iron Acton, in Gloucestershire, where we were to take up an invitation initiated between me and my childhood friend Meg Poyntz, who was the lady of the manor and a cousin of the queen, albeit from the wrong side of the blanket. For many years, My Lady the King's Mother had been a strict but kind foster mother to numerous children in need and coincidentally Meg and I had both been her wards at the same time. During the usurper's short reign, when King Henry's mother had been imprisoned in her own house for conspiring in a failed rebellion, all her wards and servants had been evicted and I had taken shelter with Meg and her husband Robert Poyntz.

Subsequently, Robert had been knighted after fighting in King Henry's victorious army and as we neared his domain I was amazed to see what changes had been wrought by the rewards he had received. For this was now a land of quarries, where the highways and villages were threaded between huge excavations, which had transformed the landscape. Then, as we neared the village of Iron Acton, there was evidence of another industry, where men with spades and shovels were piling earth of a deep red colour into large carts with teams of oxen in the traces. Because our cavalcade moved faster than such heavy loads could do, we found ourselves enveloped in a cloud of dust as one of them lumbered ahead of us on the roadway. The Master of Horse called a halt.

'We'll wait until the air clears,' he said, riding back to report to the queen.

She spluttered a little into the kerchief she held over her nose and mouth as she nodded agreement. 'Definitely, Sir Roger. What is this red cloud we have encountered?'

'It is red ore dust, your grace. Red ore is the source of

the iron we use to manufacture our cannons and cauldrons. This area is rich in it and the oak trees in the forest nearby provide the charcoal that smelts it. The ancients called the oak "ack" – hence the name Iron Acton.'

Lady Meg was the illegitimate and much-loved only child of Anthony Woodville, Earl Rivers, the eldest brother of King Edward the Fourth's controversial queen, Elizabeth Woodville, hence Queen Elizabeth's cousin, and she and Sir Robert had named their first child Anthony after him, who in due course had become squire to my husband, Sir Richard. This second Anthony had reached his majority as the century turned and made an advantageous marriage and I was hoping to hear news of him, as well as looking forward to refreshing my friendship with his mother.

When we arrived at Acton Court, the Poyntz manor house, I was delighted when that same young man rushed forward to hold my stirrup as I dismounted from my palfrey. 'My lady Guildford!' he cried, dropping to his knee and kissing my hand, in the same exaggerated greeting he had frequently made when living in our household as a squire. 'Welcome to Acton Court! It fills my heart with joy to see you again after so long.'

I felt the blood rush to my face at this effusive greeting and glanced ahead at the queen to check whether she had heard him, relieved to see that she had her back to us and was being assisted from her chariot by Anthony's father. With amused chagrin and a rapid shake of the head I shook my hand free from his and murmured, 'Thank you, but please rise, Anthony, and save your enthusiasm for your queen.'

I had forgotten how dazzling his smile was, showing teeth gleaming white with the youth and health reflected in his eyes, which sparkled like sapphires. I had treated him as a member of our family for years and taken his appearance for granted but a period of separation had given me a fresh appreciation of his voice and features – strong brown-gold hair and a voice that was deep and musical. He was almost the image of his mother when she was the girl I had shared a bed with in Lady Margaret's household, only with masculine additions such as a small beard and a muscular build. All these thoughts flashed through my mind as he rose and turned to the sound of his mother's voice.

Meg Poyntz came to upbraid her son in an undertone. 'I know how much you revere Lady Guildford, Anthony, but you should really greet the queen first. Go on and do it before she takes offence!' As he briefly bowed his departure, grinning all the while, she took the same hand he had held. Like his, it felt warm and friendly in mine. 'Joan, you are so welcome! Ignore my preposterous son – he has read too much French poetry and swears you are his courtly lady. But you must know that, and to be sure it is not unjustified, since you saved his arm and his life after the Battle of Blackheath, for which we can never thank you enough.'

For once I was grateful not to be a pale-skinned woman for I could feel my face flaring but knew it to be barely obvious under my dark Mediterranean colouring. 'You have thanked me in writing, Meg, I cannot count how many times, and much of his recovery was due to his own determination. I am glad to see him show no obvious scars, although I know they must still be deep on his arm.' Anthony had been appallingly burned when a cannon exploded on firing during the defence of London against Cornish rebels.

'It is I who should thank you for coming to my rescue and inviting the queen to stay.'

'Coming to your rescue? It was an honour to be singled out by her grace. We are so looking forward to caring for her, for we hear she has been unwell recently.' She leaned nearer to whisper. 'Are we supposed to know she is pregnant?'

I bit my lip and gave a small shake of my head. 'The king knows, of course, but it has not been officially announced. However, she may do so now for the babe kicked during a rather rough Severn crossing – such a relief!'

At this point Meg's husband Sir Robert brought the queen to our side and we both made a curtsy. 'I am admiring your house, Lady Poyntz,' Elizabeth said. 'I love the colour of the bricks.'

'Yes, we are very proud of our red earth here, your grace. It makes beautiful bricks as well as smelting into pig iron.'

'Pig iron? What is that?' The queen turned to her host and his son, who was hovering behind him.

'It is the rough metal that forms when the ore is made extremely hot, your grace. When it cools it forms blobs which look rather like piglets.' It was Anthony who spoke.

The queen laughed. 'Really? And then my master of horse tells us clever blacksmiths melt the pigs again and turn them into useful articles – like cannons and cauldrons.'

'Yes, just so, your grace,' Meg intervened. 'But if I may, let me escort you to your apartment, where I trust you will find everything you need for your comfort and convenience. We may be country bumpkins but I hope no one will ever say we do not know how to make guests comfortable and entertained.' As we passed through the open, and suitably iron-studded, main door of the manor house she expanded on the theme of entertainment. 'And when you have rested after your journey I hope you will be ready for a light supper and we will all enjoy listening to the music of your minstrels, who I see you have kindly consented to bring with you.'

'I travel nowhere without them, Lady Poyntz,' the queen admitted. 'Prayers, music and the saints are my mainstay at this time. But I also confess that I enjoy a hand or two of cards before I retire for the night. Do you play?'

Meg shot a slightly amazed glance at me, following behind. 'I'm afraid not, your grace. But my son Anthony does and I'm sure he would be honoured to join you, if you so wish.'

9

Acton Court

August 1502

ANTHONY POYNTZ LOST FIVE pounds at cards that night. I wondered just how he managed to engineer her victory so surreptitiously but the queen was ecstatic. So happy in fact that she ordered the minstrels to play a galliard so that she could console her opponent by partnering him in the dance. 'I hope you are a better dancer than a card-player, Master Poyntz, because I haven't danced for some time but I do love a galliard.'

'Sadly I am not yet acquainted with it, your grace,' the young man admitted ruefully. 'But if you were to show me the steps I expect I could pick it up quite quickly.'

He was as good as his word, absorbing in a matter of minutes the hops, skips and leaps that had made the galliard so popular at court, accompanying the lesson with much laughter and exaggerated arm movements. I had not seen the queen so animated since Prince Arthur's death. The cards may have cost Anthony five pounds but the dance gained him much prestige.

While accompanying the queen to the stool-room as I did every night before bed, she became almost effusive.

'What a pleasant and intelligent young man Master Poyntz is, Joan,' she said, 'and handsome, too. Why do we not see him about the court? I think he would be an asset.'

'He has only recently married,' I told her, 'and before that he was completing his law studies, as well as serving in my husband's retinue. I doubt he would have had time to attend court.'

'Well, I shall bring him to the attention of the king.' She bent her head to allow me to loosen the clasp of the mourning reliquary she wore in her dead son's memory. 'If you had anything to do with his upbringing you are to be congratulated, Joan.'

'Well, I may have encouraged his love of reading, your grace, but I think you can attribute his manners and appearance entirely to your cousin, his mother.'

Her expression became pensive. 'Yes, he has something of the Woodville looks and charm. My mother was very fond of her brother, his grandfather. I remember her bitter tears when she heard of his execution.'

Elizabeth rarely made mention of her Woodville relatives and I thought it wiser to make no comment. She gave a shake of her head, as if to clear it, then thoroughly caught my attention with her next remark. 'I saw Master Poyntz kneel to greet you on our arrival, Joan. He obviously admires you greatly.'

I frowned. 'I think "admires" may be too strong a word, my lady. He is grateful because he believes I saved his life.' And I told her how I had treated his burned arm after the Battle of Blackheath. 'He's a romantic soul and a great believer in the French tradition of courtly love, as are so many young men these days. You will doubtless receive your share of his devotion after your dance tonight.'

This made her smile. 'Well, I'll look forward to that.'

I'd been wondering why Anthony had not brought his wife to meet the queen and enjoy the entertainments, and the following day after Mass and prayers in the small Poyntz chapel at the local church of St James the Less, I asked him how he was enjoying married life. His evasive reply surprised me. 'That is not an easy question to answer. Is there a time of day when you are free from royal duties? I would like to show you around the Acton Court demesne. There have been a few changes since you were last here, as you can imagine.'

After a brief pause I nodded. 'The queen likes a rest in the afternoon. If we are not travelling, it is usually soon after dinner. Would that be convenient?'

Taking my hand, he kissed it briefly, smiling. 'I will seek you out, my lady.' I noticed with some relief that he had stopped calling me Mother Joan, as he had used to do in his early teens, copying Richard's children when living in the Guildford household.

Queen Elizabeth and her hosts had begun their return to the manor house and I hurried to catch up with them. While the rest of us took our exercise walking the red road, the queen had elected to use her chariot and with the hood down she was able to look around her and enjoy the sight of children playing on the village green and stopping to wave as she passed. Women with spindles tucked into their belts even paused their spinning and dropped rough curtsies to the fine lady in the chariot.

Walking behind it, I overheard Meg and Elizabeth planning the evening's entertainment, while Sir Robert Poyntz trudged along on the other side, occasionally turning to raise an eyebrow in my direction. I later learned that he had agreed to lend the queen a substantial sum to tide her over financially until her return to Richmond. All her saintly offerings and gambling losses were clearly proving beyond her available means. I only hoped Sir Robert's generosity would work to his advantage because I knew how hard it was to persuade the queen's Chancellor to pay her gambling debts.

Dinner that day in the great hall was treated as a grand occasion. It would be the queen's only main meal at Acton Court and every effort had been made to make it a memorable banquet. The minstrels played soft, digestive music from a carved gallery, freshly painted murals of Poyntz emblems and coats of arms encircled the plastered walls, while fragrant scents wafted up from the herb-strewn rush matting and delicious smells drifted from the slices of venison swirled into a rich red sauce, which were distributed in silver dishes at the high table and, in wooden bowls, even down to the lower orders. When over-excited hands shook as they spooned up their portions I feared for the white linen festooned with summer flowers, which covered the trestle boards. There were sugared figs and creamed onions to accompany the venison, salads and spices to freshen the palate and costly Bordeaux wine poured from chased silver flagons. A good many pigs of iron had been smelted to finance the Poyntzs' lavish hospitality.

Queen Elizabeth appeared duly grateful, clearly relishing her meal. Her doctors had told her that venison was a sovereign meat for pregnant ladies and everywhere she went her hosts were encouraged to serve it to her in any form: hot, warm or cold. Equally, if they wanted to curry further favour, the best way to do it was to despatch a live deer, or preferably more than one, to Richmond Palace to boost the winter supplies for her table.

After such a sumptuous meal, the queen was eager to take her rest and so it wasn't long before I was released from my duties and able to stroll out with my book into the dappled shade of the home orchard and find a seat under a tree already flush with apples.

IO

Acton Court

Late August 1502

M Y EYELIDS WERE ALREADY drooping drowsily when I felt rather than saw someone sit down beside me on the bench and heard a familiar voice say, 'It is not like Mother Joan to nod off with a book in her hand.'

I smiled as I felt the book being gently removed from my loose grasp and the same voice remarked, 'Aha, *The Treasure of the City of Ladies* – how many times has my lady read this well-thumbed volume? It's no wonder she falls asleep over it.'

I straightened up indignantly and turned to face my intruder. 'I was not asleep, I was merely resting my eyes.'

Anthony Poyntz nodded sagely. 'Of course you were. And no apple would dare to wake you by falling on your head.' He glanced upwards as he spoke and as if to illustrate his point a big rosy apple dropped to my feet with a thud. 'This was not the best seat to choose,' he added. 'Let me show you my favourite hideaway. The place I used to flee to when my tutor called me to my Greek studies.' He held out the book and I reached for it but he took my hand to pull me to my feet before letting me take it.

'Did you hide there from me when you were four and I

was trying to teach you Latin?' I asked, brushing down my skirt. 'You were too young really but you still managed the declensions.'

'Did I? How precocious. I don't really remember being four but I can't imagine I would have run to hide from you. I only recall you being kind and showing me many interesting things around the gardens and orchards – birds' nests and beetles and butterflies. And now it is my turn to show you something. Have you sensible shoes on?'

I tucked my book into the pocket of my skirt and lifted the hem to expose my buckled leather shoes. 'As long as the ground is dry these should be fine.'

He nodded. 'Yes, they should. Please follow me.'

Paths had been cleared between the trees and the way was open through the pears and cherries and medlars, but when we passed through an arch in a hedge, the scent of roses became intense and thorny branches reached out on every side. I stopped to detach my sleeve from a fiercely armed stem and one of its sharp weapons drew blood from my finger. As I sucked it clean I had a sudden vivid memory of a more serious wound being inflicted on the same hand by the fearsome beak of a raven when, years before, I had foolishly tried to stroke it. My stomach gave a sudden lurch and the dinnertime venison threatened to reappear.

Sensing I had dropped back, Anthony turned and must have seen my discomfort. 'What is it? Have you a scratch? Here, take this.' He drew a clean kerchief from his purse.

'It's nothing compared to the damage that can be caused by a raven.' I took the kerchief and dabbed at the thorn wound, then raised the thumb. 'Remember this one?' An inch-long scar divided the soft inner pad.

He gave me a curious look and nodded. 'I remember you telling me the story. Which is a good introduction to what I want to show you. I used to hide among those tall conifers at the end of the rose garden. Watch them closely and you might spot something familiar.'

At first I could not see what he meant but before I could admit it, a large black bird flew in and settled on a high branch. Then I watched another land beside it.

'Ravens! How wonderful! I don't remember any here years ago.'

'These only arrived this year, probably migrants from Wales.' There was a note of triumph in Anthony's voice. 'I knew you'd be pleased. Most people are horrified when they know we are sheltering ravens but you have always been different. Perhaps you might persuade my wife of the ravens' worth.'

I gave him a sharp glance. Ever since arriving at Acton Court I'd wanted to enquire after his marriage, trusting to hear that he had found happiness with the rich heiress his parents had chosen for him. But his words and his tone did not give me cause to hope. 'Does she fear them then?' I asked.

'Not fear them; nothing much frightens Elizabeth. She hates them.'

'But does she love you, Anthony? And do you love her?'

He gave me a puzzled look and sighed. 'Actually I believe she despises me. And hard though I try, I cannot bring myself to love her. But she is carrying our child and we have to make the best we can of our marriage, whether we like it or not.'

'But you are kind to her, aren't you? Women's humours

are often erratic when they're with child.' I had always thought of Anthony, boy and man, as a gentle soul and could not imagine him being angry or violent.

'I don't shout at her, if that's what you mean, but her mood can change very suddenly and sometimes I have to leave the room when she starts up.'

On the verge of asking what he meant by that, I had second thoughts. He was only twenty-two and might never have considered that she could be concealing apprehension about the birth under a defiant attitude. 'You say she is fearless but all women fear childbirth, I think, especially the first time. There is so much that can go wrong. When is the baby due?'

I could detect the level of his anxiety by the way he began to wring his hands. 'She does not seem certain but she looks quite big.' His hands made a round shape in his stomach area. 'The midwife said it looked like an August birth. We only live a couple of miles away at our manor of Frampton, but Elizabeth wouldn't come here to meet the queen in case her labour started. My lady mother thinks it could happen any time now.'

'Does she have a female companion she can trust? Anyone who would support her?'

'The midwife in the village will come as soon as she is sent for. Elizabeth has met her and seems satisfied. There are no female relatives she can call on because she was an only child and her mother died when she was young. My eldest sister Margaret would help but she only recently gave birth herself and has her own babe to care for. Otherwise you have met my three teenage brothers and two younger sisters and will realise that they are either the wrong sex or too young. My mother offered to be with her but Elizabeth refused.' He sighed. 'They don't really get on.'

'Then you must go back to her today, Anthony. Whatever she says, she needs you there for the birth.'

He nodded. 'I will leave before dark but the queen has commanded me for one more card session after supper. There has been no word from Frampton so I'll lose a few more pounds to her grace and then ride to my wife.'

'I would come myself but I cannot leave the queen. It's not official yet but she is also pregnant and needs my care.'

'Yes, I know. My lady mother told me in strict confidence.'

'Her child is not due until the New Year but she does not carry her babies easily and she is no longer young. We must all pray for her, and for your Elizabeth.' I took both his hands and squeezed them encouragingly. 'Look after her, Anthony, and be gentle with her moods. Whatever you think, she does need you and perhaps she will discover how easy you are to love. I will pray that she does.'

I released him and gathered up my skirt to leave. 'I must go back now. Thank you for showing me your hideaway – and the ravens. I hope they stay. They will bring you luck.'

When I reached the hedge arch I turned and saw that he was watching me, his brow still furrowed. I touched my lips and gave him an encouraging wave.

While he played cards with the queen after supper I asked his mother about his wife and the impending birth.

Meg sighed and leaned nearer to murmur her response. 'Sir Robert was determined Anthony should marry Elizabeth Huddersfield because her father was Attorney General to the king and had asked him to look after her interests after his death. He died two years ago and they married soon after, as you know. She is a strange girl. I offered to be with her at the birth but she turned me down.'

'Yes, Anthony told me. It's unfortunate because she seems to have no female relatives of her own,' I said.

'Actually her stepmother is still alive but she's taken a vow of chastity and retired to a convent. Elizabeth inherited her father's manors in Devon so Anthony is not short of income.' Meg cast a glance at the card table and smiled ironically. 'At least he wasn't until her grace came to stay.'

'He's investing in a future at court,' I reassured her. 'The queen is very taken with him and I must admit I'm not surprised. He has great charm but appears unaware of it, which is very endearing.'

'Hmm,' Meg said, laying a hand on my arm. 'You see that, Joan, but unfortunately it seems his wife does not.'

II

Langley Lodge and Westminster Palace

September–October 1502

AFTER ACTON COURT, THE latter stages of the queen's
progress were subject to a number of prolonged stays
at various noble houses due to her recurring bouts of weakness and fatigue. I became so worried about her health that
I wrote secretly to the king, advising him of the situation, and
when we reached his private hunting lodge at Langley he was
waiting to greet her.

He summoned me to his chamber when Elizabeth had
settled for sleep. 'She looks like a ghost, Lady Guildford
– so pale and thin. Under her smock, the babe protrudes
like a gall on a sapling!'

I could only agree. 'Yes, I'm afraid it's true, your grace. She
has pushed herself too hard. But some weeks of rest and good
nourishment should return the roses to her cheeks. I have
sent for Master John Grice, her apothecary, and he will be
meeting us here very soon with remedies and restoratives.'

The king's brow creased with concern. 'Perhaps I should
also send for her physician.'

'If it is your wish, sire. But as a rule physicians do not
attend to matters of childbirth. Master Grice is consulted by

all the best midwives in London, including Mistress Massey, who I assume will attend the queen as she has done before?'

He nodded with a stern look. 'Well, let us wait to hear what the apothecary has to say. Please advise me when he arrives and I will send for him.'

He left me wondering nervously if he considered me responsible for the queen's condition.

Master Grice appeared on the evening of the following day, his assistant leading a laden packhorse, its panniers stuffed with bottles and jars and glass mixing bowls, all wrapped in straw to protect them from the hazards of the road. Although I told him of the king's wish to see him on arrival, he insisted on visiting the queen first. Afterwards he, too, expressed surprise at her condition but was optimistic that he could treat her successfully. 'Nevertheless I wonder that she wished to travel so far and so fast at such a perilous time in her life. After all she is not young.'

'She wants to provide the realm with another prince, Master Grice, and has prayed at every shrine in her path for heavenly assistance in her mission. I suppose there is nothing in your panniers that would ensure the birth of a male child?'

John Grice knew me well enough to scoff. 'If I had such a miracle at my command I would be a wealthy man, Lady Guildford, so I hope the king understands the futility of asking me for one. It is always in God's hands.'

'I'm sure he does. And if prayer can achieve it the queen has definitely done her best in that regard,' I told him.

'Then I will do my best to repair the physical damage all that praying has done,' he said glumly. 'But do not tell the king I said that.'

It took three weeks of Master Grice's ministrations to restore Elizabeth to sufficient health to continue the journey, with frequent stopovers and further visits to shrines. The king had banned his wife from riding and arranged for her horse-drawn carriage to be delivered to Langley. I confess that I found the constant riding arduous enough myself, without the added burden of being five months pregnant. I was greatly relieved when we boarded the royal barge at Staines to complete the journey on the River Thames.

The relative comfort of the barge seemed to restore the queen's energy and mood because as soon as we reached Westminster Palace the first thing she did was to order it to collect the Dowager Princess of Wales from Durham Palace, the Thameside residence of the bishop of Durham, who had kindly lent it to Prince Arthur's young widow while she recovered from her bereavement.

When I protested that it might be wise for Elizabeth to take a few days' rest before launching into entertaining the princess and her entourage I was put firmly in my place. 'Fond though I am of your company, Lady Guildford, I now need to fulfil my duty to my daughter-in-law, who must be anxious to establish herself at court and to learn what our intentions are towards her. After all we are her parents-in-law and must treat her like the daughter she still is. I will bring Princess Margaret back from Eltham as well, so that they may become better acquainted. It will be good for her to learn something of the Spanish court before she is obliged to go to her Scottish husband. There is to be a proxy marriage to confirm her union with King James in the New Year and Margaret will travel to Scotland next summer.'

'She is still very young for such a responsibility, is she

not, your grace?' I was on tenterhooks saying this but felt it to be true. Princess Margaret was not yet thirteen, and while she would be that age by the time the proxy marriage took place, it was still very young to contemplate leaving everything that was familiar and starting life as a wife in a strange country.

Elizabeth closed her eyes and heaved a sigh. 'Yes, you are right, she is, but the marriage is to seal a Treaty of Perpetual Peace between Scotland and England – a truly magnificent concept – and the king is anxious that it be confirmed as soon as possible. For their part the Scots wish their queen to be present in her new realm when it is ratified. I asked Henry to persuade King James that he should delay consummation until she is fifteen and I have every hope his agreement will be forthcoming.' Her hands strayed to her swollen belly, as if to protect the child within from hearing these details. 'For that and many other reasons I have decided to ask you to accompany Margaret to Scotland when she goes – *in loco parentis* as it were. I know this will take you away from your own family for many months but she admires you so much and I'm sure your presence at this crucial time in her life would greatly ease her transition from princess to queen.'

She gazed at me enquiringly, waiting for an answer, while I took a deep breath and considered my response. I had little inclination to go to Scotland with Margaret. If I agreed to go it would mean more long hours in the saddle and probably many more advising and consoling a very anxious young queen. I decided to refuse.

Sensing my hesitation the queen spoke again. 'The king is relying on your help in this matter, Joan. He is very concerned for his daughter's well-being.'

Years of loyalty to the crown swirled in my mind. I was my mother's daughter; she who had abandoned everything, even her children and her adopted country, to serve the deposed Queen Marguerite of Anjou until she died. Against my first instinct I found myself nodding. 'It will be my honour to attend the Queen of Scots,' I said.

Elizabeth smiled. 'It is a great weight off my mind to know you will be with her.'

Richard was furious. 'You did not have to say yes, Joan! You have daughters here in England who also need your help and advice. Why do you choose to favour the queen's daughter over them?'

It was hard to reply because I did not really have an answer that would satisfy him. And the one I chose to give merely made him angrier. 'We also have a son who is making his way high into the favour of the prince who, God willing, will be the next king. We both need to preserve the Guildford name in royal esteem, as much for him as for ourselves. Besides, how many times have you been long absent on royal business? No, don't answer that because they are too numerous to count.'

His face was a picture – eyes wide and lips pursed in displeasure. 'And what about our marriage vows – your debt of duty to your husband? Do you give no thought to that?'

I gave him what I hoped was an engaging smile. 'Clearly the king and queen do not. And after all we are not young lovers any more, Richard. But as I recall our reunions have supplied some of our most loving moments.' I cast a meaningful glance at the tester bed in the courtiers' chamber we'd been assigned in Westminster Palace and then waved at the sturdy oak door. 'Perhaps we should push the peg in the lock and take this opportunity to store up some more, in order to sustain us while we are apart?'

12

The Tower of London

January–February 1503

HAVING RECEIVED MY PROMISE to accompany the Queen of Scots to her official wedding in Scotland, the queen chose not to ask me to attend her lying-in and delivery, which was due in mid-February. Her chief lady-in-waiting was not happy about this. 'What shall I do without you, Joan?' Beth Stafford grumbled privately. 'You know far more about childbirth than I do! At least you have experienced it yourself.'

'One of the duties of a wife is occasionally to spend time with her husband,' I told her, 'and I have other family commitments besides.'

Richard and I spent the New Year celebrations with his daughter Maria at the Haute family seat near Canterbury but when we returned to Halden Hall we received a summons back to royal duty. Two years previously, King Henry had commissioned another new tower extension to be built onto the Royal Palace at the Tower of London. It was to be called the King's Tower, to provide the monarch with a very grand bedchamber, a personal bathroom with hot running water, and on the ground floor a guardhouse and an extensive library. There was to be a royal inauguration of this new tower at the end of January with ceremonial organised as usual by Richard, to include an archery competition, jousting and a twenty-one-gun salute. Queen Elizabeth's baby was not due until the middle of the following month and, despite her enduring dislike of the Tower, she accompanied him there and they stayed for a Candlemas service on the second of February, prior to travelling back to Richmond Palace the following day for her to begin her lying-in.

Unfortunately her labour began unexpectedly early in the middle of the High Mass being held in the Chapel of St James at the top of the White Tower. All the elaborate preparations that had been made for the royal lying-in at Richmond went for naught as the pains struck so intensely that her legs buckled under her and she had to be carried from the chapel by the king to the nearest chamber, which happened to be the chaplain's retreat. I had been attending the service and of course accompanied Elizabeth there along with Lady Stafford, who looked aghast at the situation. Luckily, the midwife, Alice Massey, had been hired for a month and was already residing with the royal household, so a page was immediately sent to bring her to the queen's aid.

Despite her considerable discomfort, Elizabeth could not bear to fail in her duty and as soon as she had been laid on the bed and the pain had receded somewhat she pressed into my hands the velvet purse of coins she had been intending to offer at the altar. 'I cannot disappoint the Virgin so please offer this in my stead, Joan. It will provide candles for the chapel for the whole year. We cannot consign it to the dark and the Holy Lady will surely sustain my travail and grant me the boy I so ardently desire.'

'It will be my honour to do so, your grace,' I said sincerely, thinking impiously how it would surely be churlish of Christ's Holy Mother to refuse the desperate pleas of a pilgrim who had prayed and made offerings at almost every shrine between London and the Welsh March. 'And Mistress Massey will be here very soon to help you.'

As I made for the door I found myself wondering why Elizabeth's pains should have started so suddenly and violently and not developed with the usual gradual increase in intensity most common among mothers.

'I think her grace may have been experiencing mild discomfort for some time, Lady Guildford,' Mistress Massey explained in a soft, confiding voice when I returned ten minutes later. 'It is not uncommon for older and experienced mothers to put minor twinges down to the womb being stretched as the babe grows and not recognise them as the start of labour, especially if they are not due for some days or weeks. In this event the more violent onset of the later stage of their labour can take them by surprise.' She glanced at the pale, exhausted face of the queen. 'And the sooner this birth is over the better, for her grace is very weak. She will need a long rest afterwards.'

All the necessary linens, lotions and vessels had been assembled in the unfamiliar chamber and when the baby did come, little more than an hour later, it too was weak and very small and the midwife swept it off to the chapel font, which had been filled with cold water in case of the need for a treatment sometimes prescribed to shock a premature baby into breathing. Elizabeth was unaware of this for her eyes were closed and sunken, deep in shadows, only little puffs of air from her lips reassuring us that she still lived. The midwife's assistant was watching for the afterbirth but we were all waiting anxiously to hear the baby's cry. When it came at last it was meagre and plaintive, a feeble protest at such insensitive treatment. The midwife returned with the child warmly wrapped and so thus far none of us had been able to observe its sex.

'A little girl, your grace,' said Mistress Massey, placing the tiny child in the crook of queen's arm.

My heart sank. After a long and fraught pause, a tear slipped slowly down Elizabeth's cheek. Neither mother nor child made any further sound or movement and I hastened to use the midwife's mirror to check again for breathing, while Mistress Massey rushed back to the other end of the bed at the urgent behest of her nurse. Lady Stafford hurried off to inform the king of the far-from-triumphant delivery and a tense hush fell in the small room.

I made the sign of the cross, my lips moving in a silent Ave Maria. As I did so I realised that it was still February the second. Although the delivery had been traumatic, it had at least been quick. The candles would still be burning in every church in the land to commemorate the purification of the Virgin Mary after the birth of baby Jesus. To me it seemed achingly sad that despite all those prayers to Christ's Mother for a son, on this her special day there was no inclination to celebrate this unexpected delivery in the Tower of London.

Because of the tiny infant's frailty there was no time to prepare the usual pomp and ceremony of a royal baptism. Even the chrisom veil, infused with holy oil, which had featured at the baptism of all the king's other children, could not be brought from Richmond in time.

While accompanying the queen on her pilgrimage, I had watched her become utterly convinced that she was carrying the male child she had promised to King Henry during the dark days following Prince Arthur's death. Now her body, which had grown so frail, gradually became consumed with fever, seemingly unable to summon the strength to resist it, and I sadly shared the day-and-night vigil over its gradual but apparently unstoppable decline. In the early hours of February the eleventh, on her thirty-seventh birthday, Queen Elizabeth of York drew her last tremulous breath. Afterwards, believing her to be safely ensconced in the heaven she truly deserved, I fervently hoped she never knew that little Princess Catherine, the child she had prayed so hard to be a boy, would survive her by only a week.

PART TWO

13

Colleyweston Palace

1503

'I HOPE WHEN I finally meet my real husband face to face, he is not as old and ugly as the Earl of Bothwell!'

The Queen of Scots' proxy wedding to the Scottish king had taken place at Richmond Palace two weeks before her mother's death, and visiting the new young queen in her chamber at bedtime afterwards, I could not help sympathising with her.

When the earl had processed into the crowded Presence Chamber between two splendidly clad bishops, to play the part of King James the Fourth, Margaret had been unable to conceal her dismay. Already well over fifty, the king's leading diplomat was a hardened soldier with a scarred face and a grey beard. Although he wore a cloth of gold doublet to represent King James, he was very far removed from the romantic bridegroom his teenage proxy bride might have preferred. Nevertheless he had performed his role with fatherly kindliness and attempted to assuage her evident disappointment by describing her genuine spouse to her in glowing terms as 'the comeliest man in Scotland'.

Five months later we set out from Richmond Palace in

the company of the king, only recently recovered from his total prostration following the death of Queen Elizabeth, on the first leg of our journey to Edinburgh for the real marriage celebration. Most of King Henry's close relatives joined this early cavalcade, which after several days on the road stopped for a few nights at Colleyweston, his mother's extensive country estate in Northamptonshire. Aware that she was unlikely ever to see her namesake again, Lady Margaret Beaufort wished to give her beloved granddaughter a memorable send-off to her new kingdom. Banquets, jousts, dances and religious services had been arranged and Margaret, Queen of Scots, was listed as the guest of honour at all of them.

A beautifully inscribed vellum scroll describing these events had been left in the visitors' chambers and reading it at the start of our stay, I wondered if it might all look rather overwhelming to the young queen. Therefore, later that evening, I was not surprised to receive a visit from her.

Not being used to sleeping alone, Margaret had chosen to share her bed and chamber with Catherine Gordon, the young Scottish noblewoman who King James had given in marriage to the handsome stranger who had been announced in his court as Richard, Duke of York, the younger of the two disinherited boys who had disappeared from the Tower of London during the reign of the usurper. After being captured following his failed invasion of England, this same man had been exposed as a pretender from Flanders called Perkin Warbeck and executed on Tower Hill. His unfortunate widow had accompanied him to England and was inevitably also arrested, but she found favour with King Henry and was placed in the queen's household at about the same time as the young Princess Margaret also joined it. Despite a five-year age gap, the two teenage newcomers had formed a close friendship.

My chamber at Colleyweston was next to Margaret's and conveniently connected by a door, through which she was able to make a surreptitious entry, closing it quietly behind her. Mildy had been about to help me prepare for bed but the quiet and careful way my visitor closed the door told me that she was seeking a private meeting and so I quickly sent the maid away.

'Kitty is asleep and I don't want to wake her, Mother Guildford,' Margaret said, already clad in a chamber robe and clearly ready for bed herself. She'd chosen to call her friend Kitty because of the number of Catherines at court. 'I need to speak with you privately.'

Thinking she might wish to discuss the entertainments, I indicated the table on which I had laid my scroll and the two chairs beside it. 'Please sit, your grace, and tell me the problem.'

Comfortably ensconced, she indicated the scroll. 'My grandmother has made me the guest of honour at every special event, Mother Guildford,' she remarked.

'Is that not because she wants to honour you?' I suggested. 'And also perhaps to accustom you to being the focus of attention, which is, I'm afraid, the destiny of queens.'

'Yes, I know that, and I've become more accustomed to the idea as I've grown older. Besides I like the things that go with being a queen; the clothes and the jewellery, the hawks and horses – particularly the horses. I adore the golden palfreys my father has given me to carry my litter.'

Her solemn litany of the advantages of royalty made me smile. 'So what can be your objection to being your grandmother's principal guest? My advice would be to make the most of it, because after this the journey becomes more tedious. You will pass through one town after another, where every mayor will welcome you with a long speech and every citizen and his children will come out to clap and cheer you through the streets in your beautiful litter, come rain or come shine; and there are many miles and many towns between here and Scotland, your grace.'

Margaret shook her head vigorously. 'All this I know, Mother Guildford!' she exclaimed. 'What I came to discuss with you is the fact that I think I have made a mistake in bringing Kitty Gordon in my train.'

This admission took me completely by surprise. 'Oh! Really? Are you sure?'

Her response was vehement. 'Yes! I am very sure. I know you, like everyone else, thought she would be helpful in describing the way the Scots live and speak – and she has already told me a great deal. But that is not why I no longer require her company. My mother told me that she asked you to accompany me to Scotland *in loco parentis* and so, as her representative, I have come to you to solve my difficult problem. How do we get rid of Kitty?'

The very proud queenliness with which she uttered this last remark reminded me that there was a great deal of her father in Margaret. King Henry had a decisiveness about him that had served him well during his reign and I hoped it would be of equal use to Margaret in hers.

I took a deep breath. 'Well, first of all, I think you had better tell me the reason for it.'

Margaret put her elbows on the table and said simply, 'Basically, she is too beautiful.'

I couldn't stop my eyes opening to their widest extent as I stared at her and there was a long pause before I voiced my reaction. 'Well, yes, she is very attractive, it's true. But you have always known that. Why should it suddenly offend you?'

She shook her head. 'Oh, no, I'm not offended, Mother Guildford. I like Kitty very much and she likes me. We get on well, as you know, and I love having such a beautiful friend. But I have learned things from some of the Scottish ladies who have travelled down here to join my train. Things that make it foolish for me to take Kitty back to King James's court.'

She sounded so serious, so wise beyond her years, that I found it hard to believe she was still only thirteen. 'This sounds like gossip they are spreading. It's never a good idea to heed gossip, your grace. Tell me who these ladies are and I'll speak to them myself. What do they say?'

It was her turn to breathe deeply before she replied and her voice shook slightly. 'That King James is besotted with Kitty. He has been ever since he laid eyes on her when she came to his court as a girl of my age. They were amazed to see that she was among the ladies in my entourage. He used to write passionate letters to her. They believe she became his mistress. It would not be sensible to take her back really, would it? I'm sure my mother would not have advised it.'

I screwed up my face in disbelief. 'I'm sure she would not, if it's true. But if Kitty was his mistress, why would the king have married her to the man who said he was the Duke of York?'

'Because that man and Kitty had fallen in love and married secretly anyway. You can do that in Scotland, I'm told. The ladies said the king was distraught but he must have understood that being married to a man you believed to be a duke might seem preferable to a woman rather than being merely the mistress of a king. So he gave them a public wedding, then supplied them with an army and a ship and sent them off to invade England. I think he must have known they were unlikely to succeed, don't you?'

I was so astounded by the whole extraordinary story that I fell silent, but Margaret filled the void: 'So should I just tell Kitty that she must return to King Henry's court? And do I tell her why, or do I just say I no longer require her company? That is my awful dilemma, Mother Guildford.'

14

Scotland

August 1503

MARGARET DISMISSED CATHERINE GORDON as gently as she could, waiting until the party at Colleyweston was over and choosing the day before the king departed, allowing her to travel back among the other members of his court. I did not ask her what she had said to Kitty but it helped that King Henry told her he had decided he would not allow Kitty to leave his court while Richard, Earl of Suffolk, the last York pretender to the Tudor throne, was alive somewhere in Europe.

Saying goodbye to her best friend and all her closest relatives at once took its toll and although Margaret managed to remain composed through all their tears and embraces, she invited me to share her departing litter and collapsed into my arms as soon as the procession had cleared the Colleyweston gatehouse.

'I'll never see them all again, shall I, Mother Guildford? They will be alive but they are already dead to me. It's so cruel! How can I bear it?' Her protests came in desperate jerky gasps and all I could do was hold her close and let the tears flow. It was the moment when I realised how wise

Queen Elizabeth had been to so earnestly request my promise to accompany her young daughter to her destiny. But at the same time I also had to remember that it was only twenty-five miles to the next stop on our northern journey, when the great and good of the town of Grantham would be waiting to greet the new Queen of Scots. While I would give all the comfort I could to my sobbing charge, I had to remember that her next royal appearance was only a matter of hours away.

This was when I learned just how well Margaret had come to understand the duties of a queen, for by the time we reached Grantham she had dried her tears, accepted my application of an unguent to smooth her puffy eyes and blotched complexion and emerged from her litter to greet the welcoming party with dignity intact and exuding royal splendour. The cheers were deafening and only the first of a succession of similarly enthusiastic welcomes as she travelled the Great North Road from town to town. When we reached the city of York it took our cavalcade two hours to make its way through the excited crowds that filled the streets from her entry at the Micklegate Bar, where she was invited to touch the monarch's state sword, to the beautiful Minster church, where the Archbishop of York held a Mass. By the end of July, to the sound of a royal gun salute from the town's walls, we had crossed the river into Berwick upon Tweed, where a farewell banquet was planned.

Margaret was surprised to find that she had not yet entered Scottish territory. 'I thought the River Tweed was the border,' she whispered to me before her litter came to a halt.

'Twenty-one years ago, before the death of King Edward,

his brother Richard of Gloucester took the town back from the Scots after a siege,' I told her. 'Did I not teach you the history of your own country? *Mea culpa!*'

Queen Margaret laughed. 'There you are, you see, Mother Guildford – you were too busy teaching us Latin! So when do I actually cross into my new kingdom?'

'A few miles up the road at a place called Lamberton. A welcome party from King James's court will meet you there.'

The sound of trumpets and pipes and neighing horses alerted us before we rounded a corner into the small hamlet of Lamberton and were confronted by an array of tents and pavilions. Scottish knights in armour, bearing their colourful coats of arms, were lined up ready to show off their jousting skills in a flag-decked tourney ground laid out in front of a small church. Two bishops and Lord Renton, the local laird, were waiting at the lych-gate to welcome the Queen of Scots into her kingdom at the start of a noisy and cheerful episode, which had Margaret enjoying refreshments while watching the jousting and presenting the prizes to the winners. Afterwards she, and as many as could fit into the little kirk, heard Mass from the Archbishop of Glasgow before the English guards left for the south and the Scottish knights assembled to escort her ten miles up the road to her overnight accommodation.

Margaret was fascinated by Fast Castle, which was located on a high rocky promontory jutting out into the North Sea and accessible only via a fiercely defended barbican and a drawbridge over a deep ravine. Having been advised to close the curtains of her litter when we crossed the bridge, she could not resist peering out. She gasped and clutched at my arm with open-mouthed astonishment. 'It's like being on a cloud, Mother Joan! I can see nothing but rocks and water far beneath us! I'm amazed the horses aren't frightened.'

As if they had heard her, there was a sudden lurch and I had to grab the sleeve of her gown to haul her back from the open side of the litter as the lead horses suddenly leapt forward in panic to find solid ground. A mounted knight came cantering up to steady the jittery pair and then to bow before the open litter and check whether the Queen of Scots was unharmed.

'Alexander Home at your grace's service,' the young knight said. 'Welcome to Fast Castle; it is not an easy place to reach, I'm afraid.'

Margaret drew the curtain wider and smiled up at him. 'It is an adventure I am happy not to have missed, sir. You must be the lord whose name I've been told is spelt "Home" but pronounced "Hume". Thank you for letting us stay in your remarkable castle. Having survived the bridge I shall feel very safe here.'

I think Fast Castle was Margaret's favourite stop on the whole journey; partly because of its dramatic location with sweeping views out to sea and the wild calls of the sea birds nesting on the surrounding cliffs and partly due to the presence of its extremely handsome, attentive and amusing host. The following day, when he offered his cupped hands to help her mount her horse, I saw the blood rush to her cheeks before she jumped up into the saddle, and on the journey along the coast to Dunbar Lord Home rode beside her, pointing out the sights and naming the estates through which we passed. When he left the cavalcade to return to his home she rode excitedly to my side. 'What a beautiful country this is, Mother Guildford! And how kind and charming its people are. I intend to be very happy here.'

I crossed my fingers on the reins of my palfrey and sent up a silent prayer to ask for divine attention to her words. 'I'm sure King James will be delighted to hear that, your grace,' I said. 'And soon you will be meeting your real and royal husband.'

Two days later she was installed in Dalkeith Castle a few miles south of Edinburgh, where the king had organised for her to stay while she rested after her journey and made preparations for the wedding. Her chamber was a large and well-furnished apartment with windows overlooking the moat and the extensive hunting park. Despite wearing a wide-brimmed hat while she rode, the August sun had turned her exposed skin a deeper shade of pink and I was busy applying more of the calming balm to the affected places when a messenger came to tell us that the king had arrived on a whim, wishing to bid his bride goodnight.

Margaret was intrigued but hesitant. 'Is that proper, Mother Guildford? I'm in my chamber robe, ready for bed. My hair is loose. Should he see me like this before we are properly married? Or should I dress again and go down to the hall to greet him?'

I gave her a reassuring smile. 'Royal bridegrooms often choose to make an unexpected journey to see their brides before the wedding. Your brother, Prince Arthur, God rest his soul, rode all the way from Ludlow to see his Spanish princess before their church wedding. They, too, were already married by proxy.'

'And did Princess Katherine admit him to her chamber?'

'No, but she did go to meet him in a public room and

allowed him to lift her lace veil to see her beautiful face. So I see no harm in admitting King James to your chamber when we are all here with you – Oh!'

I had been indicating the other ladies and chambermaids who were in attendance when the door was flung open to admit a fine-looking man in a hunting jacket and long riding boots. 'Such good advice from a sensible woman, whoever you are!' The king – for it was unmistakeably him – gave me a brief nod of acknowledgement and strode straight up to Margaret, making her a sweeping bow. 'My beautiful queen! We were hunting in the area when we heard you had arrived, so I have come to welcome you to our kingdom! I do hope you like what you have seen of Scotland so far.'

Margaret's low curtsy was understandably slightly wobbly and he reached out to take her hand, helping her to rise and carrying it on to his lips at the same time. 'Thank you, your grace,' she said faintly. 'I am happy to be here.'

'I see you are preparing for sleep but let us share a cup and drink to your safe arrival.' He did not release her hand but led her to a table in the window where he had spotted the jug of wine and a jewelled cup, which had been set for her convenience. With his free hand he poured wine expertly, then lifted the cup to offer it to her. 'I hope you are satisfied with the properties I have allocated to you as your dower. They are among my most valuable castles and palaces and their manors will provide you with a sizeable income to support your needs. I want my queen to wear the best gowns and jewels and live in all comfort and security.'

The wine threatened to spill as Margaret held it to her lips, sipping hurriedly and at the same time casting a swift and puzzled glance in my direction. 'I think the queen has not yet seen the list of properties, your grace,' I said with a brief bob.

'But I cannot wait to see it and to visit them with you, my lord,' she assured him, handing the cup back.

'We shall take a tour together after our union has been heaven-blessed, Margaret.' King James took a healthy gulp and smiled broadly. 'I drink to my very lovely bride,' he said. 'The ceremony will be at the Abbey of the Holy Rood in Edinburgh in four days' time.' Returning the cup to the table, he bent forward and kissed her fondly on the cheek. 'Now I will say goodnight and ride back to Edinburgh a happy man. God has granted me the bride of my dreams!'

15

Dalkeith Castle and Edinburgh

August 1503

TIRED FROM HER LONG journey and the emotion of meeting the king, Margaret slept late the following morning and I decided not to rouse her when a member of the castle household confided anxiously that there had been a fire in the castle stables during the night and the two golden horses King Henry had given her had died in the conflagration. Those palfreys were her pride and joy and had carried her much of the way from Richmond to Scotland. I greatly feared their demise would cast a dark shadow over the wedding celebrations.

At supper the previous evening the Earl of Morton, who owned the Dalkeith estate, had suggested that she might enjoy some hunting in the parkland surrounding the castle and so after she rose, she grew excited as we dressed her in her riding attire but I wondered sadly if she would still feel like hunting when she learned of her palfreys' fate.

Lord Morton waited until after she had broken her fast to tell her the dreadful news, trying to soften the blow by promising that horses just as suitable would be found to carry her litter when she went to Edinburgh for her wedding.

'And I have sent a message to inform the king of the sad situation, your grace,' he added.

There was tense silence as Margaret stared at him, speechless for a long minute in utter disbelief. Then, as tears gathered in her eyes, she rose from her chair and almost yelled in the earl's face, 'No others can possibly replace those golden horses! How could this terrible thing have happened, my lord? Surely busy stables have grooms living in with the horses at all times! Shouldn't the fire have been extinguished before it could take hold?'

Lord Morton backed away from her violent anger and dropped to his knees. 'I-it was the summer heat that caused the h-hay in the loft to smoulder unnoticed,' he stuttered. 'It must have burst into flame in the early hours of the night while the grooms were asleep and the loft floor collapsed into the stalls. Two of my staff were badly burned trying to get the horses out but they were already stupefied by the smoke and collapsed. I am so sorry this should have happened while you are here, your grace. It is a disaster.'

At this stage the queen became what she truly was, a young girl of thirteen who had already faced too much death in her recent life. She threw all decorum to the wind and swung round to me, flinging herself into my arms and sobbing. 'I can't bear it, Mother Joan! I can't face staying here any more! I don't want to be married! I just want to go back to England!'

The earl was up on his feet and Lady Morton had risen from the table she had been sharing with the queen. Both were visibly horrified at Margaret's outburst and gazed in panic at each other, wondering what to say or do. I shook my head at them and guided the distraught girl towards the door, still hiding her tears on my shoulder. 'The queen will retire,' I told them. 'If you have any soothing potion in your cupboards it would be kind of you to send it up.'

Twenty minutes later, when Margaret's anguish had subsided and the tears had stopped, it was the king himself who brought the potion to her chamber. He waved it in my direction and I took it from him.

'I come to bring you comfort, my little one,' King James said gently, dropping to his knees beside the bed, where she had buried her face in the pillows. 'I too adore my horses and know how agonising it is to lose them, especially when they have served you tirelessly and well. Your Mother Guildford will pour you some calming tonic and I will dry your tears on my silk kerchief. Death is hard to bear at any age but worst of all when you are young.'

Hearing his voice, Margaret roused herself to turn and mutely accept the gentle way he applied the kerchief to her swollen eyes and as he did so I suddenly had a premonition that this marriage might prove to be a success.

Two white horses were found to bear the queen's litter and her procession to Edinburgh was met halfway there by King James, mounted on a black charger and dressed, like Margaret, in cloth of gold with colourful trimmings and glittering jewellery. Outside the city gate a palfrey was waiting for her to ride through the streets but the king decided that they should ride together and a pillion was attached to his saddle for her to sit behind him.

Their entrance into the city was met by rousing cheers as the people greeted the first queen consort of Scotland for fifteen years. At St Giles' Kirk in the High Street, they were offered an arm-bone of the saint to kiss, while a Te Deum was sung. Then the mood became merrier at the Mercat Cross where a fountain ran with red wine and we all stopped for refreshment. Processing slowly down the hill called the Canongate we viewed a series of pageant scenes from the Bible and tableaux illustrating tales from ancient history and when the royal couple dismounted at the Abbey of the Holy Rood, another Te Deum welcomed them into the church.

After a service of thanksgiving the king put his arm around his bride's waist and walked with her to the adjoining palace where there was a festive supper before he led her to the door of her chamber. While her ladies prepared her for bed, Margaret was full of praise for the king and his courtiers and the episode of the stable fire seemed entirely forgotten. However, when the Scottish ladies had departed for their own houses and only her English attendants remained, she did wonder out loud why, after the king had kissed her goodnight, he also kissed all his female courtiers before he left.

'I would not want him to do that when I am queen,' she said firmly.

The wedding took place the following day and we were all up at dawn to prepare the bride for her big occasion. The king and queen walked to the church in separate processions and met at the altar, both wearing white damask. Margaret's gown was trimmed with red velvet and had a train embroidered with English roses and Scottish thistles. Her deep auburn hair hung shining and loose down to her waist, held by a gold coronet studded with pearls. The king wore a crimson jacket over his white damask doublet and scarlet hose, a black bonnet with a ruby brooch and a sword in a magnificent jewelled sheath. Despite the difference in their ages, while making their vows at the altar they looked a splendidly matched royal pair.

At the wedding banquet the bride sat in splendour beneath a gold cloth of state and the king insisted that she be served first. There were twelve courses, many toasts and much music from minstrels in their galleries but sadly there was no room for dancing, although I knew that Margaret would have liked to show her graceful skills on the floor to her new subjects. When the time came for bedding the bride and groom, the two were escorted to their respective chambers by their attendants but as I followed Margaret's train from the hall a page came and tapped me on the shoulder.

'Lady Guildford, the king bids you to meet him in his apartment. Please follow me.'

King James was waiting in a small anteroom to his bedchamber. Through the open door his own attendants could be heard noisily exchanging ribald remarks as they prepared his night attire. 'Please forgive the inevitable bawdiness, my lady,' he said rather awkwardly as I made my curtsy.

'It is a wedding, your grace,' I said with a smile. 'And a very splendid event it has been.'

Nevertheless he appeared to be rather embarrassed and signalled for the door to be closed behind him by his chamberlain. 'Well, I have summoned you because I know that you, of all her English ladies, have the closest relationship with the queen.'

'I have been with her on and off since she was five, my lord. She calls me Mother Guildford.'

'So I have noticed.' He rubbed at his forehead distractedly. 'That is why I am asking you to explain something to her.'

I made no response but waited for him to continue.

'I'm sure you know that a marriage is not legal until it has been consummated and King Henry has asked me not to consummate my marriage until Queen Margaret is fifteen.'

I swallowed, hoping this was not leading where I feared it might be. 'Yes, my lord, I am aware of that.'

'Well, I understand the reason for it, because King Henry's mother was only thirteen when he was born, after her marriage was consummated when she was twelve. I do not intend to let that happen to Margaret.'

I felt a wave of relief, but it was short-lived.

'However, I cannot risk our marriage being declared invalid and so it is my intention to ensure this cannot happen. Our wedding night will be spent together and I will make love to Margaret just this once, to establish the loss of her virginity.' His face had coloured deeply but he pursued his theme. 'However, I will ensure that there is no possibility of her becoming pregnant, if you understand me? I will withdraw before the seed is spilled.' He drew a deep breath and continued. 'Subsequently I will visit my wife regularly, we will have a loving and happy life together as king and queen but I will not share her bed actively again until she is fifteen. I am relying on you to explain the necessity for the consummation to her, so that she understands what will happen tonight. Afterwards I will tell her my future intentions myself. I will not come to the queen's chamber for an hour, to give you time to prepare her.'

He made me a bow. 'That is all. Thank you, Lady Guildford.' He strode to his chamber door, rapped on it for entry and left the room.

I shook my head despairingly. Did all kings think women only existed to do as they were told without thought or complaint? How did he expect a thirteen-year-old girl to experience the act of love once and then wait for months in frustration to discover its pleasures, or perhaps live in fear of when the time came for it to happen again? However hard King James tried to make her content, I knew that for sixteen months Margaret would not be an entirely happy wife.

When I returned to her chamber it was not easy to spirit her away from the rest of her attendants, who were busy bathing and primping the bride ready for her bridegroom. I had to wait until she emerged from the petal-scattered water and had been patted dry with soft linen, before I could wrap her in her chamber robe and persuade her to come with me into the small oratory behind the impressive marriage bed that dominated the centre of the chamber.

At all costs I did not want to make her cry on the cusp of her deflowering so I began by telling her how proud I was of the way she had carried herself through the marriage ceremony and the banquet and asked if she had enjoyed her wedding. Luckily she was enthusiastic about the whole day and made things a great deal easier for me by saying how kind and loving King James had been.

'He is so attentive, Mother Guildford, have you noticed? I think the bedding ceremony will be quite easy.'

'Yes, I am sure it will, your grace. There will be a blessing of course from the archbishop, and then all sorts of people will probably come and kiss you both and perhaps they will give you gifts and throw flowers.'

'Yes, the Scottish ladies told me that, and some of the men

might be a bit tipsy and sing bawdy songs but I am not to listen or be offended by it. It is quite normal apparently.'

'I'm sure they will keep it mild, being aware of your young age,' I said. 'And with that in mind, are you happy about what will happen once all the other people have left and you are alone with the king?'

'We will be in bed together and I will just do whatever he asks me to do. But I believe he will not ask me to open my legs, is that right?'

Since my meeting with the king I felt that I had to adjust that advice. 'Well, as I have told you a man and a woman have to unite physically before a child can be conceived and I think you must prepare for him to do what the law of Scotland requires of a married couple, although I know he does not wish there to be a baby before you are of an age to give birth safely.'

'Some of my mother's maids of honour tried to tell me that when a couple don't want to make a baby the man does not spill his seed into the woman but I did not believe them. It sounded . . .' she hesitated, screwed up her face and dropped her voice ' . . . messy.'

My mind raced. Should I tell her not to be surprised if 'messy' happened or should I just be satisfied that her mother's young maids of honour had spared me the task of obeying King James's instructions to the letter?

Margaret solved the problem for me by making the sign of the cross at the travelling altar in the oratory and making for the door. 'I think the archbishop will be here soon so I must have my hair brushed. Will you come and do it for me, Mother Guildford? You are the best at brushing hair.'

16

Edinburgh to Colleyweston Palace

December–January 1503–4

I STAYED IN EDINBURGH with some of the English girls who had agreed to keep Margaret company while she settled in to her life as Queen of Scots but after she had celebrated her fourteenth birthday at the end of November and seemed happy enough with all her Scottish castles and servants, I decided to arrange my journey back south. Caravans of merchants from various guilds regularly travelled between Edinburgh and London and were willing to include other people in their number for a fee towards paying their hired guards and as long as they supplied their own horses, so Mildy and I joined one that left at the beginning of December, hoping to be back in London for Christmas.

The farewell with Margaret was tearful for both of us. 'I shall not know what to do without my Mother Guildford,' she declared, taking my hand to raise me from the curtsy I always afforded her. 'No one loves me as you do.'

I smiled through the lump in my throat. 'You have a husband who shows every sign of loving you and it will not be long before he does a little more than just kiss you goodnight, your grace.' We were safely alone in her chamber, her attendants having been dismissed, but nevertheless I kept my voice low. 'Please write and let me know how everything goes after your next birthday.'

She gave me a coy look. 'Perhaps not everything, but I will write discreetly so that you understand. Have a safe journey and tell me of your safe arrival. I will pray for you.'

'And I for you – that you have a long and happy reign and a nursery full of healthy children. I hope your subjects will pray for that as well.'

Our journey south started in cold, bright autumnal weather and the caravan moved at a good pace until we grew near to Fast Castle, where a freezing rainstorm rushed in off the North Sea and soaked us all. I had taken the precaution of purchasing new oiled capes, but they proved inadequate against the onslaught. We just had to hope that the sun would come out eventually but I don't remember being really dry again until we reached Newcastle three days later. Luckily as we travelled south through the larger towns the merchants wanted to do business, which meant that we stayed two nights, giving us the chance to dry our clothes over the fire at our chosen hostel.

Unfortunately, as it turned out, from York we took the road to Lincoln and, riding through the marshy fenlands between the two cities, I developed a fearsome ague, which within hours transformed me from a healthy, energetic woman into a shivering, delirious crone. Luckily the caval-cade included an apothecary who prescribed a potion to reduce the fever, but feeling weaker than a drooping lily, I abandoned my palfrey to be led by a guard and accepted being boosted into a pillion saddle behind a burly but kind-hearted merchant, who did not object when my head drooped onto his shoulder at frequent intervals. The caval-cade even took a detour to deliver me back to the king's mother's country palace of Colleyweston, where I knew I would find a welcome.

For years my mother, Lady Katherine Vaux, had been sharing the king's mother's country home with her old friend and patron, Lady Margaret Beaufort and now, bless her, as soon as she saw me she took control, summoning servants to carry me to a bedchamber where she set about stripping me of my damp and travel-stained clothes and tucking me between fresh linen sheets, where I remained for I knew not how many days.

'How long have I been here?' was the first question I asked Mildy when I finally emerged from the series of weird dreams which had inhabited my delirium, to find that my head was spinning and my limbs ached. 'I feel as if I've run all the way from Edinburgh.'

'It's been nearly a week,' the maid replied, offering me a cup of warm milk. 'Drink this, my lady. You need it. We've tried to make you swallow some gruel but you've hardly eaten. At one point your mother feared for your life.'

It was when I struggled to pull myself up to sitting that I noticed the weakness in my legs and arms and realised that I was ferociously thirsty. 'Does my mother know I'm awake?' I asked between gulps of the milk.

Mildy shook her head. 'No, because she's an old lady and she needs her beauty sleep. But I told her maid and I expect she'll be along to see you as soon as she hears the news.'

I handed her the empty cup. 'I am very lucky to have

been able to come here to Colleyweston. I don't know what would have happened if I'd been taken ill crossing the border hills. It was wild country, wasn't it?'

'Yes, but at least there weren't any biting insects up there. Those marsh flies we ran into on the Lincolnshire fens are what bring the ague.'

'Really?' I stared at her. 'I've never heard that. How do you know?'

Mildy gave me a patient smile. 'I'm a smith's daughter, my lady,' she said, as if that explained everything. 'Now, do you need help to the latrine?'

I nodded gratefully. I had been wondering how I would manage to stand, let alone walk. How I loved my pretty, practical, perceptive Mildy! She was nearly eighteen now and I wondered frequently what I would do when she married and left me.

As I shuffled awkwardly back to the bedchamber, leaning heavily on Mildy's shoulders, my mother appeared. 'Oh, Gigi, you're up at last. God be thanked!' She nearly toppled us as she rushed up to embrace me and land heartfelt kisses on both my cheeks. 'Lady Margaret and I have prayed for you at every Office and every Mass.'

'Thank you, dearest Mother, but I don't think Mildy can bear the weight of two of us!' I gasped.

She backed off, looking contrite. 'Forgive me – but I'm so pleased to see you on your feet!'

Mildy increased the pace. 'She won't be for long, my lady, if I can just get her back to bed.'

By the time I was restored under the tester and Mildy had disappeared to fetch food for me to break my fast, my mother had installed herself on a stool at my bedside. 'She's a helpful girl, that maid of yours,' she remarked after the bedchamber door closed. 'Pretty, too; how have you managed to keep her from the church porch?'

I sighed. 'I don't know. I expect she likes her independence. Can we talk of something else? Tell me what you've heard from the English court since we've been in Scotland.' I lay back and closed my eyes, hoping I'd steered her thoughts towards a sufficiently meaty subject so that I could rest my pounding head.

At first her words were a soothing stream that barely touched my interest but then I was suddenly alert as she started to relate news that definitely piqued my attention. 'Of course I can't discuss it with Lady Margaret but I believe the queen's death turned the king's mind a little. He's become very suspicious, particularly when it comes to the Exchequer. He seems to think that the nobility and gentry are milking the coffers – claiming payments for tasks they have not completed or over-charging for goods they have either failed to supply or undercut. So convinced is he of this that he has set up a new council to flush out the offenders. He calls it the Council Learned in Law and it is headed by a group of lawyers of the kind some might call slippery. I believe one of them is the Comptroller of the Mint, Sir Henry Wyatt.'

I roused myself to interrupt, my voice sharp with indignation. 'Wyatt is not a lawyer!' I could not believe what I was hearing but I was too weak to make any more protest.

'Is he not?' My mother sounded astonished. 'Well, I suppose you would know since he works at the Tower but I'm certain he is on this new council. Perhaps he's just good at checking the books.'

'He's good at cooking the books,' I muttered. Sir Henry Wyatt was a name that sent shivers down my spine. 'What does Sir Reginald think?' Sir Reginald Bray had been Lady Margaret's Receiver General for what seemed like forever and was such a loyal supporter of her son that King Henry had made him Chancellor of Lancaster and used him as his chief minister in all but name. He was someone the king trusted above all men and I could not believe he would have backed the appointment of Wyatt to any council that dealt with the law.

My eyes had flown open at the mention of Wyatt's name and I saw my mother's widen in surprise. 'Haven't you heard, Gigi? Sir Reginald died last year. It must have been soon after you left for Scotland. The king was devastated – he still is. Within twenty months he has lost his son and heir, his beloved wife, and his most important courtier. I suppose it's no wonder he feels lonely and insecure.'

At this point, Mildy returned with a jug and bowl, followed by a page bearing a cup and napkin and a platter of food. There was a fuss as my mother stood up and pushed her stool back, making room for these items to be placed on a side table and carried to my bedside. The smell of fresh bread and hot pottage suddenly made my mouth water.

As Mildy leaned in to help me sit up, the page bowed and said, 'My Lady the King's Mother bade me enquire if it would be convenient for her to pay you a visit after Mass?'

Even though Lady Margaret Beaufort had been my foster mother when I was a child and I was presently living under her roof, she was also now the highest lady in the land and I was still exhausted. In my present state of weakness, the prospect of conversing cogently with such an august visitor seemed impossible. I directed a desperate glance at my mother, who gave a brief nod. 'I'll deal with this, Gigi. You are too tired. Lady Margaret will understand.' With that she blew me a final kiss and turned to usher the page from the room.

I heaved a sigh of relief and fielded a sympathetic smile from Mildy, who placed the platter of bread and cheese on my lap and poured some of the contents of the jug into the bowl. The pottage smelled tantalisingly of chicken and garlic. 'Eat, my lady, and then sleep some more. You are not yet strong enough for exalted visitors.'

As my health improved I brooded over what my mother had told me about the king's new Council Learned in Law. I wished I could discover more details and fretted over Richard's position, especially as I knew he had been involved in some property business with Sir Henry Wyatt, although my absences with the queen and the royal children had prevented me discovering many details. Now that Wyatt was apparently a member of the king's commission investigating his nobles' affairs, I could not help fretting over exactly what their joint activities had involved. Although it had been fifteen years ago, Sir Henry probably still begrudged the fact that, rather than accepting his offer of marriage, I had chosen to marry Richard instead. I knew Wyatt to be a vengeful character and not one to forget or forgive a slight.

'Do you have any plans for the future, Joan, now that the late queen's household has been disbanded?'

Lady Margaret's question came out of the blue at the intimate supper she had arranged for my mother and I to share with her on the day before my planned departure from Colleyweston. We ate in her private dining room, which was hung with exquisite tapestries scattered with flowers and coats of arms, symbols of her own illustrious lineage, and overlooked her privy garden where carved and coloured images of Beaufort yales and Richmond greyhounds looked down over hedged flowerbeds that were presently dormant. Her first and favourite husband, Edmund Tudor, Earl of Richmond, had been half-brother to the Lancastrian King Henry the Sixth and Lady Margaret was still listed in the hierarchy of the nobility as Countess of Richmond, so the lack of York heraldry in her personal garth did not surprise me. The emblem of a small white flower, tucked among the bounteous petals of a large red bloom and known as the Tudor Rose, was the only heraldic nod to York that she allowed to be seen anywhere around her country home.

I took time to consider my response to her question, watching as the server placed several dishes on the pristine white cloth. 'For the first time in my married life, my lady, God seems to have granted me the chance to choose my own path, and my first inclination is to spend time with my family and particularly my son, Hal.'

Lady Margaret raised a well-defined eyebrow, highly expressive under the frame of the nun-like white coif and wimple she chose to wear in her secluded retirement. 'Then you'll not have heard yet that the king has recently made that less likely by removing Prince Henry from Eltham and taking him into his own household at Richmond Palace. He feels his precious heir will be more secure there and I believe your son is among those chosen to accompany the prince.'

This was not good news. I'd been hoping to collect Hal from Eltham on the way down to Kent for a few weeks' recuperation. At the same time I wanted to visit Princess Mary and see how she was faring without her mother and sister. Having been her governess for several years I was very fond of the little princess, the youngest of the king's surviving children.

'Well, I have been worried that his grace might be feeling lonely without any of his family around him, so I am glad he has chosen to bring Prince Henry into his care,' I said diplomatically, although I was not sure that the prince would be feeling the same. Having seen little of his father during his infancy, as a schoolboy I knew he had resented playing second fiddle to Arthur, the king's golden boy. Conversely, Harry had adored his mother and mourned her passing terribly, confessing to me as he wept over her deathbed that he blamed the king for encouraging her to have another child. I had tried to tell him that it was she who had hoped to bring consolation to them both by bearing another son but not only had Henry made it clear he did not believe me but he had also strongly implied that he'd no wish for a younger brother. Now that he was England's heir I suspected that he feared encountering the kind of sibling rivalry that had made life so difficult for his York grandfather, King Edward the Fourth.

'I'm sure you will be permitted to visit your son.' Lady Margaret raised the jewelled cup, which had been filled and placed beside her by her cupbearer. 'But we must drink to your new life of freedom from court restrictions. We enjoy such a life here at Colleyweston, do we not, Kate?' My mother raised her own more modest vessel and smiled agreement before they both took a sip of the wine. 'I understand that your husband gave you your dower house well in advance, so you have somewhere to call your own, should you wish to retire fully.'

I thought of Frensham Manor and all the improvements I had made which I had not yet managed to enjoy, and drew a cogitative sip from my own cup. 'Oh, I don't think I'll be retiring, my lady, although my husband might expect to see more of me for a change, as he fulfils his obligations to the king.'

'Well, I hope he steers clear of the Council Learned,' said my mother. 'It doesn't sound a very comfortable place to find oneself.'

I reached out to squeeze her hand gratefully across the table and said, 'I shall do all I can to see that he does not.'

17

The Tower of London

Spring 1504

Leaving the palfreys we had borrowed from Lady
Margaret for our ride to London at her city stables,
Mildy and I took a ferry downriver to the same destination.
Our journey had been made under the protection of guards
escorting the regular delivery of sheep-meat and fresh vege-
tables to the household at Coldharbour, along with my
travelling chest, which I asked to be sent on to the Tower.
I was greatly looking forward to reaching the familiar
comfort of the quayside residence granted to my husband
as Master of the Royal Ordnance. So as the ferryboat shot
the receding tide under London Bridge, I gripped the
gunwale and felt a surge of exhilaration at the prospect of
being back in the great city after nearly a year's absence.
Mildy and I shared a triumphant smile as the boat pulled
alongside the quay steps.

'It's good to be home, isn't it, Mildy?' I said, squeezing
her arm at the elbow as we set off through the piles of
armaments heaped on the dockside waiting to be stored in
the White Tower's cellars. 'Or would you rather be at Halden,
nearer your family?'

She gave me a sly smile. 'Oh, no, my lady. I have missed London life!'

I wasn't sure I liked the sound of that. Did she have a city sweetheart I hadn't heard about? However, before I could dwell on this thought my attention was drawn to the sight of a large black bird flying up to the top of the White Tower with its beak full of prey. Far from recoiling at this sight I felt another surge of elation, calculating that this might be one of a pair of ravens bringing food to its chicks, which indicated they must have a nest hidden somewhere up on the highest roof in London. It also meant that despite the recent and highly significant bereavements in the royal family, the legend still prevailed. The ravens had not abandoned the Tower and the Tudor throne was still secure in the kingdom of England.

Martin the steward answered our knocks, wreathed in smiles at our return. 'Welcome back, my lady! We heard you have been unwell but I hope you are fully recovered now.'

With interest I watched Mildy make a hurried curtsy to the steward and disappear through the servants' hall to the left of the entrance before replying. 'Indeed I am, thank you, Martin. My travelling chest will be delivered shortly if you could arrange its collection from the quay. I hope Sir Richard is here and not called away somewhere. I have been on the road and not able to hear from him recently.'

'He is here, my lady, but he is conferring in his office at present and I do not like to disturb him.' The steward's face had turned a deep shade of red and my immediate reaction was to move past him to the door that he had been making a futile effort to protect. It gave access to the ground-floor chamber, which Martin called Richard's office and I thought of as his den, where he did all his designing and kept his accounts. It was usually locked.

Today however, it was not. When I walked in I found two men sitting opposite each other at a table strewn with open ledgers and papers that were covered with columns of numbers. One of them was my husband, Sir Richard Guildford, and the other was Sir Henry Wyatt. Richard leapt to his feet and moved around the table to greet me. 'Joan! I-I did n-not expect you so soon!' His face was flushed with embarrassment and never before had I known him to stammer. Sir Henry swivelled in his chair, failed to rise and gave me a smile that was more like a sneer. '*Lady* Guildford,' he drawled, stressing the title with unnecessary emphasis.

'I'll return in a minute, Henry,' Richard said, taking my arm and steering me back to the open door. Once out of the chamber he pulled it to and leaned back against it, his ear to the wood, as if fearing the man on the other side might be listening. 'I can't talk now. Can you wait until he leaves?'

'What is wrong, Richard?' I kept my voice low, copying his. 'You look so stressed.'

He leaned forward to kiss my mouth. 'Thank God you are back, Joan! I have missed your sane advice.' With a sigh, he added, 'But I do not want to leave him alone in there. Wait for me in our chamber and I will come as soon as he leaves.' He shook his head with a rueful smile and his hand went to the latch as he left with a puzzling parting shot. 'You were right after all.'

With my head in a whirl and the feel of Richard's lips still on my mine, I made my way up the stair that led to our bedchamber. Just the sight of Sir Henry Wyatt had stirred feelings I hoped had vanished forever – anger, anxiety, and distrust. And they must all have been showing on my face because Mildy was in the room unpacking my belongings, my travelling chest having arrived.

'Oh, my lady, what's wrong?' she asked, pausing in her hanging and folding. 'Have you seen a ghost?'

'No, Mildy,' I said enigmatically. 'I've seen the devil!'

Nearly an hour passed before Richard came. Mildy and I had emptied the chest and she had taken all the soiled clothing off to the domestic quarters to be washed and brushed back to service, then returned with sweetmeats and a jug of small ale, which I encouraged her to share with me, not having much appetite myself. Tactfully she did not refer to my mention of the devil and I did not expand on an exclamation I was already regretting. There was no necessity to involve Mildy in past events that did not concern her.

So when Richard made his entrance, pale-faced and rubbing his brow, I signalled her to leave and she slipped out, closing the door behind her. He flopped onto the bed as if his legs would hardly hold him up. 'Dear God, Joan, where have you been? You will not believe how the wheel has turned!'

I climbed up beside him, laying my hand on his creased forehead. 'What was going on down there, Richard? Why was Wyatt here, looking like the cat that got the cream?'

He hauled his head off the pillows and leaned on his elbow to gaze directly at me. I had never seen him look so troubled and my heart went out to him as he poured out his misery. 'You've never liked him, have you? Well, you can congratulate yourself. King Henry gave him a knighthood and I assumed therefore that he must be an honourable, trustworthy man but I have been a fool, Joan, who has had the wool pulled over his eyes for years. I realise now that he is a knave and a fraudster.'

'Yes, Richard, I can believe he is both those things,' I murmured, feeling tears of sympathy welling in my eyes, 'and you are no fool. I'm sorry I have been away so long and knew nothing of your troubles. But I'm here now and will do everything I can to help you.'

Spring sunbeams through the window had warmed the room and I'd removed the riding apparel I had been wearing and donned a simple kirtle over my smock, leaving my hair looped into a net. He reached out and pulled the net away, twining his fingers in my long, dark hair. 'I have missed you cruelly, wife,' he said. 'You do not know how much.'

There was a longing in his eyes and I felt my blood stir in reply. 'Then show me how much, Richard.' I eased myself forward until I was curled into his body and he settled back into the mattress with a sigh. His arms encircled mine and his lips met my lips in a long, searching kiss. His need was obvious, even through the layers of his gown and hose and my own need was suddenly no less. Whatever threat the presence of Wyatt represented, it could wait to be confronted; at this time and in this place of privacy and comfort there was a more pressing matter to attend to.

18

The Tower of London

Summer 1504

IT WAS A MEASURE of Richard's desperation that he
accepted my help in searching his records for any weak
spot in his financial affairs and it took hours of extensive
browsing before I located exactly where Wyatt had exploited
a loophole in his bookkeeping. To my astonishment, it
originated before our marriage when, in his capacity as Royal
Master of Ordnance and Weaponry, Richard had been
granted the massive sum of eight hundred pounds from the
Exchequer to build and fortify a new defensive tower at the
mouth of the River Rother, to repel cross-Channel French
raids on the key port of Rye. Not long afterwards Richard
agreed to form a business partnership with Sir Henry Wyatt
to offer mortgages to Kent farmers and lesser landholders
impoverished by the civil wars, which Henry Tudor had
vowed to end when he took the throne. I remembered our
first Christmas, which Wyatt had spent with us at Halden
Hall, when this partnership had been formed and now
wished I had taken more interest, instead of doing all I
could to avoid contact with the man whose suit Richard
was unaware that I had spurned.

He had assumed that the interest paid on these mortgage loans would soon replace the money he borrowed from the royal grant to finance them, and for a time this proved to be the case. But over the ensuing years the king's increasing reliance on my husband's multiple skills had involved him in so many extra duties that he had taken his eye off the activities of his partner, who had pursued his own agenda without consultation. The king's eight hundred pounds had shrunk to almost nothing and not a stone of the tower had been laid.

'And then, if you remember, Joan, the king decreed that all trade with the Low Countries should cease and the bottom fell out of the wool trade.' Richard's face was a picture of misery and he pushed back his chair to stand up, beginning to pace the floor in agitation. 'The sheep farmers who'd taken out mortgages could no longer afford to pay the interest so Wyatt foreclosed on their loans and demanded land off them in payment. I would never have done that, Joan. As well as being friends of long standing, many of them are also my tenants and I rely on them in order to raise my quota of men when the king orders a muster. They will never rally to my banner now and I cannot retain their allegiance. To add insult to injury, I have just discovered that Wyatt took their lands into his own estate, cleverly concealing the arrangement from me. I was confronting him about it when you walked in on our meeting.'

'But that is fraud, Richard! Surely you have a clear legal case against him.'

He paused his pacing and gave me a rueful smile. 'You'd think so, yes, but so far his account books have proved impossible to obtain, despite Anthony's best efforts.'

'Anthony? You mean Anthony Poyntz? Have you been using his legal services?' I heard my voice rise in agitation.

He gave me a startled glance. 'Yes, why not?'

Hastily I shook my head. 'No particular reason.' Yet this was not quite true. My concern sprang from the conversation I'd had with Anthony in the garden at Iron Acton, during the queen's regrettable progress. His lack of enthusiasm for his marriage and his attitude towards his wife had alarmed me, especially when he compared her personality to mine. I feared awkwardness between us if we tackled Richard's case together. 'Except he is still quite young,' I added, 'and inexperienced.'

'He's a good lawyer.' Richard resumed his pacing. 'And he's very loyal to me – to us. I could not trust any other lawman with this case.'

He had made a good point. I gave myself a mental shake. 'You are right. There is no one better.'

He appeared to accept my change of heart but his revelations had not ended. 'However, serious though it is, the matter of Wyatt's fraud is not my chief concern,' he admitted. 'I have lost the king's trust. He no longer believes me loyal.'

'Surely not! You are among his oldest friends and supporters; Comptroller of his Household, his Master of Horse and Ordnance. Not even Lord Daubeney is held in higher esteem.' Daubeney was the king's Lord Chamberlain, head of the Royal Household.

When Richard ran his hand through his hair as he did then, it was clear that it had thinned dramatically. 'King Henry is not the man he was, Joan. Since losing the queen and the Prince of Wales, he has changed radically. For a start he is not well. He has frequent bouts of fever and a recurring and painful quinsy and feels desperately insecure with only an under-age heir to assure the Tudor succession. But instead of turning to his friends for support he has withdrawn into himself. He is guarded and suspicious. Also he has lost the steadying hand of his financial guide, Sir Reginald Bray. I hate to say it but all this has turned him into a miser. He believes money is the best form of security and pours over his books and ledgers for hours, looking for ways to fill the royal coffers and refusing to meet his officials and councillors. Two new lawyers now have his ear and attention, men who spend their days devising ways to tax the nobility for every penny they can. Yet they are commoners who are not on the council and have no official positions in the royal household. They are a law unto themselves.'

'Who are these men, Richard?' I asked. 'Do they at least have names?'

'Oh yes, they have names,' he said bitterly, 'names that are inscribed on my brain. One of them is Richard Empson, against whom I bore witness in a court case he brought for debt, which he lost. For this he hates me and I know he spins lies about me to the king. The other is Edmund Dudley, another slippery lawyer who was one of Sir Reginald's right-hand men and now sits beside the king in his study as they pour over the account books, looking for victims.'

'Are they also on this new Council Learned that I've heard about? It sounds terrifying.'

'Not officially – they stay deliberately aloof from it – but they feed it with evidence. There is not a lord or landholder who does not sit in fear of its power. Yet neither it, nor Henry's two sniffer dogs, are answerable to the Royal Council or even to Parliament.'

'But surely you can still speak to the king personally? Does he not gather his friends together for hunting and do you not talk freely in the evenings? Can you not warn him about these men?'

He shook his head. 'Those days are gone, Joan. There have been hunting parties but I have not been invited and nor has Daubeney. The court is a very different place nowadays. There is no queen to grace it and no music and dancing. And I fear that you would no longer be welcome either, because your brother is under suspicion of conspiracy with the Earl of Suffolk.'

'No!' Now I was flabbergasted. Before I left for Scotland I had congratulated my brother, Sir Nicholas Vaux, on his appointment as Lieutenant of the castle of Guisnes on the Calais Pale, which I had understood to be a form of promotion. 'But Nicholas is living on the French border, while Suffolk is holed up miles away at the Emperor's court, is he not? How are they supposed to conspire at that distance and about what?'

Richard heaved another of his sighs. 'Do you not remember? His wife's sister married Viscount Lovell, a man who fought at the Battle of Stoke to put the present Earl's brother on the throne of England. These treasonous connections are never forgotten.'

My eyes blazed. 'The king more or less ordered my brother to marry Elizabeth Fitzhugh in order to bring her Yorkist family into the Tudor fold. He cannot now believe that she has managed to turn his coat.'

Richard shrugged helplessly. 'Why not? He believes the husband of his own wife's sister is a traitor. Lord Courtenay is still held prisoner here in the Tower.'

I remembered the queen's anger two years before, when the king had ordered the arrest of his brother-in-law and the eviction of Elizabeth's sister Lady Catherine Courtenay and her children from their Devon castle. It must have fired his suspicion of others around him, which the queen had been unable to dispel and which had evidently become considerably worse since her death.

At this point the door of Richard's office opened to admit a handsome young man in a short blue gown and jaunty red cap – Anthony Poyntz. Before I had time to control it, I felt my heart flutter in my chest. Ten years ago he had been calling me 'Mother Joan'; now he was pulling off his cap, bending his knee and kissing my hand.

Richard gave a harsh laugh. 'Stand up, man! It's my wife, not the Holy Roman Empress!'

As he rose, Anthony gave him a contrite grin. 'You know she is my honoured lady, sir. I mean no harm.'

'Huh! If I thought you meant harm, young squire, I'd have you in the stocks!'

I glanced from one man to the other. If we three were to work together to save Richard from the king's wrath, I realised that I must never appear to side with Anthony more than my husband.

19

The Tower of London and Richmond Palace

September 1504

T HERE HAD BEEN NO rain since June and the stream of Richard's search for evidence of Sir Henry Wyatt's financial embezzlement of the eight hundred pounds ran equally dry. Meanwhile, Wyatt paraded around the Tower like a peacock, dressed in a turquoise gown of watered Italian silk trimmed with gold braid, a garment that blatantly ignored the strict sumptuary laws. Clearly he wished to show the world that he was not among those of knightly status who were suffering the predations of the Council Learned in Law. Richard, who had previously mocked my dislike of the man, now kept well out of his way, deliberately using paths and passages around the fortress that his former business partner did not frequent. It was Anthony Poyntz who told me that Wyatt had married a widow called Anne Skinner two years ago and was now the proud father of a son. Foolishly I began to hope this might have erased the man's resentment against me and mine.

How wrong I was! When I inadvertently ran into him on Tower Green one scorching day in September he greeted me with jutting chin, a minuscule bow and an unmistakeable sneer. He did not doff his hat, as any other gentleman would have done. Having had only the briefest of glimpses of him in Richard's office on the day of my return from Scotland, I noticed now that he no longer cut the lithe, clean-shaven figure he had in his younger days but sported a full, silver-streaked beard and carried a substantial belly beneath his lavishly embroidered doublet. He also sweated profusely from the heat.

'Lady Guildford.' He planted himself before me in a manner that made it impossible to ignore him. 'I wondered when I might have the dubious pleasure of encountering you.'

'Sir Henry Wyatt,' I responded in an icy tone. 'What an unlooked-for meeting.' I deliberately avoided his gaze.

'I wonder, have you noticed that the accursed ravens you once so avidly championed no longer use those shelters you provided?' He swept his arm in the direction of the alder trees lining the far end of the Green, his gloved hand passing within an inch of my face.

I flinched involuntarily. 'I have been otherwise engaged, Sir Henry, so no, I had not noticed. But I hear the king has been unwell. Perhaps they will return now that he has recovered.'

'God be thanked that he has,' the knight said, crossing himself piously. 'I pray daily for his good health and the stability of his throne. Not that I believe those blithering black birds have anything to do with it. Incidentally, have you heard that I am a married man now – and the father of a son?'

'I had heard, yes.' I allowed a lack of interest to creep into my voice. 'I hope mother and son fare well.'

His grin acquired a gloating quality. 'They do and I'm pleased to say that we have a *second* child already on the way.'

The emphasis he laid on the 'second' child infuriated me. I took him to be deliberately exulting in his wife's fecundity, compared with my lack of it, failing as I had to give Richard another child after Hal, and I could not stop myself making a rude response: 'Really? Well, bully for you!'

I made a swift break around his substantial form and hurried on across the parched grass of the Green to my intended destination – the little church of St Peter ad Vincula. I was still seething as I knelt before an image of the Virgin, begging her help to soothe my indignation.

That afternoon, Richard showed me a letter he had received from the king's chamber. It was a formal document, clearly dictated by King Henry to one of his clerks, had no royal seal or signature, and bore all the hallmarks of a diktat rather than a communication between a monarch and his loyal official. Richard was very obviously shaken by its content.

'I wrote to the king to request a meeting, as I have done before, but all I received in return was this stark refusal,' he said, thrusting the letter into my hands. 'It's the sort of thing that might be sent to a groom or a scullion, not to his Comptroller of the Household. I feel dead to my old friend, as if I should break my staff.'

My heart went out to him. The white Staff of Office was awarded to the senior officials of the king's chamber and was considered a great honour, to be carried on official duty. When a monarch died, holders of such a staff would break it and throw the pieces into his grave as a sign of mourning and the end of an era. 'Why don't I write to King Henry and ask for an audience?' I suggested. 'I haven't yet given him my report of his daughter's Scottish wedding and her relationship with King James. Surely he will not refuse to see me.'

Richard was dubious. 'It might be better to write for permission to visit Hal. That request will surely be granted and you could seek a royal audience when you get there.'

Fanatical about security, the king had moved his thirteen-year-old heir from his relatively informal childhood quarters at Eltham Palace into apartments in his own closely guarded and formally staffed chamber wing at Richmond and Hal had gone with him. So far I had not been able to visit them there but Hal and I had exchanged letters in which he had hinted that the relationship between the royal father and son was fractious. Perhaps Richard was right, I should approach the matter of a visit to my son through the office of the Lord Chamberlain and hope that I might obtain an audience with King Henry while I was there.

Thus it was that a week later, armed with a pass into the chamber wing and an allocation of accommodation in the palace, Mildy and I took a ferry upriver to Richmond. We disembarked at the main palace quay and Hal, bless him, was waiting there to meet me. I could hardly believe my eyes when I saw him, inches taller than when I had bidden him goodbye eighteen months ago before leaving for Scotland and wearing clothes tailored with much more of a nod to the latest fashions than those I had supplied him with – a gown of green worsted with gold silk sleeves over a dark blue doublet.

'Goodness, Hal!' I gasped, when he released me from a

fierce hug. 'Was it wise to grow so tall? You must tower over the prince by several inches now!'

His wide pearl-toothed grin had not changed. 'I'm making the most of it, Mother, because he is growing equally fast and will soon outstrip me, I'm sure. Besides, Charles Brandon is much taller than any of us so he's the one who should watch his step.'

He gave orders to a nearby porter to collect our baggage and Mildy began to issue him with instructions about their destination, so I felt perfectly able to leave her to it and tuck my arm into Hal's. 'Is Master Brandon still lusting after Princess Mary or has he learned his lesson?' I asked him.

Hal gave a snort of derision. 'He'd have a problem! We hardly see anything in a skirt around here. The princess is still at Eltham and we're all forbidden to leave Richmond unless we have written permission from the Chamberlain's office. The rules are much tighter here and they're driving the prince mad.'

'So you're all locked in, are you? I should be grateful that you came out to meet me.'

He shrugged. 'Not actually locked in – we're on trust not to leave. And I'm not too bothered because apart from missing my dearest mother, this place is amazing. There's fabulous hunting and we have brilliant masters and coaches teaching us all the skills we need with weapons and horses. Honestly, I couldn't ask for a better place to learn chivalry.'

'Hmm.' I tweaked the soft silk of his gold sleeve. 'And you seem to have acquired some sumptuous apparel. There are good allowances for clothing then?'

'If you think this sumptuous, you should see what the

prince wears. Even at thirteen he's clothes-mad. The king abhors his sartorial whims and frequently sends him off to change if he doesn't like what he's dressed in.'

Sartorial whims! I was impressed with his highly developed vocabulary but refrained from remarking on it. 'They're still at loggerheads then, as you said in your last letter?'

'To be frank poor Harry doesn't stand a chance in an argument with his father; he may be well educated but the king is the king and can't be crossed. Harry has taken many a beating on the orders of his father. Recently he was obliged to watch one of his pages take it for him, which he couldn't bear. He had to beg the king to stop it and has been careful not to anger his father so much again.'

I pictured the situation and smiled grimly, lowering my voice and leaning closer to my son's ear. 'Well, King Henry always was a cunning negotiator but that sounds as if he's swapped cunning for intimidation. When we can be safely alone I will tell you how he has contrived to strike fear into your father.'

The long façade of the royal apartments at Richmond Palace was built of pale stone and topped with rows of chimneys and turrets built of red brick. The combination reminded me of a marchpane subtlety, laced with cream and strawberries, and I wondered if any of the bricks had come from Iron Acton. The rest of the palace, including the visitors' accommodation, was constructed entirely of the red brick and, being situated behind the royal chambers, lacked the sweeping views over the River Thames, which the superior rooms enjoyed. I had stayed there previously, when I was still a senior lady-in-waiting to the late queen, but the room I was allocated this time was not nearly as comfortable.

There was no discreet close-stool behind a door and it was a good walk to the nearest latrines. Clearly my status as wife of the Comptroller of the Royal Household did not bear the cachet it once had.

Mildy had immediately set about unpacking and Hal suggested we took a walk in the prince's privy garden, to which he had access. 'Prince Harry is with his tutor until dinner so we should have a chance to have that safe talk you mentioned,' he said, lowering his voice.

I caught the anxiety in it and nodded agreement. It was only days until his fifteenth birthday; he was rather young to carry the weight of his parents' concerns but he had a sensible head on his shoulders and every right to hear the substance of his father's plight.

20

Richmond Palace

September 1504

PRINCE HENRY'S PRIVY GARDEN was arranged more like a sports field – a hedged space, which contained a bowling green, a skittle alley and a wood-walled section that was netted for tennis practice, the full courts being situated further afield. A pathway down the middle was lined with late-flowering plants and by the time we had walked slowly up and down its length three times I had managed to outline the various reasons for Richard's fall from grace. Laying it before my son as plainly and simply as I could made me face the seriousness of his plight myself, in a way I had not done before, and I began to think I should not have burdened Hal with it after all.

The strength of that summer's sun had tanned his skin but underneath this mask of health I could see that the blood had drained from his face. 'How could he have allowed his affairs to become so disordered, Mother?' he murmured, glancing around to ensure that no one was within earshot. 'He is Comptroller of the Royal Household, with responsibility for checking the annual accounts of the king's chamber. If his own books are so muddled, how can the king possibly trust him to clear his?'

I gave a heavy sigh. 'Well he can't, of course, Hal. But some blame must surely go to the king for loading him down with so many responsibilities, which Richard felt unable to refuse. The worst aspect of it all, though, is the way Sir Henry Wyatt has managed to manipulate everything concerning the loan business so that it all looks like your father's fault, when it was actually Wyatt who embezzled the castle-building fund and enriched himself at the king's expense. But we have so far been unable to obtain written proof of his larceny.'

'Will they arrest my father?' Hal's question emerged as a shaky croak.

'I very much hope not. But since Prince Arthur and the queen died, it seems the king is on a crusade against his knights and nobles, suspecting many of having taken financial advantage of the crown. And your father is among them because although he appears to have spent the money granted for new defences at Rye, there is no sign of a fortress having been built.'

Hal halted abruptly and removed his arm from my grasp. 'I don't understand why he did not do it, Mother! He designed that huge sea wall along the north bank of the River Rother. A defence tower on the other shore should have been no problem for him.'

I would have liked to describe to Hal the extraordinary amount of other work the king had loaded onto Richard's shoulders in the early years of his reign but our opportunity for private discussion had ended. Over his shoulder I noticed the iron-studded door from the palace fly open to admit the Prince of Wales and behind him a noisy group of attendants, some carrying heavy baskets of bowls and others stringed tennis racquets.

'It is Mother Guildford!' Prince Harry raised his voice above the chatter behind him and increased his stride along the flower-lined path to halt before me. 'I have not seen you since the departure of the Queen of Scots. I long to hear your version of her wedding splendour.' By now I had sunk into a deep curtsy as his rank demanded. 'Please rise, my lady.' For a thirteen-year-old boy his style as he bent to raise me was immaculate. I was tempted to wonder why his father ever took objection to his manner and appearance, until I noticed the pearl in his ear, the bright turquoise of his doublet and the jewelled aiglets on the laces that attached its cream puffed sleeves. This new heir to the throne was becoming a style setter, while I assumed his father still dressed in long plain black gowns and sober gold chains. A clash of characters was vividly demonstrated right there.

'I believe I must congratulate you on your betrothal to the Dowager Princess of Wales, my lord,' I said with a smile, which he did not return.

His response began rather petulantly. 'Yes, but I don't like to hear her called that, correct though it may be, Lady Guildford. We correspond frequently and I address her as Princess Katherine. Sadly we do not have much opportunity to meet, even though she now lives in London.' He turned to Hal. 'My tutor has let me out for some exercise. I'm going to knock down a few skittles. Will you join us?'

Hal made a rueful nod. 'I would like to, sir, but first I must escort my mother to the Chamberlain's office. She wishes to seek an audience with the king.'

The prince frowned and cast me a quizzical glance. 'That's not easily achieved at present. Would you like me to accompany you, to put a little pressure on?'

My heart lifted. I'd been dreading the prospect of my request being refused out of hand. 'That is a very gracious offer, sir, but what about your game? I wouldn't want to interrupt your exercise routine.'

He gave a shrug. 'I'll walk briskly there and back. I'm eager to help the lady who first introduced me to the joys of Latin. Come – we'll go now. I'll return very soon to skittle the rest of your scores.' This last remark was addressed to his companions, who made deferential scoffing noises.

I had to jog along to keep up with the pace of the two youngsters as we negotiated several stairways and passages to reach the royal apartments, which afforded the king's chambers a panoramic view of a long stretch of the River Thames as it wound its way towards Windsor. The Lord Chamberlain's office occupied a suite of rooms just outside the imposing entrance to King Henry's private quarters. Confirming the presence of royalty inside, four Yeomen of the Guard of the King's Body stood in their tawny household doublets, hatchet-faced, with their halberds crossed against any entry. On sight of the prince they drew up their weapons in salute but subsided when he turned in the direction of the Lord Chamberlain's door, which was instantly opened by a duty guard in a leather gambeson.

Breathless from chasing after Hal and the prince in my heavy skirts and court shoes, I would have given a silver shilling for a chance to sit down, but there were to be no offers of that sort in the office of the king's chamberlain. Lord Daubeney being predictably absent, it was under the charge of a deputy, a young knight whose name I never discovered and whom I hoped never to encounter again. Although the prince was able to cower him somewhat, merely by dint of his exalted rank, his presence did not succeed in achieving automatic entry for me into the king's Presence Chamber.

I considered the deputy's tone unnecessarily scathing. 'I have never heard of Lady Guildford, my lord, but if she is any relation to Sir Richard Guildford, who is on this list of undesirables, there is no chance of her getting past the Yeomen Guards.'

Prince Henry drew himself up to his not yet considerable height. 'Lady Guildford was Lady Governess to the royal children for several years of my childhood, sir,' he declared in a determined tone. 'She does not need to be anybody's relation to be a close personal acquaintance of my father's. Also she was lady-in-waiting to my mother for many years and present at her death in the Tower of London. There could not be a more worthy visitor to the king's chamber.'

Hal and I exchanged glances, sharing our amazement at the young prince's manifest strength of will. The deputy's bluster appeared to crumble before its authority. 'Well, I suppose if you vouch for her, my lord . . .' he said hesitantly.

'I do. Please authorise her entrance at once and issue her a pass to the duty usher. Otherwise the king will wonder why she was not admitted on sight.'

As the deputy chamberlain turned away to dictate a pass to his clerk, Prince Henry turned his back on him and treated us to a smile and a wink. His voice was still authoritative as he said, 'We can return to our pastimes now, Hal. Mother Guildford should be well taken care of.'

With that he strode to the entrance, surprising the page, who'd been watching proceedings wide-eyed and had to scramble around him to open the door. 'I will see you at dinner in the great hall,' Hal murmured to me as he followed the prince out.

At the mention of dinner I felt my stomach rumble. Having left the Tower soon after Prime, so far Richmond Palace had not provided me with any sustenance and the day was wearing on. I could only hope my visit to the king's chamber would at least supply some words of comfort I might convey to Richard.

21

The King's Chamber, Richmond Palace

September 1504

IN ALL MY NINETEEN years of serving the royal family I had never felt so nervous about an encounter with the king. After the death of Queen Elizabeth, King Henry had literally fled into isolation at Greenwich Palace and collapsed, both bodily and spiritually, leaving the arrangements for her funeral to the three people he trusted most: his mother, Lady Margaret Beaufort, Thomas Howard, Earl of Surrey, and my already over-burdened husband, Sir Richard Guildford, who had taken charge of organising all the solemn processions and secular ceremonial. It had been another example of the reliance King Henry had always placed on Richard's organisational skills. I could not imagine why that trust and reliance had been so rapidly replaced by distrust and rejection and was determined to remind the king of their twenty-year friendship and Richard's steadfast loyalty.

My pass gave me immediate entrance to the king's chamber, a complex of rooms in which he could be certain of privacy and security, but when I was greeted by one of the royal ushers he informed me that I would have to wait until King Henry chose to invite me further in.

'His grace is with his financial advisers and cannot be disturbed at present, my lady. May I offer you some refreshment while you wait?'

Ten minutes earlier I would have jumped at the chance of some wine and sweetmeats but now my stomach was so tight with nerves I felt unable to swallow anything solid and accepted only a cup of watered wine and a seat on a bench against the wall. I had expected there to be others waiting on the king's pleasure and was surprised to find that I was the only one. Prince Henry's intervention had clearly been of extreme influence. I wondered if his father would be informed of his son's intervention and whether he would approve it.

Hours passed and my nerves were gradually replaced by indignation at being ignored, even by someone as important as the king. Moreover hunger once more gnawed at my stomach and there had been no further offer of refreshment. Hal would wait in vain for me at dinner. After my early start that morning I began to grow drowsy and was jerked out of sleep by a rough hand on my shoulder. It was a different usher that stepped back and waited for me to focus.

'His grace will see you now, my lady. Please follow me.'

Fifteen months had passed since I had last set eyes on King Henry and the change in him was profound. He had always been slim but now he was almost skeletal, his face hollow, his expression haggard and joyless, as if he had not smiled for years. Except for ceremonial occasions, when he wore his jewelled crown and carried his gold sceptre, he had always dressed soberly but now he was clad from neck to foot in black velvet, devoid of ornament save for a heavy gold cross on a gold Tudor Rose chain. His brimmed hat was trimmed with a plain gold bar brooch, hung with two red drop rubies, shaped like tears. He might have been a sorcerer.

As I curtsied my face must have registered the shock I felt. 'Yes, Lady Guildford, I see that you recognise the change in me,' he said. 'But in you I am pleased to see no change. Please rise.'

'You have suffered much sorrow, your grace,' I said as I straightened up. 'And when the queen died I, too, lost a friend. I pray that I have not lost your friendship as well.'

Deep creases appeared between his brows and his tone of voice was cold. 'Kings cannot afford to have friends, my lady. It exposes them to exploitation.'

My heart thudded painfully in my chest and I had to force words out. 'But surely before you became king, my liege, you relied on your friends for support, did you not? And after you took the crown you needed them to help you keep it. How can you manage that now, if you have no friends to rely on?' I knew I was taking a risk asking such a direct question but Richard's future depended on the answer I received.

To my distress the royal frown deepened. 'I have found that friendship cannot be relied on. But fear can. The constant threat of losing royal favour keeps my throne steadier than the cultivation of friends.'

I stared at him, aghast. His eyes held mine, icy blue. There was no sign of the warmth they had contained when his wife had been alive. The kingdom had lost more than its subjects knew when their queen died. I felt tears welling and lowered my head so that he would not see the effect of his words. In that moment I sensed any hope of restoration for Richard slip from my grasp. However, I did not want the audience to end, so I shook myself mentally and pursued the conversation.

'I have had the honour of meeting with the Prince of Wales today, your grace,' I remarked. 'How fortunate it is that he lives here with you at Richmond now. It must be a great comfort to have the company of such a promising son to give you hope for the future.'

King Henry suddenly began to wring his hands and I noticed that the bones of his wrists stood out like gnarled sticks. 'You might think that, yes, but the boy is flippant and pleasure-seeking – too eager for sport and not keen to concentrate on his studies like his brother was. Although he does attend daily Mass and regularly makes confession. I'm also pleased to say that your son is a good influence in his life, Lady Guildford.'

'I am proud that you think so, sire, but puzzled to hear that the prince neglects his studies. When I was governess to his sisters I found him a very bright boy, already well read and able to converse fluently with learned visitors to Eltham Palace. Perhaps now he is at a crucial stage in his life, when he is adjusting to his radically changed status.'

'Life is radically changed for the whole Tudor family, since God chose to claim its heir and its matriarch. Elizabeth brought the music and dance into court. How can it ever be the same?' He was so disgruntled and embittered, as if he almost blamed his wife and son for their own deaths.

I felt sorry for young Prince Harry if, due to his father's despair, he was permitted no gaiety in his life. 'Not the same perhaps, your grace, but if young people have no joy they surely cannot thrive. Dancing and music, sport and competition are essential parts of their development.'

'You think I am blighting my son's development?'

The intensity of his indignation was daunting but I pursued my theme. There might be little hope of forgiveness for Richard but if I could encourage some levity in the palace it might improve the relationship between king and prince, and improve Hal's lot as well. 'Not intentionally I'm sure, my lord, but your own deeply felt desolation might be having such an effect.'

There was a long silence, when the king put his right hand to his forehead and shielded his eyes as if to hide their expression from me. I waited for the curt dismissal I fully expected as the king turned his back and walked towards the dais where stood the canopied throne on which he received his diplomatic visitors. It was draped in red silk embellished with gold fringes and symbols of Tudor and Richmond: red and white roses and pale greyhounds. When he was seated he beckoned his duty squire from his position at the privy entrance.

'Bring a stool for Lady Guildford, Francis, and then send for some wine and spices. We have much to discuss.' When the stool was brought he had it placed beside him on the dais and beckoned me over. 'Please sit. Forgive me, my lady, I had forgotten your insight and wisdom, the very reason why the queen appointed you governess to our daughters. I would welcome your advice about Prince Henry but first I wish to hear your account of the Queen of Scots' wedding.'

I took my place beside the king, careful to ensure my head did not rise above his, for he was not a tall man. 'Well, sire, you may already know that it would not have taken place at all, if your daughter were not a lady of iron character. Because as if the journey had not been taxing enough, only a few days before the wedding there was a terrible fire in the palace stables and the two golden horses you gave her to carry her litter died in the blaze. For a girl of thirteen, with a passion for horses, it was a disaster and she was understandably distraught. For a time I feared she would not recover enough to take part in the arranged festivities but fortunately her bridegroom, King James, came to console her, listing the string of castles he would grant her after the wedding, among them Stirling and Linlithgow which, as you must know, my lord, are among Scotland's most magnificent palaces.'

King Henry's lips spread into a brief smile, the first I had witnessed during our meeting. 'Margaret has always been very conscious of her status – a good trait in a queen.'

'Well, only two days later she made her entrance into Edinburgh to rousing cheers and rode pillion behind King James through the city before attending a service in the church of the Abbey of the Holy Rood. The next day she walked through crowds of cheering citizens to the abbey, where the marriage was blessed and confirmed. She looked glorious, my lord, in a gown of white cloth of gold with a train of embroidered scarlet. As a good omen the sun was shining and her long, red-brown hair gleamed and was much admired. I am sorry you were not there, your grace, you would have been so proud of her. I'm sure it would have lifted your spirits and the people certainly seemed enchanted by their new young queen, as did the bridegroom.'

At this stage the king held up his hand to interrupt. 'I promised her mother that consummation of the marriage would not take place until she was fifteen. I believe you attended the bedding ceremony, Lady Guildford. I trust you ensured that King James held to this pledge.'

I was embarrassed by this query, especially in view of the Scottish king's loose interpretation of that agreement. 'I saw them blessed and bedded, my lord, and anything further was according to his conscience, although he did confess that he longs for an heir for the Scottish throne. I was told he keeps a mistress in a house close to Edinburgh, whom he visits frequently and there is apparently a nursery of his illegitimate offspring, which at least proves his own fertility. I suppose it is inevitable that a man of his age and status would not be entirely celibate. I think there is every hope that he and his new queen will be well suited when the time comes.'

'Let us pray that she proves fertile anyway,' he said solemnly. 'We will know if he has broken his pledge if there is a child within the next year but it matters most that Margaret can provide an Anglo-Scottish heir, so that our two countries might co-exist in peace for the foreseeable future.'

'Well, she may be young, sire, but I assure you that she is only too aware of her duty in that regard. When the time comes there is every likelihood that their union will fulfil your hopes. Several of her English friends have stayed in her household to keep her company and King James visits her frequently. Aside from the persistent dampness of the Scottish weather, I'd say that his queen has all the comfort and company she could want.'

'Except her beloved horses,' he observed gloomily. 'I will send her a trained mare to replace her golden ponies. Now, let us discuss the Prince of Wales. You implied that I should not chastise him for spending too much time at sport and pleasure.'

I groped in my mind for what I had actually said. 'I think

I suggested that sport and dancing and outdoor pursuits should be encouraged, your grace, not curtailed. Boys of the prince's age and inclination need to compete in order to develop their minds and strength and if they urge each other on with shouts and friendly mockery, that is all part of it. I'm sure you remember your own experience in the tiltyard.'

'Yes, Lady Guildford, I do, but I was in exile and did not have all the privileges and companions my son has. I had my Uncle Jasper to thank for any skill I acquired with the lance but I would not have dared to yell insults at him as my son's friends do to each other. Nor did I have the privilege of music lessons and dance classes or the run of a library full of books. Henry does not appreciate his good fortune.'

I tried my best to respond to his last remark tactfully. 'Perhaps he doesn't understand just how much he owes to you for providing his good fortune, my liege? Which I would suggest is down to his age, not his character. Outwardly he appears sophisticated and clever but he is only thirteen – still a child. He wants to be loved and cherished like any child and therefore misses his mother as much as you do. You have that in common a least.'

'Yes, but consider this. His sister Margaret was the same age when she married the King of Scotland. You have just told me that she showed remarkable strength of character and composure in her new role and yet I find no sign of such traits in her younger brother. Prince Arthur too showed remarkable promise of leadership before his regrettable demise but I again cannot find any such evidence in Prince Henry.' He rubbed his forehead distractedly. 'It vexes me to say so but I hold it to be the case.'

My mind harked back to the way the prince had handled the question of my admission to this very meeting and I was tempted to use this as an indication of his father's misapprehension of his second son's worth, but decided against it. I felt that I had done my best and was anyway distracted by the offer of wine and sugared fruits by the duty squire. It was then that I suddenly recognised him as Francis Poyntz, the younger brother of Richard's former squire and present legal adviser, Anthony. The Poyntz family was clearly moving up in the social hierarchy.

The arrival of the refreshments changed the tone of the audience. The king abandoned the intimate discussion we had been having and turned instead to polite platitudes about the colour and type of horse the Queen of Scots might prefer to receive, an enquiry about my journey back to England and concern for my health after hearing of the attack of ague. Within a short time he stood up, indicating that the meeting was over, and the squire escorted me to the exit.

Away from the royal presence, Francis became quite conversational. 'As I think you know, our father is Chamberlain to the Dowager Princess of Wales and my brother Anthony has been acting as his legal aide over the matter of her betrothal to Prince Henry. He is here at Richmond meeting with the king's lawyers and I took the liberty of informing him of your audience with the king. He is waiting outside the Privy Chamber to see you.'

22

Richmond Palace

September 1504

PERHAPS IT WAS THE wine I had drunk on an empty stomach but I felt strangely elated at the prospect of seeing Anthony. While we had both been trying to help my husband prove his innocence over the misuse of the royal grant for the castle to defend Rye harbour, we had consistently treated each other with polite deference. Even Richard had noticed it and privately asked me if we had fallen out over something. Now however, unrestricted by his presence, we freely exchanged warm kisses of greeting.

Anthony stepped back from the embrace to study my face. 'You look flushed, Joan,' he said with concern. 'Are you not well?'

I gave a shaky laugh. 'To be honest I think I'm a bit fuddled. I have eaten nothing but a sugared plum or two since I left the Tower before dawn this morning and the king's wine is very strong. I suppose there is no chance that supper is still being served in the great hall?'

'The great hall is presently full of intoxicated lawyers and diplomats making the most of the king's wine cellar while they commiserate over their failure to persuade the Spanish to pay the second half of the Dowager Princess's dowry. I know because I've just escaped their bibulous company.' Anthony turned to his brother. 'Can you find something a bit more substantial than a comfit from the king's kitchen, Francis? And is there somewhere we can sit and talk while Lady Guildford saves herself from starvation?'

Francis indicated a deep window embrasure at the side of the gallery leading from the Privy Chamber. Stone benches lined its walls. 'That's about as private as you can get at Richmond Palace, brother.' He gave me an enquiring look. 'Although I presume Lady Guildford has been allocated a bedchamber?'

I frowned, unable to decide if there was a hint of innuendo in his query. 'The window seats will be perfect,' I said coolly. 'And don't spend too much time finding cooked meats when you must have duties to attend to Francis. Just some bread and cheese would be very welcome.'

He nodded, bowed and hurried off, while Anthony and I exchanged puzzled glances. 'I don't know what wild thoughts inhabit that boy's head,' he remarked as he took my arm to escort me to the window. 'At least the benches have cushions for some comfort.'

The gallery ran along the front of the palace and overlooked the Thames where the royal dock protruded into the river, the flames of lighted torches reflecting off the surface of the water. Even after dusk, several ferryboats were tethered there, waiting to take visitors to their homes, the oarsmen lounging together in the passenger seats, gossiping to pass the time.

'Is one of those waiting for you?' I asked Anthony.

His gaze followed mine. 'Probably. But there's no hurry. Tell me how your audience went with the king.'

I sighed. 'Not well. I think I may have ruined Richard's chances of a pardon.'

'Surely not; only four years ago you were King Henry's celebrated Lady of the Ravens – the saviour of the kingdom! We heard that story even in Iron Acton.'

Encouraging though he intended them to be, these words prompted a rueful smile. 'That was then, Anthony. Everything has changed. His beloved Arthur died and then the queen and now I hardly recognise the man who is our king. He is a different creature – cold and lonely and resentful. Also he has been very ill and is exceedingly thin. He seems to have lost all compassion and is morbidly concerned for the future. I sensed that he almost despairs of the Tudor throne surviving after his death.'

'Well, he may have cause to think that.' Anthony's expression was bleak. 'Sir Richard is aware of several conspiracies in the York camp, especially among landholders like him, who feel the claws of the Council Learned.'

My heart sank. It seemed that Richard had confided in the young lawyer things that he had kept from me. 'What conspiracies? I am not aware . . .' I halted abruptly as Anthony raised his arm in warning and stood up as Francis reappeared through the entrance to the Privy Chamber carrying a basket.

'No need to break off on my account.' His tone could only be described as a snigger. 'I've brought bread and cold meats for Lady Guildford.' He placed the basket on the bench beside me. The smell of meat made my mouth water. 'There is also a jug of small ale to dilute the effect of the king's wine. I must go now because he is about to retire. Just leave the basket under the bench and I'll collect it in the morning.' He swivelled round to his brother. 'There's also a message for you, Anthony. Your ferryman says he'll leave within the hour and he wants paying. Don't forget to do it, even if you don't leave with him.'

He strode off briskly, leaving Anthony and I staring after him. 'Ha! Does he think we are lovers or something?' I asked with a puzzled laugh. 'Whatever can have given him that idea?'

To my surprise, Anthony's face had flushed, whether with anger or embarrassment I could not decide. 'Well, he knows things have gone sour between me and my wife,' he said, slumping back down onto his bench. 'But I've given him no reason to think I'm intending to stray.'

My smile was ironic. 'Not with a lady old enough to be your mother anyway.'

His brow furrowed. 'No one would think that to look at you.'

I felt my heart flutter and willed it to stop. 'Now you're flattering me, Anthony, and if anyone heard you say that, they'd instantly be suspicious. Anyway you have a new baby boy, have you not? How is he?' After the birth of a daughter, called after his mother, Meg Poyntz had written to tell me there had been a boy but I couldn't remember his name.

His face darkened. 'Little Ferdinand died. Elizabeth is devastated and blames herself but it was no one's fault. He just caught an infant fever and was dead within a few days.'

'Oh dear, I'm so sorry. When was this?'

He removed his hat and ran his hand through his thick hair. There were tears in his eyes. 'Only a few weeks ago. There was no comforting Elizabeth. She shut herself away in our chamber and told her maid not to admit me. When I insisted she became hysterical and told me she never wanted to have another child. But later the maid said she thought her mistress might be pregnant again already. I had to leave to attend this meeting with the Spanish lawyers and to be honest I don't really want to go home.'

'But of course you will, Anthony.'

Despair deepened in the young man's eyes. 'Telling me I must go home is like me advising you to go back to the king, throw yourself at his feet and beg for mercy for Sir Richard, when you know it will do no good. But I will go home, eventually. Now, why don't you eat and drink what is in that basket? Then we could both take the ferryboat downriver to the Tower to continue fighting your husband's desperate cause.'

The smell from the basket had already stirred my appetite and so I delved into it and extracted a manchet loaf in a napkin. I also lifted the jug of ale and passed it to Anthony. 'I'll eat and you drink,' I said. 'But then I think you should take the ferry to London. My maid will be waiting for me in my guest chamber, where I also hope to find a message from my son Hal. The poor lad was expecting me to meet him at dinner in the great hall hours ago. We are not free agents, Anthony.'

There was a brief pause while he took a deep draught from the jug, then he lifted his head and gazed at me for a few heartbeats before speaking. 'You are right, of course. It is better if we don't leave together. Francis would get the wrong impression and then gossip would spread like wildfire.'

I nodded. 'Which certainly would not aid Richard's cause. King Henry disapproves of scandal even more than his mother does.'

23

The Tower of London

Spring 1505

IT WAS SPRING BUT still chilly and the previous few months had been miserable. Anthony had worked on and off with Richard, combing the Guildford accounts for anomalies until the beginning of Advent, when he finally returned to Gloucestershire. The books had been submitted to the Council Learned, as everyone now called it, and we'd heard nothing from him or it since. Meg Poyntz wrote to say that Anthony was back living at his manor of Frampton and his wife had announced her third pregnancy.

'Elizabeth has grown so large so quickly that I very much fear it may be twins,' Meg had written, and I wondered how God could be so cruel to a struggling couple. Twins were double danger and double trouble. I had to quash the urge to write and sympathise with Anthony but Elizabeth Poyntz and I had never met and I did not want to be responsible for causing more strife between them.

Christmas had been a sad affair at Halden Hall with Richard's eldest son and heir Edward Guildford and his wife Eleanor, who came up from the Sussex coast, where they lived on one of the Guildford manors. When she married Edward at the age of sixteen, I had thought Eleanor West a rather wild, conceited girl but seven years of marriage without children had subdued her considerably and as a house guest on this occasion I enjoyed her company, finding her pleasant and helpful. She even provided a moment of joy for Richard when she was finally and unexpectedly able to announce that she was expecting a baby.

'At last!' It was a rare pleasure in those days to see Richard smile, but he stirred himself from his persistent gloom to embrace his daughter-in-law and kiss her cheeks. 'May God grant us a boy, dear lady – an heir for the Guildford estates.'

'Eleanor is adamant that a girl should be equally eligible to inherit,' said Edward, 'and I tend to agree with her. A healthy living child is all we need.'

I was pleased and surprised to hear him say this but noticed that Richard's perpetual frown had settled once more on his brow and so I made no comment, except to kiss the expectant mother and wish her well.

On our return to London it was not long before a smug-looking, over-dressed Sir Henry Wyatt made his appearance at the Tower House just as we had sat down to our midday dinner. His staccato rap on the armoured entrance door drew me swiftly from the table to the porter's spyhole to see who was there, fearing the dreaded sight of a sergeant at arms come with a summons. As Wyatt raised his arm to rap again I could have sworn that the lining of his winter gown was ermine.

I did not want the taste of his name on my tongue. 'It's the Comptroller of the Mint,' I said quietly to Richard, returning to the hall as Martin the steward came through to admit him.

Richard's face blanched and he stood up. 'I'll see him in my office.'

As I made to accompany him, he stopped me. 'Alone, Joan. Your presence always annoys him,' he complained, 'and then there is no chance of reasoned discussion.'

'That's because he knows I can tell when the wretch is lying.' I tried to keep my voice light but my mood was dark. Richard knew, as well as I did, that the threat of royal vengeance increased every day and so far we had been helpless to stop it.

I sat beside the hall fire and fretted, while Hugh the server cleared the uneaten dishes and removed the cloth. Then I tried to distract myself by moving to a window and looking out over the Tower Quay, watching tenders bringing cargo from ocean-going ships anchored in the Thames Roads below London Bridge. Often when I indulged in this activity I tried to imagine the places these sturdy three-masted ships had come from and the kind of goods they brought – oranges from Spain, wine from Gascony, silks from Florence – but on this occasion all I could think of was the ferryboat that might come to take Richard upriver, under the bridge, to face a secret court somewhere in the City.

I had not married Sir Richard Guildford for love but because the king had more or less ordered me to do so, if I did not wish to remain forever a lowly spinster maid of the queen's chamber. But over the years of our marriage I had come to realise that we shared a relationship that could survive frequent separations, sporadic disappointments and enjoy occasional passionate interludes. Richard had come to tolerate my fierce defence of the Tower ravens and I had learned to live with his masculine belief that women were inferior creatures. I even hoped I had managed to alter this misconception somewhat. And in the course of all that compromising, it was inevitable that we now recognised how much we depended on each other for support. We had found love of a practical kind that was nevertheless based on deep but rarely expressed emotion and I could not bear to think that, slowly and insidiously, along with Richard's health and self-esteem, it was being destroyed.

As I pondered this unhappy situation, a couple strolled into view along the quay and my eyes widened in surprise. It was my maid Mildy in a pretty hood and gown I had not seen her wear before and beside her – very close beside her – was Sim, the boy now become a man, that I had rescued from starvation and exploitation when I found him, ragged and fearful, lurking in our home wood at Halden Hall. Mildy carried a basket, its contents hidden under a cover, so there was no reason why Sim, who was staying at the Tower to refurbish the raven nest boxes, should not have escorted her to the market to buy provisions for our cook. But the way they walked and talked together, heads leaning close and smiles never far from their lips, suggested there was more intimacy between them than simply sharing an errand.

I watched them turn in through the rear gate of the house, which led to the back yard and the separate kitchen quarters, considering whether I might ask some pertinent questions of Mildy when she came to help me prepare for bed. But this line of thought vanished completely when I heard angry voices rising from Richard's office below. A few swift steps took me through the hall door to the top of the stair. Directly below I could see my husband and Sir Henry Wyatt standing face to face, their belligerent attitudes speaking volumes as they continued to argue their contested points. Then my attention was drawn to the emergence through the open office door of Anthony Poyntz, whom I had believed to be far away in Gloucestershire.

He raised his voice to interrupt Wyatt, who was still fulminating. 'Allow me to see you out, Sir Henry. Sir Richard's steward is clearly otherwise engaged and it would be unfortunate if you missed fulfilling your obligations elsewhere.'

'I want a word with you anyway, young Poyntz,' Wyatt said brusquely, abandoning his confrontation with Richard and grabbing Anthony's arm to make for the heavy exit door. 'We can talk as I walk to the Mint.'

Could Wyatt be attempting to entice or corrupt Anthony away from his loyalty to us I wondered suddenly, as the heavy fortified door of the Tower House clanged shut behind them? A thought that jangled in my mind as I walked down the stair to Richard. 'Did you manage to make any progress at all?' I asked him.

He shook his head morosely. 'Wyatt was here merely to gloat over a debate about my case that was conducted by the Council Learned. Him being there at all is farcical of course because he has no training in the law but his membership gives him freedom to suggest victims and conceal his own culpabilities. He is numbered now among the few land holders who have entirely escaped the attentions of Dudley and Empson.'

'I was surprised to see Anthony. Did you know he was coming back?'

'He had not warned me but I was grateful he was there for he knows every member of the Council Learned and how they operate.' Clearly Richard had no thought of the possibility of Anthony actually being suborned by one of those members. 'How could the king possibly have endorsed Wyatt's membership?'

'Perhaps he isn't aware of it? Does he ever attend their sessions?'

'Not that I know of. You could be right. He only looks at the growing list of fines in his ledgers and endorses further and fiercer penalties for non-payment. He makes no allowance for the character or loyalty of the people involved.' His voice suddenly grew hoarse. 'Henry never speaks to me now, even at Privy Council meetings, to which I am only summoned because Sir Thomas Brandon chairs them and he still believes in me.'

I moved forward to put my arms around him. Along with the original eight-hundred-pound missing grant, almost every other expense Richard had claimed over the years – for tournaments organised, ships built, engineering services rendered and arms procured – had been scrutinised and queried and officially found to be in some way flawed, to the Exchequer's loss. I had checked these expenses myself and knew they could not possibly be faulty, unless someone had altered the corresponding entries in the king's ledgers, which I now suspected might be only too likely. The fines consequently imposed were astronomical – impossible to pay, without taking out a crippling loan from the bankers of Lombard Street.

Richard must have read my thoughts. 'Wyatt has done his evil work well. He has turned every Italian banker against me, poisoned my reputation in the City and even succeeded in blackening my name among the legal fraternity. I have no hope of meeting the sums demanded by the Exchequer, which now number more than twice as much as the original grant to build the bastion at Rye.'

I realised that the situation was desperate. Edmund Dudley and the Council Learned had got Richard in their sights and persuaded King Henry of his chronic financial misconduct, which could only have further inflamed the monarch's wild suspicions about his one-time ally's loyalty. Twisted logic might have led him to believe that if Richard had once organised a Tudor invasion of England, if he'd turned his coat to York, why could he not now be organising another for Edmund, Earl of Suffolk? There was no knowing what the charges would be against Richard when they came, as they inevitably soon would, if we couldn't find some way of proving corruption and gross misconduct on the part of Wyatt and the king's 'financial advisers'.

At the risk of jeopardising my mother's close relationship with the king's mother I decided to seek support from a source King Henry was unlikely to ignore.

To My Lady the King's Mother, greetings from your former ward and humble servant,

I write to you in desperate hope of obtaining justice for my husband, Sir Richard Guildford. At present he is under scrutiny by the Council of the Learned in Law and in imminent danger of being arrested for financial misconduct; but even more unbelievably, possibly also for suspected treason. I hope and pray you would agree that these are charges completely alien to a man who has been

King Henry's faithful friend, ally and councillor for over
twenty years; charges which have been falsely
compounded and presented by a network of council
members who bear a grudge against him. Friends of his
who have tried to defend him have found themselves
similarly under attack and all his letters to the king
protesting his loyalty and faithful service have been
ignored, even possibly intercepted.

Honoured lady, you are our greatest hope of support
and reliable contact with the king's majesty. Sir Richard
Guildford is no traitor and any mistakes of a financial
nature are easily explained and rectified if the friendship
and trust between him and the king can be restored.

On Sir Richard's behalf I entreat your help in seeking
restoration to his grace's favour and removal of the
threat of a dangerous and menacing miscarriage of
justice.

I remain your grace's humblest and most loyal
servant,
Joan Guildford

I did not tell Richard I had written the letter and sent it by
courier to Colleyweston, hoping against hope that it would
give us time to avert his arrest.

24

The Tower of London

September 1505

ONE MORNING I WOKE early with terrible toothache. It was still dark and I lay still, willing the appalling pain to go away. But my moaning must have been louder than I thought because Richard stirred. 'What is it, Joan? Are you ill?' he asked.

I sat up, feeling my cheek. It was hot and swollen. 'Toothache. I'm going to find some oil of cloves.' He grunted and rolled over.

I gathered my kirtle and gown from the clothes pole where they hung and carried them out of the room. Quickly I opened the shutters and dressed as best I could in the empty chamber where the Guildford boys had once slept. The pale dawn light creeping through the narrow slits in the spiral wall supplied just enough light to see my way down the stair and once I had gathered the fragrant oil from the spice cupboard in the kitchen quarters and rubbed it on the swollen gum, I knew that I would need to make a trip to the barber surgeon.

The knowledge that this would probably mean losing the tooth depressed me. Perhaps it was the pain I was in that made me despondent but I saw this as a first sign of age. I was forty-one and although my complexion had thus far remained smooth, I now anticipated wrinkles spreading on my face, dragging my cheeks into jowls, and I would lose the one advantage I treasured of being half-Italian and having olive Mediterranean skin and abundant raven-black hair. My court contemporaries, formerly admired as 'English roses', now covered their grey streaks under coifs and veils and desperately tried to disguise their lined complexions with creams and unguents, which dried and cracked as the day wore on. At least I was still able to let my hair show under my hats and headdresses and relish the admiring glances I occasionally received from men young and old.

At this point, Mildy made an appearance, surprised to find me up and about. 'My lady, you are an early riser today. Is all well?'

'No, Mildy, I have a terrible toothache. When you have completed your morning duties I will ask you to accompany me to the barber's shop. I'm afraid I am going to have to lose a tooth.'

'Oh, poor madam! Toothache is such a wretched pain. I will get Hugh to set the fire and go and fetch my cloak. The barber always opens as soon as it's light so we can go now.'

She was right; the shop was open behind its red and white striped pole and already busy with apprentices giving trims and shaves under strict supervision by the licensed surgeon-barber, who took one look at my infected tooth and ushered me into his operating booth. I had overseen a few extractions performed on the young Guilford children and considered all the screaming and fussing rather excessive but with my head already bursting with the pain I now realised that my censure had been cruelly unfair. The sight of the pincers he brought sent my stomach churning, so that I thought I might disgrace myself by vomiting all over him. But even if I had it might not have been noticed since his apron was far from clean, displaying the bloody results of what must have been the week's extractions. However, the pain was so acute that I decided even the work of pincers that looked big enough to remove a horse's molar was preferable. I closed my eyes and opened my mouth.

'From now on I shall make much more effort to clean my teeth every day, my lady.' Mildy still looked pale and shaken as we left the barber's shop, even though she had turned away as soon as the instrument of torture appeared and refused to look round again. Understandably I made no response; indeed I did not expect to speak again for some time and considered it likely that I would not emerge from my room for days, even if I managed to walk as far as the Tower House.

Fortunately the house was unusually quiet when Martin the steward admitted us. 'Sir Richard has gone to the City, my lady,' he revealed. 'He would not let anyone accompany him but said he would meet with Master Poyntz at the Middle Temple.'

'Thank you, Martin,' I mumbled and gathered up my skirt to climb the stairs.

I heard Mildy explain my situation to him briefly before following me. The rest of the day was spent restlessly and uncomfortably, by turns propped up on the pillows and rising hourly to rinse my throbbing mouth with diluted poppy syrup. Certain it would be impossible to eat anything, I refused to descend to the hall at dinnertime and heard from Mildy that Richard had not yet returned. In the afternoon I fell into a restless sleep and woke to find darkness had fallen. The hole in my gum where my rotten tooth had been throbbed less than before.

There was a lamp burning on the nightstand and I saw that Mildy had exchanged the bloody water in my washbowl for fresh, so I clambered down from the bed to perform another rinsing routine. As I did so I realised that the dizziness I felt was probably from the poppy juice and reduced the strength of the dose, grateful that it seemed to be doing its work. It took courage to use my hand-mirror but the swelling on my cheek looked less pronounced and I managed to wipe away some streaks of blood. The maid had also laid out a fresh kirtle and gown, encouraging me to change from the clothes that still bore the stains of the barber's attention and to go down for supper.

To my surprise Anthony Poyntz was waiting in the hall, his expression clouded with concern. When he kissed my hand I was ashamed to see that there were traces of dried blood under my fingernails. 'Your maid tells me you have just had a tooth taken out,' he said, pretending not to notice. 'But I need to talk to you now if you are feeling up to it. I'm afraid I have bad news.'

Logic told me it had to be about Richard. 'Then I think I will sit down,' I said, moving towards the two chairs set near the hearth. As I took my seat I hoped it might be a case of Richard drowning his sorrows in a tavern somewhere with disreputable friends, as he had recently done frequently. I could not have been more wrong.

Anthony took the other seat, pulling it nearer to me. The fire suddenly blazed, as if a new log had been thrown on, but he ignored it. 'Sir Richard was called before a panel of the Council Learned today. I'd no idea he was due to go but it seemed he had received a royal subpoena a week back. Did you know about it?'

My heart was now throbbing worse than my mouth. 'No. He has become morose and secretive and when I have questioned him I receive only evasive answers. He has come to rely on you for counsel, Anthony.'

He nodded. 'I know. There were many things about the law and the way it was being used against him that he didn't grasp. He was up against some slippery customers on the council. Sir Henry Wyatt was not the most dangerous of them, I'm afraid.'

'I wish I'd been here when he left this morning but I went early to the barber's with a rotten tooth. I was in too much pain to bear it. Did he meet you before he answered the summons?'

'Oh yes, he found me but it didn't do him much good because as it turned out they wouldn't let me in. He was summoned to the Duchy of Lancaster's Chancellery, where the hearing was apparently to be held, but first we went to the Tabard Inn on the other side of Fleet Street. He said it was for "a good jug of ale to give me strength".' Anthony looked genuinely upset when he told me this, which set my anxiety level rising and my mouth throbbing again. 'At the Chancellery there were two armed guards on the door and as soon as Sir Richard showed them his summons they accused him of being late, ordered me to leave and marched him off into the building.'

'So where is he now? Did you wait for him?' I was really worried now.

'Of course I waited for him – from Terce to Sext according to the church bells, and still he didn't come out. When he did, he was surrounded by guards who marched him straight up the road towards the Fleet Bridge. I had to run to catch up with them and all he could do was yell that they were taking him to the prison.'

If I had been standing up I would have collapsed but as it was I slumped down in my chair as if my bones had melted. The throbbing in my mouth seemed to explode into my entire head. Anthony must have thought I'd fainted because he flung himself down before me, grabbing my flaccid hands, as if to stop me sliding down onto the floor. 'Dear Joan! Are you all right? Can I get you something – someone? This has been a terrible shock.'

Somehow I managed to shake my head very gingerly and was amazed to find that my voice functioned, albeit feebly. 'No, I'll be fine in a minute. Just a bit faint.' I forced myself back to an upright position, reluctantly pulling my hands from the comfort of his, to push on the arms of the chair. 'You're right, it is a terrible shock. The Fleet Prison! It's a cesspit. Sim nearly died in there once for something he had never even done. How on earth does Richard deserve that?'

'He is a Privy Councillor, Joan. I'm sure they won't put him in one of the communal cells with all the street felons.'

'I would not be so sure of that. It is only hard coin that speaks in that vile place. We must get some to him as soon as possible.'

'I will go now if you wish.' Anthony stood up. 'But I'm afraid I have little with me in London. Would there be coin in Sir Richard's strongbox? Have you the key?'

'Yes, but I fear there is next to nothing in it. Since Sir

Reginald Bray died and Richard fell from the king's favour, he has been driven to the Italian bankers for funds. Their interest rates have become criminal and I no longer serve any member of the royal family so our income has all but disappeared. We have been at our wits' end.'

'Would Master Edward have some liquidity? He shares control of the Royal Armoury with his father, does he not? And their headquarters are here in the Tower. Surely there are funds in their office?'

I frowned fiercely and rubbed at the bulging wrinkles I could feel between my brows. 'Yes, no doubt there are, but wouldn't that be compounding the offence that Sir Richard is accused of – embezzling the king's coffers? We cannot risk that. There must be another source of funds. A sympathetic member of the Privy Council, perhaps.'

There was a long silence, during which Anthony paced the length of the hall and back, scratching his head. On his return he stopped before me once more. 'Have you a messenger available? I have an idea.'

'Sim is here at the moment. He is trustworthy and will do anything I ask.'

'Sir Thomas Brandon lives on the other side of London Bridge – a big house at the far end of the Borough High Street in Southwark. Sim can't miss it. Sir Thomas is one of Sir Richard's fellow Privy Councillors and I know they are still close friends. Could you write a note to him?'

Suddenly infused with energy, I stood up. 'I'll do it straight away.' Feeling in the purse on my girdle I handed Anthony a key. 'This will open the strongbox, which is in Richard's office. I'm hoping that he gave you the key for that.'

Anthony patted his own purse and nodded. 'Fortunately

he did. Are you sure you are all right? Only a few minutes ago you looked very pale.'

I ignored his query. 'I'll call for Sim. I hope he isn't busy elsewhere.'

A sudden memory of Sim and Mildy crossing the Tower Quay came to my mind and just as it did she entered the hall and dropped a brief curtsy. 'The cook wonders if you're ready for supper, my lady?'

'Yes, in a short while. Can you tell him Sir Richard will not be here but Master Poyntz will.' I heard Anthony close the hall door as I spoke. 'He'll be back very soon.'

Mildy bobbed again. 'Yes, madam.' Then she peered at me more closely. 'Are you quite well?'

'I'm fine, Mildy.' I was growing impatient. 'Can you find me some paper and a pen? I need to write a letter.'

'There's some in the steward's cupboard. I'll fetch it.' She made for the screen door.

'Good. And when you have, tell Sim I wish to see him urgently. I think you will know where he is. And send Hugh to set up the trestle.' Mildy shot me a backwards glance before she disappeared but I had no wish to tax her about her relationship with Sim at this moment – if indeed there was one. Even my aching jaw had slid from my senses. Getting Richard out of the dreadful Fleet Prison was all that mattered.

25

The Tower House

September 1505

WHEN THINGS GO WRONG, they go wrong with a vengeance. I remember nothing of what happened after Sim left with the letter I had written to Sir Thomas Brandon and Anthony returned from his search in the strongbox to pronounce it completely empty. I'm told that he caught me when my knees suddenly buckled and I would have dropped to the floor in a faint. Then he carried me up to my bedchamber, Mildy close behind with a candle to light the way, when I vaguely heard her explaining about my awful visit to the barber but she did not yet know about Richard's incarceration, and neither of them was aware of the tendency of certain agues to recur violently when a body is under stress. Apparently I babbled a lot of nonsense, sweated a great deal, slept fitfully and messily swallowed a few spoonfuls daily of bread soaked in milk. I was not to return to cogent reasoning for nearly a week.

When my wits at last returned, no one was more relieved than poor Mildy, who was my guardian angel for the duration of the fever. 'I feared you might never recover, my lady! You have been ill for days and you must be starving, for you have eaten next to nothing for a week.'

'Well, I hope you did not waste any of our scant resources calling a physician, Mildy. This has been my first attack of what I fear may be several more bouts of fever. I'm told on good authority that they should become steadily shorter and less violent and I pray that will be the case.' I made an attempt to pull myself up on the pillows but found my arms too weak.

Mildy hurried forward to help, chatting as she did so. 'Master Poyntz has called every day to enquire after your health and he is here now. Will you see him? Or shall I suggest he come tomorrow?'

I found it hard to concentrate on anything but the effort required to sit up. 'Yes – no. Oh yes. Let him come up but help me into my chamber robe and a chair first, Mildy. And give my hair a brush.' Despite my confusion of mind I desperately needed to hear news of Richard's plight, feeling a surge of guilt that so much time had passed since his arrest.

On entering, Anthony drew up a dressing stool beside me and sat down. 'You look as if you have been through the mill, Joan,' he said. I noticed that he rarely addressed me with my title these days and found it strangely pleasing.

'Thank you, Master Poyntz,' I responded demurely. 'So good to receive a compliment.'

He blushed. 'I meant it sympathetically, my lady. Your maid said she was about to bring you up some nourishment and I'm sure you need it so I won't stay long.'

'But long enough to give me news of Sir Richard, I hope.'

I may have sounded a little peeved and he hastened to

placate me. 'Of course. Sir Thomas Brandon was glad to offer help financially and sent a purse of ten pounds in coin, which was very generous, I thought. He couldn't come in person because he, like you, is suffering from the ague. It must be the season for it.'

'I don't think there is a season for it, Anthony. It just strikes when you're already down. Sir Thomas has my sympathy. I will write to thank him.' I paused. Suddenly I remembered that before all this I had written to Lady Margaret but apparently received no response. Nor had I heard from my mother, who I was sure would have read the letter and sent me some sort of sympathy; at least told me whether Lady Margaret had written to the king, or even just that the letter had arrived? But had it? The room seemed to close down on me and I had to shake my head to clear it and focus on Anthony, sitting beside me looking worried. 'So I take it you've seen Sir Richard?' My voice sounded weirdly alien and Anthony frowned but replied.

'I have, yes. Sim and I went to the Fleet the next day. It cost us two whole marks to get him brought up from the common cells. Poor man, he looked shattered. But his first thoughts were for you. He said how glad he was you had not come yourself and he asked me specifically to tell you he did not wish you to.'

'I'm hoping we can get him out of there before I'll be well enough to visit anyway,' I said. 'Did you convince the gaoler to move him to a higher cell?'

'Yes, but a first-floor chamber cost another mark and there'll be more to pay to stay there as time goes on. It's not very big and unfortunately he has to share it with another prisoner – a priest from Yorkshire who claims to be innocent of any crime – obviously.' Anthony's voice acquired an ironic tone. 'I've met him now and I can't say I'm impressed but Sir Richard seems favourably disposed towards him. I asked what he needed me to bring him the next day and he said just his missal and his rosary, so Father John seems to have already had some influence. But of course I also took him a clean chemise and hose and have done so several times. Everything stinks in that place . . .'

His speech seemed to fade away. Feeling more exhausted by the minute, I must have slumped down because he jumped up from the stool and pushed it back where it came from. 'You should not be out of bed, Joan. You are tired. I will come again tomorrow.'

I made a vague gesture and heard Anthony bound from the room, begging pardon as he deftly dodged around Mildy who entered. 'Alas, my lady, in that short time he has tired you out I can see,' she cried, putting a tray down. 'Have you the strength to get back to bed?'

I roused myself enough to nod. 'I must, Mildy, but you might have to help me.'

It mattered little what the cook had provided because my appetite and sense of taste seemed to have deserted me. However, coaxed by Mildy, I did my best to swallow a few spoonfuls before dropping once more into the restless sleep which my body seemed to demand more than food. For at least another week I was incapable of concentrating enough even to read a book, let alone write a letter, but Anthony took the trouble to write on my behalf to thank Sir Thomas Brandon and sent word to Edward Guildford and Hal. When I was well enough to get dressed and sit by the hall fire, they all came to visit.

Hal arrived first and his shocked expression on greeting me revealed better than my mirror how much I had altered since our last meeting. 'Oh dearest Mother, you really have been ill! In all my life I cannot recall seeing you so thin. Are you sure you are quite recovered?'

'I always hankered after a chiselled jaw,' I told him with a smile. 'And now I have one. But, oh Hal! As I look at you I realise that I have missed your birthday in my stupor! You are sixteen now and the picture of a healthy, handsome, muscular squire! You must be able to beat the prince quite easily at the staff.'

He shrugged. 'I can beat him, yes. Do I always choose to? No. Never mind about the birthday – tell me about my father? I cannot believe he is in prison! Surely he would never have offended the king?'

'Not intentionally, no, you are right. They have long been friends. But times have changed and the king is now surrounded with sharp-eyed lawyers who sift through his ledgers adding two and two and making five. Richard is accused of misusing royal funds but the original blame lies elsewhere. I cannot say with whom but he has been trying to prove it for months now, to no avail.'

'At court a number of the king's knights have been similarly accused but they have paid the fines the court imposed, even if it empties their coffers. Could Father not have done that?'

'How soon must you return to Richmond, Hal? That is a long story.' In truth I wanted to change the subject, not wishing to load the father's troubles onto his teenage son's shoulders. I thought that as the eldest son Edward Guildford should bear that burden.

'I took two days' leave because I thought I might be able to visit him. Will that be possible?'

I pondered this, wondering if Richard would want Hal to see him languishing in the Fleet. 'To be honest I don't know. He has forbidden me to visit him but when I have the strength to walk the streets again I fully intend to go. All I can say is you should go tomorrow with Anthony Poyntz and try your luck. If you are waiting at the gate, it is my guess that your father won't refuse you.'

However, by a happy coincidence Edward arrived from Kent that night and the next morning, after attending to matters at the Armaments Office, agreed to take his young half-brother with him to see their father. While they were gone, Sir Thomas Brandon appeared at the Tower House and I was able to thank him profusely for the ten-pound loan.

'I do not know what we would have done without it, Sir Thomas. My husband would have spent far too long in the dank and crowded common cells of the Fleet. He has been ailing of late and I fear his health would not have stood it.'

Sir Thomas raised his hand in a dismissive gesture. 'I pray you not to mention it, Lady Guildford. I could not allow harm to come to my good friend Sir Richard, who has supported me consistently at meetings of the Privy Council. I am only sorry that I could not bring it to you myself last week, being under the influence of a recurring ague, which I now understand also affects you.'

'Yes, we are fellow sufferers, Sir Thomas,' I confessed. 'And I have every sympathy for you because it is not a pleasant experience.'

He was older and greyer than I expected, although I

should have realised that he and Richard were much of an age, both having supported King Henry twenty years before in his campaign against the usurper.

'I believe your son Hal is one of the squires of Prince Henry's chamber in the royal household,' Sir Thomas continued. 'My nephew Charles has mentioned him often but I have not come across him at court.'

'This morning Hal and my stepson Edward have gone together to the prison to visit their father,' I told him. 'They should return in time for dinner, when you would be very welcome to join us, Sir Thomas. Of course I hope for good news but as you know the king is not known to reverse the sentences issued through the Council Learned and so I fear he is unlikely to order Richard's release at this early stage, even for a veteran of Bosworth.'

Sir Thomas cleared his throat rather nervously. 'Indeed. Tell me, Lady Guildford, if you are in financial difficulties would you like me to arrange a more substantial loan? I'm afraid Sir Richard's royal appointments are all to be cancelled, so you may be obliged to leave this house and his estates may soon be confiscated, cutting off any income from them. I'm sure you will want to remain close to the Fleet Prison. I could offer you accommodation at Brandon Place if you wish.'

At this moment the full significance of Richard's fall from grace became clear and I felt an almost uncontrollable surge of anger – at the king, at the council and, regrettably, at Richard himself. For it was not only him that had been shamed and stripped of all honour and wealth but also me and his undeserving children.

26

The Fleet Prison

October 1505

A FEW DAYS LATER I gathered my strength, donned one of my best gowns and asked Anthony to escort me to the Fleet Prison. I had gratefully accepted Sir Thomas's offer of more financial help but, conscious of gossip and speculation, refused his offer of accommodation at his home. As Sir Thomas had warned me I soon received notice that Richard had been stripped of his offices and lost not only the house on the quay but also the rental from the houses behind it. However, having shared the post of Master of Armaments with his father, Edward Guildford was confirmed in the post, as well as taking over the office of Master of Ordnance, so although the house was no longer mine, he offered to let me to remain there, albeit not as mistress of the house but in one of the lesser bedchambers, which for the time being I was obliged to accept.

On arrival at the entrance to the Fleet Prison, I drew to an abrupt halt in order to allow my sense of smell to adjust to the reeking stench that permeated the surrounding air. It was a mixture of the pungent sewage clogging the river, which barely flowed alongside the crumbling building, and the malodorous bodies that crammed the crowded cells within. The scented kerchief I had taken the precaution of bringing was no match for such an offence to the nose and I soon abandoned it, forcing myself to breathe through my mouth and pray that the fetid air did not contain too many evil poisons.

Choking on the imagined corruption passing down my throat, I turned to Anthony in distress. 'How in the name of God can Richard be surviving in this sinkhole?' I asked him, hand over my mouth.

'You will find him much altered, my lady. You should prepare yourself for that.' I tried to read his expression but his face was set in a fixed mask. 'I'll wait for you in the Belle Sauvage Inn behind the prison. Visits are only for half an hour and you will need all of that, I imagine.'

'Yes, thank you, Anthony. I only wish we were here to take him out but I fear it might be some time before we can do that.'

Edward and Hal had also tried to prepare me for the change I would find in Richard but the spoken word is never as informative as face-to-face observation. By wearing my fur-trimmed velvet gown I had intended to bring some element of refinement into his drastically transformed world but climbing the stair to his first-floor cell I regretted my decision, because the copious skirt trailed into the deep layers of dirt gathered in the treads. Besides, when the gaoler unlocked the iron-barred door and I saw my husband stooped under the low, damp-blackened ceiling of his prison, all thought of such frivolous matters vanished.

A straggly grizzled beard, the inevitable result of three weeks' uninhibited growth, could not disguise his hollow cheeks and from beneath his grubby flat-brimmed hat his shaggy grey locks hung longer and sparser than ever. I had to force myself to kiss his dry, cracked lips and as I did so my hands felt his shoulder bones, prominent under the loose fabric of the now grimy but suitably grey doublet he had worn to the hearing of the Council Learned. I struggled to find words of greeting but he plunged right in.

'You are so thin, Joan. There is no flesh on you,' he said accusingly. 'Why have you not been eating?'

I gave him a rueful smile. 'I might say the same about you. But we both know why. I have been ill and you have been duped.'

He was once a proud knight. I had never seen him hang his head before. 'Yes. You cannot know how sorry I am.'

Through the lump in my throat I nodded acknowledgement of the apology and held out the covered basket I carried. 'I brought you some freshly cooked food. You look as if you need it.' He did not take it, still deliberately avoiding my gaze. 'It is not all your fault, Richard, as we both know. You have been sent to this horrible place as a scapegoat; an example to show the rest of King Henry's nobles and officials what will happen to those who fail to pay what his so-called "learned lawyers" decree he is owed. Queen Elizabeth would never have allowed it.'

To my surprise he gave a vehement shake of his head. 'No, Joan, you are wrong. I deserve to be here. God has shown me the error of my ways. Edward has been called before the king, who ordered him to build the fortress I should have provided years ago. I did not guard the royal grant sufficiently closely and King Henry has been noble enough to pay my son to do it instead. He could have made him do it without payment but he did not.'

'Really? Edward did not tell me that.' I wondered if this gesture, and the appointment of Edward to replace his father in Weapons and Ordnance, had anything to do with my audience at Richmond Palace.

Richard reached out and took the basket from me, placing it on a bench, which with a table and chair appeared to be the only furniture provided. 'Thank you for this. I will share it with my cellmate. Father John has shut himself away in the cupboard in order to give us some privacy.' He gestured to a dark corner and a door I had not yet noticed. 'That is where he prays and where he chooses to sleep. There is barely enough room to lie down and he has no mattress but he says that is his penance. So I have the only bed, if you can call it that.'

I had perceived a pallet leaning up against the wall. The canvas was stained and, judging by the faded yellow stems sticking out of a series of small rips, it was stuffed with barley straw. 'It looks very uncomfortable. Have you blankets?'

He jerked his thumb towards the cupboard again. 'They are thin and dirty but this chamber is so much better than the crowded pit I shared with a score of others when I first arrived. I have you to thank for that.' He put his hand up to scratch his head and I saw a louse crawl out from his hair. Expertly he snatched it away onto the trampled rushes on the floor. 'I brought some passengers up from down below,' he said ruefully. 'Everyone has them here, even the gaolers.'

'Have you anywhere to wash?' I asked with concern. 'Shall I get Sim and Hugh to bring you a tub?'

I felt quite insulted when he laughed. 'No, no. The water

will be taken from the Fleet and its effects are worse than the crawlers. Anyway, Father John says lice are God's creatures and are sent to test our devotion to the Almighty. If we love Him sincerely we will not notice them.'

My mind whirled like cartwheels. Was this the same Richard I had married? The forceful soldier-gunner who had to be persuaded to come to Mass more than once a month and had scoffed at the numerous visits to shrines I made with Queen Elizabeth I had been going to tell him about Sir Thomas Brandon's offer of a loan but suddenly decided against it, uncertain what his reaction would be. It seemed this Richard was already not the same sophisticated Privy Councillor and Knight of the Garter with whom I'd lived for nearly so many years.

Instead I said, 'I would like to meet this Father John,' and moved to take a seat on the bench beside the basket. 'It cannot be very comfortable inside that cupboard.'

'He treats bodily discomfort with the same patience and penitence as he harbours lice. But I will ask him to come out if you wish. Remember, he too was convicted on false accusations, rather like me.'

Richard chose to call him Father John but his name was John Whitby – or Prior Whitby, as he told me he had once been known. 'And still should be, if there were any justice in England.'

'Yes, I have heard that you too were arrested on false accusations. How did that come about?'

He was a small man, not of a size to suffer too severely in a cramped cupboard but quite happy to take a seat in the only chair, leaving Richard to squeeze onto the bench beside me. At first I wondered if it was just his lack of height that made him look quite plump in his loose grey habit but decided otherwise when I observed how his eyes feasted hungrily on the basket.

'I've not eaten since yesterday noon, Lady Guildford, and have not the energy to relate the sad story until my fast is broken. Might there be food in there?'

Richard withdrew the napkin. 'My lady has brought provisions, Father John. Help yourself.'

The priest almost pounced on the basket and extracted a cheese tart, which he proceeded to consume with remarkable speed, beginning his tale of woe as he chewed. 'Sir Richard knows that I was the victim of a scurrilous conspiracy surrounding the monastery of which I was Prior.'

I tried to ignore the crumbs that sprayed from his mouth as he uttered the sibilants in his account. After all a man of a certain age is not to be blamed for his lack of teeth.

Richard broke in, giving his cellmate a chance to swallow the remainder of his pastry. 'Father John was elected head of the Priory of Gisburn in Ribblesdale, way up on the Yorkshire and Lancashire border. There was a vote among the twenty monks and nuns and he was the chosen Prior. But the Superior of the mother-house wished his own candidate to have the position.'

John Whitby nodded gloomily. 'Just so – and I'm sorry to say there was nothing Christian about the way he went about ensuring that he got his way, my lady. He persuaded a member of my flock to remove one of the priory's treasures from the strong room and secrete it in my chamber, an act of burglary of which I, of course, was entirely unaware. After the item was discovered to be missing it was a dreadful surprise when searchers found it in my chamber.'

'And what was this treasure?' I asked, watching the monk lick his lips and send another enquiring look to Richard, who nodded.

With another tart in hand the cleric snatched swift bites as his tale unfolded. 'A Book of Hours, my lady, containing beautifully painted scenes from the Gospels. It was donated to the priory by a member of the Clifford family of Skipton Castle, who I believe brought it home from France after the battle of Agincourt. It is a hundred years old and very precious. I am an ordained priest. I would never have stolen such a thing.' He gazed at me with wide grey eyes as his teeth closed on the final morsel of his treat.

'Of course you would not!' Richard spoke with indignation. 'And now the book has miraculously landed in the abbot's library – for "safe-keeping". It was an infamous intrigue, from which Father John came out worst. He was taken before the ecclesiastical court in York.'

'And none of my former flock dared to give evidence in my favour,' the monk broke in. 'All too frightened of being evicted by the abbot if they did.'

'So how can it be that you are here in London? And even worse, in the Flect Prison. It's a long way from Yorkshire.'

John Whitby must have heard the sceptical note in my voice and sensed my impatience. He pushed himself up from his chair, quickly tweaking a honey-wafer out of the basket as he did so. 'That is a story for another day, Lady Guildford. Or perhaps your husband will tell you. You do not have much longer together and I can hear the Blackfriars' bell ringing for Sext so I must say the Office. Excuse me please.' With a quaint series of jerky bows he backed across the room to his cupboard and disappeared within.

'He keeps up his priestly obligations then?' I observed. 'But surely he has been defrocked, has he not?'

Richard sighed. 'A bishop may order the defrocking of a priest who is declared guilty of burglary but the priest concerned does not necessarily lose his faith in God or his adherence to Church teaching. Since Father John fiercely maintains his innocence, he has come to London to face the secular law of the land, hoping to clear his name. But since he cannot provide any witnesses willing to swear to his innocence I fear the attempt might prove fruitless. Nevertheless I am satisfied that he has been subject to malpractice and therefore to my mind he remains a holy man.'

'And so you call him Father John,' I said, trying to keep the scepticism I felt out of my voice. 'Will you confess your sins to him?'

'I already have, and been given absolution.'

'Really? Has he given you a penance?' I could not disguise my disbelief.

'No, but he has made a prediction.'

'Oh? Is he a soothsayer as well as a priest?'

My husband gave a thin smile. 'No, but I shall believe he is both if his prediction comes true. He says I will be given a pardon and when I am, my penance will be to make a pilgrimage to Jerusalem and take him with me.'

I was astounded. 'I thought you didn't believe in pilgrimages,' I reminded him.

'That was in another life, Joan,' he said sadly, rummaging in the basket. 'Meanwhile the little priest has not left me a tart.'

'I'll bring more tomorrow,' I said.

*　　*　　*

When I saw Anthony again after leaving the Fleet hellhole I wanted to fall into his arms and weep on his shoulder, seeking comfort where I instinctively knew it would be given. Had we met in a private place I might very likely have done so but the taproom of the Belle Sauvage Inn was crowded and instead I gratefully accepted his offer of a mug of small ale and recounted the details of my gaol visit.

27

Blackfriars, London

November 1505

'IT SEEMS VERY ODD to be back here again,' I said.

Mildy and I were unpacking my travelling chest in my mother's small apartment in the Blackfriars' enclosure, a square surrounded by small tenements, one of which she had qualified to rent as the widow of a soldier killed on the battlefield. When she had retired to the country with My Lady the King's Mother, she had kept it on, telling me that it was at my disposal if ever I should need it – and that time had come because Blackfriars was only a short distance from the Fleet Prison.

My life at the Tower of London was over. I thanked Edward and Eleanor for housing me while I adjusted to my reduced circumstances but was secretly pleased to be independent again and not beholden to them. The bulk of my belongings and furnishings had been sent to Frensham, the manor Richard had bought for me after our marriage, which remained legally mine even though his own Kent lands, manors and tenements had all been requisitioned by the crown and held in limbo until any trial the king might choose to subject him to. Only Edward's manor in Sussex remained a Guildford holding and home to his wife and family, he now being the proud sire of a boy named, perhaps unfortunately, Richard after his grandfather. He knew he was lucky to keep it.

'It was kind of your mother to offer you accommodation here,' Mildy observed, ignoring the fact that there were only two rooms and a kitchen and scullery. 'It means you will be able to continue visiting Sir Richard regularly.'

'Yes, but you will miss Sim, will you not?' I had been careful not to investigate how close she and Sim had become because although I was delighted that they seemed to be friends, at this stage in my life I did not want to lose Mildy's services. Selfishly I hoped she would stay with me for a while longer but now that Sim had gone down to Frensham with the furniture I wondered if she might be pining.

She gave me a look of surprise. 'You know about me and Sim?' she asked. 'I'm sorry that you do, my lady. We didn't want to tell you while Sir Richard was in the Fleet.'

'I saw you together once, walking very close, and I guessed. You are not pregnant, are you?'

Mildy looked quite shocked. 'No! We intend to marry first.'

I wanted to hug her but something held me back. 'How lovely! I hope it will not be too long before we can all celebrate your wedding together. I suppose I shall have to think about finding another personal maid though, and you will be very hard to replace.'

'Why would you need to replace me? I'm not thinking of leaving and neither is Sim. And we wouldn't think of getting married until all Sir Richard's troubles are over.'

'But we have no idea when that will be. I can't expect you to wait for ever!'

'Surely it won't be that long, my lady? The king cannot mean to leave him in prison indefinitely.'

I felt my eyes fill. 'No, Mildy, you're right, he surely cannot.' Try as I might, I obviously didn't look confident and I certainly didn't feel it. I brushed a tear away impatiently. 'But heaven help us – this won't get the chest unpacked!'

I had written of our troubles to my mother at Colleyweston and discovered that either my letter to Lady Margaret had not been delivered or she had not shown it to her companion. We had not seen each other since she had nursed me back to health on the way back from attending the Queen of Scots at her wedding but I had written to ask her about the letter to Lady Margaret and kept her informed of Richard's incarceration in the Fleet and the confiscation of his properties and offices so I assumed she would also describe it all to her royal mistress. I did not feel I could write again to My Lady the King's Mother but hoped that now she might at least be putting a little pressure on her son to reconsider Richard's position.

Mildy hadn't made any comment about the accommodation but she was clearly wondering how I would adjust to living in such humble circumstances as she picked my best miniver-trimmed worsted gown from the chest and shook it out. 'Perhaps we should leave these court gowns and robes in the chest, my lady, rather than hanging them out where moths and mice might harm them. You'll not be wearing them for your prison visits. I'll just take out the bed linen and covers and your kirtles, cloaks and stoles, shall I? Then I'll see about making a fire. It is quite cold in here.'

I sent her a look of fond gratitude. 'Yes to all that, Mildy. Meanwhile I'll go to the nearest pie shop and buy us some dinner.'

Of necessity, apart from Mildy, our main servants from the Tower House had dispersed; Martin and Sim to supervise the removal of our household goods to Frensham, where they would stay until the future looked more settled, but the kitchen and stable staff were to stay on in Edward's household. I could not bear to lose Sim and I knew Martin wanted to remain available to return to Richard's service, whenever that might be possible. Hugh the server was married and lived with his wife in the city, where he would easily find employment in another household.

Anthony had returned to Gloucestershire for the birth of his expected twins and so my short walks to visit Richard in the Fleet would continue to be done alone. But despite the king's best endeavours to unite the people of England under Tudor rule, London was still a dangerous city. Guild gangs continued to fight out their differences in the streets, thieves lurked in the narrow lanes and alleyways and conspiracies against the crown festered in many upper rooms, among supporters of the House of York. Their claimant to the throne, Edmund, Earl of Suffolk, had fled to Europe and remained under the protection of the Holy Roman Emperor Maximilian, no doubt much to King Henry's continued consternation.

Foolhardy or not, my inclination had been to buy a poniard and wear it in a sheath tucked into my walking boots. After several sessions of practising its swift removal,

I wasn't sure whether I would ever be brave enough to use it but it boosted my confidence as I made my way out of the city via the Ludgate to pay my first visit to the prison since leaving the Tower. I carried a basket over my arm like a market woman, so that I could stop at a baker's shop on Fleet Street to buy hot pies and a loaf to take to Richard and, reluctantly, his cellmate.

Although I had found him an irritant at first, over the early weeks of Richard's imprisonment, I'd become used to the little defrocked priest always being there. Indeed I had come to realise that he was an essential element in preserving my husband's fragile sanity, which might otherwise have been shattered by the indignity and discomfort of prison life. The monastic rule under which the little monk had lived and worshipped since a boy had equipped him with a faith and philosophy that sustained his existence. It was a simple and enduring belief that whatever happened to him in life, God would have a reason for it and it was up to him to discover it. Unfortunately it sometimes took him a long time to do so and meanwhile he was perfectly content to survive on regular recitations of the daily Church Offices and whatever free nourishment the Almighty might provide to keep his body in its rotund shape. So far this had resulted in Richard becoming thinner while Father John became plumper, because Richard absorbed Father John's maxims, while the ex-monk consumed the bulk of the baked offerings I brought in so regularly.

When I remonstrated with Richard, suggesting that he consume his fair share of the supplies, he had just smiled and said that he did not have the appetite to eat much and Father John might as well eat what he could not. 'I have discovered that man does not live by bread alone, Joan, and Father John has nourished me with the enlightenment to be found in prayer and a true belief in God and His saints. You have always had it but it is a revelation to me.'

Sadly on my first lone trip from the Blackfriars enclosure I forgot the rules of walking the London streets alone. These were to hide anything of value and never to carry anything that smelled edible. There were always hungry mouths lurking in the alleys near a butcher's or a baker's shop and not all of them were prepared to beg nicely for alms. After I left the Fleet Street baker's shop I found the thoroughfare had become crowded and I was unaware of a man close on my heels, until I felt a heavy tug on the basket that hung from my elbow and made the mistake of turning to see who had made it. At once the basket was ripped off my arm and a figure in a brown hooded tunic dodged away from me through the throng of people and disappeared down an alley.

'Oh no! He's got my basket! Stop him!' I yelled to an unsympathetic crowd but if anyone even looked up, they quickly turned and hurried on their way. I bent to finger the outline of the knife in my boot and toyed briefly with the idea of unsheathing it and making pursuit but quickly realised there was no point. The thief had vanished into the alley and I dismissed any idea of following him into such unknown territory as too dangerous. Besides, wielding a knife openly in such a busy thoroughfare might easily have caused injury to some innocent person and lead to my arrest. I could only hope that the fragrant meat pies and still-warm loaves of bread were destined for a starving family and not a nest of thieves who might already have grown fat on the spoils of such easy plunder.

I returned to the baker's shop to replace the stolen food and made sure to hide my purchases safely wrapped in my stole, which at least kept me warm on the last short stretch of my journey.

28

Blackfriars and the Fleet Prison

December 1505

As I CONTEMPLATED THE lonely Christmas that loomed
ahead at Blackfriars I chastised myself for such selfish
considerations when poor gaunt Richard would be confined
in his cold cell, eking out the meagre supply of firewood
left to him once the gaolers had stolen what they considered
their share of the logs I had arranged to be delivered for
burning in the small hearth. I knew that most of the candles,
which I hid among my clothing and only revealed after the
cell lock was turned after my arrival, were also apt to vanish
to the guardroom, however hard the two prisoners tried to
conceal them from their turnkeys; as did any clean, warm
clothing I might have managed to smuggle in. Richard told
me that one particular gaoler would even refuse them a
burning taper to light their fire unless some form of bribe
was offered, usually the choicest cut of any meat or cheese
I had brought that day. I never sat beside the blazing fire
Mildy set in our Blackfriars hearth without feeling guilty
at the thought of Richard shivering beside his feeble flame.
I prayed constantly for his release and the king, whom I
had once admired so much for bringing peace and wealth

to the kingdom, plunged to the depths of my estimation for the harm he was inflicting on one of his most loyal friends.

Christmas grew closer and I still heard nothing from Lady Margaret in response to my letter. But as winter started to take its grip, she sent instructions to her London Master of Horse to supply me with a mount and an escort to take me daily to the prison, for which I was extremely grateful because days of torrential rain had churned the London streets to slippery streams of mud and ordure. Each day, while I held his horse, the heavily booted groom was kind enough to dismount and collect my regular order from the bakery, so that I managed to arrive at the Fleet with my skirts and boots relatively clean. Later I learned that the sight of his Beaufort livery also served to put the fear of retribution into the thieving guards, so that fewer candles were stolen and less fuel was spirited away to the guardroom.

Richard remarked on my relative cleanliness as soon as he saw me walk in. 'I was hoping you would not come, Joan, because the streets must be foul, but look at you! Have you flown on wings like the angel you are?'

As was his habit, John Whitby rushed forward to receive the wrapped food parcels, which I removed from among the layers of my clothing, carrying them to the table with un-disguised glee, while Richard and I exchanged our usual kiss of welcome.

'You sound cheerful for someone who I see has no fire in this freezing damp place,' I said, frowning. 'I have not yet learned to fly but Lady Margaret has kindly let me have the use of a horse and a groom, so my feet have hardly touched the ground. I feel very honoured.'

'It is no more than you deserve,' he said, actually signalling the little monk from the lone chair so that I could occupy it. 'And I have good news too. Edward has received a letter from the king's secretary, telling him that his grace will be reviewing my case in the New Year.'

'How is that good news, Richard?' I found it impossible to forgive King Henry for exposing his faithful friend to such dangerous and demeaning imprisonment, when I knew in my heart that Queen Elizabeth would have persuaded him to give a Knight of the Garter the benefit of the doubt. 'He might at least have granted you bail while you wait for trial.'

Richard shook his head and perched on the bench. 'It is not just about the missing grant now, Joan. Apparently the king also has evidence that I have been conspiring with agents of the Earl of Suffolk.'

My heart began to flutter in alarm. 'Surely you would be in the Tower if that were so!'

'Several treason suspects *are* in the Tower and one of them is a man from my own village of Cranbrook, whose services I have used in perfectly innocent dealings. Nevertheless the connection has come back to bite me.'

'Who is this man? Do I know him? And why have you not told me this before?'

'The matter has only just arisen because Edward learned of the conspiracy and the names of the suspects at court and, knowing that I had employed one of them, put two and two together. I am no Yorkist spy and never would be – you can be sure of that – but with Suffolk attracting discontented Englishmen to his refuge at the Emperor's court, the king is convinced there is a major movement gathering against him in Europe. I have been caught in the frenzy of his suspicions.'

I felt that he was not telling me the whole story but I had grasped enough to realise that Richard was not going to leave the Fleet with a pardon of any kind while more suspected spies for York were being questioned in the Tower. 'You say that you have had absolutely nothing to do with any Yorkist movement, Richard, but would you put your hand on the Bible and swear it?' I had to ask him this, for I had plans of my own and I did not want to be caught up in even a whiff of conspiracy.

Richard said nothing but exchanged swift glances with his cellmate, catching him with a fish patty halfway to his mouth. Clearly the monk had been listening carefully to our conversation because without abandoning the patty he rushed off to his cupboard to return with a small leather-bound volume, which looked extremely well thumbed. 'I do not have a bible, Lady Guildford, but would you accept the services of my ancient missal? It has received many an oath during its turbulent existence.'

I realised I had asked for the impossible. A bible would not be readily available in the Fleet Prison and there was no chance of taking Richard to a church to swear his oath. John Whitby placed the book in my hands. The scratched and battered leather cover did not promise much inside but when I opened it I was astonished by the quality of the paintings contained between its pages of skilfully illuminated script. 'These are beautiful images, Brother John,' I told him, holding the book open at the Adoration of the Magi, vivid reds, blues and greens enhanced by the gleaming gold of the Virgin's halo and the guiding star.

'It was my mother's,' he said proudly. 'Her name is on the frontispiece.'

I flicked over to the title page and there, written in somewhat childish script, were two words – Annet Clifford. 'You are a Clifford, John? One of the Cliffords of Skipton?' Lady Margaret had been careful to teach her wards the names and status of all the noble families of England.

Brother Whitby's round face coloured a deep pink. 'Not exactly. My mother was a Clifford by birth but I am the son of her second marriage – to a mariner from the Yorkshire coast. I regret to say that I have never set foot in Clifford Castle, my lady.'

'We have that in common at least,' I said, offering back the missal. 'This beautiful book will serve very well as an oath taker.'

He shook his head. 'But the hand of a defrocked priest would not be suitable to hold it. Let it lie in yours.'

After due consideration I gave a nod of agreement and held the book solemnly out to Richard, balanced on both my hands. He slipped from the bench to his knees and kissed the worn leather, putting one hand on the book and the other underneath, cupping my fingers. 'In the name of God I swear that I remain a loyal Knight of the King's Body and of the Order of the Garter, and may the Almighty smite me dead if I lie.'

It was rough and ready but the tight squeeze of his fingers on mine beneath the book satisfied me almost more than the oath itself that he would not be forsworn. That day I rode back to Blackfriars with determination. If Lady Margaret was kind enough to keep my feet out of the mud, it was worth one more effort to seek her even more valuable help.

To the Right Royal and Noble Margaret, My Lady the King's Mother, humble greetings,

I do not know if you received a letter I wrote to you last year but since then things have moved on and my husband Sir Richard Guildford KG is at present held in the Fleet Prison in London awaiting the mercy of King Henry for misuse of royal funds, even though they were misused by another person and not by him. However, recently I have learned that the king has ordered further investigation into Sir Richard's loyalty to the crown, apparently suspecting that he has been in conspiracy with individuals under the pay and influence of the renegade Edmund, Earl of Suffolk. I have today personally witnessed his solemn oath, given on a holy book, that he remains as firmly loyal and faithful to his grace the king now as he was on the battlefield, when your son was victorious over the usurper Richard of Gloucester. I can vouch for the fact that he has never conspired against him, nor wished him ill in any way, but on the contrary given his grace and the kingdom twenty years of constant loyal service. I therefore beseech you to remind your son of this long service and the crown's extensive use of his considerable military, architectural and engineering skills on land and sea. There are evil forces at work against Sir Richard, which your own agents may well be able to confirm to you.

I leave my entreaty in your grace's hands, hoping that our long association might move you to plead with the king for a pardon for Sir Richard, before his failing health places him before the judgement of the Almighty.

I am, as I ever have been, your loyal servant and foster daughter,
  Joan Guildford

I scattered sand blindly over the last words I had written, feeling that this might be my last hope. For safety I tucked the letter in one to Hal at Richmond and asked him to address it and send it on to Colleyweston through the royal courier service. I trusted that if the seal of Prince Harry's household was on it, it would not be tampered with.

29

Blackfriars and Durham Palace

January 1506

A WEEK OR SO after the New Year I received the letter for which I had been pining, written in a hand and style I recognised with a leap of the heart.

To Joan Guildford from Lady Margaret, the King's Mother, greetings,

I am recently returned from spending the Christmas season at Richmond Palace, when your mother accompanied me as usual. Firstly I am happy to report that both she and I remain well, despite a treacherous journey through rain and winds back to Colleyweston. Truly winter travel grows less and less congenial with age.

Now I proceed quickly to the point of this letter. Despite all the Christmas Masses, processions, mumming and feasting, I did have some times alone with my son and, among other matters, brought up the subject of Sir Richard's incarceration. At first I thought my intervention might be pointless because King Henry was adamant that the investigations of his lawyers had been thorough and upheld the veracity of the mismanagement of Sir Richard's accounts and the loss of eight hundred pounds of royal grant. (A horrifyingly large sum it must be said.) However, when I asked whether there had been any investigation of possible third party interference in the account he admitted that he had not heard of any. I then mentioned the question of Sir Richard's loyalty and reminded him of the twenty years' loyal service he had given the crown in multiple areas of expertise, most recently facilitating Prince Arthur's wedding and the Queen of Scots' journey to Scotland, to say nothing of making leading contributions to his grace's many victorious military endeavours on land and sea. I think I can certainly say that I gave my son pause for thought and received his promise to review his suspicions about Sir Richard's loyalty before ordering any further legal investigation.

I hope to have more news in the near future but this interim report might relieve your anxiety somewhat.

I have penned this missive personally in order to preserve the contents for our eyes alone and pray for the health of both you and Sir Richard.

Margaret, Countess of Richmond

Underneath, in my mother's familiar hand, was added:

You should know that Lady Margaret wrote this letter despite suffering severe discomfort due to a wrench of the wrist during our journey home. Now she reminds me to impart what pleasure we both had in encountering my intelligent and charming grandson Hal, in the company

of the Prince of Wales at Richmond. Truly he was the
life and soul of the festive celebrations!
    Your ever-loving mother

Shortly after I had absorbed the welcome contents of this missive, I received a visit from Sir Robert Poyntz, which intrigued me because it was nearly five years since I had stayed with Queen Elizabeth at his manor of Iron Acton.

'Thank you for receiving me so promptly, Lady Guildford.' He made a bow almost as perfect as those of his son. 'It was Anthony who suggested I should come.'

'He has been a legal tower of strength to us, Sir Robert, and it is through no fault of his that Sir Richard is suffering in the Fleet.' I indicated chairs set beside the fire glowing in the hearth. 'Please sit. Anthony left us in order to support his wife through the birth of their twins. When are they expected?'

'Very soon, I believe. We hope they will lift Bess's spirits after the sad death of little Ferdinand.' Watching him lower himself carefully into the chair I assumed that age was stiffening his joints. 'I'm staying upriver at Durham Palace so I came by ferry; it is very cold on the river at this time of year,' he remarked, as if in apology. 'You know that I am Chancellor to the Princess of Wales?'

'Yes, of course, Sir Robert. How is the princess?' I signalled to Mildy, who was hovering at the service screen. 'Will you take some refreshment? Some mulled wine perhaps?' Mildy noticed the knight's grateful nod and hurried into the kitchen to fulfil the order.

'It is about Princess Katherine that I am here,' Sir Robert admitted, waiting for her to make her exit. 'She is greatly distressed by the king's treatment of her and, as my son told me of your husband's misfortune at the hands of the Council Learned, I thought you might have much in common. I'm very sorry to hear that your Guildford properties have been confiscated and Sir Richard is in the Fleet.'

'Thank you for your sympathy, Sir Robert. There has been little shown by members of the royal court, with the outstanding exceptions of My Lady the King's Mother and Sir Thomas Brandon, who have both offered me great kindness. But I admit I am still desperate to get Sir Richard out of his unjust confinement.'

At this moment, Mildy returned with a jug of wine laced with dried fruit and a pair of silver cups. She pushed a poker into the embers of the fire and tactfully stepped back out of earshot while it heated up but the knight remained cautious. 'The Thames was sluggish today as I was rowed downstream,' he remarked conversationally, rubbing his hands together. 'I wonder if it might freeze over soon.'

I felt bound to follow his lead. 'I do hope not, Sir Robert. I find snow and ice in the city streets very inconvenient.'

We lapsed into silence for a minute while Mildy plunged the red hot poker into the jug and the wine sizzled enticingly, then I waved her away with a word of thanks and leaned down to pour the hot, fragrant liquid into the cups, passing one across carefully by the stem. 'It is pleasant to have company to share a drink with, Sir Robert,' I said, raising my cup to him. 'I do not like to drink alone, even during the festive season.'

'Then you have a lot in common with Princess Katherine.' He returned the salute and took a good gulp of his warm wine. By now Mildy was out of earshot and he opened up a little. 'She, too, spent a lonely Christmas, with no invitation to court, since the betrothal to Prince Henry was cancelled and she roundly rejected what I consider to be a very ill-advised suggestion from the king that she might marry him instead.'

My jaw dropped in surprise. 'No! He didn't?' At his nod in response I sat back in my seat. 'This confirms what I have long suspected, that the queen's death has severely affected King Henry's mind.'

He nodded. 'You may be right. Although I believe he did it because he is loath to repay the considerable dowry that filled his coffers on the princess's wedding to Prince Arthur.' Sir Robert took another draft from his cup. 'He also refuses to pay her widow's portion, maintaining that if she was legally not a wife she cannot be a widow. The result is that Katherine is almost penniless and cannot pay her household, so most of her Spanish servants have been obliged to return to Spain. Only four are left, two of them Moors, originally of the Muslim faith but now baptised Christians. They will not leave because in Spain they are classed as slaves and would not be paid anyway. I very much hope that you will come and visit the princess. I'm sure she would welcome your sage advice and she will be glad of your fluent Latin. Her English remains rudimentary.'

'I would be glad to, sir. I have not seen her since I left the newlywed's household before they travelled to Ludlow.' I drained my cup and reached for the jug to offer him a refill. 'How long will you remain at Durham Palace?'

'Only a day or so. I don't like the look of the weather and need to get back to Gloucestershire.'

'Yes, of course. Would tomorrow after dinner suit her, do

you think? It would give me time to visit Sir Richard in the morning.'

He smiled and nodded, tellingly taking care not to show his teeth. 'I may be engaged elsewhere but I will give instructions to the princess's household.'

We finished the jug of wine between us and as he rose to leave he kissed my hand and made an unexpected remark. 'Anthony admires you greatly, you know. He would not fight your husband's legal battles with such vigour if it were not so. And I understand his feelings.'

The look he gave me then rang an alarm bell in my head. 'We owe him a great deal, Sir Robert,' I said hurriedly. 'I will pray for his wife's successful delivery.'

'We are all doing that, Lady Guildford. Twins are double danger, I fear. I will arrange for a ferry to collect you tomorrow.'

'That would be kind. Thank you.' I bade him goodbye, pondering the implication behind his remarks about Anthony's admiration. Had I been careless in my familiarity with him? Scandal spreading in the court about his wife would definitely not help Richard's cause.

30

Durham Palace

January 1506

DURHAM PALACE EXUDED A forlorn air. Weeds grew in the gravel path that led up from the guarded dock and passing through the porter's gate I noticed a lack of outdoor staff: gardens untended, unpicked fruit rotting in the long grass of the orchards. I did not encounter another soul until I reached the main entrance where a liveried manservant evidently knew who I was and ushered me up a dusty stone stairway to the princess's first-floor solar.

On entering, my first impression was of a stuffy wood-panelled chamber filled with dark furnishings, including thick window drapes that blocked any view of the Thames. Cheap tallow candles emitted a dim light accompanied by smoke that caught at the throat. I was announced in Spanish and made my curtsy to the sad-faced lady seated at the hearth, dressed in black with occasional touches of white, including a short lace veil shadowing her face. She seemed older than I knew her to be, having been seconded to her household during the preparations for her wedding to Prince Arthur five years previously. Then she had been just sixteen, which meant she had only recently become twenty-one.

It must have been the dark clothes and the veil that made her look older, still worn I assumed in mourning for both her husband and her mother.

Princess Katherine greeted me in her Catholic Latin. 'You are welcome, Dona Guildford. It is good to see you again.'

'It was your Chancellor who suggested that I come, your grace. Sir Robert thought you would welcome some English company.' I tried to adjust my pronunciation to hers but I could see her struggling to understand. 'You may remember that our Latin pronunciations are a little different. I hope you can follow me.'

Even through the shadow of her veil her smile was radiant. 'I understand it better than the strange English most of my new servants speak,' she said, waving me towards another chair placed near the fire. 'I think they must all come from the northlands or somewhere. Please sit down.' She lapsed back into Spanish to give an order to a dark-skinned woman hovering nearby, which sent her scuttling from the room. 'I am lucky that my Moorish girls decided to stay with me because at least we comprehend each other,' she continued. 'I know that I should learn English but it is so difficult.'

I settled myself down, grateful for the meagre warmth of the struggling fire. 'I managed to teach you some English before your wedding and would gladly help you further if you wished, your grace.'

She gave me a peevish frown. 'I do not expect to need it for much longer, Dona Guildford.' I smiled inwardly at the way she pronounced my name, which I thought made it sound rather glamorous. 'I wrote to my father asking him to arrange for my return to Spain and he replied that he would send a ship as soon as King Henry returned the dowry money paid on my marriage to Prince Arthur. When will he do so, do you think?'

This was an awkward question and I was steeling myself to tell her that I thought it highly unlikely King Henry would do so at all, but was forestalled by the arrival of an unmistakeably high-ranking Spanish lady who made a graceful curtsy. 'This is my kind and faithful friend Dona Maria de Salinas,' Katherine announced. 'She has stayed with me here in England, even though I can barely afford to pay her the wage due to a junior maid.'

The elegantly clad lady was followed by two dark-skinned girls carrying bronze trays of delicate cups and platters of sweetmeats, which they proceeded to arrange on a nearby table covered with a fringed red cloth. Both young women looked vaguely familiar and also very similar, dressed alike in long fawn-coloured tunics with white veils wound around their heads, rather like exotic nuns. I felt sure they had been in the princess's entourage when she first arrived from Spain but had functioned in a more menial role than they fulfilled now.

Princess Katherine reached out and drew her Spanish friend forward. 'Dona Maria came to support me here in England and replaced my original duenna, who had to return to Spain. So you did not meet her at my wedding. Maria has been my rock ever since, especially after my mother died.'

I rose to make a curtsy to the Spanish lady, reflecting that she appeared younger and much less severe than the rather domineering Dona Elvira I remembered. Clad in bright colours, she displayed a more cheerful attitude and a welcoming air.

'God's greeting, Dona Guildford,' she said pleasantly, before breaking off to stoke the dying fire and throw on another log. 'I hope you like pomegranate juice. It is the princess's favourite drink, the pomegranate being her personal emblem.'

'I can't say that I have ever tasted it,' I confessed, impressed with Dona Maria's Latin, finding it considerably easier to follow than that of her mistress.

'It is not possible to acquire pomegranates here in England,' the princess remarked. 'But the Spanish ambassador manages to import them from warmer climes and always brings me some. Kat and Lina prepare the juice and it is truly delicious.'

I made a quick assumption that the dark-skinned girls must have been baptised after the princess, Katalina being the Spanish version of the popular saint of Alexandria. Being the daughter of an immigrant myself, these two young women piqued my curiosity.

'It also has great benefits for your health,' Dona Maria added. 'The princess tends to suffer one ague after another.'

'And now the ferrymen say that the Thames will freeze over.' Katherine shuddered and pulled her black woollen stole closer around her shoulders, while one of the Moorish girls placed a delicately engraved glass of bright red juice on the table beside her. It had clearly been warmed, for a light steam rose from the top. 'I declare that I shall not leave the palace until the spring.' She picked up the glass and I waited until she had taken a sip before lifting my own, which I almost dropped when she made her next remark. 'Sir Robert tells me that your husband is in gaol for offences against the king, Dona Guildford. Has he been conspiring with the English lord who has run away to the Emperor's court?'

I hastily put down the juice untasted. 'No indeed, your grace, he has been one of King Henry's loyal officials for many years but he is the victim of false accusations, which I pray will be rectified very soon.'

She leaned forward, her brow creased with concern. 'Well, Dona Guildford, you may be sure that I would never stain a wife's reputation with the actions of her husband, whether or not they are proved to be true.'

'Thank you, your grace.' Solemn-faced I raised my glass in salute and took a gulp of the pomegranate juice. 'You are absolutely right, this drink is delicious.'

I noticed that the Moor girls put their hands to their mouths to suppress their giggles of pleasure and gave them a smile.

Dona Maria pulled up an upholstered stool and joined our circle at the fire. 'Sir Robert told us that you stayed at his house with Queen Elizabeth not long before she died. That was a terrible loss for the king, was it not?'

I nodded solemnly. 'Terrible. I think he may never recover from it. I have served the royal family for many years and spent some time as governess to the king's children. Only recently I returned from accompanying his oldest daughter Margaret to her wedding to the King of Scotland.'

Princess Katherine chimed in. 'I believe you also taught Prince Henry when he was younger, so you must know him well.' I pondered whether to mention the prince's rejection of their proposed marriage and decided against it but the princess continued. 'I find him a very confident young man. He will make an excellent king, I think.' There was a pause before she went on, growing more animated. 'Did you know that I was promised to him soon after Prince Arthur died? But the contract was rejected last year. It was the start of all my problems, Dona Guildford. That was when the king suggested that I marry him instead but I knew it was only because of the money – he did not want to return the dowry or pay me my widow's portion. He does not even invite me to court any more, even though I am still his daughter-in-law.'

Dona Maria leaned forward to speak gently to her. 'Your father will sort it out, *Princesa*. Soon you will go home to Spain.'

Princess Katherine's veil trembled as she shook her head. 'I do not want to go home to Spain! All that way over the waves, feeling sick, and then miles and miles over rivers and mountains to Granada! I do not wish to return now, Maria – not now my mother is dead. I wish to be betrothed to Prince Henry and become Queen of England, just as she planned. That is what I pray for and that is what will happen, if God wills it!'

I felt a surge of pity for her. It seemed such an unlikely future to hope for when the cards were so stacked against her. But I quashed my instincts and voiced my support. 'Therefore I think you should improve your English, your grace. And I will help you, if you will allow me to.'

31

Blackfriars and the Fleet Prison

January–February 1506

THERE WERE WEEKS IN January when the north wind
blew so cold and so hard that few dared to risk breaking
bones trying to walk the icy streets and the same applied
to the legs of Lady Margaret's palfrey. So it was impossible
either to visit my husband or to attempt to begin improving
Princess Katherine's English. All I could do was stoke the
fire in the Blackfriars hearth and fret about Richard, trying
to take my mind off imagining his circumstances in the
Fleet Prison by reading and rereading my small selection of
books. At least I had fuel enough to be able to pay one
of the novice monks to carry a few loads in a thick blanket
to the Fleet and just pray that at least some of it got to
Richard. In December I had sent Mildy down to Kent
to see Sim and to spend Christmas with her family and she
had been unable to return, so there was only myself to feed
and the friars allowed me to obtain meals and ale from their
kitchen for a small offering.

When at last the ice melted under a period of kind
February sun, Lady Margaret's horse and rider immediately
reappeared at my door and I began my visits to the prison

again, hating to think how badly the deadly weather would have affected Richard's health. Would he even have survived?

He looked terrible; gaunt and grey-faced, his ragged clothes hanging off his limbs like seedpods on a winter ash tree. When I hugged him, I worried that the sharp bones I felt running down his spine might crumble. Yet I was loath to let him go. 'Jesu, Richard, you feel like Old Father Time. Where is your scythe?'

He showed no inclination to release me either, seeming to absorb all the warmth he could from my body into his. 'If I had one I might have eaten my own flesh by now, Joan. Thank God you have come at last!'

I looked over his shoulder. 'Where is the plump monk? Has he shrunk away?'

He shook his head, his arms still tight around me. 'No, but the guards let him give the last rites to dying prisoners. The local priests stopped coming when the ice made the streets impassable and they asked him to do it.'

'But he's not a priest any more.'

Richard let me go at last and stepped back. 'No, but the dying don't know that and he still looks like a monk. He brings them some solace, I suppose. If you hadn't come soon he might have had to salve my sins.' He reached for the saddlebag I had put on the table and undid the buckle. 'Whatever you've brought, I'll eat it. I could even eat the leather of the bag.'

I had managed to preserve the bakeshop bread and pies from the guard on the gate who had been too busy grabbing some of the logs from the full pannier I had loaded onto the horse but most of them were still left for me to carry in. 'How long is it since you had a fire? Shall I light one?'

'The ashes died and we haven't had a flame for a day or two.' He was sinking his teeth into a meat pie, which muffled his voice. I felt a lump form in my throat. Could I have come any sooner? Luckily I had thought to bring a flint and tinder with me and I set about using them. 'But today I have received a letter from Edward, who's at court,' he added, pulling a much-folded paper from the front of his threadbare velvet doublet. 'Here, read it.'

I scanned the note as fast as I could decipher Edward Guildford's scratchy writing on an ink-spattered page. Firstly it said that the king had asked him to join a jousting team for a tournament at Greenwich Palace. Apparently, Archduke Philip of Burgundy's ship had been driven onto the Dorset coast by Channel storms on its way from the Netherlands to Spain and, as the son and heir of the Holy Roman Emperor Maximilian, he was being generously hosted and entertained by King Henry while waiting for repairs to be made. But in the second part of the letter was the news that Edward had been taken aside by the king's secretary, Bishop Foxe of Winchester, and informed that the Privy Council would ratify a royal pardon for Sir Richard Guildford at its next meeting in March.

I could scarcely believe my eyes, which instantly filled with tears of relief. For a minute or two I closed them and lifted the cross around my neck to whisper a Deo Gratias, then held the letter out to return it. 'At last! This is wonderful, Richard.'

He did not appear as gratified as I expected. 'A pardon is not forgiveness, Joan. It will not restore me to my former position or return my honours and properties. I might only get out of prison to take up life as a pauper.'

'But you will be alive and if you stay in this dreadful place much longer they will be granting a pardon to a corpse.'

He waved the last morsel of his pie. 'Not if you can keep bringing me these – and the fire!'

I forced a smile. 'And as long as you get to the food before Father John does!'

On my return to Blackfriars I sent a messenger to Durham Palace to ask if Princess Katherine would permit me to visit her again, in order to fulfil my offer to help with her English. However, the messenger returned with a verbal reply that the princess had been invited to join the king at Greenwich, where he was presently entertaining Archduke Philip and Archduchess Juana, who was Princess Katherine's sister. It pleased me that the king had invited his daughter-in-law, even if it was only out of an obligation to let her meet with her sister. I hoped they might have been able to enjoy a happy reunion but later, Hal, who had accompanied Prince Harry to the same court event, wrote that the archduke had kept his wife under close guard in his apartments and also refused even to dance with Princess Katherine. It seemed that the alliance between England and Spain was hanging by a thread and I worried for the future of the young woman who had once been so fêted and praised when she married Prince Arthur. Perhaps she had been right; it was not worth her learning English.

I would have loved to be able to visit Hal at Greenwich but I needed to remain in London so that I could deliver nourishment to Richard. I thought how sad it was that he had not been involved with the organisation of the tournament in which his son was taking part, having planned and built all the tourney fields of King Henry's reign so far.

My friend Sir Thomas Brandon was kind enough to write to me at Blackfriars, revealing to my horror that the Privy Council meeting, at which the king was to officially announce Richard's pardon, had been postponed.

The reason is that the Earl of Suffolk is still being sheltered in the Austrian court and the king is insisting that he be returned to England. In fact the matter of his repatriation has been the principal subject of negotiation during Archduke Philip's stay in the kingdom, because King Henry's chief concern since Prince Arthur's death has been the increasing number of Yorkist conspiracies centred on Suffolk's tenuous claim to the throne. So although the archduke has been treated as an honoured guest, he is kept under close guard and will not be allowed to sail for Spain until Suffolk is safely locked up in the Tower of London.

I read this, feeling as if the world had landed on my shoulders. There was no knowing how long the delay might be and my eager expectation of getting Richard out of gaol was swamped by bitter disappointment. When I married him, as well as becoming a lady-in-waiting in Queen Elizabeth's household, I had adjusted into his family life, running his houses, organising his motherless children and almost dying giving birth to my own son. Life had been eventful, busy, and occasionally traumatic but I had never felt lonely. Now loneliness swamped me.

Apart from my visits to Richard, suffering and starving

in the Fleet, I had not had a meaningful conversation with anyone for weeks, except for communicating with a few servants and messengers and the Beaufort groom who escorted me to the prison. Very occasional letters from Hal and Edward and my married stepdaughters were highlights but they were no substitute for the busy life I had spent in the courts of the kingdom. Even the absence of Mildy and Sim contributed to my sense of isolation. I actually felt jealous of their presence at my manor of Frensham, yearning to be with them, running the house and even talking to the ravens, which still nested thereabouts. In February and March they would be building their nests and laying their clutch of eggs and I would be energised by the signs of new life. But all alone in my stark monastery almshouse, I felt almost as much a prisoner as Richard.

32

Blackfriars and Frensham Manor

April 1506

KINDLY, SIR THOMAS BRANDON informed me that Edmund, Earl of Suffolk, was delivered to the Tower of London in mid-March and Philip of Burgundy was allowed to sail for Spain. Edward Guildford received his father's pardon on April the second and arrived at Blackfriars the following day to give me the good news. He wanted to go straight on to the Fleet but I thought Richard would not want to be seen out in the city in his soiled prison garb and so I insisted he wait while I opened the chest that held his father's court clothes and selected a black fur-trimmed velvet gown, a padded grey doublet and a black hat with a white feather. I also included a fresh chemise, clean hose, and his leather riding boots, which had been polished to mirror brilliance by Martin the steward before he left the Tower House.

Packed into two panniers, they were loaded onto the spare mount, which the groom led and would be the horse that would carry Sir Richard Guildford back into the outside world again.

However even in the smart apparel I had brought, Sir Richard was far from being the same man that had once been Master of the Royal Ordnance and Armoury, Comptroller of the King's Household, Privy Councillor, Knight Banneret and Knight of the Garter. Not only did his rich clothes hang from his shrunken frame like washing pegged out to dry, but try as he might he could hardly hold his head up to keep his hat on, so that it fell off within minutes and had to be saved from disappearing into the murky waters of the Fleet River by the agile groom. I rode beside him and at times could hardly refrain from taking the reins because he seemed to have barely enough energy to steer his steed. Most of what he could summon had been expended on his cellmate, John Whitby. Their farewell had been emotional and effusive but held in whispers, like a conspiracy. We were soon to find out why.

I had borrowed a tub from the friars and after he had consumed a Lenten meal of pounded fish and bread soaked in milk to protect his loosened teeth, he soaked for an hour before a roaring fire and I tried with pumice stone to remove some of the dirt that clung to his skin. By this time he craved sleep above everything but I would not let him lie in clean sheets until I had cut his hair short, treated his head for lice with a tincture of delphinium and wrapped it tightly in linen soaked in lavender oil. All this treatment he took meekly and without complaint. He was barely the Richard I recognised until he made suddenly made a speech, which brought him vividly back.

'I cannot stay here long, Joan. Tomorrow we will go to Kent, to your manor of Frensham, and I will prepare to make a pilgrimage to Jerusalem. I cannot live in King Henry's kingdom until I have atoned for my sins and washed my soul of its transgressions.'

It was the longest utterance he had made since leaving the Fleet and I recalled his exchange with John Whitby about a pilgrimage at the start of his sentence.

'Your head has been turned by your "Father John", Richard,' I reminded him gently. 'But you should remember that he was defrocked and debarred from his priory for a reason. He may not be a cleric you should put your trust in. Besides, he is still locked up.'

He shed the towels he had used to dry himself and I held out a clean shift of mine for him to cover his nakedness. It fell loosely on his shrunken frame but would serve better as a nightgown than those that had fitted him before.

'Not for long, I think,' he said to my astonishment. 'Nor will he be disgraced. Father John attends a hearing of the court of common law tomorrow and expects to be exonerated and released. If he is, I will collect him and take him with me to Frensham. Edward has arranged horses and I am assuming you will not refuse us shelter at your manor until we leave for the Holy Land?' He crossed himself and leaned forward to kiss me on the cheek. 'Thank you for your enduring care, Joan. You have supported me in ways I could never have expected. And now I cannot wait any longer to sleep in a comfortable bed!'

Speechless at what I had just heard, all I could do was knit my brows and watch as he pulled the covers over himself. He was asleep in moments.

The following day, Richard was up before I woke and 'stole' a few groats from my purse, doubtless to buy breakfast before meeting his son and riding to the court, held at the Guildhall, off Cheapside. Edward returned to Blackfriars at dinnertime without him and explained his absence. A jubilant John Whitby, whose Yorkshire convictions had been overturned, had taken Richard with him to the Crutched Friars, a religious order that occupied buildings on ground behind the gallows on Tower Hill.

'They are the brothers who wear brown habits with red crosses on the back and carry staffs topped with crucifixes. You'll have seen them about the city, I'm sure, Mother Joan. Their Prior will rededicate Father John to the Catholic Church and the friars themselves specialise in preparing people both spiritually and practically for pilgrimage to Jerusalem. As I think you know, both my father and Father John have vowed to go there. In fact I have booked places for them on a ship sailing from Rye in a week's time.' Edward seemed to see nothing amiss with the fact that all this had been arranged between the three men without referring to me at all.

'Pilgrimages cost money, Edward,' I said, trying to keep the anger from my voice. 'How do they propose to finance a journey of that complexity and risk?'

Colour rose in his face. 'Well, I expect they will seek alms on the way, as all pilgrims do, but I have paid for their crossing to France. The king has made a contribution as well. He added ten pounds to the money he granted me to build the tower to defend the port of Rye; the money that my father somehow lost. Work has begun already.'

I had to turn away to hide my reaction to this. Clearly there had been a conspiracy to remove from the royal court one of their number who had let the crown down. And Richard was complicit in it. His wife was apparently of no importance. I was a mere female who did not merit consultation or consideration. How did they think I was supposed to survive, I wondered? I'd already had to borrow money to support myself, and Richard's transgressions had also cast me from the shelter of the king's favour and any hope of further royal employment. But he seemed unconcerned about how I would survive while he was roaming the world to make atonement for his sins. Perhaps he thought that I would be able to return to court and take up where I left off – but I feared that was never going to happen. The closest I could get now to the royal household was through my son's letters and my lessons with Princess Katherine, who was as removed from the court as I was. In fact I felt obliged to send a note to her to explain that I would not be available for those lessons for some time.

Our journey to Frensham was slow, mostly because of Whitby's inability to control his hired horse, which kept wandering off to crop the grass at the side of the track. Frustrated by the pace of our journey, Edward left us as soon as we neared Halden Hall. He had received a royal order to achieve the return of the confiscated Guildford properties and took off with relish to evict the bailiff who had been sent by the king's sheriff to take over the manor. Richard had shown no interest in serving this notice himself, having thoughts only for the pilgrimage.

Edward's departure left me riding alone, following the two self-absorbed pilgrims at their painfully slow pace, solemnly receiving the blessings of other passing travellers because they were clad in their brown Crutched Friar robes with the red cross on the back. At least they and the staffs they also held, with the crucifix at the top, probably protected us from any roadside bandits, who might otherwise have considered us easy prey.

When we finally arrived at Frensham Manor it was a joy to find Martin the steward at the door and Mildy inside to greet me. Martin was justifiably puzzled when Richard refused to follow me to the chamber we had usually shared and requested that another be prepared for him and his companion, with the curtained bed dismantled and removed and two pallets laid on the floor. 'We leave in three days on a pilgrimage, Martin,' he explained. 'There is no point in us reclining in luxury now if we are to spend the next year sleeping rough under the sky, or at best on straw in hospice dorters.'

Mildy heard this with widening eyes but waited until we closed the door on what was apparently now to be my own lonely chamber to ask the obvious questions. 'Why is Sir Richard going on a pilgrimage, my lady, and who is that strange man?'

I heaved a great sigh and sank thankfully into the cushioned window seat. 'Oh, Mildy! You may think that man is Sir Richard Guildford but you would be wrong. That is a man who has been robbed of his freedom and his honour, starved and frozen and humiliated, and now believes he must atone for the sins he has committed in order to merit divine absolution. He sees that "strange man", as you so rightly call him, as the one who will lead him to the Holy Land, where he will be restored to God's grace and thus readmitted to the favour of the king.'

Ever practical, Mildy asked, 'So what will happen to the Guildford lands, my lady? At present they are ruled by a man who calls himself the king's bailiff and waves a document with the royal seal. All the villagers who were employed by Sir Richard have been dismissed, the stock has been sold and Martin has been prevented from checking the estate ledgers. I don't know where he is finding the funds but at least we are not yet starving here at Frensham.'

The anger that had been growling in my gut all the way from London became a raging beast. That some strange member of the king's yeoman guard had been sent to sack the Guildford staff was suddenly to me like a red rag to a bull. I stood up. 'Please get started on the unpacking, Mildy. I'm going to speak to Sir Richard.'

However, when I went in search of him I discovered that he and his fellow pilgrim had set out, walking up the lane to the local village of Rolvenden. 'I think Sir Richard wishes to show Brother Whitby the Guildford chapel in the church of St Mary the Virgin, my lady,' Martin told me, his refusal to grant him the accepted priestly title of 'Father' revealing his true opinion of the re-frocked priest. 'The master is much changed, is he not?'

'Yes, Martin, it is quite a recent alteration and I am as perplexed as you are. But Mildy has just revealed the worst aspect of it and that is his apparent indifference towards the plight of his servants and farmhands. I am afraid the crown has taken advantage of the confiscation of the Guildford properties and holdings and has swiftly moved to profit from them by dismissing the workers and selling the stock. Master Edward is even now repossessing Halden Hall from the bailiff but I'm afraid there are no Guildford funds available at present to rehire the estate workers. I really don't know what I can do about it, being very short of funds myself. What I do have left in coin will have to feed this household and eventually, somehow, be paid back to the kind donor.'

Martin gave me one of his rare smiles. 'I am very glad to hear that Master Edward is taking responsibility for the Guildford holdings now, my lady, but you are forgetting that Frensham is entirely your property. It does not belong to the Guildford holdings and your tenants paid their rents at Michaelmas as usual, so that there is coin in your coffers here, only waiting for you to release it.' He handed me a heavy metal key. 'I have taken the liberty of inspecting the farm accounts as well and although the reeve is not literate he has taken the tally sticks to the local priest and all the receipts are entered. Your shepherds and ploughmen, house and stable staff have all been paid and if you use the key you will see how much is left to see you through the rest of the year.'

Frensham had proved to be the one thing Richard had done right – given it to me as my dower, and it would save me and my faithful servants from penury. I did not stay to count the contents of the strongbox when I opened it but I noted that there were piles of groats and even a few of the new silver shillings, minted no doubt under the evil eye of Sir Henry Wyatt, plus the glint of gold from a small stack of angels. We would not go hungry, as Martin had implied.

Therefore, as Richard's mind was completely made up and there seemed no point in trying to dissuade him, three days later I stood on the dock at Rye and watched his ship sail off under a brisk north-easterly breeze. Since leaving the Fleet he had barely spoken to anyone except his re-frocked companion. Certainly he had expressed no regret or apprehension to me. The only positive thing he had done was to make a will, which now lay sealed in the Frensham strongbox with the household funds in which he had shown no interest. Try as I might, I could feel little emotion at his departure. The Richard I had unwillingly married and come eventually to love had evolved into an obsessive pilgrim, who barely even kissed me farewell.

'You will write, won't you?' I shouted as he mounted the gangway but he gave no sign of having heard.

PART THREE

33

Frensham Manor and Halden Hall

May 1506

EDWARD INVITED MARTIN TO move up to Halden Hall and take over stewardship of the Guildford holdings, which left me free to appoint Sim as the new steward of Frensham Manor. It demonstrated my faith in the boy I had rescued from the forest sixteen years before, and the wages he would earn and the occupation of the steward's accommodation meant that at last he and Mildy could marry and support a family. Their wedding at the church of St Mary the Virgin in Rolvenden, followed by a celebration meal at the manor house, was a high point for all of us as blossom frothed on the fruit trees and lambs began to gambol in the fields beside the sheep-pens. Spring heralded new life everywhere; there were chicks in the hencoops, ducklings on the pond, calves in the meadows and even young ravens in the nest at the top of the conifer at Halden, where Jack and June, the pair I had brought to Kent from the Tower of London, continued to hold sway over the home wood.

However, try as I might I seemed to be the only living being who did not feel the joy of life renewing itself. It did not surprise me that I had heard nothing from Richard but it soured the pleasure I genuinely wanted to feel at witnessing the love between Mildy and Sim as they made their marriage vows. When darkness fell after the feast, the wedding party lit the couple's way with torches, singing bawdy bedding songs, as they crossed the back court to the lath and cob cottage that was their new home.

I knew that inside the cottage Mildy's boisterous brothers would have hidden prickly teasels and spiky twigs of holly between the sheets of the marriage bed and hung mistletoe from the bedposts as a symbol of fertility, while her sisters would throw dried rose petals over the blushing couple as they were stripped to their shift and chemise before they climbed beneath the covers. Then the village priest would sprinkle them with holy water and her family would kiss them good-night, while the rest of the guests chanted ribald rhymes and danced around the bed. I forced myself to join in the fun and watched them smile patiently at their tormentors, hoping they were holding hands under the blankets and waiting until the noisy party left so that they could remove the thorns and prickles and embrace each other eagerly, in the knowledge that their loving was wholesome and legitimate at last.

Next morning, Mildy surprised me by bringing a warm posset to my bedside. 'I told you to take a few days off!' Surprise may have lent my exclamation a slight hint of ingratitude.

She smiled, undeterred. 'Force of habit, my lady, besides there is so much to do. Sim wants to call a meeting of the manor tenants but he can't do that until the manor house is clean and polished after the wedding. He hopes you won't need to use the hall and solar today. We plan to set to with mop and pail.'

'And what if I need you to brush up my gowns and mend my smocks? Does Sim have first call on you now that you're married?' She looked so disconcerted that I had to laugh. 'Fie on me! I am joking, Mildy. Sim's meeting in a clean hall is far more important than a few gowns and shifts. But first of all I want to hear about your wedding night. Was it all as you could have wished?'

Again I caught her unawares and she blushed, as any bride might. 'We are both very happy, my lady. And thank you for leaving before my brothers' language became too crude. Our mother had to clip a few ears to make them remember their manners.'

'They are blacksmiths, Mildy, not angels. Anyway a few rude rhymes are expected at a wedding. Were they all your brothers and sisters? I lost track of names, there seemed to be so many of them.'

I was out of bed now and sipping my honeyed posset as she collected up the elements of my apparel for the day, chatting as she did so.

'I have two older brothers, John and Mick, who work in the family forge. Both are married and so their wives were there. Of course I have no need to introduce Hetty, who you might have noticed is pregnant again – that will make three children. And then there's Dot, one of my two other sisters, who is married too and her husband Jethro also works in the forge.' She paused to hand me a clean smock. 'And then there's the youngest sister I want you to meet properly – Rose. You may have noticed her. She is neat and pretty and also reads and writes really well – better than me. She's only fifteen but I think she would make a very good personal maid for you when I have to stop.'

'When you have a baby, you mean? But I shall always want you back between children, Mildy.' I found it hard to imagine a time when she would not be part of my life.

She gave me a doubtful look. 'Of course I will be here as long as Sim is. But you may not always be here, madam. You need someone who will travel with you and Rose is keen to see the world.'

My doleful expression must have spoken as loudly as my words. 'I'm not sure I will travel much further than Halden Hall now. There is no queen to serve and my husband is persona non grata at court, which firmly closes that door for me. Also I am neither wife nor widow and I have no London home, therefore no one of status will invite me anywhere. So I'll not need a travelling maid, Mildy, you are safe at Sim's side.'

She handed me a soft cloth soaked in lavender water and warmed by the fire for me to wash my face and hands as she revealed something unexpected. 'I will always be that, my lady, but there is something else that prompts me to introduce you to Rose. I was not a virgin bride and my babe is expected in the autumn.' She avoided my gaze as she handed me my smock. 'So Rose's services might be needed sooner than you think.'

I made a quick calculation. 'A Christmas conception? You could not resist when you heard the nativity hymns! And why should you? Come here!' I pulled her into a tight embrace before letting go in order to cup her face between my hands. Her eyes asked for forgiveness but I shook my head. 'Congratulations and God bless you both. That is the best news I have heard in what seems like years!' Due to the lump in my throat I could add no more but with the scented cloth I gently wiped the tear she shed. 'Bring Rose to me. I'm sure she'll be perfect.'

Apple blossom was still falling when Anthony Poyntz arrived at Frensham without warning and had to be sent on to Halden Hall, where I was sitting in the wood behind the house I had once called home, talking to the ravens I had brought from the Tower, who had also made it their home. Their chicks were squabbling, balanced on twigs protruding from the ragged nest high in the conifer above me, and their parents, Jack and June, were calling back with sharp admonishments in between swallowing the treats of trapped vermin I had collected from the stables.

'They're telling their children to step away from the edge, I warrant. I guessed I'd find you here.'

There was a click as the gate to the wood closed and the familiar male voice drew nearer behind me. I leapt up from the log where I always sat to commune with my ravens and Jack and June immediately spread their glossy black wings protectively over their treasured treats but they did not send out alarm squawks. We all knew who the incomer was.

'Anthony!' I said, turning with a delighted smile.

He bowed over my hand and kissed it fleetingly. 'Joan – Lady Joan,' he said. 'The Lady of the Ravens.'

'Not any more; those days are long gone.' I made a gesture towards the birds. 'But Jack and June remember you. They have long memories.'

'I went to Frensham and was pleased to be greeted by your new steward. Sim carries the responsibility well.'

I nodded. 'He is my rock. Did he tell you that he and Mildy are married and expecting a baby?'

'He did. I will pray for a successful birth.'

The way he said this made my heart lurch. I reached out to touch his sleeve. 'Your— don't tell me . . .?' I could not complete the question.

He turned his face away but I knew his eyes had filled with tears. 'Twin boys. Born in the New Year and did not see the spring,' he said, his voice breaking.

I murmured, 'God rest their souls!' before folding him into my arms. With closed eyes I breathed in the masculine aroma of his leather gambeson and found it disconcerting and enticing at the same time. I drew back hastily. 'I prayed so hard for you all. That is cruel indeed.'

He too pulled back but not away. 'It has confounded Elizabeth. She has fled to her estates in Devonshire and taken little Margaret with her.' One hand went to his forehead, covering his eyes as if he was trying to hide a memory. 'I may never get them back, Joan.'

Gently I pushed him off. He had come to me for consolation. It was not right for me to seek it from him. 'Have you tried, Anthony? Have you been to Devon?'

He stepped back, his booted feet causing a flurry of protesting kwaarks and flapping wings from the ravens, which had drawn nearer out of curiosity as we embraced. 'Yes, yes, I have. But she would not see me, or even admit me to the house. Of course all the servants there are loyal to the Huddersfield family and although as her husband I am legally the landholder, they march to Elizabeth's tune.'

Elizabeth Poyntz was a mystery to me. All I knew of her was what Anthony had told me and I was painfully aware that there were always two sides to any story. I quietly returned to my seat on the log and watched the ravens snatch up the remains of their treats to fly up to the nest and feed them to their young. They clearly thought the drama was over but I was not so sure. Anthony stood silent, breathing heavily as he fought to control his emotions and I waited until he succeeded, leaning over to brush twigs and bark from the other end of my makeshift perch; he sat down, straddling the log.

'What do you think I should do?' It was the question I had been expecting but to which I had no answer.

I shook my head. 'I have no magic salve for your very sad situation, Anthony. Of course prayer often helps, although it has not worked for me lately.'

Suddenly he looked stricken. 'Oh, forgive me!' he cried, pounding the bark between us, causing his knuckles to bleed. 'Sir Richard has abandoned you and broken the laws of chivalry. How could he?'

I greeted that with a hollow laugh. 'Something I ask myself every day! But there is no explanation I care to contemplate. I console myself by remembering that it was he that gave me Frensham Manor – he said it was a token of his love and gratitude. He was a different man then but Frensham has been my lifeline. Without it I would be begging at the church door.'

'I'm sure his children would not allow that! Nor would the king for that matter. All his own children have benefited from your teaching and sage advice – as indeed have I. You have been a wise counsellor to all of us. I for one would never let you go lonely or hungry.'

He reached across to touch my sleeve then noticed the bloody knuckles and stopped, a gesture that made me smile as I responded, 'I know that. As for the king, like Richard, he is greatly changed. The queen was his wise counsellor and my friend. Today I am certain he feels nothing for me – or indeed for any of his subjects, except as sources of wealth for the crown.' I glanced swiftly around the clearing, suddenly aware that I was speaking treason. 'I even worry that Hal lives under the king's control at Richmond Palace. Like his father, my son has only to put a foot wrong to ruin his entire future.'

'But Hal is not like his father, he is like you – clever and kind and resourceful.'

Praise from anyone had been in short supply recently and to my alarm I found myself wanting to throw myself into his arms and kiss him. I clasped my hands tightly in my lap to prevent myself moving. 'Stop being nice to me, Anthony, or I shall dissolve into a sobbing mess,' I ordered.

'Then we could cry on each other's shoulders. I would find that very comforting.'

'Maybe, but I would find it very disturbing.' I turned a challenging gaze on him.

He studied my face in silence while my heart thundered so hard in my chest I was certain he must hear it. 'Count the years between us, Anthony – there are sixteen. When you were that age you called me Mother Joan.'

'I do not call you that now – and never will again. For one thing you do not look any older than you did then and you do not deserve to be lonely and deserted as you are now.'

I gave him a grateful smile. 'I know you say that to cheer me up and I must admit that it does. We are friends, Anthony, just friends – and always will be.'

'If you say so.' He suddenly blushed and put his hand to

the purse on his belt. 'Heaven forgive me, I almost forgot. I have a letter for you from my father. Now there is a man who is also one of your admirers. I met with him at Durham Palace when I passed through London and he gave it to me to deliver. I think he writes on behalf of Princess Katherine.'

He passed me the letter and our fingers touched. It felt like a hot brand had singed my skin. Anthony stood up, a momentary expression of shock fading from his eyes. 'I must go. I have duties in Bristol.'

'Will you not stay for dinner?' I rose, too, though more slowly.

'Thank you – but no. I am learning navigation and my ship sails in two days.' He spoke with false brightness.

My laugh had a harsh edge. 'You are running away to sea!'

'Yes,' he said.

'Well, that may be wise. I'm sorry you're leaving but I wish you *bon voyage.*'

'I'll come again when I am back. I hope you enjoy being mistress of your own manor again.'

'Yes, I believe I shall.' As he waved farewell from the gate I felt a sharp sense of loss.

34

Frensham Manor

Summer 1506

To start with Sir Robert Poyntz's letter came as a pleasant surprise. In it he enquired whether I was in a position to renew my personal English lessons with Princess Katherine.

> *Having attended court when Archduke Philip and her sister Juana, his archduchess, were here, there have been subsequent events, which I cannot here reveal but which have brought about a new desire to become more fluent in English. Therefore she has tasked me with enquiring if your offer still stands to renew the lessons you began earlier in the year. She spoke very highly of your method of teaching and even more highly of your pleasant company, an observation with which I entirely concurred. Of course there would be accommodation for you at Durham Palace should you require it . . .*

The letter continued with sad details of the Poyntz family's desperation at the loss of Anthony's three little sons and the inevitable worries concerning the inheritance of their considerable holdings and investments. However, it was the brief mention of 'unrevealed events' that I found very intriguing and it set me wondering how I might discover more about them before I committed myself to a lengthy stay in the princess's rather gloomy Durham Palace household. I sent an enthusiastic reply to Sir Robert with a caveat that I could not begin before I had seen the harvest in at my Kent manor.

Meanwhile the onset of summer had brought improvement to the roads and tracks, encouraging visits from my two nearest stepdaughters Maria and Lizzie, anxious to discover the reason for their father's unexpected departure for the Holy Land and disappointed to hear that there had been no communication received from him since his departure. More happily, they brought their babies to meet me, and thoroughly enjoyed each other's company for the first time since their respective marriages. For this reason and because I was keen to re-establish my personal management of Frensham Manor, I was loath to go to London before the autumn.

Then fascinating information concerning the reason for Princess Katherine's renewed interest came from the much-hoped-for arrival in early August of my own flesh-and-blood son. When I heard his familiar voice greeting Sim in the courtyard beneath my solar window I fled down the stairs like a heedless teenager, pleasing myself at how swiftly I could do so, lifting my long skirts high.

'Hal! Oh, Hal, you've come at last! It's so good to see you.'

I almost collided with the stable boy, who had come forward to take the horse, which skidded to a halt as Hal leapt from the saddle, crying, 'Beloved Lady Mother, I have managed to escape the Richmond Palace prison at last!'

His voice had dropped to a deep tenor and his arms felt as taut as rope as he pulled me into a bear-like hug. Hours spent training in the tiltyard had built his once-boyish muscle into a soldier's brawn. He would be seventeen next month and to my dismay I found uncontrollable tears pouring down my face as I clung like a limpet to his unrecognisably broad shoulders. Since I had last seen him he had changed from a lion cub into the full-grown beast. A thick dark mane of hair fell from under the narrow brim of his jaunty bright-feathered hat and the polished leather cuirass he wore for protection on the road glinted gold in the bright summer sunlight. The proud drumbeat of my heart must have been heard in Rolvenden.

But pride did not prevent me treating him to some motherly concern. 'You have surely not ridden from Richmond all alone, Hal. Have you not brought a companion?'

He released me with a crowing laugh. 'Ha! Such maternal fussing truly tells me I am home! No, my lady, I did not ride alone, I came with Edward, who has dropped off at Halden to inspect proceedings there – and doubtless to collect some much-needed funds to pay our jousting fees. You will be proud to learn that we have both been selected for the prince's tournament team.'

Impatiently I brushed the evidence of my tears from my cheeks but could not prevent a new surge of pride surfacing at this news. Considering that Edward was fifteen years older than his young half-brother, with at least ten years more tourney training behind him, this made Hal's achievement even greater. I tucked my arm into the crook of his and squeezed the iron-hard flesh. 'Well done both of you and may God protect your jousting. Come inside; as is your habit you have arrived at dinnertime.' I steered him through the carved front door and added as we made our way into the hall, 'Is Edward leading the team? He must be one of the oldest members.'

Hal made a face. 'Sadly no; that honour goes to Charles Brandon who, it must be said, is the most skilled and fearless among us. But Ed and I have the task of organising the tournament and, as the prince is away on a progress with the king, we have been given this leave to make our plans. It is to be a "joust royal", which means fast and furious and attended by the royal family and all the foreign ambassadors. It is quite a responsibility.'

'How exciting! When is it to take place?'

'Not until next spring, but King Henry wants it to be the most spectacular event of the decade. One that will be famous all over Europe.' He grinned round at me. 'Cheaper than going to war with France!'

'And the king is all for hoarding money!' I remarked ruefully. 'If he were not your father would not be seeking atonement in the Holy Land.'

At this point, Sim appeared from behind us to welcome Hal and show him to his place at the table. Gleaming white linen had been laid as if to welcome the Prodigal Son. 'It looks like a handsome spread, Sim,' Hal said. 'You've learned your stewarding skills fast.'

Sim grinned his appreciation of the praise and left to organise the presentation of the wine, while my son broached the subject that had obviously been uppermost on his mind. 'Have you heard anything from Father?'

I could not reassure him. 'No, nothing. He just boarded the ship at Rye and vanished.'

Hal chewed his lower lip and frowned. 'I was so sorry not to see him before he went but his release and departure all happened with such speed that there was no time. It's been over four months though; shouldn't he be in Jerusalem by now?'

'He could be in darkest Cathay, Hal, for all I know. You might as well be fatherless and I am neither wife nor widow. What does Edward say?'

'He won't speak of him and is doing his best to restore Halden to a functioning manor. The king's bailiffs stripped it of all its assets. I wonder if Father knew what was happening to his holdings while he was in gaol.'

Before Hal's arrival I had been keeping Richard firmly at the back of my mind, finding this the best way of dealing with my feelings. But now I was dangerously close to tears once again and I beckoned the server who was waiting at the screen with the bowl for hand-washing. 'Let us change the subject and prepare for our meal. Tell me, how is Prince Harry? He was such a help to me when I was trying to see the king at court. Even at his young age, he was a force to be reckoned with.'

Hal blew air through his lips and sank his hands into the bowl of water. Picking up the towel, he turned back to face me. 'In truth, there are two princes, Mother. One is called Harry and he is a tour de force. He grows at the speed of light and already threatens to outstrip me and most of his other household companions.' He handed the towel back to the server, who moved on to offer the water to me. Meanwhile his pangs of hunger took over and he reached for the manchet loaf on the board beside us to cut two portions. 'Let us say grace before I tell you more because I could consume this whole loaf. Edward and I set out at dawn and did not stop except to water the horses.'

I quickly used the towel and waved the server away because I could tell by the tone of my son's voice that he did not want to speak further of the prince in a servant's hearing. 'Take some of the stewed hare as well,' I suggested, watching the man leave the room and saying a quick 'Deo Gratia'. 'And Sim will now come to pour the wine but I assure you his lips are sealed regarding anything said in this hall.'

The steward entered with a flagon and proceeded to fill our cups as Hal made swift work of his bread and meat. 'That stew is very tasty, Sim,' he remarked, picking up his napkin to wipe his fingers. 'Has Jake taken residence in the Frensham kitchen?'

Sim paused on his way out. 'I'm afraid not, Master Hal. He stayed in London and I've heard that he's working in Sir Thomas Brandon's kitchen now.'

I was able to confirm this. 'So he is. When he dined at the Tower House while Richard was in prison Sir Thomas was impressed with Jake's cooking. After we found the Guildford coffers empty he was very generous with a loan and good advice. I've only recently been able to repay him. But while we're alone, Hal, tell me more of the prince; I sense that you have much to relate.'

Hal took a fortifying gulp of wine. 'As I said, it's a tale of two princes,' he began. 'In his private quarters and at the tiltyard and tennis courts he is still Harry and much like the boy you remember from the Eltham days when you were governess to his sisters – taller and stronger of course and still highly competitive, determined to excel at everything but always ready for a laugh and a song and a chance to tease the young ladies. However, the moment he is in the king's company he becomes Prince Henry and a completely different character. His father likes to walk with him in the evenings and discuss the business of the kingdom and you might never see a more attentive and serious fellow. Obviously he does not reveal any details of these conversations to us but afterwards he usually stops by the royal chapel to pray or consult his confessor and he always returns in a pensive mood. The king was taken very ill during the spring and there was genuine fear that he might not recover. The Queen Mother even came to Richmond from Colleyweston to supervise his care and court gossip was rife with rumour that he was on his deathbed.'

I broke in here. 'That's when the royal pardon came through for your father, Hal! Perhaps it was a near-death effort by the king to assuage his guilt at subjecting his loyal subject to such harsh treatment.'

Hal shrugged. 'Maybe; certainly it was a very tense time at Richmond. After the prince had been permitted to visit his father's bedside one evening, Will Compton, his Page of the Chamber, and I were preparing Harry for bed as usual when he suddenly declared that he was not ready to be king and did not think he could ever be the kind of monarch his father expected him to be. He even burst into tears and threw himself into Will's arms, moaning that he wished his mother had not died and left him to carry the burden on his own. "My lady mother would have understood my fears!" he moaned. "She would not have called me weak and light-minded, as my father did tonight."' Hal paused.

'Harry may be tall and strong for his age but he was still only fourteen at the time. That was not a good way to treat your only son, was it, lady mother?'

I sighed, wondering who this Will Compton was, who seemed to be such a close comforter of the prince. 'No, it was not, but perhaps the king's mind was affected by his illness. I know that he experiences the cough and the quinsy and these can be agonisingly painful when suffered together.'

'Hmm.' Hal looked dubious. 'Anyway the king recovered and took Harry off with him on his summer progress, probably to get him away from all his young friends who lead him astray. So here I am, free to visit my dear old lady mother!'

I rapped his knuckles with the side of my hand. 'Not so much of the old lady, thank you! And what's this I hear about the prince having changed his mind about marrying his brother's bride?'

His face fell. 'How did you know? Harry's sworn us all to secrecy about that! The king would be furious.'

'Hah! Up to now I just suspected – but now I do know. Luckily I'm just your dear old lady mother, who won't spread it around. But you must be more careful with your master's secrets, my darling boy!'

35

Durham Palace

Autumn 1506

Hal encouraged me to pursue Princess Katherine's interest in perfecting her English, so once the harvest was in at Frensham, I joined him and Edward on their return ride to London, leaving Sim and Mildy in charge at Frensham. Riding her pony at my palfrey's heels was Mildy's younger sister Rose, nervous and excited at the prospect of serving in a royal household. Mildy, expecting to give birth in September, assured me that she had taught her sister all she needed to know to perform the task of lady's maid and certainly in the few weeks that the teenager had shadowed Mildy, I could not fault her. A quiet girl – much quieter than her sister – but dextrous and obliging and undeterred at the thought of leaving her extensive family for the wider world; I hoped she would not have her head turned by the glitter and fleshpots of London.

Things had changed radically at Durham Palace. It no longer exuded an air of abandoned grandeur but was primped and polished, the gardens and orchards weeded and neat, with fruit plentiful on the trees. Inside, the window glass was polished and the curtains drawn back to allow the busy panorama of the River Thames to feature in all the principal chambers and, as if to reflect the fresh brightness of her surroundings, the Dowager Princess had abandoned her drab gowns and mourning veils and reverted to wearing the wardrobe of bright silks and floating lace she had brought from Spain.

I also discovered an apparently altogether altered character and soon learned of the reason for it from her two dusky handmaidens, Kat and Lina. At the end of my first week, while the princess enjoyed the afternoon rest she called her 'siesta', the two girls hesitantly asked me if I would like to observe the way they prepared her pomegranate drink and I was delighted to spend the afternoon with them in their specially fitted room beside the dairy. They worked at processing the ripe pomegranates from Spain, while next door a team of English milkmaids made cream and cheese from the milk provided by the small herd of cows that cropped the grass of the palace orchards. It was from these local lasses, hired from the nearby farms, that the two Moorish girls had learned their English and while it was reasonably fluent, from their rough vocabulary and the bawdy stories the dairymaids told each other, I could appreciate why Sir Robert Poyntz would not have considered them a suitable source from which the princess should acquire her grasp of the language.

By the time I had watched the messy business of peeling and stripping the pomegranates of their skin and pith and the careful removal of the flush of juicy seeds within, it was clear to me that the task was not one I would wish to be required to perform daily as Kat and Lina were, when the fruit was in season. It struck me as a painstaking and tedious exercise and the flavour of the resulting drink hardly worth the effort involved. However, the process gave me a chance to learn more about the eventful lives of the two women.

Both had been born in the city of Granada, the capital of the Muslim Emirate of the same name, which from the start of their young lives had been under attack by the neighbouring Catholic kingdoms of Castile and Aragon, ruled by Princess Katherine's father and mother, King Ferdinand and Queen Isabella, who had sworn a joint oath to bring all the Spanish kingdoms under Christian rule.

'Which they did, when we were both young girls,' Kat concluded. 'Our Emir fled into exile and the Spanish king and queen moved into his fabulous palace, declaring that Muslims must convert to Christianity.'

'And what happened then?' I asked, somewhat shaken by what this revealed of the despotic nature of Princess Katherine's parents. 'Did your families convert?'

'Well, yes – and no.' Kat's expression darkened. 'My father had made arrows for the Emir's army but he refused to supply the Spanish and the soldiers beat him so badly that he became crippled and could not work at all. My mother took him and my brothers into exile across the Middle Sea and left me with an aunt who promptly sold me to the royal palace as a kitchen skivvy.'

'You were *sold*?' I echoed. 'As a slave?'

Kat nodded and Lina broke in. 'Me too. We had no choice. We had nowhere else to go. Of course we had to be baptised but at least we were fed and clothed. Many other Muslims starved because they could not work to feed their families.'

I had been about to exclaim that slavery was wrong and

that there was none in England, then I remembered that Sim's father had sold him to a boatman on the River Medway when he was ten. Sim had not been paid a groat for all the physical work he'd been forced to do and his face had been a picture when I offered to pay him a few pennies for looking after my ravens. So instead I asked, 'How old were you both then?'

Kat answered. 'I was twelve and Lina was ten. We met and became friends in that massive kitchen, which was full of male cooks and scullions who saw any young girls as prey.' Her face was screwed into an expression of disgust, so that I had no trouble knowing what she meant. 'I rescued Lina from one of the pastry cooks, who already had his hands and more up her skirt when I hit him from behind with a sieve.'

Lina nodded gravely. 'I was so scared and he was so strong! When Kat hit him he fell back and we ran to the chapel, where one of the priests took us to the queen's *casa*. Queen Isabella was very strict about such behaviour and decided that we should be removed from the kitchens and set to work in her household instead. That's how we ended up serving the princess.'

'But now we are in England and we feel like freaks when we walk in the streets. People stare at our dark skin and sometimes they call us devils and spit on the ground behind us,' said Kat. 'The princess is lucky; both her grandmothers were English, so she has red hair and blue eyes.'

'And fair skin,' Lina added with twisted lips. 'English men love pink-skinned girls! The prince hardly sees us but he stares at our mistress; you can see that he thinks her beautiful.'

This remark confirmed what Hal had let slip at Frensham. Yet only two years ago, days before the prince turned fourteen, he had personally cancelled his betrothal to Princess Katherine on the grounds that it had been contracted without his permission, which as he reached the age of puberty he was refusing to give. It had been this rejection that had cast Katherine into depression and left her in limbo and penury, as her royal allowance was withdrawn. Officially she had not seen Prince Harry since and so I feigned surprise. 'Have they been meeting, then? I thought the marriage had been cancelled.'

'Those meetings are secret!' Kat scowled at Lina. 'You should hold your tongue!'

Lina recoiled, hand on mouth, and I hastened to reassure her. 'Don't worry; I will hold mine. But just tell me, do the meetings please the princess?'

Lina shook her head, her hand still firmly in place, but Kat's face became wreathed in a wide smile. 'Oh yes, my lady. Nothing could please her more!'

The following day I was surprised to receive a visit from Hal, who found me in the rose garden behind the palace chapel taking my outdoor exercise while the princess took her siesta. I had spent the morning trying to improve her English accent while reading passages from *The Golden Legend*. I would read them out to her sentence by sentence and she would try to copy my words. But on this occasion she seemed unable to concentrate and became cross when I corrected her pronunciation. Clearly there was something else on her mind but I did not like to ask what it was. At dinner she picked at her food and snapped at the servant who failed to notice that her wine cup was empty. We were all quite relieved when she retired to her chamber.

I frowned at my son's unexpected arrival. 'Whatever are you doing here, Hal? I thought you were at Richmond.' My tone was still tetchy as a result of the morning's language session.

He gave me a quizzical look and made an exaggerated bow. 'And a very good day to you, too, dear lady mother,' he said. 'Do I find you a little *distrait?*'

'Ha!' His excessively courtly address made me laugh before replying. 'As *distrait* as a teacher may be with a touchy student on her hands! But you haven't answered my question.'

'I have not come alone. At this moment your touchy student will be smiling shyly at some pleasantry uttered by her latest admirer, all safely chaperoned in the utmost secrecy by a certain Dona Maria de Salinas. So you see the princess's "siestas" are being put to good use. Meanwhile I am dismissed from the prince's presence to twiddle my thumbs while Cupid fires his arrows.' He made a vague gesture indicating our presence together in the garden.

I gave him a kiss of peace, only mildly offended at my company being considered a mere 'thumb twiddle', because I was so delighted at the notion of Prince Henry renewing the prospect of another English–Spanish alliance. It seemed to me the most suitable settlement of Princess Katherine's anomalous position, living as she did a shadowy existence on the outskirts of the English court. 'But why all the secrecy?' I asked. 'Does it not please the king that his son has changed his mind about the princess?'

Hal's finger shot to his lips, alarm colouring his face. 'The king does not know. It was under his father's instructions that Harry reneged on the original marriage contract and until recently King Henry was pursuing the idea of remarrying himself, making covert moves on Princess Katherine's elder sister, the Dowager Archduchess Juana, which would have made a marriage between Harry and Katherine impossible, of course.'

Soon after being permitted to leave England and arriving in Spain, Archduke Philip had succumbed to some mysterious ailment and died. Poison was suspected but never proven and Juana was once more on the European marriage market.

I threw up my hands in exasperation. 'What a sticky web these royals weave! Their paths are as thorny as the roses all around us. But how come you and the prince are able to escape from Richmond? I thought all your moves were monitored.'

Hal nodded. 'At Richmond they are, but as part of his Duchy of Cornwall, Harry holds the park and palace of Kennington and has persuaded the king that it is the best place for organising the teams for the big tournament next spring. It's close to London but secluded from the public gaze and thus very suitable for gathering contenders and keeping practice sessions secret. The prince wants the spectacle to be a glorious surprise, so those of us involved in the planning have moved across the Thames to accommodation in the small palace hidden away behind Lambeth. It's only a short row across the river from there to here and Prince Harry and I can make the crossing without involving any oarsmen who might recognise him and be susceptible to earning a silver coin or two by spreading the word to the pamphleteers. Hence the dullness of our apparel.'

He indicated his unusually plain jacket and hose. 'It goes without saying that the prince looks much more handsome in disguise than I do. The princess certainly thinks so anyway – judging by the letters she writes him.'

My brows raised in surprise. 'Does he show you her love letters?'

Hal's shoulders heaved. 'No, of course not, but he does read me a sentence or two occasionally. They both write in very flowery French, rather like some of your "knights and ladies" romances.'

I gave a little snort. 'Huh! No wonder the princess finds *The Golden Legend* rather tedious. Perhaps I should look out some of Mallory's Arthurian prose, then she might be more eager to improve her English.'

'Good idea.' He tucked his hand in my elbow and led me down one of the winding paths of the garden. 'I think it would be very much in your interests to cultivate Princess Katherine's favour, Mother. After all, there is every possibility that she will be our next queen.'

With Hal's words in mind I borrowed a copy of Mallory's wordy but emotional account of *The Death of Arthur* from Lady Margaret's Coldharbour library and as a result the princess's attention and her English pronunciation were much improved, although I concluded that she would never entirely lose her Spanish accent, which happily added a charming idiosyncrasy to her conversation. Her afternoon 'siestas' continued to be interrupted by regular visits from the prince and I enjoyed more of Hal's company than I had for years.

36

Frensham Manor

Winter 1506–7

Towards Christmas, Princess Katherine received an invitation to attend the festivities at Richmond Palace and made her preparations in a state of high excitement, a condition that also infected her female attendants. Dona Maria remained relatively composed but Kat and Lina fell to chattering so loudly and constantly about the prospect of all the feasting and dancing and being in the presence of male servants and courtiers that they had to be reprimanded in chapel by Father Diego for making too much noise during Mass. He was the new confessor who had been sent from Spain to serve the princess.

He asked me rather pompously one morning, in his weirdly pronounced Church Latin, whether he might attend the English classes I was holding with the princess. 'Although my French and Latin is perfect Dona Juana,' he boasted inaccurately, 'I think if I am to stay here for some time I should improve my communication with the common people. I mean of course the servants and even some of the guildsmen who attend her grace, the tailors and goldsmiths, who seem to speak only English. It is fortunate that you are already teaching her and I could perhaps attend your classes?'

'At present they are entirely private, Father Diego,' I replied, 'and so of course I would have to ask the princess. I will let you know her response.'

Princess Katherine looked horrified when I put his request to her. 'Oh no, Dona Joan! Have the Franciscan monk sit in on our female privacy? He is my confessor but I do not wish to confess that we are reading *Le Morte d'Arthur* together – a volume I do not think he would approve of! We are just getting into the Book of Sir Tristram of Lyonesse, when the witch leads Sir Lancelot to Princess Elaine's chamber, and I suspect that we are about to find them in bed together. I shall be very interested in the outcome of that story but not if I have to read it in front of Fray Diego!'

I had to laugh. 'Indeed not, your grace! I see your problem. We shall not admit the friar into our class.' I picked up the heavy volume to which she had referred and opened it at the page mentioned. 'There may be a word here that you have not yet encountered – for example "enchantress". I shall read the passage aloud and see if you are able to guess the true meaning.'

She listened intently but bearing in mind her expressed wish to marry Prince Henry I thought her answer was more wishful thinking than accurate.

'I think an "enchantress" must mean a beautiful lady, perhaps an Aphrodite, who can make any man she wants fall in love with her. Was Elaine an enchantress and did she put Sir Lancelot under a spell in order to conceive his child?'

I knew about the meetings and letters that had passed between Prince Harry and Princess Katherine, but she had not confided this activity to me, so I had to bite my lip and give her the true gist of the story. 'Not quite, your grace. It was the enchantress Lady Brusen who put Sir Lancelot under a spell to make him think he was bedding Queen Guinevere, whom he loved. The result of their one night together was to be Sir Galahad, the knight who eventually wins the Holy Grail.'

'Well, I'm glad Elaine was not the enchantress because she was a princess, whose child would be a king.' Her wish fulfilment was evident so I did not correct her.

At the end of this lesson I became quite despondent when she announced that she was going to Richmond Palace in a week's time and suggested that I might like to make arrangements to spend Christmas with my family. 'But I hope we may continue our lessons in the New Year, if you are available,' she added. 'I shall miss our entertaining lessons.'

Her tone was light-hearted however, as she would be spending time at court, close to Prince Henry, and I knew there would be fun and games because Hal sent me a note to say that he would not be able to spend any time at Frensham over the festive season. The prince wanted his help in arranging entertainments and disguisings for the royal celebrations. Fortunately, Edward Guildford took leave from his duties at the Royal Armoury and I was able to travel down to Kent with him and his family. I spent the last days of Advent decorating the Frensham great hall and preparing games and treats for the children of the staff, including little John, the baby boy born safely to Mildy and Sim in mid-September.

'We have a special favour to ask you, Lady Joan,' Mildy

said, as she placed the gurgling child in my arms for the first time. 'Please feel free to say no if you do not like it.'

I smiled at the baby and then at her and cast an enquiring glance at Sim, who hovered at Mildy's side. 'Well of course I will say so if I disapprove, but I think it very unlikely that I would deny anything to a couple who have kept my manor in such a neat and tidy state in my absence. So please, tell me what is this favour?'

It was Sim who spoke up. 'In all the time I have worked for you, my lady, I've just gone by the name of Sim. I never told you my family name in case you contacted them and my father made trouble. But now I am a father myself I want my son to have a proper formal identity. So Mildy and I would be honoured if you would allow us to take the name of the land we live on. The baby has been baptised John, after Mildy's father, but if you don't think it cheek, we'd like our family name to be Frensham – with your permission.'

I couldn't answer straight away because a large lump developed in my throat. This was the boy I had caught in the Halden woods, watching the ravens eating the kitchen scraps I had brought out for them while his own stomach rumbled with starvation after several days running from a brutal master. How I wished Richard were present to hear Sim's request, showing as it did what an upright and worthy citizen he had become, simply because we had demonstrated faith in him.

Clearing my throat, I managed to find words to make him smile. 'Master Sim Frensham sounds a very honourable name indeed and you have earned every right to use it. I'm sure that if Sir Richard were here he would agree with me, but since he is not I shall take it upon myself to acquire for you the legal documents to prove you and your family are faithful retainers of this manor and well suited to carry its name.'

Never usually one to make flamboyant gestures, on this occasion Sim fell to his knees. 'Thank you, my lady!' he declared, placing his hand on the small body of his son, resting in my arms. 'Mildy and I will ensure that John Frensham grows to be a worthy holder of the name.'

'I have no doubt of that,' I said, kissing the baby's rosy cheek and handing him back to his hovering mother, who murmured her own fervent agreement to carry out Sim's promise. I felt moved to add, 'And I hope that in due course there will be a happy and healthy family of young Frenshams filling the yards and fields with their shouts and laughter. This manor is your home and their home to come. When Sir Richard returns, I shall need you all to keep it running smoothly while I perform my duties back at Halden Hall.'

Sim rose to his feet. 'Have you any idea when that might be, my lady?' he asked. 'Has there been word from Sir Richard?'

I sighed. 'Sadly not, Sim, but then there is no easy way of communication between here and the Holy Land, so we must just keep faith that quite soon he will be arriving back here from some distant port. Perhaps he might get word to Master Edward to send a ship to bring him across the Channel, giving us time to prepare a proper welcome.' My words rang hollow to my own ears but they seemed to satisfy the Frenshams, probably too happy to have heard their new name spoken to mark the diffidence in my tone.

Hearing my husband's name seemed to jerk my emotions

into action. This would be the second Christmas I had spent without him and his absence and silence had begun to reinforce my belief that he may never return at all. All manner of doubts occupied my mind during the religious ceremonies I attended at the church of St Mary the Virgin, sitting with Edward and Eleanor in the Guildford chapel, where the family arms of a black saltire and four black martlets on a gold ground evoked memories of Richard's many military sorties in support of King Henry. Although I frequently saw a version of it worn by Edward Guildford, his bore the label of the eldest son and lacked the surrounding Garter belt.

I shared the cheerful games and laughter organised by Eleanor to amuse her infant son and the other children of the estate but their careful avoidance of the mention of Richard's name, and their failure to even raise a toast to his health, somewhat spiked my ire. They had moved in to Halden Hall and assumed the running of the house and lands in a way that suggested they would have no wish to relinquish control of the Guildford holdings, even when Richard did return.

It was not until after the first snows of January had fallen and thawed that Edward rode into Frensham Manor with a crumpled letter on which the seal remained miraculously intact. 'It's amazing that it has reached us because the address is almost indecipherable,' he said, holding it out. 'But I thought we should open it together.'

I took it from him with a shaky hand, squinting over the faded ink. 'Well, it is addressed to me, so that thought was only right but it is not Richard's writing.' I steadied myself and broke the seal, which was damaged and fell easily apart. When I caught sight of the text I carried the letter to a seat at the hall table, waving Edward to join me. 'It is written in Latin – and in an unusual script. I may take some time to read it.' But I had already caught sight of three crucial words, *'eques'* – knight, *'peregrinus'* – pilgrim, and *'Guildford'*.

I rubbed my forehead distractedly, becoming more and more distressed as the crazy Latin revealed the sorry end to Richard's pilgrimage. 'I'm afraid your father is dead, Edward. The Warden of Mount Zion writes to tell us of his demise in the pilgrim's hospice only two days after arriving in Jerusalem. Apparently he and John Whitby were held hostage in caves outside the Holy City by armed bandits called Marmaluks, who demanded a ransom to release them. He and the priest were both already ill but they paid whatever was demanded and made it by camel to the pilgrims' hospice where the Prior expired that very night. Richard survived another day but also died before he was physically able to go to the Church of the Holy Sepulchre and make his offerings.'

I lowered the letter as the awful truth sank in. 'So he never made his peace with God or received absolution for his perceived sins and he was buried that night by the friars of Mount Zion.' Words failed me then and my head sank onto my arms as the tears began to flow.

Edward sprang from his chair and snatched the letter off the table. 'Damned Latin! I never could get the hang of it. What does it say caused their deaths? Was it poisoning or some terrible desert disease? They were in a hellish hurry to bury him, weren't they? That suggests foul play but I suppose we'll never know.' He flicked angrily at the fragile parchment and a small part of it dropped away onto the floor. 'Who is this Warden of Mount Zion, anyway?'

'He's the Pope's man in Jerusalem,' I said hoarsely, pulling my kerchief from my sleeve. 'Not an easy task these days, I'm told, with Saracens swarming over most of the Holy City. If you want to contest the burial you'll have to go through the Vatican, I believe. But personally I'd rather leave poor Richard in peace. At least he died where he wanted to be, even if he didn't manage to atone for his sins.'

Edward gave an angry snort. 'What sins? He worked loyally for King Henry in a dozen different ways and never demanded enough recompense. Those months in the Fleet broke his spirit and that clown of a priest took complete advantage of a broken man. I'm glad he died as well. It would be terrible if he were to come prancing back from Jerusalem without my father! Far from being sinned against, King Henry is entirely to blame for the death of one of his most loyal subjects. Fortunately he'll soon be passing his crown to a younger and better head.'

'Hush, Edward!' I raised my head in alarm. 'You speak treason. Any of the servants might hear you.'

'Let them,' he said and I saw tears glistening in his eyes. 'My father was an honourable man.'

How could I disagree? 'Oh yes,' I said, 'indeed he was.'

37

Frensham Manor

Spring–Summer 1507

AS SPRING WARMED THE land, bluebells carpeted the woods and cowslips nodded in the fields, which usually brought joy to my heart, but not this year. There was no question of returning to Princess Katherine's household yet. I had half-expected to be made a widow by Richard's foolish pilgrimage, but before I received the letter from the Warden of Mount Zion, Richard's absence had been like a thorn in my thumb – a constantly recurring irritant, reinforcing the anger I'd felt at his leaving. Now that I knew he was dead I found myself remembering the good and loving times we had spent together and my bed felt cold and empty. I did not even have the satisfaction of seeing his body and having a grave to visit and a tomb to commission.

Young Rose proved to be exactly the confidante needed by someone whose emotions veered out of control at frequent intervals and was regularly to be found weeping in dark corners. She located the address of the London apothecaries who had supplied the cures for Queen Elizabeth's delicate health and sent them an order for a potion that might calm my nerves, which she administered whenever she detected the approach of one of my 'turns', as she called them. She also firmly advised the other Frensham servants to avoid mentioning Richard's name, which on the whole they did. As a result, with the advance of spring my condition improved.

Then one drizzly June afternoon a small cavalcade trotted down the Frensham entrance avenue: three horses, two ridden and one laden. Alerted by the sound of hoof beats, I caught sight of them from the window seat in the great hall, where it was my habit to sit and read on dull days, and instantly recognised Anthony Poyntz. When I went out to meet him in the porch I was still carrying my book. As he had done in the past, he took it from me.

'It is no surprise to find you burying your grief in literature, Lady Joan,' he said, eyeing me with his sympathetic blue gaze. Then he glanced down at the spine of the leather-bound volume. 'But despite its title, I do not believe Dante's *Divine Comedy* will bring you any light relief.'

I swallowed hard on a surge of emotion and tried to laugh at his wry humour. 'You are wet, Anthony! And so is my book. Come inside.'

One of my stable lads came to take his horses. 'There are more and newer books in the saddlebags,' he told his retainer. 'Have them brought in to my lady. And take the venison to the kitchen.'

I ushered him into the hall, dashing rain and tears impatiently from my eyes. 'Venison? From which royal park have you stolen that?'

'I stopped at Croydon Palace on my way from London, on the orders of My Lady the King's Mother,' he said with a rather smug grin, letting one of the house servants remove his rather odorous oiled cloak. 'It comes with her condolences.

I've been mixing in exalted company, attending the spring tournament at Greenwich; where incidentally your son Hal greatly distinguished himself. I had hoped you might also be there.'

'Hal begged me to go but I couldn't face it. As you see, it takes very little to make me cry and tears are not well received in court circles. Besides I don't think I could trust myself not to accuse the king of causing Richard's death.' At this moment Sim made his appearance, having been appraised of Anthony's arrival. 'I know you will remember Sim,' I said. 'He is now my steward here at Frensham.'

'Yes, so Hal told me.' Anthony nodded at Sim. 'He said the manor had never flourished so well. Congratulations.'

They were much of an age, these two young men, and if I detected a faint note of disdain in Anthony's words of praise I set it aside. 'Master Poyntz will be staying overnight, Sim. Would you have a chamber prepared for him? We will need some refreshments now and please tell Cook there will be an extra place at supper.'

The steward gave a brief nod of compliance. 'Company will be a nice change for you, my lady. I'll tell Mildy about the chamber.'

Anthony watched Sim leave then turned to me with a raised eyebrow. 'He's become rather familiar for a servant, hasn't he?' he said and echoed Sim's comment in a country burr. '"Company will be a nice change, my lady."'

I frowned and waved a hand towards seats at the hearth. 'Oh, Sim is Sim. He's married now, you know, and has a baby son. Tell me, how is your family, Anthony?' I probably shouldn't have asked, but his mocking of Sim's Kentish drawl had irritated me.

'Well,' he said, taking a deep breath and sitting down, exhaling slowly, 'there was a change at Christmas, when I went down to Devon to share it with Elizabeth and little Margaret, although Margaret is not so little now – nearly six. And Elizabeth seemed happy, running her two manors and enjoying the hunting and hawking on the moors surrounding them. So much so that there was something of a ceasefire between us.' He went rather pink as he said this and I soon discovered why. 'As a result she is expecting another child later this year.'

'But why do you frown, Anthony? Is that not wonderful? Perhaps this time it will be a healthy boy? I know your father prays for an heir.'

'Yes, I gather you have been recently in his company and that of the Princess Dowager.' He sighed. 'Elizabeth had believed the twins left her barren and now she is terrified of facing another birth. I have been in Gloucestershire and did not hear of it until just before I went to Greenwich for the tournament. She told me not to come back to Devon.'

'Well, you are man and wife and she cannot legally refuse you access to your children. If the baby was conceived at Christmas she must be well into her time already.'

'You are right and I will go back but I wanted to come and see you first. Hal told me you had taken the news of Sir Richard's death very hard.'

At this point I was grateful that Sim reappeared with refreshments, placing the tray on a small table beside me. 'I took the liberty of broaching the cask of malmsey, my lady. And Nat was almost tongue-tied at the sight of the venison. He said he would roast it for the midsummer feast, if that would please you.'

'If he doesn't think that would be too long to hang it, Sim. Nat is our cook,' I explained to my visitor. 'And the malmsey will be just right for a wet day, will it not, Master Poyntz?'

'I can enjoy a cup of malmsey any day.' Anthony raised a hand to halt Sim, who was backing away. 'I hear you have a son and a wife now. Congratulations are due once more.'

'Thank you, sir.' There was a pause. 'They even came in the right order.'

Silence fell as Anthony frowned, so I intervened. 'Of course they did! First the wife and then the son; Mildy does everything right, doesn't she, Sim?'

Sim made a little bow. 'Yes, she does. Will that be all, my lady?'

With a smile I nodded. 'Thank you, Sim.' When he had gone, I added, 'There is a very loving couple, and a very loyal one. Do you know, they delayed their wedding until Richard was freed from the Fleet.'

Anthony gave me an ambiguous look – neither admiration nor disapproval. 'I remember him as an uneducated youth, willing but needing to follow orders. What changed?'

'Nothing changed. It just took him a while to learn to trust his own judgement. You come from a privileged family and have no idea what it's like to be treated like dirt. Until he came to us, Sim only knew violence and hunger, but his affinity with the ravens showed me that there was gentleness and intelligence behind the fear in his eyes.'

'He was lucky it was you who found him. Had it been anyone else he would have been thrown into gaol and forgotten.'

'Is that what you would have done?' I asked. 'I don't think so. I see the light of gentleness in your eyes, too.'

'Do you, Joan?' He looked startled. 'You are being kind.'

I picked up the wine jug, filled the two cups provided and handed him one. 'Take it from me, Anthony, when you have a healthy boy in the cradle everything will be different. So here's to him!'

He took a good gulp and smiled appreciatively. 'This is delicious! But I did not come here to seek your sympathy; I came to offer comfort to you.'

'And you have,' I said. 'When I hear other people's problems I realise that mine are trivial.'

'You call the loss of your husband trivial!'

'No, I call the way I have been weeping over his loss trivial. My mother lost my father at the Battle of Tewkesbury but she wasted ten years of her widowhood wiping the tears of Queen Marguerite, who had lost freedom, crown, husband and son. I learned from their example that excessive mourning can become a selfish weapon.' I raised my cup to him. 'You have stirred me out of self-pity, Anthony.'

He gave a wry laugh. 'Hmm, your faith in me may be misplaced. The truth is I came to seek your advice, as much as to bring you comfort. And of course robust advice is what I have received and I love you for it.'

The words 'I love you' fell on my ears like rain in a desert.

38

Frensham Manor

End of June 1507

THE FEAST OF ST John the Baptist heralded the true
start of summer and we dined on the venison Anthony
Poyntz had brought. The following day was warm and in
the afternoon he and I took the opportunity to do some
hawking. In the strip fields the seed crops were beginning
to turn gold and on the common land up on the hill behind
the manor house, shepherds and their dogs were busy
rounding up the sheep for shearing. Ignoring the rules of
falconry we took a sparrow hawk and a hobby out to the edge
of the warren and waited in the woods nearby for the rabbits
to emerge for their evening foraging. After the two young
hawks had made some spectacular, and occasionally
successful, chases and stoops, we were able to pack two brace
of summer-fat bucks into the saddlebags. We decided to
feed a few titbits to the hawks then hood them for a rest
while we refreshed ourselves.

Shadows were beginning to lengthen under a nearby thicket
of birches but it was still warm. Soon dusk would bring
perfect conditions for the two agile birds to hunt among the
trees but for the time being they were settled, hooded and

quiet, on the pommels of our horses' saddles to wait for the game fowl to come in to roost. Meanwhile, from my pannier I lifted a bag of cheese and cherries, two cups and a skin of wine and, at the edge of the trees, we chose a fallen log to sit on and enjoy the last beneficial rays of the sun.

Anthony, who was still with us, picked up a handful of cherries and selected one reflectively before remarking, 'This reminds me of the occasions when I accompanied Sir Richard out hawking. He usually took one or two of his children and a couple of falconers with him though, and of course a dog or two to sniff out the prey.'

'I've thought about getting a dog,' I said, squeezing wine from the skin into the two cups, balanced on the log between us. 'Richard gave his favourite pair of spaniels away to a local farmer before he set off on his pilgrimage. I think he was more upset to leave them than me.'

I passed him a cup and he took it with an exclamation. 'I cannot believe that to be true!'

'But you watched him sink into despair as you worked with him to try to prove his innocence.' I picked up the other cup and sipped before placing it on the ground at my feet. 'By the time you left, when there was no proof to be found, he was hardly the same man and after his spell in gaol he was entirely changed. The only person he believed in was his cellmate, John Whitby. God rest both their souls.' I crossed myself briefly then reached for the wedge of cheese I had folded in a napkin and began to unwrap it. 'Until you arrived I've been too glum to contemplate adopting a pup.'

'And now?' His brows rose in enquiry. 'If you intend to stay here at Frensham, might it not be a distraction to train a dog? Or maybe even two? You have the kennel.'

I mused on his suggestion, spreading the napkin on the log and laying the cheese on it. 'It's possible, although I have a standing invitation from the Dowager Princess to return to Durham Palace and I don't think it would include a dog. But why do you assume I would get a hunting type? It might be a lapdog.'

This time he snorted derisively. 'No! I can't see you with a lapdog, Joan.'

'Why not?' I jerked my head up, rather indignant. 'Ladies have lapdogs. Am I not a lady?'

He assumed an exaggerated expression of contrition. 'I did not mean to imply that you are not a lady. Of course you are – just not the sort of lady that keeps a poor little lapdog under her skirt, or tucked up her sleeve.' He moved to face me on the log. 'You are a lady who strides out. Not one that trips along, simpering. I have always admired that about you.'

'Really?' I broke a piece of cheese off the wedge and held it out to him. 'What else have you admired about me, Anthony?' I meant the question to be flippant but nevertheless felt an unexpected surge of anticipation.

As he took the cheese his fingers touched mine and a sudden shiver shot up my arm. Then I caught his eye and a flash of wild desire engulfed my entire body. With a gasp I withdrew my hand but he brushed the cheese aside and took it back, linking his fingers into mine. In a low voice he said, 'The list is too long and I don't know where to begin, Joan.'

Under the cloth of my sleeve the hairs on my arm rose, as if disturbed by a hot breeze. But there had been no hot breeze and every part of me was focused on the connection of our flesh, where his thumb began gently to stroke mine. Gradually he bent his elbow, pulling me nearer and nearer until first our breath mingled and then our lips met. The effect was explosive, like the slow match meeting gunpowder when a cannon is fired. Warm honey seemed to spread through my veins, stirring my blood and sending my senses reeling. Time stood still while two hands and two pairs of lips wreaked havoc.

When I finally managed to pull away, I pressed my offending hand to my treacherous mouth. My eyes opened wide and stared into his in disbelief. Words hung between us that could not be expressed, for fear they might prove cathartic. Eventually I expelled air and cried, 'No! No, no, no, no, no; that – just – did not – happen.'

Anthony's response shook me to the core. 'Why not, Joan? You know I have always loved you.'

I shook my head violently. 'Not like that, no – not like that! It won't do. It is impossible.'

His shoulders rose. 'In your eyes perhaps, but not in mine. You are my dark lady, my Guinevere, my Helen of Troy – and you always will be.'

I shook my head vehemently. 'I am none of them, Anthony. There must be sixteen years between us, and besides you are married.'

He stroked his chin, adorned these days with a fashionable pointed beard. 'So was Guinevere. I cannot deny the marriage but you know well how fragile it is. How little it offers me in the way of love or comfort. Can I be blamed for finding those essential life-elements elsewhere? Somewhere I have always found them, even as a lad. I can never forget how you saved my life, Joan.'

'You were a boy, only eighteen, my husband's squire. It was my duty to care for you as I cared for my son. It does not mean that, ten years later, I can contemplate the notion of any other feeling between us.' I looked around distractedly. 'And now I cannot continue this unfortunate expedition.' I hastily rewrapped the cheese, picked up my cup and threw the contents on the ground before pushing it back into the pannier. 'Finish the wine if you will and return the wineskin. I will take my hawk back to the mews. You can stay here if you like and fly the hobby at the game.'

I turned to head for the horses but he ran after me and caught my arm. 'Joan! Joan! Please do not reject me! I can't bear to lose your friendship.'

I stopped but I did not trust myself to turn and address him face to face. 'If we are to remain friends, Anthony, you must leave tomorrow and go back to your wife. If she turns you away again, find yourself a mistress but do not ever expect me to perform that role.'

I felt him release my arm and suffered a sharp stab of regret; but I took a deep breath and plunged away into the trees, towards the horses. His voice carried to me on the still evening air. 'Very well, my lady, I will do as you say, but never forget that I will always love you. *Always*, Joan.'

39

Durham Palace

September 1507

Anthony had departed at dawn the day after our
unfortunate hawking expedition and I did not see him
before he left. But the episode prompted me to decide to
take the Dowager Princess up on her long-standing request
to renew the English lessons. Her Christmas visit to court
at Richmond had proved disappointing. The king had kept
Prince Henry close to him during all the celebrations and
entertainments and Princess Katherine and her small entourage were given separate lodgings in the palace grounds. It
was as if the officials had been ordered to keep her as far
away from the royal apartments as possible.

'Even Princess Mary had to make a surreptitious escape
to come and see me,' she confided when we took a walk
together in the gardens. 'She is such a beautiful girl and
kind too. Only eleven years old and with opinions of her
own about everything! I really enjoyed her company and
admired her for defying her father to visit me. She is very
fond of you, Lady Joan, and was sad to hear about your
husband's death in the Holy Land.'

'Yes, I know,' I said. 'I received a letter of condolence

from her, written in her own hand. I was very pleased to have it.'

Katherine smiled. 'She said I was lucky to be taking lessons from you and wishes you were still her governess.'

I took a risk to ask her about Prince Harry. 'And did you have any conversation with the prince at all, your grace? Or indeed with the king?'

She frowned fiercely. 'King Henry gave me one formal audience, along with the Spanish ambassador, but all he wanted to know was when my father was going to pay the second half of my dowry. He never allowed the prince to dance with me at the Christmas feasts and I was seated with my staff at a separate table. Since then he has cut off my small allowance from the royal Exchequer and I have been told it will only be restored when the dowry is paid. That is why, unless my father sends me some money, I am able to pay you so little for my lessons, Lady Joan.'

It was the Moor girls who revealed the rest of the story, talking to me during the princess's siesta, no longer a cover for meetings with Prince Henry now that the joust royal was over and the prince had no more excuses to make visits to Kennington and incognito journeys across the Thames to Durham Palace.

'Our mistress has been badly treated by the King of England, my lady,' said loyal Kat, the elder of the dark-skinned maids. 'She will probably not tell you, but he was so cross when his offer of marriage to her sister was turned down and the dowry still had not been paid, that he sent his guards to steal our mistress's gold plate as compensation. It included a reliquary containing a finger bone of St Iago, which had been given to her mother on her wedding day.

It needed mending, otherwise she would have been wearing it and it would not have been in the strongbox with the rest of the gold.'

I was horrified at this example of King Henry's avarice. 'Can she not write to the prince and ask him to get it back? I'm sure he would oblige.'

'She does not want to show any disrespect for the king to his own son,' Lina broke in. 'She still prays daily for King Henry's health, even though his death would bring her much relief.'

'Her grace is a true Christian,' I said. 'If the prince's mother were still alive she would never have allowed her to be dishonoured like this. Your mistress was the first person she wanted to see when she returned from her last pilgrimage. Young though the princess was then, she thought her daughter-in-law a strong and clever woman.'

Kat made a quick check to see that the door was firmly shut before risking her own opinion. 'The Muslim faith would say the king does not show his dead wife honour when he mistreats their son's widow.'

Very soon after this the princess was told that the Bishop of Durham had requested that his London house be returned to him and King Henry used it as excuse to remove her back into her Christmas lodgings at Richmond Palace. Presumably he had discovered that they were smaller and cheaper to run and again, far removed from the royal quarters.

Princess Katherine blinked back tears as she told me there would be no room for me in her new abode. 'And now the new Spanish ambassador is demanding that either

Prince Henry and I are married, as was planned, or else I am permitted to return to Spain. Meanwhile the king is negotiating marriages between Princess Mary and my cousin Charles, and his elder sister Eleanor and Prince Henry. I believe the Pope will never give dispensations for both unions because of consanguinity but, as you can see, at present that leaves me out. The prince is sixteen now and old enough to wed. If my father would only endorse the ambassador's demand, I believe I could be married very soon.'

'And would you be happy to marry Prince Henry, your grace?' I asked, taking the plunge.

She nodded glumly. 'Of course I would, Lady Joan. He is handsome and clever and I know he likes me. And I would be Queen of England as my mother intended. But just now it looks as if I will have to live in a cottage until I grow old, while the monarchs of Europe squabble over alliances.'

PART FOUR

40

Richmond Palace

April 1509

AFTER ENJOYING A YEAR and a half at Frensham, I was back at court, and a very different court it was. My mother and I were sharing a guest chamber at Richmond Palace, a slightly awkward arrangement because our circumstances had not allowed us much contact in recent times and we were not as comfortable together as we had been when we were both younger.

It was ten years since Kate, or Lady Katherine Vaux to use her court title, had followed the king's mother into retirement at her country palace of Colleyweston, deep in the Eastern shires of the Midlands. Both ladies were now in their late sixties, elderly and set in their ways, with aches and pains and fixed opinions. Nevertheless when the news came that the king was mortally ill, determined to supervise her son's care, Lady Margaret made the hundred-and-fifty-mile journey to Richmond Palace and of course my mother had come with her. I had brought Rose with me to serve us both because there was plenty of coming and going in a court that was preparing for the inevitable death of the monarch.

Two weeks later tempers were stretched and we were all on tenterhooks as the king's condition grew worse and worse; his consumption was raging, aggravated by the terrible quinsy of the throat that had plagued him on and off since the death of the queen and made swallowing and speaking agonising. It meant that in addition to suffering acute pain and difficulty breathing, King Henry the Seventh was literally starving to death.

Apart from organising her son's treatment and arranging his physical comfort as far as was possible, Lady Margaret was also determined to ensure that when the inevitable happened everything was prepared for a seamless transfer of the throne to her seventeen-year-old grandson, Prince Henry. At the daily meetings of the Privy Council, she and young Henry were seated together at the top of the table and nothing that was said escaped the attention of the royal matriarch. Then, after she had been to pray beside her desperately sick son and bid him goodnight, she would summon my mother to supper in her chamber to talk over the events of the day. Sharing her chamber as I did, my mother often used me as a listening ear when she had heard something that particularly worried her, and as King Henry grew weaker his moods became grimmer and his orders more autocratic.

'The whole court knew that when Princess Katherine came to visit him last week the king sent her away with a flea in her ear,' my mother began when she returned one evening, 'and now Lady Margaret says he has put a ban on any union between her and Prince Henry, telling him he must seek a marriage and a treaty with France. Would that not leave the Dowager Princess in a very awkward position?

I feel very sorry for her but you know her better than I do, Gigi. What do you think she will do? I'm not sure her father will welcome her back to Spain.'

I pondered briefly, wondering whether to spill a secret to my mother. 'I haven't seen her for some time but Hal told me that she had been corresponding with the prince and gave the impression that their letters were quite tender. Also while his tournament team was training at Kennington Palace I know he made visits to her at Durham Palace. The Pope granted a dispensation for their union on the grounds that there was no consummation of her marriage to Arthur, so there is really no reason why they could not marry. I imagine it rather depends on the prince and whether he will pay heed to his father's dying wishes.'

My mother nodded. 'He gives the impression of being quite subdued at present, which I suppose is not surprising. Margaret says he rarely speaks at Privy Council meetings and most of the councillors seem to think that when he takes the throne he'll just do as he's told, as he has done for the past four years under the king's influence. What does Hal think?'

I gave a little laugh. 'Hal and Harry are still thick as thieves and while they were preparing for the tournaments at Kennington they got up to all kinds of mischief. If his stories are anything to go by, when the time comes the Council is in for a big surprise. But if you love your grandson, Mamma, please do not say anything of this to Lady Margaret.'

My mother's mouth twisted in a half-smile. 'I would not dream of threatening Hal's position in the heir's household when he's done so well to retain the prince's trust for all these years. Anyway I have an inkling that Margaret already suspects what will happen when the king dies and secretly supports her grandson's position, whatever ideas the Council may have. Besides, it has been settled that if the prince is still under age when his father dies, Lady Margaret will officially be appointed his Protector until his eighteenth birthday, which she declares is the royal age of succession. So until the end of June it would be My Lady the King's Mother who officially runs the country.'

On the basis of this conversation, the following day I decided to try to pay a visit to the Dowager Princess but was surprised to find royal guards at the entrance to the small, two-storey redbrick house, set close to the herb garden in the palace grounds. I wondered if it had once been the head gardener's cot or an extra guardhouse. It certainly looked a very meagre residence for a royal princess.

At first the guards were reluctant to let me in and one of them went inside to seek advice. As a result, Sir Robert Poyntz appeared at the door and beckoned me up the short staircase.

'I'm sure the princess would be delighted to see you, Lady Joan, as am I. But just at present she has another visitor and we have been asked to admit no one else until he leaves.'

I had an inkling that I knew who this visitor equipped with a brace of royal guards might be but did not say so. 'Well, I could come another time, Sir Robert, if that is more convenient.'

He shook his head and pushed the door further open. 'No, come in and have some refreshment. I do not think it will be a long wait and I will enjoy your company meanwhile, if I may.'

It was Lina who brought wine and sweetmeats. She looked

surprised and excited to see me but obediently poured the wine silently and retired without speaking. I was glad that at least the princess obviously still had her faithful few retainers to serve her.

'It is a sad time for the Tudor family, Lady Joan,' Sir Robert remarked, having taken his first sip. 'And I'm sorry that you are no longer in the princess's household to support her. But at least you have provided her with a good basis of English, even if her pronunciation is occasionally a bit off-centre.'

'I admit that I used to find it rather charming, Sir Robert. But perhaps it has slipped a little since I left her.' I raised an eyebrow enquiringly as I took a sip of the wine myself. 'I'm wondering who is her mysterious visitor. Are you at liberty to tell me?'

He shook his head. 'Alas not. I leave you to guess the identity through your close friendship with my lady and even closer relationship to one of Prince Henry's companion squires. Meanwhile I wonder if you know that the Poyntz family at last has a fine and sturdy heir to our considerable holdings and businesses? His name is Nicholas.'

A nod and a smile accompanied my response to his question. 'I do know, Sir Robert, and I am delighted for you. Especially if he is as sturdy and healthy as you suggest. He must be just about walking by now.'

The grey-haired knight looked uncertain. 'I believe so, but I have not seen it myself. His mother keeps her children down at her Devonshire manor while Anthony is away at sea on the king's business. At my request he also makes sure to bring a good supply of pomegranates back from Spain every time he sails for that coast so that I can keep the

Dowager Princess supplied. He has become quite an adept sea captain now and combines trading with diplomacy, finding his legal training useful at the same time. I am very proud of my son's achievements.'

A male servant in royal livery appearing at the door and bowing spared me any response to this final declaration. 'The princess's guest is leaving now and thanks you for making the arrangements, Sir Robert,' the man announced, causing my companion to rise hastily, excuse himself and follow him from the room. Five minutes later he returned, just as I drained my wine cup.

'Her grace says she cannot wait to see you,' he said, holding the door open. 'Please follow me.'

The princess was standing beside a brazier full of red embers of charcoal in a room furnished as a solar but obviously not catching the warmth of any sun on that chilly April day. Two chairs were arranged tellingly close beside it. As I made my curtsy she covered the few steps across the floor and raised me up for a kiss on the cheek. 'Lady Joan!' Nobody at court seemed to call me Lady Guildford any more. 'It is so good to see you again. Please, let us sit.' She gestured to where cushions were heaped on a deep window seat and we both made ourselves comfortable. 'Kat will move the brazier nearer.'

My heart was in my mouth as the maid succeeded in lifting the red-hot brazier across the room. It was not far, for the room was not large, but I would never have expected anyone, let alone a woman black or white, to lift such a heavy and dangerous object any distance. I wanted to protest but held my tongue and merely breathed a sigh of relief and thanked Kat with a sympathetic nod.

When the maid had left the room at a dismissive wave from Princess Katherine, I said, 'That was cleverly done, your grace.'

'Oh, Kat does it all the time.' The princess seemed unconcerned. 'It is so cold and wet at present, do you not find? The world seems to be crying for King Henry before he is dead. But it will not be long now.'

'So I believe.' I indicated her attractive pale blue gown, embroidered with love-in-a-mist flowers. 'And we are not in mourning yet, I see. I have also learned that I am not your only visitor.'

Her cheeks coloured prettily. 'No, you are not and if you have guessed who it was then I ask you not to reveal his visit to a soul. Even from his deathbed the king can issue unpleasant edicts. He still refuses to return my mother's reliquary.' She paused to lean forward and whisper. 'I shall not mourn him, however black my apparel.' Then she sat back with a smile. 'I heard you were here at Richmond and I hoped you would come to see me. What do you think of my present accommodation? Now you see why I could not let you stay with me. Kat and Lina are sleeping in the scullery.'

'But you still manage to have visits from a certain person? What does he think of your apartment? Has he complained about it?'

She shook her head with a resigned sigh. 'He says it would do no good and anyway, we will soon have castles and palaces to choose from.'

'You will be married then? Even though the king forbids it.'

'He will not be here to do so. But again I can trust you

not to mention our meetings to anyone, can't I? All my staff know, of course, but I can trust them and I am sure I can trust you.'

'That goes without saying, but I will swear it if you wish. Is he sure he can trust his guards though? There were two at your entrance who nearly wouldn't let me in.'

She laughed. 'They above all will not tell! All his servants know that good times are coming, as long as we all keep our lips sealed.'

41

Richmond Palace

23 April 1509

FOR THE NEXT DAY or so a pall seemed to hang over
the palace. Everyone knew that in the royal wardrobe
lengths of black cloth were being hastily sewn into mourning
livery for the king's household and in their apartments senior
courtiers were being measured for their funeral attire.
Beeswax mourning candles were placed in the chapel and
the audience chambers, ready to replace the everyday lighting
and the children of the royal choir had travelled to Richmond
from St George's Chapel, Windsor, ready to sing Masses
and dirges when the king's soul was heaven bound.

But before any death was announced, the twenty-third
of April arrived and with it the annual celebration of the
Order of the Garter on the feast day of their patron, St
George. Along with a crowd of courtiers and ladies, I stood
in the great hall and watched the knights in their long blue
cloaks and hoods slowly and proudly parade its length on
the way to the king's Presence Chamber, where Prince Henry
was to preside in his father's stead over the ceremony of
welcoming two new knights into the exclusive Order. Lady
Margaret also attended, the last Lady Companion of the

Garter, since the dying king had discontinued the practice of appointing women. After dinner they all attended a long Mass in the chapel before returning to complete the day with a supper and toasts.

I relate all this because it was not until the end of these ceremonies that the Archbishop of Canterbury announced that the king had actually died at that very hour two evenings before. When the gasps died down from those who had not been in the know, which seemed to be most of us, there had been a ceremonial trumpet flourish for the seventeen-year-old prince as he was proclaimed King Henry the Eighth and the appointment of Lady Margaret as temporary Protector of the Realm. It was not until the following morning that the solemn tidings were declared in the City of London and couriers set out to spread the word throughout the kingdom. In the afternoon the new young king, dressed in royal blue mourning, rode through the city streets on the way to the Tower, to the sad toll of church bells and the acclamation of the gathered crowds.

Meanwhile the first plans of the Royal Council had been put into action and before the city awoke the two shady lawyers who had done most to bring men before the much-loathed Council Learned were hauled from their beds and taken to a very different part of the Tower. Edmund Dudley and Richard Empson were the men responsible for the despair and incarceration of my husband Richard Guildford and, as far as I was concerned, for his ignominious and unnecessary death in a pilgrims' hospice in Jerusalem. Their arrest had been the first order made by the new Protector and I, for one, wanted to kiss her hand.

It was in the early hours that my mother woke me with

extraordinary news. 'Margaret has at last been able to weep for the death of her son,' she told me. 'The poor woman has been holding back her tears until the necessary arrests were made but I have at last seen her drop into exhausted sleep. All those who were at his deathbed were sworn to secrecy until the crucial arrests had been made that would demonstrate to the people that the new reign would be one of joy and reconciliation, not tainted by the grim investigative practices of the sinister Council Learned. It is now disbanded.'

'Is there now a period of official mourning for the late king?' I asked.

'Yes, a fortnight – to give time for the funeral preparations. Tomorrow there will be a procession and an overnight vigil at St Paul's, followed by a requiem Mass in Westminster Abbey, then the late king's body will lie in state until it is lowered into the vault of his new Lady Chapel to rest beside his queen. As a final offering and to mark the end of one reign and the start of another, his household officials will break their white staffs of office and throw them in after him.'

'As is the tradition,' I acknowledged, remembering how Richard's white staff had been collected and carried away by a sergeant at arms after he had been committed to the Fleet prison. 'And what about the new king? Will he take any part in all this?'

'No. If you remember none of the royal family attended Prince Arthur's funeral. Prince Henry . . .' A frown creased my mother's brow. 'I mean King Henry the Eighth, of course! Margaret says that for his safety he will remain at the Tower of London until the obsequies are over.'

'Which is where I will go to seek my tilt-mad son,' I announced, 'and relieve you of a chamber-mate who has grossly overstayed her welcome.'

Lady Vaux demurred, as I knew she would, even though it was the truth. 'It has been a relief to have your company through this sad event, Gigi – a real boon to have someone trustworthy to talk to. But where will you stay? My little home in the Blackfriars demesne is always available but it will be cold and bare.'

'That is a kind offer, Mamma, but I think I will throw myself on the new king's mercy. I'm sure there must be empty chambers in the Queen's Lodging at the Tower. I'll send a note to Hal to warn him of my arrival and hope he can acquire one.'

42

Greenwich Palace

May 1509

THINGS DID NOT WORK out quite the way I had anticipated, for my letter to Hal sparked an unexpected response.

To my dearest lady mother,

I write in reply to yours, which asked me to approach the king on the matter of your visit to the Tower of London. King Henry invites you to stay in the Queen's Lodging but begs a favour of you in return.

Once the solemnity of the late king's funeral has past, his grace wishes to despatch you on a barge to collect the Dowager Princess of Wales from Windsor Castle, where she has been staying of late and bring her here to join his court. The princess has particularly asked for you to join her company of ladies and King Henry is anxious to accede to her wishes. As soon as the funeral is over, he intends that his court should depart downriver for Greenwich Palace. Mourning garb will be worn on formal occasions, so if you should need any extra clothes bringing up from Frensham I could send a messenger to collect them for you and any other items that you might

*require. I think the princess hopes you will remain with
her for some while. King Henry asks me to impress on
you that the entire content of this letter should remain
strictly confidential.*

*Meanwhile I send you my enduring love and look
forward to our imminent meeting.*

*A barge will collect you at Richmond early on
Saturday morning of this week, so we may have a day
or two together before you set off for Windsor.*

*Written on Tuesday the second of May at the Tower
of London,*

Henry Guildford

I read the letter several times in order to be sure that I had
absorbed its content. It was hard to believe that the
boy-prince I had sent my young son to serve nearly ten
years ago was now in a position to change my own life
completely. And what is more who trusted me enough to
keep the secret of his obvious intention to ignore his father's
deathbed instruction regarding the princess who had once
been his elder brother's bride. If Harry was taking Katherine
to Greenwich, his own birthplace and favourite royal palace,
did he intend to make her his queen there – even before
he had been crowned? Would this be the first evidence of
Harry no longer being the compliant young prince but
showing the world just how he intended to rule as King
Henry the Eighth of England? Was Katherine of Aragon
to be the bride he chose himself; not one he might wait for
a committee of old men to choose, as the most suitable
match to boost the kingdom's prestige?

If this was indeed the step he intended to take, then I

could only applaud his boldness and wish the couple a successful marriage. At the same time there was no escaping the fact that Katherine was twenty-three years old, while Henry was two months off eighteen. Barring illness or accident he could have forty years of fertility ahead of him, whereas Katherine might have less than half that and although her mother had borne six children to adulthood, only one of them had been a boy and he had died at eighteen. As one who had witnessed and nursed Harry's beloved mother Queen Elizabeth through her heroic efforts to establish the Tudor dynasty, I feared that her son was following his youthful passion rather than considering one crucial responsibility of kingship, to sire a healthy number of boys to ensure the future of the Tudor throne.

During the days of mourning the mood at the Tower of London had been serious and sombre but from the moment the new and carefully selected young courtiers stepped out of the flotilla of barges onto the white stone dock at Greenwich a tone of youthful exuberance was established that was to prevail throughout the next few weeks and months. England had a new young king and the years of threat and fear were over.

In her chamber at Greenwich Palace and in great secrecy, Princess Katherine was fitted for a very special gown. Details of the wedding ceremony had been kept strictly secret, scheduled for early June, but all who filled the palace with laughter and games were well aware of the love that had blossomed between the king and the princess.

Regular outdoor amusements often involved hide and seek in the gardens, when secret kisses would be stolen in the shrubberies, followed by musical evenings of singing and dancing in the great hall, when the new king demonstrated his talent for playing a variety of instruments. He also partnered a succession of young ladies but whenever the music turned to the energetic volt, the only partner he would take was Princess Katherine.

Their first performance of this new dance received enthusiastic applause from the whole company, for they had clearly practised its leaps and complex steps that ended with a high and swirling lift of the lady by the gentleman, which drew a charming blush to the princess's cheeks. At dinner the following day, to a flourish of trumpets, King Henry personally presented her with the heart of the stag he had killed out hunting during the previous week, cooked and laid among a carpet of wild garlic picked from the forest. Whether or not she was sufficiently delighted with the gift to actually eat it we were unable to see from below the high table, but her smile gave every sign that she was overcome with shy pleasure at the romantic message it conveyed.

Among the attendants the princess had brought with her to Greenwich were of course her friend and duenna, Dona Maria de Salinas, and also the two Moor chamber women Kat and Lina, whose intriguing colouring stirred much attention among the male courtiers. However, during my own attendances on Katherine, I learned that Kat had wisely married a musician from among the royal minstrels who, as well as playing the sackbut, was a strong and muscular fellow with some fiendish fighting techniques learned during his wanderings through the military camps of Europe. Not only was he responsible for the swelling belly beneath Kat's flowing gowns but his reputation also protected young Lina from any lewd attentions from drunken guardsmen.

On duty in the robing chamber during one fitting of the special dress, I watched Katherine twisting and turning in order to view herself in the magnificent looking glass that was a feature of the room. A seamstress rose to her feet and stepped back with a curtsy, having finished pinning the hem of the train. The white cloth-of-gold gown was reaching the stage when it might be sent to the embroiderers for embellishment.

Katherine turned briefly away from the mirror to catch my eye. 'In Spain white is not a colour for weddings, Lady Joan. It is usually red for luck and sometimes black for a second wedding. Are you sure this will be acceptable in the king's eyes?'

I gave her a reassuring nod. 'I am certain it will, Princess. In fact I think any colour would be acceptable to the king if you are wearing it but white will set off your beautiful auburn hair, which of course you should wear loose.'

She touched the thick plait that was presently wound around her head like a smooth snake. 'A sign of my virginity, is that not the message it conveys?'

Bearing in mind the fuss there had been seven years ago over whether her marriage to Prince Arthur had been consummated or not, I made sure that the smile and the emphatic nod she could see in the glass expressed no hint of doubt. 'Indeed it is, Princess. But tell me, are you happy with the length of the train?' I asked the question in order to turn the subject swiftly to other matters. 'It is important you are not distracted by any fear that you may trip.'

Her chin lifted and she made an athletic turn, her foot sweeping the heavy train behind her with practised ease. 'I have no fear at all about this marriage, Lady Joan,' she said.

'I am lucky to be marrying for love, as well as for the privilege of sharing the throne of England. But I was born and raised to be a queen and I will not trip.'

Her words gave me a sudden recollection of another bride destined to become a queen – the new king's own mother, Elizabeth of York, who had expressed exactly the same sentiment almost word for word to a younger me, before her marriage to Henry the Seventh. The new King Henry had adored and admired his mother and now he was set to marry another beautiful auburn-haired woman who also believed she was born to be a queen. Surely it was a good omen.

When I first saw the white gown on its return from the embroiderers I was astonished. It had only been away for a little over a fortnight and the gleaming fabric had been transformed. An intricate trail of golden roses wound its serpentine way around the bodice, skirt and train, at intervals framing images of ripe pomegranates depicted in blushing shades of pink. So freely grown in Spain, the pomegranate was the symbol Katherine had chosen as her personal emblem. A large embroidered version formed the centrepiece of the gown's train, bursting with the scarlet seeds that packed the centre of the fruit, forming an unmistakeable icon of fertility and plenty. There was no doubting that this bride understood what was expected of her first and foremost in her role as Queen of England.

In my avid absorption of literature I had also read that the pomegranate was recognised as a symbol of love and power, a heady combination when united but dangerous if at odds. And it made me think of Anthony Poyntz, which was dangerous in itself.

43

Blackfriars and Westminster Abbey

Midsummer Day, 24 June 1509

'I'M NOT VERY HAPPY about Margaret,' my mother said as we hurried down Water Lane towards the River Thames, skirting the shadowy height of the western city wall. We had ordered a ferry to meet us at the Blackfriars steps at Prime and the church bells were just beginning to ring. 'She's been ailing since before the old king's death but she soldiers on without rest, chairing Privy Council meetings, organising her son's funeral and now arranging her grandson's coronation. She's sixty-six, Gigi, not a spring chicken like you!'

I grimaced, stretching my arm, still cramped from sleeping in an awkward position. My mother and I had shared the bed in her small apartment in the Blackfriars' enclosure and my sleep had been erratic. 'I don't feel like a spring chicken, Mamma. Why did we not rate a chamber in Westminster Palace?'

'Because it is full of people more important than we are; that's why Margaret chose to stay at the Abbot's House.'

I almost stopped dead in astonishment. 'Surely no one is more important than Lady Margaret! For another four days she is still the ruler of England.'

'That's true but the palace is packed full of the king's lively young gentlemen and the queen's new young ladies, all celebrating the coronation and the fact that it is Midsummer's Day. There will have been fireworks and bonfires and barrels aplenty. We can only hope that their heads are clear enough to remember the roles they have to play in today's ceremonies. Whoops!' She swerved to twitch the braided hem of her silk skirt hastily clear of a suspicious puddle on the otherwise dry path and gave me a look of disgust. 'Why can't people piss in the Fleet? It's only a step away. Imagine if I'd gone to the coronation banquet stinking like a latrine!'

I laughed. 'Really, Mamma! You sound like a Winchester Goose.'

Lady Vaux put on her palace voice, the one she used on royal duty. 'Goodness me! I hope they don't let any Bermondsey whores across the river on this auspicious day.' Then she noticed the boat moored at the foot of the steps, the Thames speeding past as the tide flowed upstream and an anxious ferryman gesticulating in our direction. 'Look, the ferry is waiting. Quick, Gigi! We can break our fast at Margaret's table before going to the abbey.'

As we were seated at Lady Margaret's table in the abbot's refectory I saw why my mother was worried about her friend. On this festive day of her grandson's coronation the Countess of Richmond and Derby looked shrunken within the folds of her richly trimmed crimson robe and her smile of greeting was given with weary stoicism. 'God's blessing on you both,' she said, pushing her bowl of bread and milk aside. 'I have no appetite this morning but you must fortify yourselves for the day ahead. I was offered pigeon pie so you should have some. Who knows when the coronation banquet will be served.'

I nodded at the server who hovered, waiting for our wishes, and asked for small ale to go with the pigeon. 'And bring the same for Lady Vaux,' I added, for my mother was busy trying to encourage our hostess.

'You really must have a few mouthfuls, Margaret, or you will disgrace the king by fainting in the abbey.' She turned to the servant with a fierce expression. 'Bring her grace some warm broth or curdled eggs; something more nourishing than this cold pap.'

The young man left, rolling his eyes silently, but was back in minutes with the pie and the requested egg dish. Meanwhile Lady Margaret had been persuaded to drink some ale and looked a little cheered by her friend's bossy presence. 'I feel better for your company, Kate,' she confessed. 'And yours, Joan. The abbot's bed is too wide and so soft that I felt lost among the covers. I needed more bolsters but my maid snored on her pallet and I didn't like to wake her to fetch them, so I barely slept a wink.'

I thought that not waking her snoring maid didn't sound at all like the powerful Lady Margaret I had known and loved and I could see from my mother's expression that she felt the same, but neither of us said anything. However after we had all eaten and drunk as much as we needed, which in her case was very little, the royal grandmother summoned her train bearer and led the way back to her grand chamber where we were to make ourselves ready to take our place in the abbey.

'She doesn't look as if she will last the day, Joan,' murmured my mother, anxiously shaking her head. 'I've never known her look so fragile.'

'Surely there is a herbalist in the abbey who might have some restorative potion we could acquire?' I suggested. 'I could go and ask the guestmaster while you help my lady with her headgear.'

'Yes, that's a good idea, Joan. But don't be too long.'

The guestmaster directed me to the hospital, where the infirmarian offered me a strong infusion of valerian and angelica, sweetened with honey, which I hoped the lady might willingly take. 'But the patient should consult a physician if the exhaustion continues,' he advised. 'It is often the precursor of something more serious.'

I feared he could be right but reflected that it was rest that Lady Margaret needed, which she would not find today. It took a good deal of persuasion before she agreed to take a dose of the potion but when she tasted it fortunately she liked the flavour and so I tucked the phial into the pocket of my gown, against further need. She established a surprisingly fast pace as we set off for the special viewing box in the abbey clerestory, where twenty-four years ago she had watched her son's coronation. It gave her a bird's eye view of proceedings, without subjecting her to the curious gaze of the courtiers and clergy gathered in the chancel, but there were a lot of steps to get up there and we had to stop several times for her to catch her breath as we climbed.

I felt a pang of envy as I watched the newly married and soon-to-be-crowned king and queen walk side by side onto the beautiful mosaic pavement in front of the altar, because the young ladies carrying Queen Katherine's train were all carefully chosen daughters of high-status courtiers.

Although she had been apologetic, I was considered too old and widowed to be included among them. But I had to admit that if I could not be down among the participants, my position viewing from Lady Margaret's eyrie was the next best place to be.

Gold candelabras lit the altar, illuminating the beautiful frontal, which had been embroidered especially for this one occasion and depicted the Tudor Rose and the pomegranate side by side in beautiful scarlet, white and shades of pink. Two golden thrones awaited their occupants on either side of the chancel, facing the choir and the long nave, which was crowded with citizens eager to hail their new king and queen as the crowns were placed on their heads. Knights of the Garter would hold a cloth-of-gold canopy over each of the new monarchs as they took their coronation oath and were consecrated with the holy chrism, so this most solemn part of the ceremony was hidden, even to us gazing down from above, but presumably not to an all-seeing God.

I was seated with my mother behind Lady Margaret so I could not witness the depth of her feeling when the gem-studded crown was settled on her grandson's head, but I could see the expression on Katherine's face as the smaller coronet was placed on hers. No tears were shed but a look of almost celestial gratitude lit her face and her lips moved slightly, perhaps with a prayer of thanksgiving to mark the long-awaited realisation of the promise her mother, the warlike Queen Isabella of Castile, had made to her as a child – that she would one day be Queen of England.

44

Westminster Hall

24 June 1509

AT THE CORONATION BANQUET, music and song filled
the vast great hall of Westminster Palace, making
conversation almost impossible, but there were so many
extraordinary sights to marvel at that it did not seem to
signify. The Duke of Buckingham rode up and down the
aisles between the tables dressed in his usual excessive finery,
which for once seemed appropriate, his glossy black charger
trapped in fur-trimmed cloth of gold. Behind him walked
the king's new Royal Steward, wearing his brand new
embroidered tabard and bearing his white staff of office,
leading a long, snaking procession of kitchen varlets bearing
vast gold and silver platters of seldom-served creatures, all
cooked and re-dressed in their skins and feathers: a stag
with antlers attached and gilded, a porpoise on a sea of
salad leaves, its skin studded with jewels like drops of water,
a swan and her cygnets swimming on a tide of green jelly
and whipped cream spume, a pig with its skin sizzled into
golden crackling and its head crowned with rubies. Behind
all these came a series of subtleties concocted from coloured
marchpane to celebrate the marriage and coronation and

demonstrating a dozen ways of doing so. But ironically, while my eyes marvelled at the wonders, I felt my appetite disappearing further with every passing extravaganza.

My mother and I were seated on the new queen's reward table, which was situated on the dais behind the high table. And so although we received a close-up sight of these culinary wonders as the procession wound its way towards the carvery, where they would be portioned and distributed along the trestles, we only had sight of the backs of the throne-like chairs of the royal party, who of course faced down the hall, overlooking the crowd of courtiers and citizens seated below.

'I can't see Margaret at all,' my mother whispered in my ear. 'How will we know if she is all right?'

I tried to reassure her. 'There are numerous pages scattered around who can bring us a message if necessary. But it's my guess that she will hold herself together at all costs, at least until the dancing starts.'

I tried to sound confident but in truth I wasn't certain of this at all. However, all went well as the meats were served and cleared; then as the sweetmeats were being circulated I spotted Princess Mary making her way towards us. Lady Margaret had been sitting in a place of honour beside the queen, with the young princess on her other side, and my heart missed a beat when I spotted her approach. However her beautiful face was serene, giving no hint of alarm, so I laid a reassuring hand on my mother's arm as I rose to greet her with a curtsy.

'Isn't this a wonderful occasion, Mother Guildford?' Mary was elated. 'It is so long since I saw you and so I took the chance of having a word before the next course is served.'

'I am honoured, your grace. Is it about my lady Margaret, by any chance?'

'No – why should it be?' She looked puzzled. 'This is her finest moment, to see her grandson on the throne, the continuation of the Tudor dynasty. Perhaps she's a little tired and she hasn't eaten very much – just a sliver of cygnet I think, but I expect she'll make up for it with sweetmeats. That's what I usually do at banquets.'

Her winning smile with its pearly white teeth was captivating. 'Well, I'm very happy to hear that,' I said, 'but I have some restorative tonic with me. Just send a page if you think she needs it.' She nodded but seemed unwilling to leave. 'Did you want something else of me, Princess?'

She spoke in a rush of words. 'Yes, Mother Guildford, I very much want you to come back to me at Eltham Palace. Things have never been so good as when you were there as governess and I know the king will agree. I realise that your husband tragically died in the Holy Land and you may not yet feel ready to take a royal post, but as soon as you do, please let me know.'

She was so earnest and complimentary that I wanted to embrace her but of course I resisted the temptation. 'I am touched that you should want me to return, your grace, and I will give a great deal of thought to your offer. But it could not be straight away because there are several other matters requiring my attention at present. I hope you understand.'

I could see the disappointment in her eyes but she nodded briskly and even gave a little curtsy, which I hastily returned. I watched her walk back to her place at the high table, head held high.

My mother had overheard the conversation. 'How could you turn her down, Gigi? She so obviously regards you as a mother figure and needs your support now that she is alone at Eltham.'

'She is far from being alone, Mamma.' I took my seat again. 'She shares her life with several other young ladies and a nurse and a governess. Just now I feel responsibility towards both you and Lady Margaret, to say nothing of the queen, who has also asked me to take a position in her household. But it is lovely to think that the princess recalls my presence with fondness.'

'Well, I hope you will remember her offer when you have finished dealing with your elderly charges, although there is really no need.' Her tone was indignant. 'We have managed pretty well together so far.'

I felt a twinge of guilt, because I could not say that I feared she might lose Lady Margaret quite soon – and then what would she do? I hoped she would come to Frensham with me. But I said nothing of these things and merely remarked, 'Of course you have, Mamma!' and blessed a passing server who at that moment delivered a platter full of sweetmeats and filled our cups with wine.

Out of the corner of my eye I noticed a familiar figure approaching from the high table, where he had been speaking briefly to Queen Katherine. It was her Chancellor, Sir Robert Poyntz, and he stopped beside me to make a bow. 'How good to see you again, Lady Joan,' he said in greeting. 'And congratulations on the improvement you've made to the queen's English pronunciation.'

I stood up to return his bow with a curtsy. 'I think the king may have had something to do with her renewed efforts,

Sir Robert,' I said with a smile. 'They seem to get on remarkably well together.'

He glanced back to where he had come from. 'Yes, they do, but I think most of their private conversation is conducted in French. The advantage of her speaking more fluent English is mainly in dealing with her new household, in which I now have the honour of being promoted to vice-chamberlain.'

'Oh, it is my turn to congratulate you then. I did wonder whether Queen Elizabeth's former chamberlain might have become a little too old for the task.' The Earl of Ormond, who had held the post for the late queen, was now in his eighties but apparently still held it in an honorary capacity. 'I had expected to see Anthony here among the king's squires. Was he unable to come?'

'Yes. Instead he has sailed for Spain on a mission for the queen. She hopes he will return with a cargo of oranges and pomegranates, among other things.'

I smiled. 'Her grace will greet that with a big smile when it comes, I'm sure. Tell me, how is the young Poyntz heir?'

Sir Robert's smile almost outdid the myriad candles lighting the dais. 'Young Nicholas, yes. He is a sturdy little boy – already running about. And I've recently been told that Elizabeth expects another child in Advent.'

At this news my heart seemed to miss a beat but I tried to show pleasure to match his. 'Goodness – so Anthony has two reasons to make a quick return from Spain, one to please the queen and the other to be there for the new arrival. I shall pray for two safe deliveries.'

'Thank you.' He looked amused but gratified. 'Happily

since the last birth proved easy, Elizabeth does not seem so anxious about the next one.'

'Forgive me . . .' Over Sir Robert's shoulder, I had spotted a page heading towards us. 'Are you looking for me?'

The boy nodded. 'If you are Lady Guildford, then yes, I am; Princess Mary is asking for you.'

Abandoning the queen's new vice-chamberlain, I hurried round to the high table, where the princess was looking out for me anxiously and pushed back her chair when I arrived. 'Thank you for coming so quickly, Mother Guildford; I think my lady Margaret needs your help.'

Behind me I felt rather than saw my mother arrive. 'Is my lady ill?' She bent over the throne-like chair in which her friend seemed to be asleep. 'Margaret? Are you sleeping? It's Kate. Wake up.'

She had kept her voice low but the familiar tone obviously alerted the countess, whose eyes fluttered open. 'Kate? Have I missed Mass? I'll come now . . .' Confused, she tried to raise herself from her chair but fell back, dazzled by the noise and the bright flames of the candles on the table.

My mother dropped to her knees to take her friend's hands. 'No, there's no need to move, Margaret. You just fell asleep. You're tired. I think we should get you home.' She looked up at me. 'Joan, can you get hold of a litter, do you think? Hal might know of one.'

I nodded and turned away to look for my son, who was acting as one of the king's cupbearers during the banquet. Luckily the throne-like seats at the high table were spaced well apart so that the king and queen were not disturbed but Princess Mary rose to intercept me. 'I think it would be quicker if I speak to Sir Thomas Brandon,' she said, showing wisdom beyond her years. 'As the Master of Horse he can quickly summon a litter. You stay with Lady Vaux and bring the countess to the royal stairway. It is just through the privy door and I will meet you there.'

Before I could stop her she had sped away to the king's household reward table at the other end of the dais where the court officials were seated. Within moments, Sir Thomas had risen at Princess Mary's urgent request and they both hurried away through the privy entrance. I turned back, realising that it would need both me and my mother to support Lady Margaret from the dais without drawing attention from the crowded hall and that was something My Lady the King's Grandmother, Protector of England, definitely would not abide.

45

The Abbot's House, Westminster Abbey

June—September 1509

THE SOUND OF THUNDERING hooves and splintering lances penetrated the open window of the Abbot's House, causing the slight figure in the impressive crimson-hung bed to stir, but not to wake. There had been almost constant jousting activity on the specially built tourney ground between Westminster Hall and the abbey ever since the banquet came to an end and was followed by a rush of knights and squires to catch the remaining light of Midsummer's Day and get the coronation tournament underway. Lady Margaret had slept through it all, as she was still doing four days later. But sadly it was not a sleep of peaceful rest but of a gradual passing. Kate Vaux's lifelong friend was in the valley of the shadow of death and as I helped my mother tenderly care for the lady's failing body and watched her pray beside the bed for her thirsting soul, I feared that she too might go with her.

We had managed to help Lady Margaret walk slowly to the privy door at the back of the dais and waited at the top of the stair. Princess Mary hurried back to the banquet to explain to the king that his grandmother was weary and needed to rest and Sir Thomas Brandon appeared within minutes, ignoring the protests of the matriarch as he picked her up bodily and carried her down the steps to the waiting litter, where two brawny royal guards waited between the carrying poles. During the brief journey from the Hall to the Abbot's House, Lady Margaret had become very agitated and pulled my mother down to whisper urgently in her ear, a message I could not hear. But as we assisted her from the litter I noticed a telltale damp patch on the cushion and a similar one on the back of the countess's satin gown. I heard Kate whisper, 'There's no need to worry about that, Margaret. Let us get you to your bed. What you badly need is rest.'

I couldn't help thinking that this sudden loss of bodily control was an ominous sign and my fears were proved right only moments after we reached the abbot's chamber, when the fragile body we were supporting between us suddenly went rigid and then slumped into unconsciousness. 'Oh dear heaven, she has had a seizure, Joan!' my mother cried. 'We are going to lose her.'

However, the lady who had passed her royal blood to her son and grandson was made of sterner stuff than her tiny frame indicated. Her physician was sent for and her confessor, Bishop John Fisher, arrived as if summoned by God or angels, to minister to her soul, a task which my mother continued between his regular visits with almost constant prayers as the days passed. Although the celebrations of their marriage continued unabated, the new king and queen came daily too and on the evening of his eighteenth birthday, Thursday, 28 June, Henry was accompanied by Sir Thomas Brandon, the most senior member of the Privy Council, who with Bishop Fisher performed a short ceremony at her bedside, officially passing the sceptre of power from the sixty-six-year-old Protector of the Realm to the eighteen-year-old King of England.

Despite her apparent lack of consciousness perhaps Lady Margaret had somehow become aware that her great responsibility had now passed to the crowned king, which freed her of the burden, for as evening moved into night and Bishop Fisher still prayed at her side, her eyes suddenly opened and she reached out her hand to his. Quickly he signalled all of us from the room and in peace and privacy he administered the last rites.

Darkness fell and a full moon had risen to fill the midnight sky with its pale light when Lady Margaret Beaufort, Countess of Richmond and Derby and mother and grand-mother of kings, took her last breath with one hand on her crucifix and the other clasped in those of her oldest friend. It was then that my mother began to cry.

She cried quietly throughout all the necessary rituals of washing and dressing the dead, and did not stop as we walked to Blackfriars, leaving the lying-in-state and funeral arrangements to the officials of the royal household. For days afterwards I tried to console my mother, assuring her that her friend was now at rest and at liberty to enjoy the fruits of the exemplary life she had undoubtedly led in her latter years, but no words would bring her comfort.

'We always said we would go together,' she moaned, using the hem of her smock to blow her nose, now that her supply of kerchiefs was totally depleted. 'I have no consolation in the fact that I outlived her.'

'You have me and Hal,' I reminded her, only slightly miffed that she obviously did not consider this much compensation, 'and Nicholas and his children. You are not without family who love you, Mamma.'

When a letter arrived revealing that the king had granted her an annuity of twenty pounds I still could not entirely quench the flow of tears, hard though I tried. 'You could hire a couple of servants to look after you with that or you could rent a bigger apartment here in Blackfriars. But I'd really rather you came down to Frensham with me, at least for the rest of the summer.'

Her head shook slowly. 'I have a grave plot reserved here,' she mumbled, as if that settled the matter. She even refused when my brother Nicholas arrived to invite her to come back with him to Harrowden, the manor where she'd spent the early years of her marriage, before exile and my father's death in battle had robbed her of her happy family life and where I had imagined she would like to be buried. Eventually I hired a married couple as cook and maid, installed them in a nearby apartment in the Blackfriars enclosure and at last managed to make my return to Frensham in time for the August harvest. As fate would have it Katherine Vaux did not keep Margaret Beaufort waiting long for her company. In early September my brother sent one of his servants to fetch me back to London to attend our mother's funeral. The maid said she had found her dead in her bed, making her passage to heaven in much the same way as her friend had done but, to my everlasting regret, without any close family there to witness it or to fetch a priest for the last rites.

During the ride to London I constantly castigated myself for not insisting that she accept my offer to come to Frensham, where she would have died a comfortable death attended by at least one of her scattered family and where the Rolvenden priest would have been close by to bring her the last rites. The guilt I felt at this sorry ending for such a famously kind and beloved lady was exacerbated by the fact that when the will was read she had left the lease of her Blackfriars apartment to me. Although a London base would always be useful, I seriously wondered whether I could bear to be regularly reminded of the fact that I had not been there at my mother's deathbed.

Some consolation was to be had from another excellent grain harvest at Frensham and from frequent playtime with Mildy and Sim's two adorable babies, the second being a little girl they had flatteringly named after me. Little Joan was a tiny fairy of a babe with Sim's tow-coloured mop of hair and Mildy's bright brown eyes and I was only too happy to have her company in my arms when I took walks around the Frensham demesne. Her brother John had already earned the nickname Rave because Sim had a habit of taking him to visit the ravens at Halden and so 'Rave' had been his first word, and he learned to walk and run chasing the latest fledglings around the home wood, just as Hal had done as an infant.

While these things made a happy distraction, when I had watched the Frensham babies together I couldn't help thinking of Anthony and wondering if he, too, made time to play with his children. The information Sir Robert Poyntz had revealed, that another baby was expected in Advent, had come as a surprise and even though I had encouraged Anthony to reconcile with his wife, an evil imp of jealousy kept gnawing at my heart. It was one thing to tell Anthony to do the right thing and quite another to hear that he had done so. I told myself that these thoughts were just the result of loneliness but his parting words, 'I will always love you, Joan!', seemed to have carved themselves into my mind. That kiss in the birch wood had done more damage than I cared to acknowledge.

46

Richmond Palace

December 1509

'GOD GIVE YOU GOOD day, Lady Guildford.' I turned to a voice I did not recognise but which held faint tones of one that I did.

'Sir?' I replied with an enquiring raise of the eyebrows. A young man in a subdued but well-tailored brown fur-trimmed doublet had emerged behind me among a crowd of courtiers milling about in the Presence Chamber waiting for King Henry the Eighth and his new queen to hold an audience.

He made a courtly bow. 'Francis Poyntz at your service, my lady. I did not expect to find you here. My brother gave me to understand that you were living in Kent.'

I could place him now; he was handsome, with dark hair and features but not particularly tall, resembling his father, Sir Robert. 'You are Anthony's brother!' I exclaimed. 'We met once before here at Richmond.'

'Indeed we did, Lady Guildford, when you attended an audience with the late king. I am now a Squire of the Body to the new king, so if I can help you in any way please let me know.'

'Thank you Master Poyntz, it is always helpful to have a friend in high places.' I bowed my head in a gesture of gratitude but also to hide a frown, remembering that the younger Francis had appeared to hint that his brother and I might be involved in a liaison. 'But tell me, how are Anthony and his family?'

His expression grew solemn. 'Perhaps you have not heard. His wife Elizabeth died, soon after giving birth to their latest child – a girl called Mary. The midwife said she'd had a seizure of the lungs.'

My hands flew to my chest, where I feared my own heart might fail at this news. 'Oh dear God,' I said hoarsely, 'that is terrible news. I am so sorry to hear it.' Disturbingly I felt as if there had been a death in my own family. 'But the child lives?'

Francis nodded. 'Yes, a little girl, quite healthy I believe. Anthony has hired a wet nurse. But you look pale, Lady Guildford. Perhaps you should sit down?'

I shook my head. The flutter in my chest had receded. 'No, it was just a shock to hear these sad tidings. How is Anthony? He must have been distraught.'

'It was only last month after a slightly premature birth and of course he was devastated. After losing three of their baby sons it was a great blow to lose the mother as well. Childbirth is terribly cruel to some families, isn't it? At present he is on the high seas.'

I was not surprised to hear this. 'The sea has always been his refuge, has it not? Is it a trade venture or just a voyage of recovery?'

'A bit of both, I think. He has a cargo of iron for King Ferdinand's foundries in southern Spain but I believe he also carries letters from Queen Katherine to her father.'

'So the Poyntz family stands high in royal favour. I am pleased for you.'

'Thank you. Yes, the new regime has been good for us. And you? Are you here as a guest or have you joined the queen's household?'

'The queen has invited me for Christmas but since it was announced last month that she is pregnant I think that might have something to do with it.'

At this point the door of the Presence Chamber opened to reveal a clutch of trumpeters and two ushers moved to a clear a path to the royal dais. All chatter died as a fanfare announced the approach of King Henry and Queen Katherine.

I had not seen Katherine since Lady Margaret's death, after which she had set out with the king on a royal progress and I had returned to Frensham. The tailors and jewellers of London had hurried to glorify the new queen and for this appearance, in celebration of the end of Advent, she was wearing a loose gown of pink velvet bordered with white mink, over a cream kirtle with tight sleeves. On her head a gold coronet proclaimed her rank and under it a lace-edged French cap framed her sweet round face. Pearls and diamonds adorned her breast and rows of rubies glinted on her white leather shoes. Tall and handsome though the young king was and equally magnificently crowned and clad, all eyes were on the woman with whom he had chosen to share his throne and who was now carrying the Tudor heir. He treated her as if she was made of gossamer, holding her hand up the steps of the dais until she had settled herself in her throne and not even relinquishing it when he took his own seat beside her. He was ensuring that everyone in the room saw how precious she was to him.

It was Katherine's loyal friend and attendant, Dona Maria de Salinas, who searched me out to invite me to the queen's chamber later that afternoon. I found it full of ladies and young maids busy embroidering, their chatter almost drowning the music of a band of musicians. Clearly anticipation of all the dancing and disguising, feasting and frolicking of the Twelve Days ahead was too exciting, especially for the young ones. When the queen spotted my arrival she rose from her gilded chair close to the fire and came to greet me. It was some time since I had made a deep curtsy and I was grateful that I had put in some practice the previous evening in my luxurious guest room, which was even fitted with a Venetian looking glass.

'I am so happy to see you again, Lady Guildford.' Although her English was now quite fluent, Katherine's voice remained attractively laced with the charming lilt of her Spanish heritage. 'Come, we will retire to my closet so that we may talk more easily.'

I followed a step behind her through the chattering throng and a yeoman usher threw open the carved and polished door that led into the rest of the Queen's Lodging. This was a suite of rooms located in the main keep of the new palace, reserved entirely for the queen's own use and vaguely familiar to me from my time with Katherine's predecessor. We passed through the dining room and the solar with its mullioned south-facing oriel, before plunging into the passageway that linked the spacious bedchamber, the robing room, the bathing room and the privy. The final chamber at the far end was called the closet, where meetings could be held in secure privacy. It was furnished with a table and chairs and a ready-laid fireplace, to which the usher quickly set a flame. Once he had closed the door behind him Katherine threw her arms around me in a warm embrace.

'I have not properly thanked you for all the help you and your mother gave me before the coronation. And afterwards you both took such wonderful care of Lady Margaret on her deathbed. The king was so grateful. Tell me, how is your mother? I know she and his grandmother were very good friends.'

To my consternation a lump formed in my throat and my eyes filled with tears. I shook my head wordlessly and the queen led me to a chair. 'Oh dear, what is it, my lady? I liked your mother so much. Is she hurt or ill?'

I just managed to say, 'No, but she followed her friend to the grave a few weeks later and I was not there at her deathbed,' before burying my face in the kerchief I pulled from my skirt pocket.

Katherine took another seat. 'Oh, I am so sorry. I know exactly how you feel. I was also distraught at my mother's death but word only reached me a fortnight after it happened and I too felt terrible guilt. Come, let us share a drink and some comfits and talk together.' The queen rang a bell on the table beside me and shortly it was answered by Kat, the maker of pomegranate juice. On the tray she carried stood an enamelled Spanish jug, cups and a bowl of preserved fruits.

I managed to dry my tears and tuck the kerchief away as Kat put the tray on the table and began to pour the drinks.

'It's nice to see that familiar faces are still with you, your grace. And how is Lina? Is she still with you?'

'Oh yes. They are both maids of my chamber and the king admires their embroidery, does he not, Kat? But you may leave us now.'

Having pulled myself together I could see that the queen was anxious to broach the subject she had brought me here to discuss and as soon as the door closed again, she did so. 'I suppose you have heard that I am pregnant, Joan?'

'Oh yes, your grace! Let me congratulate you. The king must be delighted.'

A radiant smile lit her pretty round face. 'Of course he is. But as a young and virile man he expressed no surprise when I told him. He just nodded and said he knew it would not take long. He is very confident and – what is the right word? Ardent, I think. But you will know how important it is for a king to have a fertile wife, which of course his mother was.'

I thought of King Henry's father and mother in the early days of their marriage and how ecstatic he had been when she too had been able to tell him of her first pregnancy, surprisingly soon after their marriage. But the process of building a dynasty had proved troublesome and often heart-breaking for Elizabeth. I fervently hoped it would prove easier for Katherine.

Of course I said nothing of this but nodded and spoke encouraging words. 'As was her mother and your own mother, your grace. So there should be no problem between you and King Henry.'

She gave me a doubtful look. 'I rather wish he had held back longer from making it public, but it was hard enough getting him to wait until the baby quickened. My mother always kept it a secret for as long as possible; I assume because before the Moors were expelled from Aragon there was always a war to fight and she needed to continue riding. She was a warrior queen.'

'Which I take it you are not?'

She jumped on this remark. 'I would not say that. Queen Isabella always said that women were affected by war as much as men and therefore should be involved.'

I wondered what Henry would think if his new queen demanded her say in any future English council of war.

'And the king agrees,' Katherine added as if reading my mind. 'He knows I was brought up to be like her.'

After the years this widowed Spanish princess had spent being ignored and even scorned by the late king, I hoped his son would continue to support her radical views.

'However, I have not asked you here to discuss war, Joan. I know that you retired from royal service after Queen Elizabeth died but you came to my assistance for my wedding and you supported the late queen through many of her pregnancies, so I very much hope that you might lend me the benefit of your experience.'

She paused, clearly puzzled when I did not immediately express any sign of eager acceptance. She could not know that although I loved children, I did not seek to witness their arrival in this world. I had served Queen Elizabeth in this matter because she and I were friends and of similar age and but I had done it out of love and the duty I felt towards her and the Tudor cause.

'Perhaps you have other commitments,' she suggested. 'Another marriage perhaps, or family duties?'

How could I admit my justified fear of childbirth to a woman who was hoping to successfully bear the heir to the throne of England? She needed advice and support at this time, not aversion and reluctance. I could not flatly refuse her.

'I would be honoured to attend you for your lying in, your grace. However Princess Mary has asked me if I will return to Eltham Palace as her governess and I think she may already have received the king's approval for this.'

Queen Katherine looked rather irritated. 'He has not mentioned it to me but I see that you are in demand, Lady Guildford. I will discuss it with the king and perhaps we can reach a satisfactory solution that pleases us all.'

47

Westminster and Greenwich

Winter 1510

AFTER CHRISTMAS, THE KING and queen moved from Richmond to Westminster Palace, but before she took the royal barge further down the river to return to her schoolroom at Eltham, Princess Mary stayed on for a few weeks in the royal household at Queen Katherine's request.

'What with the wedding and the coronation, the king and I going off on our progress and then all of us attending the Christmas entertainments, you and I have not enjoyed much of each other's company, Mary, and a few more weeks away from your lessons will not do much harm, will it?' I overheard her say. 'You can help me sew the layette for the coming child.' Katherine was very keen that items of intimate attire should be handmade by her ladies and already took pride herself in regularly producing beautifully stitched and embroidered shirts for her husband.

Dutifully, Mary showed polite enthusiasm for this proposal but I suspected that she was rather more interested in sharing her brother's leisure activities.

Henry was an early riser and expected his advisers to adhere to his daily routine. 'I will devote all my attention to the affairs of the realm from Prime until dinner,' he had apparently told the Privy Council. 'But I will not spend hours poring over account books as my father did. That is the task of auditors and comptrollers. And afternoons are for pleasure and exercise.'

There was no hunting to be had from Westminster but he kept a full stable at his palace of Kennington and in clement weather he would command his royal barge and lead his companions across the Thames either to the tiltyard there or into the vast hunting park behind Lambeth. Otherwise he would enjoy the company of his friends, playing instruments, cards or chess, composing music or writing poetry. If he felt like dancing they would invite some of the maids of honour to join them, when I frequently accompanied them as chaperone. I found it a good opportunity to spend brief moments with Hal.

'Can you keep a secret?' he asked me one afternoon in the middle of January when an icy squall of rain had forced the young men indoors.

I gave him a motherly look. 'Must I?' I asked.

'Yes, because it will spoil a royal surprise if you do not.' His cheerful smile belied the note of warning in his voice.

'Well, if it's a royal decree I must obey, of course. What are you planning now?' Hal was in charge of amusements in the king's household.

He cast a swift glance around the room but everyone else seemed occupied one way or another, mainly squabbling over who would have the next dance with Princess Mary, by far the best dancer in the room.

'Something that you can help me with, dear mother; it is to entertain the queen.'

'In that case, how can I refuse? So, what can I do?'

He took a folded note from his purse. 'Talk to her minstrels and tell them to practise these tunes if they don't know them. But don't let the ladies know what you're doing; especially the queen.'

I took the note from him and turned my back on the room to open it up. It listed a dozen musical titles, some of which I recognised and several that I did not. 'Who is Loyal Heart?' I asked, tucking the note away in my sleeve. 'The name seems to feature quite a few times among the composers.'

Hal made a vague gesture. 'Oh, it's just a name chosen by someone who doesn't want to be recognised. Perhaps worried that the tunes won't find favour. But it's important that the musicians practise those tunes particularly. And they only have a week to learn them.'

'Why? What is happening in a week's time?'

He made that infuriating gesture of tapping his nose with his finger. 'Wait and see,' he said. 'And don't forget it's all a secret. Tell the minstrels to practise some distance away from the royal apartments and not to breathe a word to anyone.'

'Minstrels are notoriously prone to gossip. What if they let something slip?

With a gruesome smile, Hal drew his hand across his throat. 'You can put the fear of God into them, lady mother. I know you can.'

That had been on the Feast of St Agnes and, sure enough, seven days later on the eve of St Thomas Aquinas, when we were all settled in Queen Katherine's chamber making stars from cloth of gold to adorn the saint's statue in Westminster Abbey, the double doors were flung open to a chorus of fearful yells, to reveal a band of hooded and masked men dressed in Kentish green and waving dangerous-looking swords and bucklers. Queen Katherine made much of appearing terrified, abandoning her sewing and rising from her chair to confront the intruders, placing herself bravely in front of the squealing maids of honour, arms spread like a mother hen sheltering her frightened chicks.

'How dare you disturb our leisure, sirs!' she cried. 'Please leave immediately.'

The leader stepped forward and took a stubborn stance. 'Not before we have danced with your ladies.' His voice was muffled by his mask but vaguely familiar. 'It is lonely in the greenwood and we would have music and company. Surely you will not deny us one dance, your grace?' He turned to the minstrel men. 'Can you play a galliard, maestros?'

Queen Katherine held up a commanding hand. 'No, sir, we will not have holding hands and jumping. We will permit one pavane and then you must leave. You are lucky to be granted that, rude men from the forest that you are!'

It was becoming obvious that the queen was not fooled by the green disguises but more than willing to play along with the charade. She turned to her maids of honour. 'You may choose your own partners. We cannot have these inter- lopers taking over completely. I will dance with this impertinent one myself.'

'Then I demand to choose the music,' declared the hooded leader. 'Play the pavane tune by Loyal Heart minstrels, so that everyone may hear it first before we dance.'

By now all the ladies and girls were well aware that they

were in the midst of a disguising, a popular entertainment in the Tudor court. Expressions of alarm resolved into knowing smiles as we all fell silent to listen to the tune we were to dance to. When it ended the masked captain of the Green Men approached the queen and bowed.

'Will the beautiful lady deign to take my hand to lead the dance?' The pavane was a stately dance with a steady rhythm and one that all the participants knew well but the tune was new to us all and held a few surprises as it advanced, which led to some missteps and much giggling. The mood had been set for a good session of fooling about and pretending to be fooled.

I was claimed as a partner at an early stage by a well-hooded Hal but, like everyone else, preserved the secret of the Green Men and acted as if I had never met him before. 'Pray tell me who is the expert composer of this music, sir?' I asked as we stepped out in the line of dancers. 'I thought I heard the name of Loyal Heart before we started.'

'Loyal Heart is the leader,' he replied solemnly, as we both took a small hop in the dance. 'We are like Robin Hood and his Merry Men. Prepared to love and laugh and ready to dance but with sword and shield at hand.'

I glanced at the pile of their weapons, all propped against the chamber wall. 'They don't seem to be "at hand" right now, sir,' I remarked with a smile.

'Oh, those are pretend items, my lady, not serious weapons of war. We are not here to bring trouble, only to bring joy.'

Suddenly the rhythm of the music changed to the faster and more animated tempo of the galliard, confusing most of the dancers except the queen and the one who called himself Loyal Heart. Everyone moved back, leaving the floor clear, and soon we were all applauding as he began a series of leaps and spins, which grew higher and faster until they came to a flourishing end and Queen Katherine began her response moves. Her contribution was less athletic but equally dramatic, demonstrating a sequence of more elegant but similarly swift turns, accompanied by arm and hand movements, which I recognised as being of the Spanish style I had occasionally seen her execute during dance sessions at Durham Palace. I made no comment as their dance ended but concluded that she and the main Green Man might have found an opportunity for some practice. Without further ado the rest of the men took fresh partners and paraded onto the floor for the next dance, which was announced by the lead minstrel as an allemande, a mercifully slower-paced and statelier affair. As we all set off two by two in a line I noticed with a frown that Princess Mary was partnering the same tall Green Man for the second time.

By the time all the tunes on the list I'd given the minstrel leader had been played we were all out of breath and 'Loyal Heart' was calling for refreshments – or at least urgently signifying to the queen that she should do so.

'I will order ale and cakes, sir, when you and your men throw back those hoods and reveal your faces,' she retorted with determined smile.

To a chorus of feigned female gasps of amazement, the outsize green hoods were flung back to expose the red cheeks and perspiring brows of King Henry and his band of merry gentlemen of the chamber. However, rather than laughing with the other ladies and maids, my frowning gaze was fixed on young Princess Mary, laughing and teasing the partner she had been dancing with throughout the 'disguising'.

It was Charles Brandon, the king's favourite jouster and one of his best childhood friends. This would have been unimportant, had I not known that Mary had been infatuated with Charles ever since she could tell a boy from a girl and clearly still was, even though he was now a married man in his mid-twenties with two young children and a reputation as an infamous adulterer.

48

Eltham Palace

1511

'I AM SO GLAD the king insisted that you come back here to Eltham as my governess, Mother Guildford! We have been happy together here, have we not?'

With an escort following at a discreet distance behind us, Princess Mary and I were riding side by side under the bare-branched trees of the extensive Eltham hunting park. It was February, a year since I had gathered my courage and approached King Henry regarding his sister's obvious and long-standing infatuation with Charles Brandon. I'd had to wait for some time after the disguising because only a few days later Katherine had suffered a miscarriage of the much-anticipated child she had been carrying. She had been understandably distraught; especially when one of the king's physicians suggested that it might have been due to the strenuous exercise she took while dancing for over an hour with the energetic Green Men. However, Henry had dismissed that idea and, having been told that the lost foetus was female, assured her it proved that together they could successfully conceive a child and they should simply continue to enjoy that process and pray to God to grant them a son next time.

Although I had frowned at this callous proof that he considered a girl to be utterly inferior to a boy, I'd welcomed the comfort it seemed to give Katherine and his attitude was justified when their prayers were granted and a boy was born on the following New Year's Day to great public rejoicing. A month later the queen emerged from her confinement at Richmond Palace and travelled to Westminster where the king had ordered a magnificent tournament in celebration. Mary was still sulking at the fact that she had not been invited to attend.

'I am honoured to hear you say that, Princess,' I responded, 'and completely agree that it has been a very happy arrangement. And although you are not at the tournament you must be delighted that there is now a new generation of Tudors.'

She tossed her head, making her palfrey shy. 'Yes, but I'm surprised the queen was willing to leave her baby so soon, even for a tournament.'

Having had the luxury of keeping my own son by my side until he could walk, I tended to agree with her but refrained from saying so. She was a princess and already contracted to marry Charles the Fifth, Archduke of Austria and heir presumptive to the vast empire of the Hapsburg family, which included Burgundy and, eventually, Spain. He was four years younger than her, but if all went well Mary was destined to become an archduchess and probably an empress; at any event extremely unlikely to nurse her own children. 'Being both a queen and a mother is not easy,' I reminded her. 'Your own mother found that her wishes and the duties of monarchy did not always coincide.'

'My mother was a saint,' declared Mary. 'At least that's

what my brother tells me. When she died I was a little too young to understand how saints were made.' Growing impatient, she cast a glance back at our escort and shortened her reins. 'Come on, Mother Guildford! Let's shake up the guards!'

I was perfectly willing to follow her at the gallop; anything to take her mind off the tournament and Charles Brandon, the champion jouster. And after all, I too was once again missing the sight of my son Hal competing with the big names at the Westminster joust.

Sadly little Prince Henry's time in this world did not last long, for a week later his overnight nurse woke up to find him dead in his cot, his tiny swaddled body lying cold in the morning light. Mary was heartbroken and wanted to attend the funeral at Westminster Abbey but again was not invited. She was suffering sorely for daring to demonstrate her affection for a philandering adulterer but luckily she did not take it out on me for being the one who had pointed this out to the king. I was discovering that there was more of the Tudor in the beautiful princess than many people realised and formed the opinion that although Charles Brandon was the long-standing object of her affection, she also harboured a desire to be an empress and didn't want to spoil her chances.

The upshot of being confined to Eltham was that she attended to her studies and took great pride in conversing regularly with me in Latin and French and devouring volumes of European history. Beautiful and wilful she might be but she was also very bright.

Of course, Mary was not entirely without companions of her own age. Several girls of noble family came and went but none of them seemed able to form a close relationship with their royal hostess, who perhaps treated them more like servants than friends; until this year, when a girl arrived who knew how to play servant and friend, as I had done with Queen Elizabeth and Hal had done with her son. Mary Boleyn was the daughter of a knight, Sir Thomas Boleyn, an expert jouster and one of the new king's most valued diplomats, and his wife Elizabeth, who had replaced me as a lady-in-waiting to Queen Katherine. They lived at Hever Castle on the western border of the county of Kent, only a day's ride from Halden and when Richard was alive we had occasionally visited each other's homes for celebrations. As the eldest Boleyn child, this Mary had reached the stage when she was old enough to be sent away to another household to further her education and experience, so her mother's appointment to the queen's chamber had rapidly led to her daughter's arrival at Eltham Palace.

It helped that Mary Boleyn was a year or so younger than the princess, which meant that she deferred to the older girl and made sure not to outshine her, despite the fact that she was also very pretty. Neither did she object when her royal companion gave her the nickname Bolly, 'Because it is too confusing, us both having the same name.' They both liked dressing up and the Boleyns had supplied their daughter with a wardrobe of beautiful gowns and headdresses, any of which she willingly lent to Princess Mary. The two girls delighted in putting on masks and each other's clothes and swapping identities in order to tease their dancing master.

They tried the same trick on my son Hal when he made

me a visit but although he played along for a while, making effusive bows and compliments to Mary Boleyn and completely ignoring the princess until, just before she became annoyed, he changed tack and made a comical show of suddenly realising his mistake, throwing himself to his knees at her feet, calling her 'Madame Empress-in-waiting', 'Europe's darling', and his own 'Honoured Lady'.

'How could I fail to recognise the beautiful princess who presented me with a gold ring at the Christmas joust!' he protested, extending his right hand. 'See, I wear it all the time.'

This performance set both the Marys giggling and insisting that he join them at their game of indoor bowls, which of course he did. So it was not until later that evening that I learned the reason he had come to see me. We had taken our supper in the spacious suite of rooms I occupied as the princess's governess and settled down to a void of nuts and fruit and a jug of wine.

'I am finally going to war, lady mother,' he told me casually. But seeing my horrified expression he hastened to clarify. 'Well, I'll be marshalling an army of men to sail to Spain in support of the queen's father, King Ferdinand, who has pledged to help us to retrieve Guyenne from France. But my real purpose in coming to see you is to tell you that I have decided who I am going to marry.'

Now I stared at him in astonishment. Hal was not yet twenty-one and so had not officially reached his majority. Even when he did he would have few resources to support a wife and family since his half-brother Edward had inherited all the Guildford properties and what little wealth Richard had left. He had always known that he would have to make his own way in the world, although Edward and I still frequently subsidised his activities. For him marriage was not strictly an option at such a young age.

He ignored my shocked countenance. 'Her name is Margaret Bryan and you will love her, Mother. You don't know her because she only joined the queen's maids of honour last year when her mother became a lady-in-waiting but she's pretty and lively and clever. The only problem is that her father, Sir Thomas, insists that she marry a knight. The son of a knight is not good enough apparently, so I intend to come back from Guyenne with a sufficiently glorious reputation to impel the king to dub me on my return.'

I frowned, offended by a man who did not consider my son enough of a catch for his daughter. 'Bryan is not a name I'm familiar with, Hal. Who is this knight who does not consider my son good enough for his daughter?'

'They're a Hertfordshire family. She is the youngest child and her older brother is like me, a Squire of the Body to King Henry. I don't think you've met him. Margaret is only fifteen at present but she will be old enough to marry once I return from action in Spain.'

My stomach did a flip at the mention of action. I knew it was inevitable that Hal should put all his knightly training to the test on some field of battle but the prospect of losing my only child was agonising. So distracting was this thought that I almost missed Hal's next pronouncement.

'Oh, and I nearly forgot – Anthony Poyntz was back at court from some secret voyage to Spain for the queen and told me he has asked for permission to pay you a visit here at Eltham. He had some legal work to do in the city but otherwise I think he'll be hard on my horse's heels. Did you know that he lost his wife in childbed? That is one aspect of marriage that I do not like to contemplate.'

49

Eltham Palace

Spring 1511

IT WAS ONLY A morning's ride from London to Eltham, depending on how busy the traffic was on London Bridge, and so Anthony arrived at the palace just as the Marys and I were concluding a lesson in diplomatic Latin, which Mary Tudor had clearly relished but 'Bolly' had struggled to follow. We were taking our places at the high table for dinner when I spotted him walking into the Great Hall and stepped down from the dais to greet him.

'Hal told me you were coming, Anthony,' I said, as he pulled off his flat felted hat and bowed over my hand. 'You've just missed him. He left this morning to begin his recruiting drive in Kent.'

'I caught up with Hal at court. It is you I came here to see.' When he raised his head I realised with a sudden shock that he had visibly aged. His hair was still thick and blond but there were lines in the skin of his brow and although his beard was neatly trimmed, a few telltale white threads nestled among the brown.

'And it is very good to see you.' As I spoke the words I realised that they were true. Despite my outward calm my heart had leapt at the sight of him. 'However, I must supervise the princess's meal and there is a music lesson after dinner that I have to chaperone.' I gave him an apologetic smile. 'I'm sure you understand. But after that I will be free. If the weather allows I usually take a walk in the afternoon. Will you meet me in the Pleasance at the None bell?'

His reply had an ironic twist. 'We have something of a history in outdoor encounters, Joan. But I will be there.'

I pretended to ignore it. 'Meanwhile do not go hungry.' I waved to the duty steward. 'Dinner is being served, please be seated.'

I fidgeted through the music lesson, distracted by anticipation of the meeting ahead. At night my dreams were still frequently visited by memory flashes of the kiss Anthony and I had shared on our hawking excursion at Frensham and now, while the Marys plied their lutes and the French music master made Gallic exclamations, equally of delight and despair, these echoed my own feelings as I pondered the reason for Anthony's appearance. Could he really have come merely to check if I was still alive? This did not seem realistic and yet I baulked at the notion that he might still harbour feelings for me, when I had made it clear that I did not welcome them. Or had I? Were these recurrent reminders of that incident under the birch trees indicative of the fact that whatever words I had used to reject him then, they had not been genuinely felt or entirely believed?

When the music master left and the girls had wandered off to the tennis court to work off some energy I stepped outside, just as the liquid chime of the chapel bell began sounding for the afternoon Office. It was only a short walk to the Pleasance, an area of shrubs and flowerbeds, surrounded by a high hedge and laid out in a geometric pattern to encourage a gentle stroll in a fragrant setting. Only one occupant was visible at the far end, pacing slowly, studying the ground beneath his feet. For several seconds I stood and watched him, wondering whether I was occupying his mind, just as he was disturbing mine.

He had raised his head before I reached him, observing my approach with an expressionless gaze. The None bell stopped ringing. 'Perfect timing, Joan,' he said. 'I think you make a very good royal governess.'

'Is that a compliment or a criticism?' I asked.

'Neither. It is just something to say, because I don't really know why I'm here and I expect you are going to ask me.'

'Yes, I am. But first let me express my condolences on the death of your wife. I never actually met her but she was the mother of your children and you have much reason to grieve her passing.'

He pressed his hands to his temples as if struck with sudden head pain. 'And I do, believe me I do. But I also regret that we never made each other happy as husband and wife. She deserved better from me.'

'And you from her, I would suggest. But one should never speak ill of the dead. Have your sea-going adventures provided any consolation?'

Anthony lunged forward to take my arm. 'Let us walk and talk. It will ease my discomfort and prevent any wrong impressions, if anyone else should enter the Pleasance.'

I adjusted my steps to his pace. 'In that case you had better let go of me,' I said gently. He jerked his hand from my sleeve as if it had scorched him and a brief silence fell.

We took several paces before I broke it. 'Now I will ask the question. Why are you here, Anthony?'

When he turned to reply I could see that there were tears in his eyes. 'I had to find out if your feelings had altered towards me.'

I searched my mind for some innocuous reply but could not find one. 'Because your wife has died, you mean?'

'Yes.' The creases between his brows had deepened. 'Is that very crass of me?'

'No, Anthony, but it implies you thought my only objection to your declaration was the fact that you were married. Whereas perhaps you might recall that I also pointed out the considerable difference between our ages and the fact that at one time you had called me "Mother Guildford". Does that not imply that you saw me in a maternal light?'

'You think my affection for you incestuous?' He shook his head so violently that his hat fell off and he stooped down to retrieve it. When he straightened up we had both stopped walking and rising blood in his cheeks declared his irritation. 'No, Joan, nothing could be further from the truth! As a youth I saw you as my honoured lady, in the poetic tradition of the French troubadours you had encouraged me to read. But that changed completely when I grew to manhood and especially after you tended my burned arm following the Battle of Blackheath.' He hurriedly rolled up the loose sleeve of his gown and the tighter ones of his doublet and white linen shirt to expose the gnarled red scar that covered his left arm from wrist to elbow. 'I fell in love with the woman who saved my life.'

The sight of the scar inspired another surge of memory, especially of the fear I had felt that the dreadful festering wound, caused by an exploding cannon, might well go on to claim the life of a young man still three years short of his majority, who had spent much of his teenage life in our household as Richard's squire. 'But that was surely gratitude,' I protested. 'Very different from an unquenchable desire, which is what you seem to be implying.'

His eyes blazed. 'Seem to be implying!' he repeated. 'Oh no, Joan, that is what I have fought to smother all my life since. It is what I thought marriage might finally eliminate, had my parents chosen the right wife for me; one who knew how to banish the image of the one who had stolen my heart. But Elizabeth did not have a character to compare with yours. She was self-absorbed, materialistic and comparatively uneducated. All of which I could have forgiven had she had any sense of humour or zest for life.' He halted abruptly, pulling his sleeves back over the scar. 'She could not bear to look at this because I told her how I owed you my life when you commissioned a special basket-cover to allow the air to seal the wound and stop the rot from spreading.'

I gasped and put my head in my hands. 'You should not have told her that, Anthony! No bride is going to forgive her bridegroom for eulogising another woman.'

His face crumpled. 'I realise that now but it was only later that I learned how much it had poisoned our relationship. Ironically it made me treasure your memory more. I am deeply sorry, Joan, if that does not sit well with you.'

Somewhere inside me something shifted. I looked at his disconsolate expression and felt a surge of sympathy. I suspected that apart from his awkward penchant for me he was also very lonely and I had to admit that at times and in certain situations, so was I. At least we had that in common. But was there any more than that, on my side at least? There was one way to find out.

'You said earlier that we had something of a history in fresh-air encounters, so why don't you come for supper with me in my apartment this evening and we can have some civilised conversation in comfort, where it does not threaten to rain at any minute.' I glanced up at the sky, which was heavy and lowering with grey clouds.

Anthony's eyebrows rose noticeably. 'I thought you did not want anyone to get the wrong impression.'

'It was actually you who said that,' I pointed out, adding, 'the governess's apartment here consists of two chambers – one for sleeping and one for entertaining, which I often do. If you say you'll come I will ask the kitchen to send up refreshments.'

His face lit up. 'Of course I will come. Thank you for the invitation.' The first drops fell as he took my arm again. 'Come, let us race the rain to shelter.'

We went to the tennis court where the two girls were still playing. It was built out from the wall of the palace under a slate roof, so the rain did not interrupt play and we watched from the netted penthouse that ran under the wooden service slope along one side of the court. The sound of the served ball bouncing erratically off the penthouse roof into the opposite court vied with the rattle of the heavy rain on the outside tiles. Having noticed our arrival, Princess Mary immediately asked me if I would call the score. 'I cannot hear her when she calls it from the other end, Mother Guildford!'

Hearing her use the form of address he had once used

himself drew a raised eyebrow in my direction from Anthony, who also received curious glances from the two girls. When the game ended with the princess inevitably victorious, I introduced Anthony and she immediately challenged him to a game. 'But I warn you I am a good player,' she told him.

He inclined his head. 'I will bear that in mind, Princess.'

While they first refreshed themselves from the jug of ale at the back of the penthouse I asked him when he had last played a game of tennis. 'Only last week at Westminster Palace,' he admitted. 'I had brought a personal letter from the King of Aragon to deliver to Queen Katherine and found her while she was watching King Henry play. To my surprise I was honoured by a challenge from the king himself.'

Princess Mary was clearly impressed but tried not to show it. 'Henry will take on anyone,' she said. 'Who won?'

Anthony gave her a rueful grin. 'He did, I'm afraid.'

'Oh, don't be. He's a good player.' She frowned suddenly. 'You didn't let him win, did you?'

He looked astonished. 'Of course not, Princess! Any more than I shall let you win.'

Mary Boleyn was standing close beside me. 'He would be wise to do so though,' I heard her murmur.

50

Eltham Palace

Spring 1511

I HAD ENSURED THAT Anthony's saddlebags were delivered to a comfortable guest room and so when he arrived at my apartment for supper he had exchanged the sweaty shirt and hose in which he had played Princess Mary for a fashionable doublet of grey-blue silk and clean white hose. 'I'm surprised you have not been evicted from the palace,' I remarked, showing him in. 'When I went to bid goodnight to the princess she was still sulking about her defeat, claiming that it was not entirely fair since she had already played a set with Mary Boleyn.'

Anthony laughed. 'Well, she has a point. I hope she will forgive me eventually though.'

'I wouldn't rely on it. She is very like her brother in that regard.' There was a clatter of dishes from the buffet in the corner of the room where Rose was laying out the supper. 'This is Rose, my personal maid who is going to serve us.' She made a curtsy in reply to his brief nod of acknowledgement. 'You may remember her sister Mildy, who is married to my steward Sim at Frensham.'

'Ah yes, your manor is quite a family affair as I recall. Do

342

you manage to get back there from time to time?' He took the seat I indicated at the trestle and turned to make use of the bowl and towel Rose had brought for hand-washing.

'Not as often as I'd like,' I said, taking a seat opposite him and following suit, smiling up at the maid. 'I think we'll have some wine straight away, Rose, if you please. Is it fish for supper again?'

'Yes, my lady, but the cook has sent a cream sauce to go with the roasted tench, and there are leeks poached with mint.'

Anthony and I exchanged satisfied glances. When most people in the kingdom would be eating cheese and onion for supper, this was a standard Lenten menu in a royal household with access to a fishpond and a winter vegetable garden. 'We are honoured by the cream sauce,' he remarked. 'My lady is obviously held in high regard in the kitchen.'

The maid brought wine and bread and two of my silver cups and suddenly I felt that three was a crowd. 'Thank you, Rose, just bring the dishes to the table and we will serve ourselves. Then you may go.'

I poured the wine as the door closed behind her and passed a cup to Anthony. 'Rose is discreet but our conversation is private, is it not?'

'If you say so.' He waited for me to lift my cup and offered his. 'A toast,' he said. 'To truth and a happy outcome.'

Outside it had grown dark. In silence I let my gaze roam his face in the candlelight and sensed that while I did his deep blue eyes never left mine. I noticed that a fan of lines had formed in the fair skin of his cheekbones; perhaps a legacy of his recent sequence of sea voyages as well as some deeply felt regrets. He was definitely no longer the carefree impressible youth who had followed Richard into battle but a man of experience and empathy, whose countenance revealed a trail of successes and setbacks.

I touched my cup to his. 'To truth,' I said, 'and hope of a happy outcome.'

We drank but the wine was sour and disappointing. 'You portion the bread and fish,' I said, pushing back my chair. 'This wine needs help. I have some spring water in my bedchamber.'

He reached across to catch my hand. 'If you go in there, Joan, I'll be tempted to follow you, which will be dangerous because we have not established anything and my mind is reeling. Please sit down again.' His tone was soft but insistent.

I did so, without any notion of what was to come.

It was his turn to rise and he came to my side, dropping to his knee beside my chair. 'You told me once to find a mistress because you would never perform that role but I am not asking you to do that. I would be honoured, Joan, if you would agree to be my wife.'

My hand flew to my mouth. Perhaps my eyes bulged unattractively because he laughed. 'Do not look so astounded. It is not such a terrible idea, is it? You are a widow, I am a widower and I believe there is no consanguinity between us. Why should we not marry?'

I freed my mouth to speak. 'Because compared to you I am an old lady, that's why.'

He shook his head. 'Well, you don't look like one and as far as I can see you still have all your teeth.' He smiled broadly to show his own. There was a small gap just visible on one side. 'Unlike me.'

'What a romantic way to make a proposal! But if we're counting teeth, I have lost one at the back, so we're equal.'

'Oh, good. Is that a "Yes" then? Because I think there is a stone in the rushes and my knee is stinging.'

'Stand up then, foolish man! And then please sit down again and I will give you my reply when you have answered a few questions.'

In an instant he was on his feet and rubbing at his knee, giving a sigh of relief. I could see blood on his white hose. 'Oooh! That was painful. Will the interrogation hurt, too?' He limped back to his chair and sat down. 'I shall not mind as long as the answer is yes.'

The humour of the situation had restored my equilibrium. 'It is not an interrogation. I was not expecting you to ask me your question and I want to get things straight before I give you my answer.'

He gave me what I could only interpret as a naughty schoolboy look. 'Very well, madam governess. At least I have not yet heard the word "No".'

'First of all I must make it clear that if we marry I will not be giving you any more children. Not because I am too old but because the birth of Hal rendered me barren. However, it did not make me cold or passionless, if you need reassurance on that score.'

'I do not for a minute contemplate that you could be, Joan. And as you know I already have children – next?' He was teasing me now.

Nevertheless I persisted. 'Have you discussed this proposal with your parents? It occurs to me that they have an interest, since you are the heir.'

He shook his head. 'No, but they would be delighted.

My father admires you and my mother loves you – has done since you and she were children together in the household of the late king's mother. You must know that.'

'She was some years older than me, so I looked up to her then. But it's true that she has always been very kind to me.' I paused before continuing. 'There is also the matter of my royal duties; Princess Mary has no mother or father to advise her and I have promised to remain with her until her marriage. As you know she calls me Mother Guildford and I must live up to that honour.'

He raised a hand. 'Please can we stop this now? I too have duties and responsibilities that will take me away from time to time. It is the life of people in royal employ. We are both aware of these obligations. And pray do not even begin to discuss the matter of dowries and contracts. It can all be arranged and sorted. I am a lawyer after all.' His hands reached across the table and enveloped mine. 'This will not be an arranged marriage for dynastic reasons. I love you and I believe you love me. Just say yes, Joan, and we can go from there.'

He was handsome, kind, intelligent and funny. What did it matter if the world thought it a mismatch? It was our affair and none of theirs.

'Very well,' I said. 'Yes, Anthony, I will marry you.'

'God be thanked!' He heaved a great sigh and squeezed my hands.

I stood up. 'And now I will fetch the spring water because we need a toast and this wine will not do on its own.' I walked quickly into the bedchamber, leaned on the nearest bedpost, took a deep breath and exhaled, wondering whether I had just made a huge mistake.

As I picked up the jug on the nightstand I suddenly felt Anthony's presence behind me and his fingers slipped under the short veil that hung from my headdress – a recent fashion. The hairs on my neck stirred and my heart missed a beat.

I felt his lips move against my ear, his voice soft and persuasive. 'The law of the land decrees that when a man and a woman make a verbal agreement to marry, it amounts to a contract; although of course it must be confirmed by consummation.'

Carefully replacing the jug, I turned into the circle of his arms, an embrace that suddenly seemed surprisingly natural and right. 'Has a priest no part to play then?' I asked in a whisper, remembering the many family and royal weddings I had attended.

'Later,' he murmured, his lips very close to mine. 'I think we should obey the law first, don't you?'

'Yes,' I found myself saying without hesitation. 'Yes, I do.'

The bed was right there and so we used it and all the sadness and loneliness I had not realised I had been feeling surged up to fuel the release of a passion that I did not know was in me. There was laughter as we explored the fastenings of each other's apparel, exclamations of wonder as the desire for each other mounted and elation as the euphoria subsided and we appreciated just how well matched we seemed to be.

'Dear heaven, Joan,' Anthony sighed, his head cradled on my shoulder, 'when you said you were not cold and passionless I had no idea just how hot and passionate you meant you were.'

I felt my cheeks flush. 'I have to confess I surprised myself. It must be the result of years of abstinence.' I raised my other arm to run my fingers over his perspiring chest. 'What is your excuse?'

He gave a throaty laugh. 'Fear, I think – that I could not keep up with you!'

'Huh!' I tweaked the blond hairs that nestled in the dip of his ribs and his hand came up to pull mine away. Our fingers entwined and I suddenly shivered. 'It's quite difficult to pursue a hot passion when it's really quite cold. If we light the fire we could heat up the meal and enjoy our supper. Even the wine might taste better now.' I freed my hand and swung my legs over the side of the bed. 'I'll put on my chamber robe and light the fire but you'd better get dressed again. You can't sleep here because Rose will come in the morning and I don't want to start the explanations until you have made an honest woman of me.'

He grinned as he pulled on his hose. 'It is true, you know. We are legally married. You can't back out now.'

I raised a sceptical eyebrow. 'I know some good lawyers.'

'Yes, you do. You just married one.'

'I thought you'd swapped a notary's coif for a sailor's hat these days?'

'I'm a man of many hats.' Having donned his shirt, he walked over and took the sash of my chamber robe from my hands to tie it for me. Then he gave me a brief kiss and ran his fingers through my hair, which lay loose down my back. 'Why don't women wear their hair like this all the time?' he said. 'It is so beautiful.'

'Very dark hair like mine is not generally considered beautiful.' I smoothed down his springy blond curls. 'Now your colour is the height of fashion, Anthony. You should grow it longer. Don't sailors wear plaits down their back?'

He gave a snort of derision. 'That is only pirates!'

I picked up his doublet, which had been discarded on the floor in our haste, and held it out for him to slip his arms in. 'I quite fancy being married to a pirate,' I teased.

He shrugged the doublet on. 'Pirates don't tend to get married. They prefer a girl in every port.'

I stroked one of the smooth grey sleeves admiringly. 'And they don't wear doublets made of silk, I warrant.' I collected the water jug from the nightstand and handed it to him. 'I'd better stoke the fire. You pour the drinks.'

We both made our way into the other room and went about our separate tasks. It was almost as if we had already been married for years. Almost . . .

I watched the flames rise around the fresh log I had laid on the embers. 'We still need to make our vows in public, Anthony,' I reminded him. 'Shall I approach the palace chaplain?'

'We need witnesses as well.' He brought the two cups of wine and water across to the fire and handed one to me. 'Shall we wait until we can make a trip to Frensham?'

I stood up. 'Shouldn't we go to your home? Your parents need to know and I have none to tell.'

'But you have Hal and there are your stepchildren. Where is Hal now?'

'He went into Kent to recruit men for his Guyenne force. He was planning to base himself at Frensham.'

'Then that is where we should go. The priest at Rolvenden will bless our marriage and Hal and Edward can be our witnesses.' He raised his cup and we drank together. 'Meanwhile you can still be Princess Mary's "Mother Guildford".'

'I don't think she will ever call me anything else.'

PART FIVE

51

Westminster Palace

May 1511 & Spring 1512

ANTHONY AND I WERE officially married by the priest in the church at Rolvenden but Hal had already left for France and Edward was busy in the Greenwich Weaponry, supplying arms for the Spanish force, so our witnesses were Sim and Mildy Frensham. When the event was registered in the church records it was the first time they had used their married name on an official document, which pleased me greatly.

We only had a few days together before I had to return to Eltham Palace and Anthony travelled on to London to attend to the legal contract. Then he rode on to Iron Acton to tell his parents and his children. But in those few days at Frensham I felt as if I cast off years of age and anxiety and became young again. I had learned how to share love and laughter and leisure with a companion who cherished me and with whom I was rapidly becoming hopelessly enamoured. So much so that I gave no further thought as to how others might receive our union.

Wisely I told Princess Mary first and while we were alone. I was not prepared for how shocked she would be.

'But he is young and you are . . .' Her voice tailed off and her cheeks flushed. 'I cannot call you Mother Poyntz. It simply does not sound right. And he is not a knight so you are no longer a lady. Will they let you remain my governess?'

This had not even occurred to me. Then I remembered how, when I had been Queen Elizabeth's companion before her marriage, I had been told that afterwards I could not be her lady-in-waiting because I was not of high enough rank. Did the same apply to royal governesses? For a wild moment I wondered if there was a way of acquiring a knighthood for Anthony but soon discarded the idea. Only the king awarded knighthoods, unless they were made on a battlefield, and even if Mary might manage to persuade her brother to make him one, Anthony was unlikely to accept an award he had not earned himself.

'Let us not even ask, Princess,' I said hastily. 'We can remain the same as ever and we will tell no one else that I am no longer Lady Guildford.'

There was a wicked streak in Princess Mary and it now came in very useful. She gave a girlish giggle. 'Very well, Mother Guildford, it will be our secret.'

And thus it remained for the rest of my time at Eltham. Meanwhile, Anthony and I managed to make several enjoyable conjugal visits to Frensham and, with Rose also sworn to secrecy, we enjoyed a few clandestine nights at the palace and were never exposed. In March the following year, Princess Mary reached the age of sixteen and was summoned to live at court in Queen Katherine's household. I accompanied her to Westminster Palace, where I was surprised to encounter my newly arrived son, back from Spain and full of stories of royal treachery and personal glory.

The contingent of archers Hal had recruited in Kent the previous year had joined an army of fifteen hundred fighting men who set sail for Spain. But soon after arriving at Cadiz, there had been a violent confrontation between the English soldiers and the local Spanish garrison, which angered King Ferdinand, who ordered the English back home. Not satisfied with this sudden and high-handed royal command, Hal had taken it upon himself to investigate whether there might have been more to it than met the eye. He'd also had a yen to see more of Spain than the taverns of Cadiz, so he retrieved his mount from the ship's horse-lines before it sailed and rode off to Granada.

Cautious enquiries among the servants and courtiers at the magnificent Alhambra Palace revealed that King Ferdinand had arbitrarily abandoned his pledge to help England retrieve Guyenne in order to concentrate all his own troops on reclaiming another Spanish territory, which had been annexed by France and just happened to be contiguous with his own kingdom of Aragon; hence the eviction order for the English forces. When Ferdinand discovered that some random young Englishman had discovered his perfidy, he ordered him brought before him.

'But he didn't clap me in irons, as I feared he might,' Hal enthused. 'Instead he congratulated my powers of investigation and asked me how old I was. When I told him I would be twenty-one in September he told me that my own king should be proud of me and set about dubbing me a Knight of Alcantara, which is an ancient order of Spanish chivalry. So in Spain I am now Don Enrique Guildforde!

Then he gave me this brooch of the Order's insignia, some Spanish gold, and all the relevant travel passes to facilitate my return to England overland.'

I was about to shower him with congratulations but Hal assumed a gleeful expression and hastened on with his narrative. 'Now comes the best part of my traveller tales, mother. I decided to make a detour to your birthplace of Corticelle in Piedmont and what a welcome they gave me! Your uncle Fransisco Penistone is now the Signore there and he knew my name. He said I resembled my father, who had told him of my existence when he stopped in Corticelle *on his way to Jerusalem!*' He spread his hands as if he had just performed a magic trick. 'Can you believe it?'

I was dumbfounded. 'You mean Richard visited my mother's Italian family before he took ship for the Holy Land? I never knew that! Why did none of the Penistones write and tell us?'

'They didn't know that he had died in the Holy City,' Hal explained. 'The Signore was *boulversé* when I told him – we spoke in French of course because I couldn't understand their local patois – and he ordered the priests to have Masses sung for Father's soul in all the churches. Then he arranged a welcome celebration for me in the town square and there was a banquet with music and dancing! It was wonderful – I wish you had been there!'

At this point I realised that, with the English army leaving Cadiz prematurely and Hal's unscheduled Spanish wanderings, perhaps he had never received the letter about my marriage to Anthony. 'It all sounds brilliant, Hal,' I said. 'And I wish I had been there in Granada to see you knighted. But I also wish you had been here, because I don't think you can have received the letter I sent with the military courier.'

'I received no letters from England,' Hal admitted. 'What did it say?'

'It informed you that I was marrying again and regretted that you would not be in England to witness my wedding.'

His eyes widened and his chin dropped. 'You've remarried? Couldn't you have waited until my return?'

'It seems not,' I replied, a little ruffled. 'Don't you want to know who the lucky bridegroom was?'

'Not really, to be honest. I suppose it's one of those court arrangements where the queen only wants married women as her ladies-in-waiting.'

I tried to contain my disappointment at his dismissive tone and said quietly, 'I married Anthony Poyntz.'

This certainly captured his interest. 'Anthony! But he is young enough to be my brother!'

My temper fired. 'It is not a marriage of convenience, Hal. Anthony and I are a very happy couple.'

His mouth twisted in disgust, an ugly expression and not one I had ever seen on my son's face before. 'You are old enough to be his mother. It is shameful! How could you? How could he? No one has mentioned this marriage to me here at court. Have you kept it a secret out of ignominy?' There was no sign now of the gleeful, happy Hal. In seconds he had changed into a sour-faced, judgemental paterfamilias, whom I did not recognise.

'Not at all!' I protested. 'It has simply been more conven- ient for the time being. I hope we can all celebrate it together in due course, when the opportunity presents itself.'

'Edward has not mentioned it either. He must be furious

that you have sullied the Guildford name.' Hal stamped his foot and dropped the bombshell he had obviously been saving for last. 'I cannot believe that you have done this! Just at a time when, not to be outdone by King Ferdinand, King Henry has declared that he will dub me an English Knight Bachelor at the close of Parliament next week. In the name of God, Mother, I charge you not to let your dirty secret out before that and do not dare to bring your new child-bridegroom along to spoil *my* wedding. Yes, you may look surprised. Now that I am to be knighted, Sir Thomas Bryan has relented and his daughter Margaret and I are to marry in May.'

I felt like stamping my foot in return but I refrained, torn between pride at my son's achievements and fury at his besmirching of the man and the marriage that had brought me so much happiness and fulfilment. 'I congratulate you on your imminent elevation, Hal, and wish you every happiness in your marriage, which I very much hope to attend. But I will not promise anything until you have apologised for slandering my lawful and beloved husband who, like you and I, greatly honoured and admired your father and without doubt will share my pleasure at your success.'

Hal glowered at me and pursed his mouth, showing a side of himself I had never before witnessed. 'I will leave you now, Mother. I have somewhere else to be. Rest assured I will not be spreading news of your unfortunate alliance at court.'

Anthony had written to say he was delayed with business in Bristol and since I no longer held an official position that merited guest accommodation within the royal household,

I was grateful for the use of the Blackfriars apartment, which my mother had left me. Rose and I could lodge there and spend some time wandering the streets of the City of London. We frequented the markets and workshops and I enjoyed viewing a variety of goods before I selected my purchases, a luxury denied to those of us who had long lived at court and were confined to ordering only from the leading craftsmen and traders patronised by the royals.

Marriage to Anthony had not only invigorated my love life but it had also inspired me to seek some new and fashionable apparel, in brighter colours and more luxurious fabrics than I had worn in recent years as a widow. Anger and disappointment at Hal's attitude to my remarriage had prompted a desire to defy his petulant outburst and ignore his threat to deny us presence at his wedding as a couple. As far as I was concerned we would attend it together and, with at least a month left until the happy event, there was time for me to order a new gown and headdress and even acquire some striking jewellery to set it off. At least I could impress my husband, even if it infuriated my son.

When Anthony arrived from Gloucestershire and I related Hal's reaction to our marriage, to my surprise he was amused. 'The young scamp! I'll soon sort him out. How dare he upset his impeccable Mamma? Who, I might say, is looking particularly gorgeous today. Is that a new gown?'

I did a few dance steps around the cramped space of the Blackfriars chamber. 'It might be. I had to do something to while away the days without your company so I went shopping. Also I had to have something special to wear for Hal's wedding.'

He caught my hand and gave me a twirl. 'I thought you just said that we weren't welcome.'

I halted my galliard and made him a curtsy. 'But I have no intention of obeying his unwarranted denial, have you? I'm sure the bride's family would be insulted. It is taking place at her home in Hertfordshire – a place called Ashridge – and I have never been to that part of the world.'

'I think it's quite close to Berkhamsted Castle. I'll have sorted Hal out by then anyway,' Anthony declared, flopping onto the cushioned settle, where I had enjoyed so many conversations with my mother. 'I have letters to deliver to the queen so I must go to court.'

Taking a deep breath I sat down beside him and broached the subject I had been hesitating to bring up. 'We cannot keep our marriage a secret much longer, Anthony. In two days' time when the Parliament closes, Hal is to be knighted by the king in Westminster Hall. Will you have "sorted him out" by then, do you think? Or should I go alone?'

Anthony drew himself up, his face a picture of disbelief. 'A knighthood? For being part of a military fiasco in Spain? How has he managed that?'

I explained about Hal's audience with King Ferdinand over his failure to support England's attack on Guyenne and the extraordinary knighthood he had received from the Spanish king as a result. 'Apparently, King Henry was livid and vowed that no treacherous foreign king should bribe a member of his chamber in such a way, even if he is the queen's father. So he promptly arranged an English knighthood for Hal. Obviously he isn't going to turn it down, especially when it means he can marry the girl he's courted for some time.'

Anthony peered at me with narrowed eyes. 'Poor Joan, forced to witness her son being raised to knighthood, when she has squandered her own title by marrying a mere squire. How can you bear it?'

I gave a throaty chuckle and laid my hand on his knee. 'With great difficulty; so how are you going to compensate me?'

He grasped the straying hand and pulled me nearer. 'I'm sure I'll think of something,' he said.

52

Ashridge Forest, Hertfordshire

May 1512

T HE TREES OF ASHRIDGE Forest were extraordinary. Hundreds of ancient gnarled oaks competed for light with smooth-barked beeches, while beneath them a carpet of bluebells, blooming freely in the warmth of May, stretched as far as the eye could see, studded with pollarded nut trees and patches of wild garlic. This forest had been tended and harvested for centuries by the blue friars of Ashridge Abbey, who had even stocked it with fallow deer in order to tempt royalty and the nobility, who stayed at nearby Berkhamsted Castle, to come hunting there, as well as worshipping and making offerings before the Holy Blood of Christ, enshrined in a gold reliquary in the splendid abbey church.

Antony and I had joined the rest of the guests who had been invited to attend the wedding of Sir Henry Guildford and Margaret Bryan in that very church the previous day and who were now taking advantage of the clement weather and the plentiful quarry to follow the chase. And a very exclusive guest list it was, headed by King Henry himself and several companions of his Privy Chamber. The king's favourite chaplain and confessor, Thomas Wolsey, had married the couple, and the bride's three younger sisters, wearing flowery headdresses, had made lovely trainbearers. After a couple of hours of following the hounds and witnessing two satisfactory kills, we had gathered beneath what we were informed was the oldest tree in the forest for refreshments and a great deal of laughter and noisy conversation was almost drowning the spring chorus of birds singing in the canopy above.

'I gather we must now call you Mistress Poyntz.' The voice of the king made me turn in my saddle. Seen close up, I thought the sheen of his slash-sleeved cloth-of-gold doublet and the glint of diamonds in the brooch on his hat must surely have alerted every wild creature in the woods to the presence of hunting royalty. Three years after the death of his father he appeared a totally different young man.

He raised his gem-studded wine cup. 'To your health! And yours, Squire Poyntz. Congratulations to you both on your own recent marriage. Hal tells me he does not approve but I put him right. There is no reason why the bride should not be some years older than the groom. Look at my wife and I. We are well matched, are we not?'

'Unquestionably, your grace.' It was Anthony who replied, bowing his head. 'Hal is a scamp as we all know but he will soon discover the ups and downs of marriage, whereas between us we have experienced them all.'

'It is so generous of you to attend my son's nuptials, your grace,' I added. 'And it was an honour also to witness his dubbing in Westminster Hall last month. I am a proud mother as well as a happy wife.'

At this point we were interrupted by Princess Mary, who

rode up on her white mare looking outrageously beautiful in a riding outfit the colour of the bluebells, trimmed with blonde Bruges lace and a matching hat of royal blue pinned with a magnificent pearl brooch. I marvelled how she could risk such a valuable jewel on a hunting expedition but that was typical of the girl I knew so well.

'I'm sorry to hear you will not be rejoining the queen's household, Mother Guildford. This was a lovely wedding, was it not? And he has a beautiful bride. You must be so proud of your son.' She made a bow to her brother. 'You made a fine kill today, my lord. Your spear throw was magnificent; straight to the heart of the hart.'

King Henry grinned. 'Thank you, sister. And may I say that you look magnificent yourself today; every inch the archduchess. It won't be long now before we're organising your own wedding.'

The potential bride of the young Archduke Charles took her moment to surprise me. 'And when I do marry, sir, I wish Mother Guildford to be in my train, with no arguments about whether she is of enough rank.'

The king frowned. 'Do not bother me with such minutiae, Mary. Tell Thomas Wolsey. He's the man who will arrange all that. And why are you still calling Mistress Poyntz Mother Guildford?'

My wilful princess tossed her head. 'Because I always have, and always will.' She turned to me with a flash of her perfect teeth. 'Is that not so, Mother Guildford?' Before I could respond the hounds began to cry, sensing that the huntsmen were beginning to stir. 'We may be off again,' she said excitedly. 'Are you leading the hunt, Henry?'

'Of course I am!' he yelled, spurring his horse. 'This is

excellent sport. You need to earn yourself a knighthood, Poyntz!' he shouted over his shoulder.

As the royal pair cantered away, Anthony and I exchanged glances and smothered laughter. 'That's you told.' I said.

'From the horse's mouth,' he quipped.

As the mother of the groom, at the banquet following the hunt I was seated between the bride's father, Sir Thomas Bryan, and the officiating priest, Thomas Wolsey. There was a brief exchange of pleasantries about a surfeit of Thomases, after which the men decided it was best to use surnames. However, I had heard that Wolsey had recently been appointed Canon of Windsor and so I addressed him accordingly.

'It was so good of you, Canon, to come to Ashridge and marry my son,' I told him. 'Your new post must make much demand on your time.'

To my surprise he winked at me. 'Where the king goes, I go, Mistress. As his chaplain I have the care of his soul and that encompasses the soul of England.'

'But I gather that King Henry favours war with France and makes treaties with the Emperor Maximilian and even the Pope in order to curb King Louis's ambitions. How does that square with the Catholic Church's preaching of peace to all men?'

Wolsey clasped his hands and regarded me gravely. 'Unaccustomed as I am to talking policy with a lady, I will reveal to you my intention to steer my lord king towards diplomacy in the case of France. But these things have to be pursued slowly and subtly. So, madam, shall we rather discover your hopes for your very promising son? I gather that he greatly impressed King Ferdinand and even earned himself a Spanish dubbing. Do you see him following a diplomatic career?'

I called on somewhat rusty powers of courtly conversation to fashion my reply. 'He is a young man, Canon, only twenty one, with a young man's desire for glory; so I presume he hopes to find action in France, under the king's banners.'

'Ah yes. And the king is not yet even twenty. It is clear they are good friends and the thirst for battle is strong in men of that age. Jousting does not always quench their desire to prove their courage and ability. However, I hear that your son does not approve of your remarriage, Mistress. Has it been of concern for you, as it has been for him, that you will no longer be holding a position at court?'

'I see your investigation of those on the wedding guest list is comprehensive, Canon,' I said, hoping my irritation was well concealed. 'In point of fact, rather than missing the glamour and privilege of a life at court, after this I intend to ride with my husband to Gloucestershire, where his family holds substantial lands, mines iron ore and quarries stone, to say nothing of owning a fleet of Bristol trading ships of which he is commander. I expect to be fruitfully occupied tending and educating his children and running his numerous manors, in order to enable him to expand his business activities. I myself am endowed with a thriving manor in the county of Kent, which is rich in sheep and crops and woodland. As you come from a hard-working background I'm sure you appreciate the value to the kingdom of the gentry and yeomanry of England.'

Canon Thomas Wolsey put his hands together and made a series of almost silent claps. 'I understand, Mistress Poyntz, that you are very well placed. And you are right, my father was a butcher in Ipswich. I regret he is no longer with us but he was a man I greatly admired and his success in business enabled him to fund my studies from boyhood to ordination into the Church.'

He might have spoken quietly but our conversation had nevertheless drawn the attention of the man on my left; father of the bride Sir Thomas Bryan, who leaned over and spoke across me. 'Outside the Church though, Canon, there is nothing like a knighthood to guarantee a man success, is there? I've told all my daughters that I will not permit them to marry a man who has not been dubbed a knight. I realise of course that for a woman like Mistress Poyntz, a second marriage is another matter and might perhaps be made for reasons other than rank.'

I cast my gaze from side to side, noting the same expression on both men. Whatever Canon Thomas Wolsey may have said to my face, his opinion of me was in complete agreement with his host. I was a cunning, money-grabbing widow who had seduced a wealthy younger man into marriage.

53

Acton Court and Frampton Court

October 1513

AUTUMN WAS SETTING IN and Anthony had been at sea off Brittany for months, commanding a ship in King Henry's new navy, which was preventing the French fleet leaving harbour while the monarch himself waged war on land in northern France. In the rural backwaters of Gloucestershire, information from both these theatres of war was scant and I was becoming more and more concerned for my husband's safety. Only the previous year he had taken part in a major sea-battle off the coast of Brittany, when his ship, the *Sovereign*, had been dismasted and drifted helplessly into what sailors called the Angry Sea, because with reefs of treacherous hidden rocks lurking beneath waves as high as Iron Acton's church tower, they were considered the most dangerous waters in Europe. It had only been prayer and a westerly shift of wind that had saved the *Sovereign* from sinking, blowing it back towards England and a lucky sighting by a Cornish fishing vessel, which towed it to a friendly port. On his return home Anthony had made little of it but I could tell from his frequent visits to the family chapel that he felt he had plenty to thank the saints for.

So I had taken to making a daily walk from my new Gloucestershire home at the nearby manor of Frampton to the church of St James the Less in Iron Acton, where the Poyntz chapel was situated. It had been built on to the main nave by Sir Robert's father and consecrated to the Virgin Mary, as so many prayer chapels were. But there were also images of other saints installed in various guises, among them a wall painting of St Jude in his green robe and white tunic, his halo lit with the flames sent by God at Pentecost to endow the apostles with the Holy Spirit. Jude was the patron saint of lost causes, besought by people in dire distress, and that was how, as bleak winter approached, I had begun to feel.

It was two miles to the church and although I had never made a vow to do it, the daily four-mile walk there and back in all weathers had come to resemble a pilgrimage. Every time I knelt to pray for Anthony's safety I slipped another silver shilling into Jude's offertory box, feeling guilty that I had never done the same for Richard during his absences. The truth was I had never quite felt for him the all-consuming love I now felt for Anthony; the kind of love that seemed to occupy every bone in my body and every thought in my head.

As October neared its end and the leaves started to fall from the trees I had begun to lose all hope of ever seeing him alive again, believing that this time his ship must have sunk with all hands, out of sight of land or friendly vessel. In other words, it was a lost cause. October the twenty-eighth was my birthday, the day I turned fifty and the time when all women surely felt as I did, that old age was catching up with them, especially one who had experienced her fair share of ridicule for marrying a handsome younger man. It was also the feast day of St Jude so my prayers to him on that day were particularly desperate appeals for news, even of Anthony's loss if nothing else. Anything to make me believe that our impulsive marriage had really happened, that we had shared passion and affection and love and laughter during the little time we'd had together and at least here, in the shelter of the Poyntz estates, a period of family acceptance had afforded us much joy.

It had particularly come from the children, led by Margaret, Anthony's eldest, a bright little girl with a mass of her father's blond hair and a mischievous smile. For her age she was an excellent rider and adored the chestnut pony she called Matilda, which Anthony had bought for her eleventh birthday before he went off to war. The series of childhood tragedies that had dogged his first marriage meant that Margaret's brother Nicholas was only five and her sister Mary three. Although I had never met their mother I always said a prayer for her soul, at the same time as I prayed for the soul of Elizabeth of York, the queen I had served for so many years and who had also died as a result of childbirth.

Luckily for me, Anthony's surviving children had proved to be pleased to have a stepmother who made their father so happy but at present they constantly asked when he would be home and I had to show a cheerful face and keep telling them it would not be long. Of course my own son Hal still haunted my dreams and also featured in my prayers, despite the fact that I knew very well he had not forgiven me for marrying Anthony. His dutiful and proud young wife, waiting for him at home, had written to tell me that he had featured prominently in King Henry's successful sieges of towns on France's northern border and been dubbed a Knight Banneret, with the right to recruit a force of men to fight under his own banner. I was grateful for the letter and proud of Hal but it only intensified my desperate need for news of my own husband.

The road between Iron Acton and Frampton Cotterell followed the course of the River Frome, which as well as watering the big strip fields between the two manors also powered several mills on its banks. It was a well-used thoroughfare because the river wound its way down to the bridge below the manor house and on through villages and forests to the centre of Bristol where it joined the River Avon at the busy city harbour. It was from there that Anthony had sailed six months before and should be where he would come back to, if he ever did.

Sir Robert Poyntz's wife, Lady Meg, had chastised me for walking between the manors alone but I was never in any danger because in daylight there was always traffic on the road: oxcarts carrying farm produce, workers moving from field to field and women walking to market or church, like me. And then there were the horses and riders. At first I had stopped and turned every time I heard the sound of hooves behind me, or my heart beat faster when I sighted them in front, but after a while I ignored them because it was never Anthony. Now I feared a horseman was more likely to be a courier with news of his demise and I did not want to learn that from a stranger's hands.

One of the mills on the River Frome was situated at the corner of the lane that led to Frampton Court, the manor house built of local honey-coloured stone and the place I had been happy to call home until Anthony left. If the millwheel was turning I would stop to watch, because I loved the smell of fresh flour as it slid off the grinder into the brown flax bags. The miller would greet me cheerfully with, 'God's greeting, Mistress Poyntz. Has the master returned yet?', as if he was always perfectly confident that he would. This usually boosted my mood and I would shake my head and wave but on this occasion when he called out I actually replied, shouting over the sound of the millrace and the millstone grinding, 'No, Master Miller, and I fear he never will.'

I did not turn when I heard iron-shod hooves trotting behind me because I presumed they would pass by as they always did. But this time they stopped and an achingly familiar voice said, 'Oh ye of little faith!'

Gasping, I swung round and my heart almost stopped beating. Helmetless and in half-armour, with the rays of the sinking sun causing a halo around his head, Anthony sat astride a hired horse, a groom behind him on another, its panniers bursting with baggage. Anthony was smiling and holding out his arms to me. I stood stock still, hands clasped against my chest, half convinced it was just my imagination playing tricks. But his laughter broke my incredulity.

'Ha! Don't tell me you have lost the power to jump up on my horse's pommel, Lady Poyntz!' As he spoke he pulled his foot free from the stirrup and in a flash my own foot took its place and I was up in his lap, safe in his arms, our lips sealed together. When at last they parted, he moved his to my ear and whispered, 'First I long for a tub of hot fresh water to wash the salt off my skin and then a bed, with crisp linen sheets and my beloved wife beside, around and under me!' My blood stirred and my heart pounded and I sent a silent prayer of thanks to St Jude.

It wasn't until much later I registered the fact that he had called me 'Lady Poyntz' and I was proud to hear that somewhere off the port of Brest there had been another battle. The commander of the English flotilla, Sir Thomas Howard, had knighted Anthony at sea as a reward for his spectacular navigation of his nimble ship, the *Santa Maria*, in out-sailing and crippling six French fighting carracks. But in the moments after his appearance, oblivious to this elevation in rank, I felt Anthony kick the horse on and clung to his neck as it broke into a canter along the gravelled track to our home, while the fearsome total of my birthday years slid away, no longer heeded.

54

Greenwich and Abbeville, France

September–October 1514

To my beloved Mother Guildford from a desperate Princess Mary,

    The king has ordered me to marry the King of France. Help me face this awful prospect, I beg you! For all these years I have resigned myself to marrying a boy four years younger than me but at least he was going to grow into a man. Now that cunning priest Thomas Wolsey (whom the Pope has inexplicably made a cardinal!) has contrived a peace treaty with France, cancelled my chance of becoming an empress and contracted me to marry King Louis, who only last year was England's arch enemy. His queen, Anne of Brittany, only died a few months ago, having worn herself out trying to supply the male heir France demands of its monarchs. Out of fourteen children only two have survived and they are both girls, poor little mites. And I am the new bride who is supposed to work the miracle! I tried screaming at Henry that 'I will not do it!' But he said that is treason and he would send me to the Tower. Wolsey suggested that all I had to do was give King

Louis a son before he died and then I could marry whoever I liked. The 'cardinal' has an answer to everything but although he wears a red hat he is not a man of his word and I do not trust him, or my brother. However it is all arranged, I have made a proxy marriage with the French ambassador and I am to travel to France next month. Meanwhile I am at least ordering some spectacular apparel and am promised a substantial dower by my ancient suitor. Also, apart from the promise about choosing my own second marriage, I have achieved one more – that you shall be appointed my chief lady-in-waiting. So please do not refuse me, Mother Guildford, I cannot do this awful thing without you!

I am your humble student and ardent admirer and anxiously await your reply,

Mary Tudor

Written this first day of September at Westminster Palace.

Before I received this letter I had known of Wolsey's mission to make peace with France because Anthony had sailed troops to Calais to reinforce the garrison there and guard the new cardinal during his negotiations, which took place just over the border in the town of Abbeville where King Louis the Twelfth had a palace. However, I had not known about the role Princess Mary had been elected to play. A girl of eighteen to marry a man more than thirty years older, and Wolsey had thought my marriage out of kilter! If she wanted me, of course I would attend her.

My faithful Rose was to accompany me as usual when I

was on royal duty and Anthony escorted us to Greenwich Palace, where Princess Mary was making her preparations in a predictably temperamental mood, blowing sweet one minute and wilful the next. Tailors and seamstresses were working round the clock to assemble a wardrobe of clothes and accessories, patiently altering and adjusting them, according to the whims of the next Queen of France. It was very obvious that although Mary was dreading the actual marriage, she was relishing the glamour it afforded her.

When she saw me enter the chaos of the robing room, she tore herself away from the two seamstresses who were attempting to pin the changes she had demanded to an ermine trimming and darted across to greet me. 'Mother Guildford! Here you are at last. I have been worried that you would not make the journey through all the wind and rain! It is real autumn weather, is it not? Perhaps we shall not be able to cross the Channel after all!' This notion seemed to delight her for she gave a tinkling laugh. 'Look at this headgear!' She twirled in order to give me an all-round view of the jewel-trimmed cap on her head. 'Apparently this is what they are all wearing at the French court. It's called a French hood. Do you think it suits me?'

I made a deep curtsy, assuming that her proxy wedding had already endowed her with the rank of a queen. 'Certainly it does, your grace,' I said as she gestured me impatiently to rise. 'It shows your beautiful red hair to the world.' Unlike the ubiquitous English gable hood and frontlet, this new design sat back on the head, leaving the hair at the front neatly open to view.

'And the gems are spectacular, are they not? They are from a treasure trove the French king says are for my personal use. I suppose there are some advantages to becoming a queen.'

'How many attendants will be in your train, your grace? Will I be able to handle them all? And do we have any instructions as to the protocol of the French court? I believe it is somewhat different to ours.'

Mary waved her hand airily. 'I have no idea, Mother Guildford. I leave all that to you, so long as I have enough maids of honour to carry my train. Bolly will be one of them, I know that.' She pointed out Mary Boleyn across the room, who seemed to be trying to instruct a red-faced tailor about the embroidery on a bodice. 'And her sister Anne is to join us in Abbeville before the wedding. She is only thirteen but she's been trained at the Burgundian court since she was eleven so at least she ought to know how to make a royal curtsy and carry a train.'

'And where is the wedding to be, your grace?' I asked. 'Paris, I presume.'

'Apparently we are to be married in Abbeville; heaven knows why but King Louis has a palace there.' Her expression went quite bleak when she said this. 'I fear it may be because it is the nearest one to Calais and he cannot wait to get me into bed and sire his longed-for son. But that is the cross I have to bear I suppose, in order to have the glory of being Queen of France.' Her tone did not imply that she considered it a glorious thought and she leaned in to whisper in my ear. 'What will it be like, do you think, Mother Guildford, to lose my virginity to an old man of fifty-two?'

I smiled to hide my sudden realisation that the French king was only a little older than me and tried to comfort her with humour. 'Well, at least it can only happen once.

377

And if, like I did, you fall pregnant immediately you won't have to suffer his attentions for very long.'

She looked at me with a deep frown and I thought she was going to protest but in the end she nodded and remarked dryly, 'That is more or less what my beloved brother said!'

The wedding was spectacular, it did not rain and Mary looked stunning in crimson and cloth of gold, with copious trimmings of ermine to emphasise her royal pedigree. In the streets the crowds cheered her and called out to '*la belle mariée Anglaise!*' She may have dreaded meeting him at last but King Louis actually presented himself magnificently as a silver-haired fox in white satin with a feathered hat and made it clear that he admired and adored her on sight. Telltale evidences of his age were a faintly pockmarked face and a pronounced limp, caused I was informed by painfully recurring gout in his left foot. After the wedding banquet I did not let the Boleyn girls help the bride to undress for the formal bedding but was assisted by two of the older ladies who had accompanied us from England. I had thought Mary well prepared for what was to come but the next morning I found a bride with dark rings under her eyes and more blood on the sheets than I cared to note.

'I expected him once, Mother Guildford,' she said in a shaky voice. 'But he took me three times! And then he woke me before daylight and insisted on doing it again – twice! Is that normal, would you say? I'm not sure that I can walk normally.'

'There is a warm bath prepared, your grace,' I said comfortingly, wrapping her in a fur-lined chamber robe and silently cursing the goatish king, vowing to give him a piece of my mind when the opportunity arose. Well before we were admitted to the marriage chamber by the fiercely armed French guards, Louis had left his trembling bride and been escorted to his own quarters, where no doubt he was regaling his attendants with a ribald account of his night-time exploits.

Luckily when the bathing was done we discovered that the excess russet stains on the sheets were due more to the onset of the new queen's menses rather than any injury caused by over-enthusiastic marital activity. Our arrival in France had been delayed by adverse weather in the Channel and the carefully timed wedding had had to be postponed, with the result that Mary's regular monthly bleed had begun at what might now turn out to be for her a convenient date, providing a chance for her to recover from the king's rough deflowering and desperate attempts to achieve a pregnancy as soon as possible. In order to explain all this and request a more measured approach, I steeled myself to acquire an audience with 'his majesty'. I had been instructed to use this form of address because that was how the French deferred to their sovereigns. Having learned this I was fairly certain that the new queen would probably relish being called 'your majesty' and it might not be long before her status-conscious brother would want to adopt the same style.

'I hope you have come with good news, Madame Guildford.' King Louis had granted me an audience but it was in his receiving chamber in front of several dozen people, mostly his male friends and courtiers who all fell quiet when the monarch spoke. 'Is my queen readying herself for the entertainment we have arranged?'

I had sunk to my knee before his throne and he gave no

indication that I should rise. 'Her majesty is eagerly anticipating the masques and dancing, sire, and her maids are even now completing her coiffeur.'

'I am told she is a fine dancer and musician and we are all anticipating that she will demonstrate her skills, are we not, sirs?' He raised his hands and looked for confirmation from the crowd, which was supplied with loud applause and courteous cheers.

Still kneeling as I was, I noticed that the king's feet were encased in soft slippers and that his left foot was heavily padded beneath his fine grey hosen. As the acclamation died away I raised my head and dared to ask, 'Will your majesty be partnering the queen in a wedding pavane or a perhaps a bass dance, sire?'

His pocked brow wrinkled in displeasure. 'That will not be possible, madame, but I have selected the best dancers in my court to lead Queen Mary out. She will not be lacking in suitable partners, I assure you.' He shifted his bandaged foot as if it pained him.

I took pity on him and indicated the empty throne beside him. 'I'm sure she will wish to keep company with you until she absorbs the differences between your French steps and the English style of dance,' I suggested, lifting my eyes to engage his. 'Besides she is quite weary after all the excitement of the wedding – and the late night.'

The king leaned forward with an enquiring expression and beckoned me to rise and approach nearer. 'Is she now? Not ailing, I hope?'

I moved close enough to hope the assembled company would not hear what I said. 'Only the way every woman does at a certain time of the month; I am sure you understand, sire. It would perhaps be wise to refrain from visiting her bed for a few days.' I saw panic in his eyes and interpreted his fear. 'No, your majesty, she is perfectly healthy and will soon be as fruitful as Demeter again – a veritable Earth Mother. You need have no worries of that sort. But like all goddesses she is delicate and must be treated with gentleness and consideration. That is my advice.'

His mouth pursed as he digested my words and I could see that they did not chime with his thoughts. 'I will consult with my physicians,' he muttered and turned away, flapping his hand to beckon an usher. 'You may go, Madame Guildford.'

As I was escorted from the chamber I wondered if my interference would have consequences.

55

Palais des Tournelles, Paris

November 1514

WITH REMARKABLE FORETHOUGHT WE had included a jeweller among the members of Mary's train who followed her from England, so when another casket full of priceless gems arrived from the king, our man was able to use them to embellish the gown and mantle planned for the coronation. Some were also strung into long loops to adorn her gleaming red hair, which she would wear loose down her back, as if flowing from the crown she was to receive. The ceremony was to take place in the Royal Basilica at the abbey church of St Denis on the northern outskirts of Paris, where French queens were traditionally crowned and French kings were buried. Afterwards a royal procession would travel miles into and through the streets of Paris to give the people an opportunity to view their new queen.

'And the view will be worth it!' declared the besotted monarch, who had not missed a night in Mary's bed since she had been obliged to admit him once more. 'She is the most beautiful queen France has ever had!'

'And he is the most insatiable king,' Mary had muttered

darkly under her breath, as we joined his retinue on the regular Sunday parade through the palace to Mass.

The Duke of Norfolk had led a contingent of English knights and yeomen guards from England to take part in the cavalcades and processions and among them was Anthony, who had captained the *Santa Maria* to Boulogne with a company of knights, led by my son Hal, proudly sporting his new coat of arms as a Banneret. So when we moved from Abbeville into the city of Paris we were treated to an impressive demonstration of jousting in front of the magnificent Louvre Palace when a team of French knights issued a challenge to their English guests, in which Hal's contingent were victorious. The new queen presented the prizes and returned to the royal pavilion with a wide smile, almost the first I had seen since her marriage. 'I declare your son to be the most amusing man in the world, Mother Guildford!' she whispered to me as she passed by to her throne. 'If he were not a Knight of my brother's Body, I think I would steal him as my personal jester.'

I had no opportunity to respond, other than to give her a brief smile, but in fact her remarks made me sad. Hal had neither sought me out nor spoken to me since his arrival in France, yet I had seen him joking and laughing with Anthony as they waited their turn in the lists. King Henry constantly sought his company, King Ferdinand had fallen for his charm to the extent of granting him a knighthood and now Queen Mary was also apparently under the spell of my popular son. But it seemed I was permanently out of his favour; shunned for marrying a man he considered his friend, preferring to ignore the fact that he was now also his stepfather. Perhaps his own popularity had gone to his head and because I had become a laughing stock at court he had to publicly show his disapproval of me. But was I a laughing stock? If I was, why had I specifically been invited to support the new Queen of France during her marriage? Above all I could not understand why I alone should lose my son's love and approval, while he seemed to lay no blame on the man who had pursued and proposed the marriage. Anthony constantly assured me that Hal would grow up and face the facts sometime but I was losing all hope that this would ever be the case and there was a hollow place in my heart where my only flesh-and-blood child should be.

In addition I was hiding a secret from the young queen until after her coronation, because I knew it would upset her. Before we left Abbeville for Paris the king's chief minister had informed me that King Louis intended to order his queen's entire English retinue back home as soon as the celebrations ended. When I asked why he gave me a smug smile and said, 'I think you must know the reason, Madame Guildford. His majesty wishes to have his beautiful young wife to himself and finds that one of her English servants in particular wields too much influence over her.'

Having personally received a less than enthusiastic welcome from the French royal household, I was happy at the idea of returning to England but I knew that Mary would be devastated, relying on me as she did to boost her confidence and act as a cushion between her and the lecherous and domineering king. However, this less than veiled personal accusation made it perfectly obvious that it would be useless for her to ask for me to be allowed to stay.

As far as the Master of the Royal Household was concerned it also conveniently achieved the removal of Mary

Boleyn, who in the few weeks we had been in France had managed to achieve a regrettable reputation for overindulgence in wine, flirtation and, I'm sorry to say, sowing wild oats. Her youth, beauty, and lack of restraint had attracted the attentions of a number of the young squires in King Louis' retinue and resulted in violent squabbles and even a duel, which had infuriated the king. In contrast, her sister Anne, only thirteen but more discreet and intelligent, if less beautiful, had conducted herself more obligingly and modestly and come to the notice of Duchess Claude of Angoulême, who asked me whether the younger Boleyn girl might be interested in joining her attendants. Unless Queen Mary presented King Louis with the heir he so ardently pursued, Duchess Claude's husband Duke Francis would be the next King of France, so an appointment to her retinue was a prestigious one.

'Surely it should be me who goes to the Hôtel d'Angoulême, not Anne!' Bolly complained when I told them both of their separate destinations. 'I am the elder and more experienced, so it follows that Queen Mary would recommend me rather than Anne!'

'But the duchess has asked for me,' Anne said with an undisguised smirk. 'I speak better French and have more knowledge of their court ways, having served the Duchess of Burgundy. Is that not right, Lady Guildford?'

'I did not ask the duchess her reason for choosing Anne and I do not intend to, so you will return to England with the rest of us, Bolly.'

I felt sorry for the elder girl, who had been Queen Mary's attendant for several years now, but decided that I would have to ask her to use my real name once we boarded the ship home. The fact that Queen Mary insisted on calling me Mother Guildford had led to the whole English retinue using my first husband's name and the thought of leaving the uncomfortable role she had made me play in France was very attractive. I was constantly asked to convey increasingly bizarre excuses denying King Louis admission to her bed; excuses that were almost completely ignored. So the idea of being able to retire to the captain's cabin on the *Santa Maria* with my own beloved husband was becoming increasingly attractive.

Queen Mary was furious about the king's order. 'No, you cannot leave me, Mother Guildford! The others can go if they like but I cannot do without you. Besides, you are my servant, not his. I shall tell Louis I will not allow it.'

I wanted to tell her that I was perfectly willing to leave but could not bring myself to do so, hoping that it would not be necessary since I was top of the list of people the king wished to see gone. And this proved to be the case. A week later I was bidding a fond farewell to the Queen of France, only to discover that she had made one last effort to prevent my departure.

'I have written to Cardinal Wolsey,' she told me with tears in her eyes as I approached the mounting block to take to my horse, 'begging him to convince King Louis to let me keep my Mother Guildford beside me and I'm hoping there will be an answer before you leave Boulogne. So this may not be goodbye after all.'

56

Frampton Court and Acton Court

1515–20

To my relief, no reply arrived to Queen Mary's letter and I stepped onto the deck of the *Santa Maria* with a light heart. However, my hope that I might at last have a talk with Hal while travelling back to England on the ship met with disappointment. He had told Anthony he intended to ride to Calais in order to familiarise himself with England's last French bastion, on the grounds that if he was ever sent there on a diplomatic mission he would know his way around. Sadly I concluded that the real reason was that he couldn't stomach the thought of being in close company with his mother and the stepfather he preferred to regard only as a brother in arms.

As usual, Anthony made light of my misgivings and soothed my concern with a kiss. 'Look, a crossing from Calais will take Hal directly to Kent, where his pretty wife is waiting for him, that is all, Joan,' he said. 'Whereas the *Santa Maria* is headed for Portsmouth to deliver most of the knightly contingent and then we will take a leisurely cruise around Land's End to Bristol where the crew can go on leave and we can go home to Frampton Court. The demands of the new French queen must have been exhausting for you. A week or so of sea air will do you good.'

He had been right, the Channel storms had died down and despite winter being merely weeks away, our journey was made under blue skies and fair winds. After a day of nausea due to the gentle roll of the waves, I found my sea legs and set out to learn all I could about navigation and the workings of a man-o'-war. At night I also had my husband to myself in his narrow bunk in the captain's cabin. Far from finding it uncomfortable, we discovered new ways to satisfy our desire for each other and enjoy the contented sleep of lovers. We could not have been happier.

Even the news from court that reached us at Frampton in the New Year did not blight my contentment, although it would obviously have infuriated King Henry. Because, after only three months of marriage, the beautiful Queen of France was a widow, putting a premature end to the union which had been intended to seal the peace treaty between that country and England. It seemed that King Louis the Twelfth, who had sent me home for coming between him and his urgent need to father an heir to his throne, had died in the attempt; although the official cause of death was a severe attack of gout. I sent up a silent prayer of thanks to Dorothy, the patron saint of brides, asking that Mary had not been left pregnant and that King Henry would stand by his agreement that she could make her own choice of second husband.

I had an inkling about whom she would choose and it turned out that the king played into her hands, sending his great friend and favourite jouster, Charles Brandon, recently made Duke of Suffolk, to bring his sister back to England. The new duke's marriage history was already chequered, to put it mildly. He had discarded one apparently barren but richly-endowed wife twenty years his senior through the London courts for an undisclosed reason, sired two daughters with another who sadly died, then contracted to marry his nine year old orphan ward and heiress in order to accede to her title as Viscount Lisle. But this contract was swiftly annulled when he was made a duke and learned of the French queen's widowed status.

They married in secret in France before returning to face the wrath of Henry, who still seemed to believe it was his privilege to appoint his sister's next spouse and imposed an enormous fine on them, before eventually allowing them an official wedding at Greenwich Palace two months later, which Anthony and I attended.

And she was grateful. 'Oh, Mother Guildford . . .' (She still insisted on calling me that!) 'Thank you for coming. You have no idea how much I missed you after you left. King Louis was a monster in the bedroom and I prayed every day for my monthlies to come, which they did like clockwork, thank the Virgin. When his gout finally struck him down no one was more relieved than me but they still made me wait in seclusion until my next menses. I felt like a prize heifer as they hovered around waiting to see if I was pregnant. But fortunately I was not, and now I am married to Charles! Am I not lucky?'

I knew that Brandon was a rake and a womaniser and always would be but I couldn't help smiling and kissing her cheek. 'You always had a soft spot for him, didn't you? Even when you were a very young girl I remember you slipping off to watch him at bowls and tennis, when Prince Harry thought you were watching him.'

She nodded. 'You knew, of course you did. Henry was foolish to think a twenty-four-thousand-pound fine would stop us marrying!'

I blinked. 'Was it as much as that? Goodness me!'

Mary gave an airy wave. 'Oh, we won't pay all that, don't worry. Henry will forgive us when he sees how happy I am.'

That had been five years ago and since then Mary had borne Charles three children, a boy and two girls, proving that the lack of an heir to the French throne had been entirely down to King Louis. And much had happened in our lives as well. Firstly a marriage was arranged between my step-daughter Margaret and a boy called John Newton, son of a Bristol merchant who did business with Anthony and held lands in Somerset. John had come to live with us at Frampton Court, in order to finish his education alongside the girl he was to marry and to learn the military skills of knighthood.

'Just as I did with you and Richard,' Anthony explained. 'John is a little older than Margaret and we must pray they get on, although I see no reason why they should not. I'm hoping you will undertake most of the academic teaching, Joan; he can read and write but will need to learn French and Latin and the basic laws of the land, although we can also appoint tutors for that if you find it too taxing. And if you agree, we might include my youngest brother William in your classes as well. He's thirteen now and not being knightly material, he's destined for the land. My sisters' governess is incapable of keeping him in order so if you can sort him out and get some learning into him my mother would be eternally grateful.'

So I was back in the schoolroom again and quite happy to be so. Young Margaret Poyntz, like her father before her, was an apt pupil, especially when it came to languages and literature, but her betrothed, John Newton, was a different story, taking more eagerly to his military training, although at least the two got on well together. As time went by Anthony's younger children also joined the schoolroom. Even at the tender age of eight, Nicholas showed aptitude for the law and his little sister Mary, although a scatterbrain, was the beauty of the family, bearing a distinct likeness to her father, with golden hair, a classically English creamy complexion and bright blue eyes.

'Well, we won't need to offer a large dowry to get Mary married!' Anthony crowed in private, receiving an angry scowl from me, although I knew it to be true.

There were some dark clouds however. Anthony became embroiled in a legal feud with the Duke of Buckingham over the stewardship of a local hunting park and, closer to home, his mother developed a chronic weakness of the bones, which led to some crippling breakages. The first of these problems involved Anthony in numerous journeys to the Westminster law courts and the second meant that Sir Robert Poyntz asked me if I could supervise the care of his wife, which demanded frequent trips to her bedside at Acton Court to deal with nurses and physicians and to send out the necessary orders for bandages and pain-killing potions. Although Lady Meg tried hard to remain cheerful and even made occasional efforts to attend Mass and confession in the Court's small oratory, I found it heart-breaking to watch the slow deterioration of a beautiful woman, who had once been the toast of English society and successfully borne and raised ten children. With the pain I knew she frequently suffered, if she prayed secretly for the blessed release of death I would not have blamed her.

My own happiness with Anthony at Frampton was tempered by the heartache of the apparently permanent estrangement from my son. Years went by and even though his wife and I exchanged a sporadic correspondence, which sadly brought no news of a child, Hal stubbornly failed to respond to my letters to him. I knew that he spent much time as a close companion to the king and had been appointed to a rash of important court posts – Royal Standard Bearer, Master of the King's Horses, Master of Henchmen and Constable of Leeds Castle in Kent, which is where he and his wife now made their home. He had also recently been made a member of the Privy Council. I should have been immensely proud of him and of course I was, but all I really craved was a meeting and restoration to the close and loving relationship we had enjoyed together before he cut me off.

Eventually, when Anthony announced that he was summoned to Westminster to give advice to a special meeting of the Privy Council, I decided that I would go with him to London, hoping to make contact with Hal at last. Young Nicholas and Mary went to Acton Court for a while, under the supervision of the resident governess, and I made sure that all was arranged for Lady Meg's care. Since Anthony was taking John Newton with him as his squire it seemed right that our Margaret should also come. She and I could help each other with dressing in the city gowns we would take with us, so there would be no need for a maid. A few years ago my sweet and capable Rose had returned to Kent to marry a farmer's son from the Guildfords' Halden estate and was now the happy mother of a daughter.

At my mother's old apartment in the Blackfriars' enclosure we realised we were cramped for space but the monastery hospitaller was happy to rent us a spare room for Anthony and John to share. At sunset they set out to buy our dinner of pies and ale at the Saracen's Head close by. I had not been in London for some years and the following day it was a treat to watch Margaret's eyes grow round as I showed her the sights and scenes of the big city while Anthony and John attended court.

'Did you speak with Hal?' I asked Anthony quietly that evening as we settled at the fireside, while the two youngsters played chess in the window. 'How was he?'

Anthony seemed hesitant, frowning as he sipped his cup of ale. 'I think he was determined to avoid me, Joan, because he didn't enter the council chamber until just before the king arrived and then he took a seat at the other end of the table from me. After the meeting King Henry engaged him in conversation all the way out of the room. He's obviously a great royal favourite, that son of yours. Some say that he is even allowed to borrow from the royal purse to pay his gambling debts.'

I stared at him aghast. 'I hope he's not following in his father's footsteps – failing to manage his finances?'

Anthony's eyes rolled. 'No, I'd guess Hal is a bad gambler and the king is not. Either that or Hal is a good dissembler and the king likes to win.'

I gave a sigh of relief. 'Definitely the latter! Hal has always known when it is right to win and sensible to lose. So perhaps you might see him at court tomorrow?'

My husband's negative shrug was disappointing. 'I fear not,' he said. 'The meeting was quite short and afterwards a friend told me that the king and his inner circle are heading off on a hunting trip early tomorrow morning.' He reached out to take my hand and kissed it. 'I'm sorry to be the bearer of bad news. But there is some good news. Cardinal Wolsey held the floor at the meeting and revealed that the alliance between England and France is to be celebrated at a grand festival. It will be held on neutral ground just outside Calais where a vast tented camp will grow around two golden palaces, where the kings and queens of each country will meet and hold court with entertainments and banquets, and there will be contests between their subjects in sports and creative arts. We were all encouraged to offer what skills we have and I have contracted to sail the *Santa Maria* around the ports of the south coast to collect and carry as many passengers to France as she will take. The festival will be called "The Field of the Cloth of Gold" and the whole Poyntz family is invited!'

57

The Field of the Cloth of Gold,
Northern France

June 1520

WE MUSTERED OUTSIDE GUÎNES Castle on the Calais Pale, England's last bastion on European soil; a great crowd of knights and their ladies, bishops and priests, physicians, lawyers, guild masters and prominent landed gentlemen with their wives and adult children, gossiping and laughing on horseback while we waited for royalty and the nobility to emerge through the barbican.

In order to challenge the French reputation for glamour we had been encouraged to dress with style and ornament, and the two Poyntz knights, Sir Robert and Sir Anthony, had spent eye-watering amounts on fabulous cream silk doublets, lavishly embellished with gold lace, and loaded their shoulders with gold collars and chains, while my soon-to-be-married stepdaughter Margaret and I gleamed with pearls on headdress and breast, our gowns of bright blue satin lavishly trimmed with white miniver. As if to greet the rays of the summer evening sun our horses were trapped in the Poyntz livery of scarlet and gold chevrons. Silver bells made bits and bridles jangle musically as the eminent citizens of England waited impatiently to follow King Henry and Queen Katherine to the much-anticipated meeting with their French counterparts, King Francis and Queen Claude, at the Field of the Cloth of Gold.

When our royal couple appeared my heart beat faster, not particularly because they were magnificently mounted on pure white horses and entirely clad in glittering cloth of gold but because riding in the van of the following procession was Hal, proudly displaying the Guildford coat of arms of a black saltire and four black martlets on a gold ground and carrying his white staff of office as Comptroller of the Royal Household. Tears of mixed pride and sorrow filled my eyes and I had an irresistible urge to canter my horse up to his and hail him as my son.

'Woah, Joan!' Anthony laid a steadying hand on my mount's rein and brought it back into line. 'Whatever is the matter?'

I shook my head and swallowed, unable to speak, but my gaze was still fixed on Hal, so Anthony read my thoughts. 'Yes, he's a staffer now, Joan, among the highest in the pecking order. I told you that. I think it's the king's way of compensating for his father's treatment of Richard.'

I forced back my tears and nodded. 'I know, and it is only right that he should. But Hal is my son and I want him to know how proud I am and how much I love him.'

'He'll be here for the whole three-week circus, Joan. I'm sure we'll find an opportunity to meet with him.' Anthony's head suddenly jerked up, his gaze drawn to the distant view of the shallow valley where the main camp was situated. 'What is going on over there? Why are the French guards moving out in battle form?' He turned to his father. 'Is this expected, sir?'

'They seem very agitated,' Sir Robert agreed. 'Could they possibly think we're attacking?' He glanced around at King Henry's escort of a hundred yeoman guards, all bearing gleaming pole weapons and wearing new uniform jackets of red cloth of gold in honour of the occasion. In the south the sun was dipping towards the horizon and its rays glinted off the metallic fabric and the polished steel heads of the guards' halberds. As the phalanx turned the corner out of the castle to follow the snaking ceremonial road to the camp, the king's Knights of the Body riding behind him were unaware of the warlike challenge this appeared to offer, but from our viewpoint it was very evident – almost blinding in fact.

'Perhaps someone should wave a white flag?' Anthony's suggestion was made only half in jest. 'Joan, you always carry a kerchief. Is it white?'

I handed him the kerchief I always kept in the useful pocket of my skirt, while still advising caution. 'Even if they do intend to attack, surely they will realise their mistake when they draw nearer? We don't want to look foolish.'

'The road is only a winding mile and there are men out there with crossbows,' he pointed out. 'Supposing after the next bend an arbalest was to send a bolt through King Henry's head?'

'Wave the white flag!' I said hastily.

Whether it was the sight of our rather insignificant flag of peace or the realisation that what looked like an assault army quickly transpired to be the expected royal cavalcade, the French crossbowmen lowered their weapons and retreated to their original position, guarding the impressive golden reception tent where the French king and queen were waiting to greet their visitors. Thus the first of a series of hiccoughs and misunderstandings that were to plague this gathering of long-term enemies was avoided and the two royal couples were eventually observed to embrace each other enthusiastically and retreat into the gleaming marquee to begin the process of permanent pacification.

I watched Hal follow the royal party into their summit meeting and understood fully for the first time how distanced I now was from the son I had nearly died delivering and whom I loved so dearly. In the eight years since I had watched him marry and fruitlessly sought to use the occasion to achieve reconciliation, I had nursed the notion that sooner or later our wounded relationship would heal, but now that I saw him risen to such evident prominence, I began to doubt that would ever happen.

The camps for the English and French were set to either side of an extraordinary canvas and timber 'palace' with an enormous, ever-flowing wine fountain; the English to the northwest, beside the road to Guînes, and the French to the southeast, on the outskirts of the town of Ardres. Each contained hundreds of well-furnished tents, which were allocated to the attendant knights and their families and servants. Other visitors were housed within the two towns and travelled into the main arena for the various events and competitions that were staged daily. These took place in venues specially built for each activity and a series of tented banqueting houses and their vast kitchens catered for the constant flow of hungry participants and spectators. Of course the most popular spectacles were the tournaments, held regularly in a purpose-built jousting ground set about with flag-decked viewing stands and covered pavilions for the queens and their ladies.

To avoid international incidents in the tilts and melees the two kings always jousted with the same crack team, which challenged a series of English and French volunteers, but all the usual customs applied and the various knights carried the favours of their chosen ladies, leading to a series of off-stage arguments and occasional serious injury.

Early on in the festival, when Anthony was involved in an evening melee, I was dining beforehand with my step-daughter Margaret in a communal banqueting tent and encountered Lina, Queen Katherine's Moorish attendant. Carrying a trencher of meats and a beaker of wine, she slid onto the bench beside us at one of the trestles.

'I hope you remember me, Dona Guildford,' she began nervously. 'I am Queen Katalina's servant. We met when you came to teach her English.'

'Yes, you are Lina.' I smiled. 'You showed me how to make juice from pomegranate seeds but I'm afraid I have never done it since. I was Lady Guildford then but my first husband died and now I am Lady Poyntz.'

She looked troubled. 'I am sorry for your loss. I did not know.'

'There's no reason why you should. I rarely come to court nowadays. Does your friend Kat still serve Queen Katherine also?'

She shook her head. 'No, my lady. She married one of the king's musicians and they have now returned to Spain. This is why I wanted to speak to you.'

'Oh? Do you also want to return to Spain?'

'No, I like it in England. I even like all the rain!'

She laughed and I with her. 'That's good,' I said. 'And your English is excellent now.' I suddenly noticed that

Margaret was regarding Lina with a deeply puzzled expression. 'I apologise. I should have introduced my stepdaughter. This is Margaret Poyntz. Lina is one of Queen Katherine's personal attendants, Margaret. She came with her from Spain nearly twenty years ago, when she was about your age.'

Lina nodded kindly at Margaret, whose pale English cheeks were blushing furiously. 'God's greeting, Mistress Margaret. I think you may be wondering why my skin is so dark. Many English people do. It is because I was born in North Africa where we have much sun. Our colour of skin does not burn red so easily as yours.'

Margaret found her voice. 'I have read about that in books but I have never met anyone with such dark skin before. I have to protect my face when the sun shines.'

'So does Queen Katalina. She and her mother both inherited her English ancestors' colouring. I think that is why King Henry loves her so much.' Her expression suddenly clouded over. 'At least he used to.'

Margaret's eyebrows rose and I broke in with an exclamation. 'Used to! What do you mean, Lina?'

She looked distressed. 'Oh, I should not have said . . . Please do not repeat!'

I hastily intervened. 'We knew the king had taken a mistress called Bessie Blount, and we heard that a baby boy was born to her last year. But that did not appear to offend the queen overmuch. Kings tend to do that, do they not? Did King Henry perhaps take another when Bessie became pregnant? Is that what you are referring to?' Lina waved her hand negatively but her expression was irresolute. 'Mary Boleyn came here to France in Queen Mary's train,' I mused on, 'and knowing her as I do I would not be surprised if she was sharing his bed, even though she only recently married.' Then young Margaret's wide eyes made me quickly change the subject. 'But enough of that – what was it you wanted to ask me, Lina?'

The Moor girl looked relieved to broach a less hazardous subject. 'I would like to stay here in England but I do not want to ask the queen to release me until I have found some way of making a living outside the court. I hoped you could advise me how I might do that, señora.'

For a minute I studied the handsome brown face and deep dark eyes before me, thinking how beautiful she was but how very different. And as someone whose looks were also considered unusual I knew only too well what kind of insult and abuse being 'different' could attract, even within the royal court, let alone outside in the real world.

I nodded briskly and gestured to our plates of food. 'I will certainly give it some thought, Lina, but this is not the place to discuss it and our food is going cold. Shall we arrange to meet somewhere less public in a few days, when I've had a chance to consider? And don't worry, Margaret and I will keep your intentions secret.'

58

The Field of the Cloth of Gold

June 1520

O N THE FIFTH DAY of the festival it began to rain. The tents we were living in were roomy and reasonably comfortable in warm weather and the tightly woven canvas kept out wind and sun but even drizzly summer rain found its way through the stitching and formed rows of drips that were impossible to avoid. And the showers continued on and off for three days.

'Could we decamp to Calais and have a few dry nights in the captain's cabin on the *Santa Maria*?' I suggested to Anthony when we woke up under damp sheets for the third time. Oiled canvas coverlets had been distributed in order to give us some protection but the smell they gave off when they got wet was too rancid to bear.

Anthony stood up and stretched. Even after nine years of marriage I still thrilled at the sight of his taut torso under his clinging chemise. He bent down to rummage hopefully in a clothes chest for a dry one before answering my question. 'Not if you want to watch your son fighting at the king's shoulder during today's melee,' he said. 'Time to get up, Joan. I think the rain has stopped.'

I swung my legs over the bedframe. 'I had not forgotten the melee,' I told him. 'But I fear it could be a mudbath and the kings might postpone it.' Despite the rain it was not cold and yet I shivered nonetheless. 'Is there a dry smock left in there for me?' At least the clothes chests remained weather-proof.

Anthony hauled one out of the chest and threw it to me. I leapt up to catch it before it could fall onto the wet bedclothes. 'I can see one in here for Margaret, too, the sleepyhead!' he remarked. His daughter still lay in her camp bed on the other side of the tent and he drew the privacy curtain across to strip off his chemise. 'I won't need John today so the two of them can have some time together. I think there are some wrestling matches in the big sports tent.'

I quickly pulled off my wet nightgown and used it to rub some warmth into my damp body before enjoying the comfort of the dry smock. 'I think Margaret might prefer to watch the archery, especially if the sun comes out at last.'

'Yes, I would,' came a sleepy voice from the other side of the curtain. 'Who wants to watch wrestling?'

Having donned his doublet, Anthony hauled up his hose and began tying the points, moving around to my side of the bed to let me tie those at the back, while he teased her. 'Your betrothed probably does, Margaret, but I expect, like all women, you'll get your way. Ouch!'

The exclamation was a reaction to the pinch I had given him on a tender part of his anatomy. 'Don't listen to him, Margaret!' I called. 'John is a gentleman, even if your father sometimes falls short of that rank!'

John was staying in one of the squires' tents, which were

situated close to the camp stables, where they could tend their knights' precious jousting horses. Anthony finished fastening the laces of his second-best doublet, a brown padded jacket with slits in the upper arms, through which the loose white linen of his shirt could be pulled and puffed; a service I also performed. At least the fabric of his doublet was not damp, having been hanging on a clothes rail in the only dry corner of the tent.

Having tweaked his sleeves, I crossed the tent to fetch two kirtles and gowns from the same rail to carry them across to Margaret. 'What am I going to do for a dresser when you and John marry in July?' I asked her as we took turns to tie each other's laces.

After we returned to England, Anthony and I were to move into Acton Court, where I was needed to run the much larger house, and after their marriage, Margaret and John were to set up home at Frampton Court. It was an arrangement that had been agreed with Sir Robert following the death of his beloved wife earlier in the year. Her passing had been sad for all of us but it had been a relief from pain for her.

'We shall both have to find someone, or else just wear smocks all the time, Mother Joan.' Margaret giggled. 'Perhaps I shall teach John how to dress me – as well as undress me.' She whispered this in my ear so her father would not hear and I wondered how long it would be before she realised that Anthony and I already knew perfectly well how to remove each other's clothes.

It was then that I had a sudden thought and wondered whether I might manage to talk myself into Queen Katherine's pavilion during the melee.

We put on our boots to walk into the festival centre because although the sun was out and steam was rising from the grass, it had also been trodden into mud in many places under the feet of people and horses. John had joined us at our favourite dining tent, which catered for those wishing to break their fast on fresh bread and ale and scraps of meat carved from the previous day's roasts. Conscious of the rich food that was constantly on offer, Margaret and I declined the meat in the interests of not having to let out our fashionable kirtles and gowns but the two men relished sharing a dish of hot beef and mutton shreds in gravy. Perhaps conscious of her father's earlier teasing, Margaret agreed to watch a morning wrestling competition with John before also taking in an afternoon session at the butts, so Anthony and I made our way together to the tournament ground in good time to acquire a seat on one of the front benches in the knights' stand. There was much chatter among friends and relations while we waited for the trumpets to sound and we managed to squeeze up to allow Sir Robert to join us. At seventy years of age and one of the older knights at the festival, he had acquired a bed in the hospice accommodation situated in the central castle where the injuries were treated, but he was still able to enjoy most of the events.

'Are you not taking part in any of the jousting, Anthony?' he asked his son, voicing his evident surprise at seeing him among the spectators.

Anthony shook his head and grinned with relief. 'Happily not, sir; having passed my fortieth year, I am now excused such duties I'm glad to say. I do not remember you riding the tilt after forty either.'

His father nodded. 'You're right; it's a young man's game, as is the melee. But it doesn't stop me wanting to watch. I see your son is on the royal list though, Joan.'

I frowned. 'Unfortunately, yes, it is his duty really, as the king's standard bearer, but I wish he didn't have to. And of course I feel obliged to watch when I'm in the vicinity of a melee and he's in the field.'

Sir Robert smiled. 'One of the trials of motherhood I suppose,' he said.

I wished I could reveal the scope of my maternal woes but chose to keep them to myself out of a deep sense of shame. I dreaded the blast of the trumpets, which would sound the start of the melee. I whispered to Anthony that I was going to visit the latrine tent and fought my way to the exit that led under the knights' stand. Rather than relieving myself, however, I set off for the opposite side of the tournament ground where the royal pavilion stood out proudly in a flutter of flags and banners. I was far from certain that I would be able to gain access to it but told myself it was worth a try.

My luck was in because one of the yeomen guards was a man I'd known when I was a lady-in-waiting to Queen Elizabeth. He had been quite a young man then but was a greybeard now; even so he recognised me. 'I'm hoping to speak to Lina, Queen Katherine's Maid of the Chamber. Is she in the pavilion?' I asked him.

'Better still, Lady Fitzwalter is still her grace's chief lady-in-waiting. I will send a message to her that you are here and perhaps you may gain entrance.'

'Thank you, yes.' I knew Queen Elizabeth's cousin Lady Elizabeth Stafford had married Baron Fitzwalter soon after that queen's death and, having given him three sons, had now returned to the royal household as chief lady to Queen Katherine. She and I had been on first-name terms during the eventful pilgrimage Queen Elizabeth had made before her untimely death and I hoped now that the girl I had called Beth would remember me and be favourable to my suggestion.

'Joan!' she exclaimed immediately as she arrived at the pavilion entrance and grasped my hand. 'How lovely to see you. Can you come in for a while? I'm sure the queen would love to talk with you.'

'And I would love to speak with her but I want to watch the melee with my family. My son is making his first appearance as the king's standard bearer so I don't really have time for that, Beth, but it is very good to see you, too. Can we speak briefly first?' I spoke quietly, not wishing the queen to hear.

Beth nodded readily, taking my cue to keep her voice low. 'Let us step outside then and you can tell me what it is you want.'

We could hear the noise of the spectators growing as we walked around the gaily striped canvas of the royal pavilion to the quieter shelter behind. Even so, I had to raise my voice to make sure she heard. 'I have a favour to ask and you must say straight away if my request is impossible.'

'I will. All this sounds very mysterious!'

I gave a low laugh. 'It's really not! But I happened to encounter Lina, the queen's chamber woman, the other day and she indicated that she felt it was time she left royal service and made a life for herself outside. She wants to stay in England and asked me if I could recommend any way she might support herself successfully. I said I would get back to her and I'm now thinking that I might give her employment myself as I am in need of a personal maid. But I don't want to offend the queen or let her think I am stealing her chamber woman.' I drew nervously to a halt, hoping that Beth would not express shock or anger and dismiss the idea out of hand.

She did not. 'I think that might be a good plan, Joan. Lina has been very lonely and restless since her friend Kat married and went back to Spain. Working in a smaller and less formal household might be a better life for her. Perhaps she even hopes to find a marriage, like her friend. Would you like me to sound out the queen before you approach Lina?'

I nodded, raising my voice above the growing rumble of the crowd. 'You might remind her that my husband set up a regular import of pomegranates through his fleet of merchant ships. So although I no longer serve her directly, we are still of service to the royal household.'

'And I'm sure someone else can be taught how to make the juice. Leave it with me, Joan, and I'll send you an invitation to the royal pavilion if the queen is amenable.' As she spoke the sound of trumpets forced her to raise her voice. 'I'd better get back now. By the way, you might be interested to know that Lady Guildford is in the royal pavilion today, watching her husband ride with the king's standard. Shall I give her your good wishes?'

This unexpected piece of information took me aback. 'No, Beth! That is, don't mention that we have met to anyone. It might make trouble for Lina.'

Beth gave me an enquiring look but then nodded. 'Very

well, I'll hope to be in touch soon. Good to see you anyway, Joan.'

With a quick kiss on my cheek, Beth became the queen's chief lady again and swept away.

59

The Melee, the Field of the Cloth of Gold

June 1520

'I THOUGHT YOU WEREN'T coming back,' Anthony said when I had fought my way to our front-row bench again. 'That must have been the longest latrine visit ever known!'

I laughed but with little genuine mirth. 'Thanks for not sending a search party,' I said, turning my attention to the opposing teams of knights and squires, gathering at either end of the tournament ground. The two kings, fighting on the same side, took their positions in front of their men, King Francis on the right flank and King Henry on the left, nearest to us. Then my gaze suddenly set on the knight at the king's stirrup, visually anonymous in his helmet but wearing a magnificent attire and with the Tudor red, green and white standard rippling over his head in the breeze, bringing the prominent Tudor red dragon uncannily to life. 'Oh, my Lord!' I flashed a sideways glance of disbelief at Anthony.

His slow nod of the head reflected my own amazement. 'It is Hal. He makes a fine sight, does he not? That chestnut charger must have cost him dear.'

'Worth it though,' I responded. 'It sets off the king's white warhorse beautifully.'

'Yes, they certainly make an eye-catching pair.' He gave me a sideways glance. 'And a tempting target.'

'Surely the king won't lead from the front, will he? He'll command from a rear vantage point like all good generals.' I spoke more with hope than expectation.

Anthony dashed any likelihood of that with one sharp riposte. 'Not in a melee, Joan.' Then, seeing my shocked look, he tried to soften the blow. 'To balance the odds in his favour the king will want to take out the opposition's champion immediately, and you will see that the Duke of Suffolk is leading the other side.'

Across the tournament ground the tall figure of Charles Brandon, Duke of Suffolk, was unmistakeable. He had only recently been restored to favour for marrying the king's sister and was leading the challenging side, presenting an equally impressive sight. 'But Brandon won't want to risk injuring the king, will he? After all they are brothers-in-law.'

'No, he won't.'

For a moment I puzzled over why Anthony should have made such a brief matter-of-fact reply and then the significance hit me. The duke would lead the charge and threaten the king but he would swerve off at the last minute and the next target was Hal. I could see it all in my mind's eye and my heart thundered in my chest. Hal was in a scapegoat position; worse, he would be without any defence because he had one hand on his horse's reins and the other on the king's standard, carrying no shield. The irony was that I knew Charles Brandon's father William had been in exactly the same position when the imposter king, Richard of

York, had made a deadly charge at King Henry's father in the battle they now called Bosworth Field. That battle had been a famous Tudor victory and William Brandon had died a hero, taking the lance thrust in protection of his commander.

However, this was no do-or-die battle, it was a military masque, a game played with real weapons but supposedly without malice. I could not protest or make a fuss because Hal would never forgive me. I just had to sit tight on the bench and hope knightly chivalry might prevail. After all Hal Guildford and Charles Brandon had been boys together in Henry's household. I had taught all three their Latin grammar in the same schoolroom. Surely there could be no animosity between them?

Anthony must have interpreted my sudden pallor or perhaps he heard my thumping heart because he caught my hand and drew it into his under cover of my skirt, where he held it until the inevitable happened. At the first charge, Suffolk knocked Hal from his horse and received a whack from King Henry's mace for his pains. Meanwhile the melee surged on around the place where Hal had fallen and I died a hundred deaths, certain that no man could emerge alive from such a maelstrom of iron-shod hooves.

I was on my feet in an instant but Anthony still had my hand in a tight grip. 'Where are you going, Joan?' he hissed. 'Sit down. There is nothing you can do. There are attendants specifically detailed to retrieve injured men from the ground. They will have him out before you know it.'

The people seated behind us started complaining loudly that I was blocking their view but I took no notice. With a determined jerk I pulled my hand from Anthony's and pushed my way towards the exit once more, ignoring the protests from other spectators, while the clashes of sword and shield on the tournament ground drew frenzied exclamations from all around. I cared nothing for which side was winning or who else was floored; my only concern was for my loyal, headstrong, potentially dead son. When I reached the outside and forced my way through the crowd of people trying to get in I suddenly realised that Anthony was still behind me, doggedly determined to accompany me to whatever madness I intended to inflict on anyone who tried to stop me reaching Hal.

At least he knew where to go. 'The hospital is in the great castle, Joan, where my father has lodging. This way.' Now I was glad to have his hand in mine as we half-walked, half-ran, dodging in and out of the gathering crowds, who were attracted to the cheers and groans emanating from the melee. As we approached the high arched entrance to the extraordinary canvas 'castle' we saw four men in royal livery carrying a stretcher, which contained a prone figure still in his distinctive armour.

'It is Hal!' I panted, tugging at Anthony's hand to increase the pace. 'He must be alive!'

We were stopped by the guards at the entrance but they soon let us through when they saw my anguished face and heard Anthony's name and explanation, directing us to a long room with wooden pillars supporting the ceiling and rows of curtained box beds, some of which were occupied by men in various stages of illness and injury and others empty, awaiting patients. We saw the stretcher party busy at the far end easing their heavy burden onto a high platform bed that was clearly used for treatments. Behind the liveried bearers hovered a young man in half-armour, his tabard clearly showing the Guildford saltire and martlets. He was bareheaded and his face bore an anguished expression. Hal's squire, I assumed, and rushed up to him, breathless.

'I am Sir Henry's mother. I saw him fall. Is he badly hurt?'

The lad shook his head, bewildered. 'I do not know, my lady. He is still unconscious. Perhaps when we remove the armour we will be able to see.'

As the stretcher party departed, carrying Anthony's thanks and pocketing the coins he gave them, the squire moved in to begin the careful process of undoing the straps that held Hal's somewhat battered but still gleaming attire together. Meanwhile, as I turned to watch them go I noticed a lady stop the bearers to ask them a question and then come hurrying up the hospital room towards us. With some difficulty I recognised Hal's wife, Margaret, who appeared to be in a state of anguish and an early but visible stage of pregnancy.

She rushed up to me. 'Lady Poyntz! I didn't know you were here. Henry did not tell me. How is he?'

'We don't know yet. His squire is about to remove his armour but he needs to be careful. Judging by its battered state it has been much kicked and dented.' I realised when I said it I probably should not have put it so bluntly, for the expectant mother's pallor redoubled and she swayed dangerously. Had it not been for Anthony catching her she would have fallen to the floor.

At the same time there was a groan of pain from the hitherto unconscious patient as the squire lifted his head to remove the helmet. However, although there were signs of developing bruises on his left cheek and jaw, there was no evidence of any blood and the rest of his face appeared unscathed. Meanwhile, Anthony had lifted Hal's senseless wife and carried her to a spare bed nearby. I began to remove the greaves from my son's shins but found the straps hard to shift.

Anthony came to my rescue. 'Leave that to me, Joan, and see what you can do for Lady Guildford. I don't feel that it should be a man who loosens her clothing but it might be a good idea.'

Anxious though I was to assess Hal's condition, I realised that he had a point and I also noticed a monk approaching with a bloodstained apron over his friar's robe, who might object to sharing his medical duties with a woman. I drew the curtain around the bed on which Hal's wife was now coming round and sat down beside her. She began to struggle upright but I laid a steadying hand on her shoulder.

'Just wait a few minutes before you sit up,' I said. 'You may become dizzy again.' She closed her eyes and sank back onto the pillow. 'I think perhaps you are with child. Am I right?'

Her head gave a minimal nod and she raised one hand in acknowledgement. 'About five months I think,' she murmured. 'I was going to write to you when I was sure.'

'Do you feel any pain in the area?' I asked tentatively, but she indicated not. 'It is not unusual to faint at your stage. Especially when you have had a shock. Your husband is conscious now and a surgeon monk is with him so we may soon find out how badly he is wounded. It was a horrible fall but so far the signs are good. His armour may have saved his life.'

She heaved a sigh and murmured, 'It was a present from the king. Sometimes it pays to be in favour.'

'Yes, and Hal knows that as well as anyone, does he not?'

'I'd forgotten that you call him Hal,' she said, opening her eyes. 'So does the king.'

'It's a childhood nickname.' I stood up. 'You rest here for a while longer. I'll go and see how he is and let you know.'

Most of Hal's armour had been removed and stacked under the treatment bed. The monk was feeling his head and limbs and his patient shrieked when he tried to lift and bend his left knee. There was blood on the calf below it.

I looked at Anthony. 'There's a huge bruise on his chest as well,' he said quietly. 'We haven't yet tried to turn him over or sit him up but I fear there may be more bruising. He's had a real battering.'

'But he's alive!' I made the sign of the cross. 'Thank the Lord and St Michael!'

'How's the fainting lady?'

'She's fragile. I feel a bit that way myself actually. What do you think, Anthony? If there is that much bruising, might there not be internal injuries that we cannot see? Sometimes that can be worse than blood and cuts.'

He nodded. 'We can only pray that is not the case. Brother Benedict seems very used to dealing with war casualties though. In this part of France they see a great deal of them.'

I heaved yet another heavy sigh. 'War is bad enough but why must men risk themselves playing what is merely a game?'

My heartfelt question received no answer because there was a fearsome cry from the treatment bed as Hal was lifted into a sitting position and I ran behind him to look. There had been no backplate to his cuirass, only a mass of straps to keep it in place, which had been no protection against the weight and iron shoes of a warhorse. The sheet on which he had lain was black with drying blood and his back looked like beef prepared for roasting. I gasped and looked up at the monk. His face was a mask of horror.

'We will turn him over,' he said through clenched teeth, looking from Anthony to the white-faced squire. 'Please help me. And perhaps the lady could bring wine from the fountain?'

Grateful for a breath of fresh air, I did as he asked, filling a large bucket from the ever-flowing source outside the castle entrance, knowing that wine was a sovereign treatment for open wounds. When I returned, Hal had relapsed into unconsciousness, which seemed to be a blessing but might also have been a warning. The monk had brought linen waste and was gently dabbing the dark crusted blood from my son's lacerated skin. I steeled myself to look at the rest of his body but could see no sign of further injury. His hose and braies appeared undamaged and I sent up another prayer of gratitude to St Michael. My breathing became steadier.

At that moment, Hal's wife emerged from behind the curtain I had drawn around her bed and I rushed to intercept her. 'They are treating his wounds, Margaret,' I warned, 'it might be better if you did not look. You must think of your baby.'

She raised haunted eyes to mine. 'Henry was your baby once, too, Lady Poyntz. How can you bear to see his wounds?'

'I cannot bear it, but I am not with child like you. Later you can help him recover.'

She winced suddenly and clutched at her belly, only slightly rounded under her smart green robe. 'I feel his pain here,' she said in a trembling voice. 'And I fear for our child.'

60

The Field of the Cloth of Gold and the *Santa Maria*

June 1520

Poor Margaret lost her child – my grandchild – and both she and I stayed with Hal that night in the hospital wing of the castle, where I acted as nursemaid to them both. When Hal finally emerged from unconsciousness he complained that it hurt him to breathe and Brother Benedict diagnosed a broken or cracked rib. He swathed Hal's torso in bandages but also applied oil and honey to the hoof-prints on his back so that they did not stick to the wound. The monk was a taciturn man but I admired his medical knowledge, especially when he produced a salve, which he said contained the pounded leaves of arnica, obtained from his senior-house high up in the French mountains, where the plant grew. Within a few days it became clear that the bruising on Hal's face and back was receding, although he still complained that breathing was agonising.

'You cannot know what a terrible condition your back was in when they turned you over,' I told him. 'It is a miracle that you breathe at all; yet Brother Benedict says the rib should heal in only a few weeks.'

For the first time in years I received a familiar wry smile from my son and my heart leapt with joy. 'There speaks my invaluable mother – I confess I have missed your sensible advice. And I promise not to complain any more.'

'What have you got to complain about, Hal Guildford? Are they not treating you well?'

I sank into a curtsy at the sound of the king's voice. He had walked up quietly behind me and neither Hal nor I had heard him, although the rest of the patients in the hospital were agog.

'I have come to check that you are receiving good care but I see your mother is here so I assume you must be.' King Henry gestured to one of the guards who were grouped behind him and a chair was immediately procured and placed beside Hal's bed. 'Now I wish to be alone with my standard bearer,' he said, waving us all away.

His escort retreated to the hospital entrance and I removed myself to my own cubicle and closed the curtain. I could hear nothing of the conversation that passed between them but occasionally I heard a burst of laughter and wondered how Hal could bear the pain of his own wit. After a short while there was the sound of a chair scraping back and King Henry called out to me. 'Lady Poyntz, please join us.'

He was standing beside Hal's bed when I emerged from my curtain and I made another curtsy, which he waved away. 'You have not forgotten your court etiquette I see, my lady. The queen sends greetings to you. She misses your company.'

'That is kind of her but she is well served, I think. I hope she is in good health, and you too of course, your grace.'

'We are both well, I thank you. I gather your husband has offered to sail Hal back to Kent when he is able to travel. Will you tell Sir Anthony I give you all permission to leave this magnificent festival early, but I am hoping your son will be well enough to join me in Calais in July to meet with Emperor Charles. Hal of course believes he will heal in no time and I pray he is right, for his company always seems to make these diplomatic sessions not only bearable but also successful.'

The king turned to leave but then turned back with a second thought. 'By the way, Lady Poyntz, I have told Hal that I insist he drop this foolish idea of his that your marriage to Sir Anthony is unacceptable. I have told him that I consider it admirable and if it is good enough for his king, it is good enough for him. I hope that will settle the matter.'

I gave him a smile, grateful for his royal endorsement of my marital position but secretly happy that Hal seemed to have become more or less reconciled to it anyway, even before King Henry had issued his ultimatum. 'I'm sure it will, your grace, and I, too, hope Hal will make a swift recovery.'

As the king walked away I wondered sadly whether he had offered any apology to his standard bearer for being the cause of his horrifying brush with death, and indirectly of the loss of his potential offspring and my longed-for grandchild. Presently, when I found their tent, Hal's poor wife was so prostrated by her miscarriage that she just sat brooding, attended only by a woman called Mistress Pearce, who I discovered had been her childhood nurse. I resolved to consult Hal about this person when he was fully recovered, because I suspected that her dragon-like presence in their household might be contributing to their lack of success in having a family.

Later, when I told Anthony of the royal approval of our marriage he laughed and said, 'The king wants me under orders, that's why he's given us his blessing. I am to be made Vice Admiral of his expanding navy.'

'Oh!' I could not control my sudden anxiety at this news. 'I know I should congratulate you, my love, and I do, of course. But if this means you'll be away at sea for long periods I cannot pretend that I will not miss you.'

Another snort of laughter greeted this speech. 'That is a double negative from one who taught the king his grammar! Nor is it accurate. Being an admiral does not mean I will spend months and years at sea, unless we go to war. It means I will be sitting at a desk in Bristol organising ships and their crews and commissioning new vessels for the fleet. And when I am summoned to court I will be taking you with me, expecting you to have Acton Court running like an oiled cartwheel, without your presence being required all the time.'

He was escorting me back from the castle hospital to our tent and I couldn't resist tucking my arm in his and planting a kiss on his cheek in gratitude for this reassurance, which attracted a double whistle from behind us. Anthony's quick turn to remonstrate with the perpetrator altered his frown of disapproval. 'Cheeky!' he called instead and caused us to halt, as his daughter and her betrothed drew alongside. 'What have you two been doing?'

John's face assumed a henpecked expression. 'Watching the archery. It was Margaret's turn to choose.'

Enthusiasm coloured her response. 'And it was very

exciting. The two kings were competing against each other using the same English longbow and King Henry won because the French king couldn't even pull the bowstring back far enough to get the arrow to the target!'

'A-ha! Well, the French king is younger and much slighter in build.' Anthony looked amused. 'That must have been a payback competition, because I was in the wrestling tent earlier when King Henry challenged King Francis to a bout and the French king floored him easily, despite Henry's apparently superior weight. He was very put out, so he'll be glad to have evened the score.'

I added my news. 'Before all that, though, he paid a visit to the hospital to check on Hal, who is still in much pain but refusing to let it show. And the king told me that we all have permission to leave on the *Santa Maria* when Hal is well enough to travel. So in the meanwhile you'd better make sure you take in all the sights and sports.' I made a point of not telling the young couple about Margaret Guildford's miscarriage, hoping she might have recovered somewhat from her miseries by the time we all boarded the ship. There seemed to be no point in burdening a young couple on the brink of building a future together with the possible setbacks they might encounter on the way.

The following day, after visiting Hal, I went again to the royal pavilion when I knew the queen would be presenting the prizes at another jousting competition and sent a note in to Lina to meet me once again in the dining tent after it finished. This time, Anthony came with me, after I had told him of my hope to employ the Moor girl.

Lina looked nervous as she sat down on the bench opposite us. 'Lady Fitzwalter told me you had spoken with her but I did not know where to find you until your note reached me today. I was afraid you had decided you couldn't help me.'

I reassured her, explaining about Hal's injury and my need to support his wife. 'But I certainly want to help you, Lina, and hope you like the offer I am about to make. This is my husband, Sir Anthony Poyntz, who may be able to help me persuade you to accept it.'

Lina made a somewhat comical sitting-down bob to acknowledge Anthony, who nodded and smiled in return. I continued: 'It so happens that I am looking for a personal maid, and wonder if the position might suit you. I know that you would be perfect for the job but I wonder whether you might find it difficult to swap the action and glamour of the royal court for the quieter life of a manor in the countryside.'

I went on to describe the location of Acton Court, the number of servants we employed, the number and age of the children in the household, and the size of the manor demesne, while she listened intently but gave no indication of approval or disapproval.

When I came to a halt, she said, 'You really want me to live in this lovely household? And you would pay me money to work there?'

Anthony broke in then. 'Well, of course we would pay you money, Lina! What made you think we wouldn't?'

Her brows rose in surprise. 'Many think those people with black skin will work for nothing. They do where I come from anyway, and Princess Katherine could not afford to pay us until she became the queen. We had food and a place to sleep, that was all.'

'Surely you are paid now, though?' I said, quite shocked. 'There are set fees for the various ranks of royal service, I know that.'

'Oh yes, I am paid the same as the other chambermaids. But I like the sound of living in a household that does not move around all the time and allows more of a variety than just scrubbing and sweeping and obeying summonses.' She smiled then. 'Oh, and emptying close-stools.'

Anthony laughed. 'We have latrines at Acton Court and pay men to empty the cisterns. That is not considered women's work. And there are occasional trips arranged to visit Bristol, which is a city quite close to our home, for those who like to spend some of their well-earned money. You might be surprised to know that there are quite a few people living in Bristol who have skin as dark and much darker than yours, Lina, because it is a busy port where ships dock that come from as far away as the Gold Coast of West Africa.'

Lina looked puzzled rather than surprised to hear this so I brought the talk back to the main question. 'So, does a job with us at Acton Court sound interesting to you, Lina? Please tell us now or at least let us know before we leave in a few days. I know it will be a big decision for you to make but we are leaving early to take my injured son home to recover. Perhaps you might be able to sail with us.'

She stood up, moved off the bench and made a curtsy. 'I would say yes right now, my lady, but my main worry is telling the queen that I wish to leave. She has been very kind to me. It will not be easy.'

I looked at her kindly. 'Yes, I understand but I will hope

that you can come with us when we go. You would be very welcome at Acton Court.'

A week later we were all on the *Santa Maria*, waiting in Boulogne harbour for the high tide, eyeing the weather and hoping the dark clouds in the evening sky would clear by morning. In the days before we left the camp I had received a note from Beth Fitzwalter in her capacity as chief lady-in-waiting, informing me that although Queen Katherine regretted her servant Lina's wish to leave, she would not stand in her way. The bearer of the note was Lina herself, accompanied by one of the queen's pages carrying her box of belongings. Perhaps as a consequence of luring her maid away, I had not received the promised invitation to the queen's pavilion.

Anthony and I relinquished the relatively spacious captain's cabin to Hal and his wife and took a smaller one, which irritated the daunting Mistress Pearce, who it seemed was mostly used to sleeping in the same room as her mistress but had to be content with sharing an even smaller midshipmen's cabin with Lina. 'She is not English, my lady,' she complained, registering loud gap-toothed disapproval. 'Where is she from and why is her skin so dark?'

'She is from North Africa, mistress, and she came to England from Spain with Queen Katherine. She has served the queen faithfully for nearly twenty years and will join our household when we reach home. Her English is excellent so you should have no difficulty conversing with her and I think you will find her very interesting to talk to.' All I got in response was a loud sniff.

Hal was now able to hobble along with a stick, saving

his bruised knee, which Brother Benedict had assured him would recover its strength in due course, so while Mistress Pearce and Margaret were preparing the captain's cabin for the night I was able to bring two chairs and a lantern from the officers' dining cabin and sit with my son on the main deck as evening drew in, determined to snatch the chance for a private talk before he disembarked at Dover.

It began with pleasantries and platitudes. How did he enjoy living at Leeds Castle? How long did it take him to ride to London to wait on the king? Did he socialise with Edward Guildford at Halden Hall? Might he ever have time to ride down to Frensham Manor to check on the situation there for me? It was a while before the conversation touched on his marriage.

'Castles can be damp and soulless places, can't they? And Leeds is surrounded by a moat and a lake; does Margaret feel lonely and cut off when you're away?'

This question gave him food for thought and he took a while to ponder his answer, which I found as revealing as what he eventually said. 'Why do you ask, Mamma? Has she mentioned it to you?'

'No, Hal, she hasn't. But she seems very subdued, which perhaps isn't surprising after losing the child. What I do think is that she's too reliant on her maid, Mistress Pearce. I believe she was her nurse as a child.'

Hal suddenly became animated. 'That woman is a dreadful nuisance! I've told Margaret to dismiss her several times but she never seems able to do it.'

I took the plunge and pursued the subject of children. 'Does she actually want children or is she frightened of giving birth, perhaps?'

He looked puzzled. 'All women are frightened of that, are they not? My father told me how you nearly died giving birth to me and never conceived again as a result.'

'Did he? I didn't know that. I wonder if Mistress Pearce provokes that fear? Perhaps Margaret would be better employing a younger and more light-hearted girl as a maid. Someone she could laugh and joke with rather than a sour-faced old nurse who treats her like a child. I must admit I wouldn't like to spend much time with Mistress Pearce. She's a dragon.'

This time, Hal gave what I can only describe as a guffaw. 'I suddenly recall that tone of your voice and I can't imagine why I ever stopped loving you, Mamma! I'm so sorry; I've been such a fool. Of course I'll go down and see how everything is at Frensham and let you know – I just need to get this knee better so I can mount my horse.'

'There's no great hurry, my son.' On the spur of the moment I rose from my chair and put my arms around him. It felt like the first hug we had ever shared, when he had stumbled up to me on shaky independent limbs and hugged my leg. Tears sprang to my closed eyes.

'Do you want to know what straightened out my thinking?' he asked in a voice muffled by my embrace. 'It was seeing you and Anthony together during the festival. You didn't know that I watched you going about together several times, and you always looked happy – always arm in arm and mostly laughing. Yours looked like a marriage so different from my own. I don't remember the last time Margaret and I laughed together.'

I released him and sat back down. Then I leaned forward and took both his hands in mine. 'The only thing that made me sad was lack of contact with you, Hal. I have missed your cheerful attitude to life and I want to see it again. Your Margaret is still the sweet girl you married. Just get rid of that dragon-woman who drags her down. Pension her off or something, but do it gently.'

'Well, this is a sight I've long wanted to see!' Anthony strolled up to our secluded corner of the deck. In the west the sky had turned to crimson and gold. 'Mother and son on speaking terms again.' He hunkered down to our level, smiling and quietly clapping his hands, then put an arm around each of us. 'I have sent our squires out to the town for some supper meats and there is wine in the jug. Shall we all celebrate together at the captain's table?'

61

Acton Court

Autumn 1520

'THE DOCTOR SAYS HIS heart is failing.' Anthony returned solemn-faced from seeing the physician off back to Bristol after he had examined his ailing father. 'He has not long to live.'

Sir Robert Poyntz had spent some time in London fulfilling his duties as Chamberlain to Queen Katherine after accompanying her back from the Field of the Cloth of Gold. Luckily, Anthony's younger brother Francis had accompanied him on the road home to Acton Court because towards the end of the journey he suffered a minor seizure and had to be brought the last few miles in a horse-drawn litter. Since then he had been largely bed-bound with only occasional outings into the gardens on sunny days.

'Father wants me to call his lawyer from Bristol to update his will.' With a sigh, Anthony sat down beside me on the long settle in the great hall. 'I suppose he has had what they call a good life but Acton Court will seem strange without his presence. He has been the lord of this manor for over fifty years.'

I laid down the embroidery it was my habit to sew beside

the fire now that the evenings were drawing in. The shutters were closed and a dozen candles burned to light the dark corners of the mansion's great hall but shadows still filled the rafters. 'Goodness! I didn't know he had inherited at such a young age. He can't have been twenty.'

'No – he was nineteen but already a squire to King Edward of York, after he took the throne back from the Lancastrians at the Battle of Tewkesbury.'

'So he must have fought on the same battlefield where my father was killed. It seems so long ago now. Did Sir Robert's father die in that battle, too, perhaps?'

Anthony looked uncertain. 'Well, he died in the same year but not in battle. At least I've never heard that, although I wasn't born until eight years later and no one told me much about my grandfather, even when I was old enough to understand. I suppose everything was in some turmoil during that period after King Edward died. That was when you fled here from London, wasn't it? And my mother took you in and you taught me to read. But you must remember more about it than I do, old lady.'

He leaned quickly away to dodge my indignant swipe at his arm. 'Cheeky man! I know your father had to tread carefully in order to keep the manors in the family; until he took the plunge and supported the late king's invasion.' I picked up my embroidery again. 'It was a tricky time for everyone, was it not? We are sailing in quieter waters now, Jesu be thanked.'

'We are, but they would be calmer if Queen Katherine could manage to birth a son. Word is that the king is getting more restless by the month.'

I nodded. 'By the menses you mean, or lack of them.

Poor lady, I feel so sorry for her. Only one four-year-old little girl to show for all her pregnancies! She has tried so hard for a male heir but has had to watch three boys come early or die soon after birth. It is a terrible shame.' With all my heart I mourned for her and them but secretly thanked the saints that I had not been at those births and deaths, as I had for many of Queen Elizabeth's.

'You make it sound as if her fertile days are over. Do you know something the rest of us don't?'

'Don't forget that Lina served her mistress in the most intimate of ways,' I said. 'That's all I'll say for her sake, and we should not spread rumours. What she told me was in strict confidence.'

Lina had settled in well at Acton Court. At first the rest of the servants had been rather suspicious of her but luckily Matt the cook had been apprenticed in the kitchen of a public house on Bristol harbour and become familiar with the African sailors who came in off the merchant venturers' ships, which traded ivory and cotton from the west coast of that newly discovered continent. Being a friendly man he had often shared a jug of ale with them and helped them with their English so that he could learn more about their life stories. He and Lina had quickly become friends and that had smoothed her path through the less amenable members of the household. In fact since Matt was not married I had great hopes of more than mere friendship between him and Lina.

'You like Lina, don't you, Joan? Engaging her was one of your inspired actions.' Anthony leaned over my embroidery frame and kissed my cheek. 'I love it that you're content here at Acton Court. I've long wanted to live here myself because the place holds such happy memories of my childhood and my beautiful mother.'

I caught his hand and squeezed it. 'And then you were sent to live with us in Kent. You must have been homesick.'

He lifted my hand and kissed it. 'But you know I was not. Your house was like a home from home and Sir Richard was a great knight to learn chivalry from. No one mourned his sorry end more than I did – except you and his family of course.'

I laid the embroidery frame aside again, letting my other hand lie contentedly in his. 'I think we were all bewildered by it. It was so tragic, so grotesque. I was never able to forgive the king for the way he was treated. Edward is building that tower to defend Rye, you know; the one that caused Richard's downfall. I believe it is nearly finished.'

'Yes, it's ironic really. If Richard had only built it and not invested the money in Sir Henry Wyatt's mortgage scheme instead he might still be alive. But then we would never have married, Joan, and I would never have been so happy as I am now.'

'Hmm.' My mouth twisted in distaste. 'I'd rather not hear Wyatt's name mentioned at all in my presence, let alone consider him responsible for our happiness. I don't even care whether or not he is still alive. I'm just pleased to be out of his orbit – and in yours.' I laid my head on his shoulder. 'I'm so pleased that Margaret and John are happily married and you have arranged for Nick to join the henchmen at Berkeley Castle next year. It will be good for him to be with other boys and not too far from home. Mary will miss him though. We'll have to bring some other girls into the Court to keep her company.'

'Yes, but first there's the matter of my father's imminent demise. He says he wants to be interred in the Gaunt chapel in Bristol; the one that he financed and designed. I'd rather he was buried in the Poyntz chapel in Iron Acton. That's where I'd choose to lie but his wishes must be followed, I suppose.'

'But the Gaunt chapel is where Lady Meg is lying and they had a long and happy marriage, did they not? I'm not surprised that he wants to be with her there.'

'Would you like to be buried beside me, Lady Poyntz?'

I could hear a note of amusement and hope in his voice and lifted my head from his shoulder to catch his eye. 'Don't you think it's you who might be given the choice of being interred beside me? Anyway it's not a race and perhaps we should bury your father first.'

Sir Robert died peacefully in his sleep in early November, just after the ghostly celebrations of All Souls and All Saints. He was carried on a hearse through the villages of South Gloucestershire to Bristol and interred as he had wished in the vault below the beautiful new Gaunt Chapel, where the coats of arms of his immediate family were moulded in plaster on the central ceiling boss and the floor tiles had been imported from Spain to celebrate his long service as Chancellor and then Chamberlain in Katherine of Aragon's household. All his brothers and sisters, children and grand-children who lived within reach attended the service of interment and many of them returned with us to Acton Court for a spread of funeral meats and drink. It was the first time I had attended such a gathering of Poyntz relatives and I found it rather daunting but happily they all dispersed early in the afternoon, not wishing to ride home in the dark.

When we had waved the last of them off, Anthony and I both heaved a sigh and relaxed into relieved laughter, somewhat to the surprise of the two young Poyntz children. 'Are you supposed to laugh at a funeral?' asked the heir Nicholas, who had preserved a solemn countenance throughout the proceedings. 'You told me not to tell any jokes, Father.'

Anthony wiped the smile from his face and put his arm around his son's shoulder. 'I just did not want you playing the fool, as I know you can; especially to your uncle John, who is quite a solemn soul and holds several Poyntz manors not far from here. There may come a time when you are lord of the Iron Acton estate and might regret having once told him silly jokes as a boy. You can tell me as many as you like, but not him, all right?' He winked at his beloved son. 'Now go with Mary and finish off the buffet, while Mother Joan and I take a walk of recovery through the gardens.'

Before she became ill, Lady Meg had installed a classic Tudor garden near the house, with hedged parterres packed with red and white roses and set about with striped wooden poles surmounted by a variety of colourful carved heraldic emblems: the red Welsh dragon, the Tudor Rose, the pink pomegranate of Spain, the English lion rampant, the spotted Beaufort yale and the white greyhound of Richmond. It reminded me of Lady Margaret Beaufort's intensely Tudor garden at Colleyweston.

At first sight I had thought it strange that a lady of

Woodville blood should take such trouble to openly declare a Tudor allegiance but Sir Robert had explained that his wife had always been grateful to Henry Tudor for establishing a period of relative calm in England, which had allowed her to rear their family in peace after the fear and tumult of the usurper's domination, which had begun with the summary beheading of her father, Earl Rivers.

'Ours was a love match, you know, Joan, like yours and Anthony's. Acton Court flourishes under such occupiers.' It was the nearest Sir Robert had ever come to admitting approval of our lop-sided marriage and now, as we walked through the garden after his death, I was glad to have had his blessing.

We paused by the fountain at the centre and I surprised my husband by taking his hand and dropping into a deep curtsy before kissing it. 'What are you doing?' he asked with a puzzled frown.

'Pledging my allegiance to the new lord of the manor,' I said, looking up at him solemnly. 'I believe it is customary.'

With an amused smile he bent to take my elbow and raise me up. 'You make me feel like a king, Joan! And at coronations, fealty is confirmed by a kiss on the lips. I would rather have that.' So he took it and lingered long in the taking. When it ended I was breathless.

'Now,' he resumed, tucking my arm in his elbow, 'let us leave all this formal glory and wander further afield. I have something to show you before it gets too dark.'

In the late afternoon light the autumn leaves glowed red and yellow and warm brown as we passed through the orchards, where only a few medlar fruits hung on gnarled branches, waiting to become rotten before being picked and preserved for winter eating. The other fruit trees – apples, pears, and cherries – had surrendered all their treasures and merely showed a few leaves that had so far survived the autumn winds. The sheds and cellars of Acton Court were full of fruit and preserves we had harvested to last us through the winter.

I knew where Anthony was taking me but not why. Beyond these fenced orchards was another hedged garden, which I had visited during the late queen's summer pilgrimage a few months before she died. She had come to Acton Court to refresh her acquaintance with her cousin Lady Meg, but she had spent each evening gambling at cards with Anthony, to whom she took a great shine. When I escaped to the orchard with a book while the queen rested, Anthony had sought me out. I remembered asking after his new wife, yet another Elizabeth, who was absent due to the imminent birth of her first child. His candour in confessing his disappointment in his marriage had disturbed me and I had tried to give him advice, with little hope that it would help. Then he had shown me a nest of ravens in some conifers at the far end of a rather overgrown rose garden.

When we reached it this time, the same garden proved to be even more tangled and mysterious than the last time I was there and only a few stray rose blooms remained on the stalk to send their fragrance out into the evening air. We both managed to catch our clothes on thorns as we fought our way through to the far end and there, looking fresh and newly painted a dark green, was the surprise I had been promised.

What was once a neat hedge of hazel and field maple running along one side of the garden had been neglected over the years and its plants had grown into quite tall trees. Half-hidden among these was a wooden construction, which resembled what soldiers called a belfry, used in sieges to attack the top of a castle wall. A series of short ladders led up through the branches of a maple to a small square timber house secured at the top, with an overhanging roof that sheltered what looked like a shuttered oriel window at the front.

'What is it?' I asked, moving nearer but none the wiser.

'It's a bit like a crow's-nest on a ship but I call it a "hide",' Anthony replied. 'If you sit up there in a few weeks you'll be able to watch the ravens brooding their eggs.'

I gazed at him in surprise. 'Do they still come here to breed? The same birds?'

He nodded, a wide grin splitting his face. 'Yes! But before they arrived this year I had a couple of ship's carpenters come from Bristol and build this tree house so that you could climb up level with their nest and watch them. I think they should be returning to the nest quite soon. Do you want to try it out?'

I threw my arms around his neck and we shared a brief kiss, because I couldn't wait to make the climb. 'Oh, thank you, Anthony, thank you! Yes, of course I do! I was always so jealous of Sim and Hal being able to climb the conifers at Halden and count the ravens' eggs.'

'You go first then and I'll catch you if you fall. But I know you won't.'

I felt like a young girl again as I hitched up my skirts and tucked them into my belt, before setting off up the four short ladders that led through the branches and around the trunk of a field maple, still burning with bright red autumn leaves. On the way up I marvelled at the way the carpenters had taken the trouble to embellish the sides of the ladders with little carved dormice, baby owls, and other woodland creatures, although I suspected that the idea might have been Anthony's. At the top an arched wooden door, similarly embellished, opened into the observing room, where a bench was set before a barrier beneath a pair of closed shutters. I opened them slowly and carefully in case the ravens had returned.

Anthony entered quickly behind me and we squeezed onto the bench together. We were directly opposite and perhaps less than a dozen yards away from the nest, which the birds had built among the higher branches of a pine tree, carefully hidden against predators from above and below but satisfyingly visible to us.

'This is utterly brilliant, Anthony,' I whispered. 'Are you sure the ravens won't know we're here? It would be terrible if we scared them away after you've gone to all this trouble.'

He put his finger to his lips and murmured, 'They won't leave, Joan, don't worry. And you might need this.' He handed me something cold and metallic; it looked like a polished tube, with spectacle lenses set into either end. 'It's called a spyglass and no self-respecting ship's captain should be without one.'

I put it to my right eye and gasped, 'I'm practically inside the nest! If only I'd had one of these when I lived in the Tower of London.'

'It's brilliant, isn't it? And a very new invention.' Anthony sounded slightly smug. 'I won it off a Genoese sailor playing cards in Bristol.'

As I moved the extraordinary instrument around the

rather chaotic nest, apparently built of sticks and leaves and bones and feathers, I picked out odd treasure that the ravens must have stolen from around Acton Court: a shard of broken pottery, a red ribbon, a wax seal, and even a shiny bodkin, which looked rather a dangerous implement to leave around fledglings. However, as yet there was no sign of eggs.

Then, within a few minutes, I heard a familiar 'kaark-kaark' from somewhere above the pine tree and a large black shape swooped across the lens onto the nest. I felt a thrill of excitement and lowered the spyglass briefly to cast a look of silent wonder at Anthony. For the first time in years, I was face to face with a raven.

GLOSSARY

---

attire: a knight's complete set of arms and armour for war or jousting

braies: male underwear, worn under the hose

curtain: the high defending wall surrounding a fortress

chrisom veil: a muslin cloth infused with holy oil and used in christenings

clerestory: church upper story set with clear-glass windows to light the nave

comptroller: auditor of accounts

frontlet: female headwear, a silk panel tied across the hairline and under a hood

lappethood: type of female headdress with long decorative side flaps

kirtle: a long-sleeved dress shown under an open and sleeveless or loose-sleeved robe

March: Name given to border lands between two countries or kingdoms

marchpane: a form of marzipan

oriel: a jutting window aligned to catch the sun

penthouse: a lean-to netted viewing stand attached to a real tennis court; it's roof, shortened to '**pent**' is also used as a 'slope', off which to serve the ball

pillion: a passenger seat buckled on the back of a horse's saddle

pollarded: a de-crowned tree; branches re-grow to remain in permanent reach

poniard: a short, sharp dagger

retinue: group word for servants or followers of a knight, noble or monarch

rocker: a nursery nurse hired specifically to rock the cradle

stole: in the 15th century more of a warm shawl than a bishop's stole of today

subtletie: the name given to an edible moulded image, paraded at feasts

sumpter: a packhorse

trencher: a wooden plate or thick bread slice on which food was placed

trestle: support for a plank table-top; also refers to both together

ward: a child in crown custody – father killed or captive or in prison

wherry/wherries: flat-bottomed sail-boat/s used for off-loading cargo

White Tower: the main keep of the Tower of London. It was painted with white lime-wash to preserve the stones

wickner: an officer charged with collecting the manor lord's dues and fines

yeoman: a smallholder – not landed enough to be 'gentry'; cf. King Henry VII's Yeomen of the Guard

AUTHOR'S NOTES

Even before I started writing about her, I became more and more aware from my research that Joan Vaux was worth more than just one book. Certainly, after *The Lady of the Ravens* was published, it became clear from the reviews that numerous readers found her story and her character interesting and were eager to discover what happened to her next. However, because I realise that some readers are apt to read the 'Extras' at the end of a book before diving into the story itself, I hesitate to reveal too much of Joan's life after *The Lady of the Ravens*. All I can say to them is that I hope you might already have enjoyed reading some of the ups and downs of her varied career during the early Tudor years and are keen for more!

Because there was so much more to Joan than her career in royal service and although, as the title suggests, she continues to serve several queens, I very much wanted to take her on into her second marriage, which historians treat as merely a footnote in her life, even though it lasted longer and probably made her happier than the first. History is vague about exactly when it started and even about the year of her second husband's death, except that ironically, despite him being considerably younger than her, it was at least three and perhaps five years earlier than Joan's, which was not until 1538, at the age of seventy-five. A grand life for anyone at this time in history!

So even for some thirteen years after this book ends, I imagine her living as a happy Lady of the Manor; while at the Royal Court, her former charge, King Henry the Eighth is causing mayhem, seeking divorce from Queen Katherine of Aragon and both marrying and beheading his second queen, Anne Boleyn, while dismissing the Catholic Church and dissolving the monasteries, to none of which I'm certain Joan would have given her approval! So much has already been written and discussed about that part of England's history that I decided not to add my pennyworth and to leave Joan happy at Acton Court, in her handsome, red-brick manor house, much of which still stands today and, coincidentally, happens to be only a few miles down the road from my home and thus forms part of the inspiration for this book.

If you have already done so, thanks for reading it, and if you liked it, please spread the word. And stay with me, as I have more fascinating fifteenth-century lives in sight!

Best wishes,

Joanna

ACKNOWLEDGEMENTS

Luckily, I had visited all the necessary research locations for this novel before the pandemic locked us all down, so I will begin by thanking the people who helped me access them. The Tower of London was more prominent in *The Lady of the Ravens*, but I should mention once again the help I had from the Press Office at Historic Royal Palaces in accessing its hallowed walls and iconic birds! Had the royal palaces of Richmond and Greenwich remained as they were in Joan's lifetime, no doubt the same people would also have helped me access those locations, but instead I had to use the internet and my medieval-filled imagination in bringing them back to life.

I lived in Edinburgh and its environs for over 30 years before moving back to England, so, fortunately, I had visited the castles and countryside mentioned in Joan's foray into Scotland in the train of Margaret Tudor, Queen of Scots. Little is known or documented about Lady Margaret Beaufort's 'palace' of Colleyweston but, knowing her character, I have assumed that it was built and furnished to the peak of medieval luxury, and described it accordingly.

Which brings me to Joan's own life in Kent, where I was lucky to encounter several very kind and helpful people. I was amazed and very happy to find that Frensham Manor still exists. I visited the house without any appointment on a very wet day and cheekily rang the doorbell. So I heartily thank the owner, Rob Pursey, who not only showed me around, but described in detail all the original parts of the building that would have been there in Joan's time and pointed out those that would not.

Up the road in the town of Rolvenden, the church of St Mary the Virgin still stands and remains almost as it was in the fifteenth century, except I can't believe that the people who attended it weekly then were as obliging and friendly as the ladies whose Saturday flower-arranging session I so rudely interrupted with all my questions. My thanks go to them all through the person of Judy Vinson, whose official title is the Reader, but who struck me as a lady of many parts and skills.

As did Carol Groom, Warden at the Church of St James the Less in the village of Iron Acton in South Gloucestershire. In the Poyntz chapel there is an unoccupied medieval canopied tomb, surely erected for an unnamed member of the family, which caused me to make Anthony Poyntz wish to be buried there. And he might well have been, but with the Dissolution and Reformation coming so soon afterwards, no one dared to have his image carved in stone.

Incidentally, the Poyntz mansion, Acton Court, is located only a few miles from my home and stands somewhat reduced but still proud in its redbrick glory. I have visited the house for several of the events put on there to bring the Tudor period back to life and managed to consult the fascinating book of its history, gleaning precious details of the Poyntz family and its activities, for all of which I am very grateful to the volunteers who preserve and staff it.

My thanks also go to Craig Bruun who showed me

around Allington Castle near Maidstone. Sir Henry Wyatt bought it in a semi-ruined state at the end of the fifteenth century and raised a family there – a family that included Sir Thomas Wyatt, the famous Tudor poet. I wonder whether in order to make his castle habitable Sir Henry might have used some of the money Sir Richard Guildford was granted to build a fortress at Rye? In recent years, Allington has been revived and renovated by Sir Robert Worcester and a brilliant job has been made of it.

Not least, I thank and salute my long-standing editor Kate Bradley for orchestrating the writing, production and publication of *The Queen's Lady* and the wonderful team at HarperFiction for the hard work they have all done under the trying circumstances dictated by a series of pandemic lockdowns. They are: Chere Tricot, Editorial Assistant, Holly Macdonald, who has once again triumphed with a stunning cover design, Susan Opie for her careful copy edit, Terence Caven for his elegant map and family tree, and Emma Pickard for ensuring that Joan's story reaches the public she truly deserves!

I cannot finally sign out without thanking my friend and agent Jenny Brown, who has steered my writing career for more than ten years now and always with wise advice, a big hug and a smile!

I am clapping you all!

Joanna

Read on for an extract from the first in
The Queens of the Tower series

THE
LADY
OF THE
RAVENS

I

THE CART RUMBLED PAST so close that it almost killed me. I was forced to flatten myself against the gatehouse wall or I would surely have been crushed before I had even entered the Tower of London. Limewash and mortar flaked off the masonry, smearing my gown with white dust. Then suddenly, above the diminishing sound of rolling wheels and clattering hooves, I heard the rasping 'kwaark' of a raven and a childhood memory rushed in to swamp my senses. I became my nine-year-old self, trembling under the gaze of a large black bird with a bill like the hook of a soldier's halberd and an eye that could pierce the soul. Then that fearsome beak had opened to emit a hoarse cry, bringing tears to my eyes, and I heard the gravelly voice of my escort, an elderly knight from the Tower's garrison.

'Think yourself honoured, young mistress. The ravens avoid us men because the archers use them for target practice. But there is a legend, which says that as long as they haunt the Tower, it and the kingdom will stand. Just lately they've been coming and going, so perhaps there's something in it.' At the time I didn't understand what he meant but so vividly had the raven's image imprinted itself in my mind, that the incident and his words had remained with me ever since.

Now thirteen years later another cart, heaped high and shedding fragments of its cargo as it juddered over the cobbles, made me press even harder against the wall and my heart thudded as a real raven was suddenly there at my feet, rushing in with a triumphant flap of feathers to peck up a speck of shiny discarded metal that glimmered in the gatehouse gloom. My daydream dissolved into reality. The carts were carrying gold and silver scrap to the Royal Mint and the raven scampered away with its booty, rising on beating wings as it cleared the archway. Hastening into the daylight, I watched it carry off its treasure, to secrete it somewhere high on the battlements.

I stood transfixed, admiring its fluid, swooping flight until an angry shout from behind alerted me. 'Hey! Clear the way! D'you want to get killed?' I jumped to the side again as another laden cart trundled past, the driver red-faced and yelling. 'God's blood, woman! There's no room for stupid skirts in here.'

Fearing more vehicles, I made a run for the gate at the other end of the moat bridge and took refuge through a door in an adjacent building, which I knew should contain the office of the man in charge. I felt in the purse on my belt and removed the letter within.

'Tell me, what business can a female possibly have in a military fortress?' The young Lieutenant Constable was hook-nosed and handsome, with all the hubris of noble privilege and not a hint of charm. He had given my letter barely a glance.

'I am on royal business, sir, as the letter says.' I held out my hand. 'May I have it back? I know where I am going.'

His eyes scanned the page and rested on the signature

at the bottom. 'Who is MR?' he asked, refolding the note and handing it to me.

I could have remarked that he should know but I desisted. 'Margaret, Countess of Richmond, is the king's mother – MR is her cypher.' Knowing the lady well, as I did, I reflected that it could equally be a monogram for 'Margaret Regina' but resisted the temptation to point this out.

He did not respond verbally but his curled lip and disapproving sniff were revealing. It was only weeks since Lady Margaret's son, Henry Tudor, had taken the throne 'by right and conquest', to become King Henry the Seventh of England and there were still plenty of dissenting Yorkists among minor royal officials. I didn't give this one many more days in his present post.

As I hurried along the narrow street between the twin curtain walls that defended the fortress from a river attack, I couldn't resist searching for more signs of ravens on the battlements of the main keep, which reared above me to my left. These enigmatic birds had haunted my dreams ever since I had made that first fearful childhood trip to the Tower to visit my mother. Whatever the men had said about it being no place for women, I could have begged to differ. My mother, Katherine Vaux, had lived within its intimidating walls for two years and the captive lady she had served there had once been Queen of England.

My grandfather, a doctor from Piedmont, had been physician to the Duke of Anjou's family and in her childhood my mother had been invited to join their schoolroom. When the duke's daughter Marguerite married King Henry the Sixth of England, she had travelled with her to his court and later married one of his household knights, Sir William

Vaux, becoming an English citizen. When civil war erupted and Edward of York snatched the throne, forcing King Henry and Queen Marguerite to flee their kingdom, my loyal Lancastrian parents escaped with my young brother Nicholas to my mother's birthplace in Piedmont. A few months later, I was born and baptised Giovanna, after my Italian grandmother.

My baptismal name may be Giovanna, but English is not a lyrical language like Italian is. Here in my mother's adopted country I have become plain Joan; and plain is what the English think me, as I am not pink-cheeked and gold-en-haired like the beauties they admire. I have olive skin and dark features – black brows over ebony eyes and hair the colour of a raven's wing. With my full lips and straight nose, many consider me odd, or probably, to put it bluntly, ugly. '*Jolie-laide*' is what the French used to call me, more kindly. Perhaps that is one reason why I habitually wear dark colours and am so drawn to the big black birds that haunt the cliff-like walls of the Tower and why, as I hastened to my meeting on that late September day, I was enraged at seeing one of the sentry archers on the battlements take aim at a raven as it flew close to his position on the roof of the Royal Palace. Luckily the arrow missed its target but I was still seething while I negotiated my way past another set of guards and into the fortress's intimidating limewashed keep, known as the White Tower.

'May I ask what a young lady like you is doing here?'

At least this time the inquiry was couched politely and came from a trimly bearded man of obvious status, wearing a furred gown, with a gold chain about his shoulders and a black hat pinned with a jewelled brooch. I had almost run into him in the gloom of the main troop-gathering hall, which was empty and echoing and lit only by the daylight filtering through a few high barred windows. Swallowing my first indignant riposte, I made him a brief curtsy.

'I've been sent by My Lady the King's Mother, sir.' Once again I offered my letter of charge.

'Have you indeed? Let me see.' In order to scan the script he had to squint and hold it up to what little light there was, then he made me a courteous bow. 'Welcome to the Tower of London, Mistress Vaux. I am Sir Richard Guildford, the king's Master of Ordnance, in charge of the guns and weapons that are held here. But I cannot believe they are relevant to your purpose. I see you are bidden to the Chapel of St John. For what reason, I wonder?'

I shook my head. 'We would both like to know the answer to that, Sir Richard, but it is a royal command, which one does not query.'

He inclined his head. 'Indeed.'

'I have a question for you though, sir.' I took a steadying breath before plunging on. 'If you are in charge of weapons, why are the archers wasting arrows, firing them at the ravens? What harm have they done?'

Even in the dim light I could see his cheeks flush and his next words were delivered with savage emphasis. 'Those ravens are the devil's demons – filthy scavengers and harbingers of death! All soldiers hate them and the archers are encouraged to use them for target practice. An arrow is retrievable, preferably with a dead bird attached.'

Or possibly a dead passer-by, I thought. I bit back any comment but he must have noticed my look of angry astonishment. I wondered how a man who lived and worked in the Tower could be ignorant of the widespread belief among Londoners that the presence of ravens was essential to the fortress's security and that of the city and the kingdom they inhabited. This folk legend and its subjects had stayed with me ever since I had heard it as a child from the old garrison knight and over the ensuing years I had made it my business to read whatever I could find on both the birds and the belief.

During the resulting silence he recovered his composure and gave me a brief smile. 'Now, Mistress Vaux, may I call someone to show you to the Chapel of St John?'

Although I could not bring myself to return the smile, I made an acknowledging bob. 'Thank you, Sir Richard, but I know the way.'

I sensed his puzzled gaze following me to the foot of the long stair. Like all castle chapels, it was situated above the other chambers, giving prayers a clear path to heaven, and on other visits to my mother and the captive queen I had made the climb to the top of the White Tower to find them at Mass. On this occasion two Ushers of the King's Chamber were there still wearing the blue and murrey household livery issued under the Yorkist kings, along with an assortment of other men in civilian dress. I was acquainted with one of the ushers, a landed squire called Nicholas Gainsford, and as soon as I arrived he began lecturing us on how anything we saw or heard that morning was to be considered a state secret and revealed to no one; everything had to be committed to memory and nothing written down. Having calmed my alarm on behalf of the ravens, I felt my heart flutter anew at Usher Gainsford's stern admonishments.

Bizarrely, the frame of a large bedstead had been erected

in the chapel nave and it was to this that he proceeded to direct our attention, impatiently beckoning us to gather around it. I received curious glances from the strange men as we jostled for position, aware that the presence of a woman was perplexing to them. Not for the first time I wondered what I was doing there myself.

'You are all here to learn precisely how to make the king's bed,' the usher continued, as if reading my mind. 'At present his grace is living at his manor of Kennington, a small palace over the river, which is easily secured and presently inhabited only by people well known to him and sworn to his affinity. But after his coronation he will be living in many larger royal palaces including the one located here, within the Tower of London. Such buildings are a warren of chambers, passages and staircases, containing many entrances and large numbers of people – not easy to keep secure. So when King Henry inhabits these palaces, or visits the homes of his favoured subjects, he will always have his own secure royal quarters, an area known as the Privy Chamber. Only trusted subjects who have sworn an oath of allegiance will be admitted into this reserved area, which will contain all the rooms necessary for his ease and comfort, where he can consult with his advisers and councillors in certain knowledge that what is said and done within its walls will go no further. And of course the most important of these rooms is that in which the king takes his rest – his bedchamber.'

He let his gaze roam over the gathering. 'You men have been appointed Yeomen of the Guard of the Body of our Lord the King and, apart from protecting the king wherever he goes, an important part of your duties will be to make the monarch's bed daily. To ensure that it is clean and comfortable and, most importantly, free of any hazard from hidden blades, poisonous plants, or biting insects that might cause him ill, injury or irritation. And naturally, when his grace marries he will want his queen's rest to be as free from danger and discomfort as his own; therefore we have a lady here with us.' My eyes flicked nervously about as everyone turned in my direction. 'Mistress Vaux is charged with relaying all that she sees and hears to the sworn women of the bedchamber of his eventual bride. Before you leave today, all of you will be required to take an oath of loyalty before the Lord Chamberlain of the King's Household.'

Having long lived under Lady Margaret Beaufort's roof, I was probably already as familiar as any there with the best way to prepare a bedstead for the nobility but Usher Gainsford was taking no chances with royal security. He literally started from scratch, feeling with the tips of his fingers and scraping with his nails all the way around the wooden bedframe and headboard, looking for any crack or crevice where something sharp or noxious might be hidden. Then he ordered one of the men to strip to his chemise and hose and, to the obvious amusement of his fellow yeomen, roll around on the thick rush mat spread over the ropes, to test it for needles, thorns or twigs.

'A sharpened twig soaked in the juice of deadly nightshade berries can work its way through to the sleeper, who falls into a stupor from which he does not wake,' he warned, then lifted the straw mattress and dramatically sliced open the end with a sharp knife. 'You need to distinguish between the different plants used to stuff this layer. Ladies' bedstraw is best and this one,' he picked out a dried stem with leaves larger than the rest, 'is called woodruff and has a scent like freshly mown hay.' He picked up a handful of the stuffing and peered closely at it. 'This mattress should be opened and refilled and all feather beds shaken and checked regularly. Some of you yeomen will be appointed Keepers of the Wardrobe of the Beds, in charge of storing the royal bedclothes in locked and insect-proof chests every day and responsible for ensuring that a record is taken of when checks are made.'

One of the men spoke up. 'In view of these precautions, sir, how would anyone manage to corrupt the royal bed? If everything is so carefully locked away and checked and the Privy Chambers are restricted to sworn servants, it does not seem very likely.'

Usher Gainsford cleared his throat and a flush stained his cheeks. 'One of a yeoman's duties is to report any hint of a colleague failing in his loyalty. You have all been chosen because you are known to be staunch Lancastrians but King Henry is anxious to unite the country, bringing York and Lancaster together under his rule and the Tudor name, ending the recent years of strife. So it is to him and the family he intends to have that his household will swear allegiance and obedience. This will be a Tudor reign and in due course, God willing, a Tudor dynasty but to begin with this may not content everyone. Dissidents may contrive to be appointed to the royal household. Treachery can emerge anywhere. You, as individuals, will be responsible for reporting anyone criticising the Tudor reign, or showing the slightest preference for another house, to the Lord Chamberlain or his deputy.'

I had no great sympathy with dissidents, having lost my father to a Yorkist army fourteen years ago, but I found this last order bittersweet as I took my oath of loyalty and I hoped I would not be expected to observe and report on the new queen's commitment to the Tudor dynasty that she would be expected to provide. Officially, six weeks into his reign, we still did not know the identity of King Henry's eventual queen, although the fact that his mother had selected me to attend this meeting strongly suggested that it would be the young lady currently living under her roof at her palace of Coldharbour on the banks of the River Thames.

Elizabeth of York, to whom I had almost inadvertently become servant, companion and friend, was the eldest child of King Edward the Fourth and the princess Henry Tudor had vowed to marry in order to boost support for his ultimately successful expedition to establish his own claim to the throne of England. But this had only happened after Edward died unexpectedly and his two young sons were brought to the Tower's Royal Palace to await the elder boy's coronation as King Edward the Fifth. This was because their uncle Richard, Duke of Gloucester, apparently unprepared to act as mere Protector to a boy king, contrived to get parliament to declare them illegitimate and to have himself crowned instead. Within weeks the York boys had disappeared from public view and two years later the usurping king, who as their Protector must surely have known what happened to them, had died fighting Henry Tudor's invading army without revealing their fate.

From my staunch Lancastrian viewpoint, I considered the York history a chequered one; however it also greatly concerned me that Elizabeth and her mother and sisters might never discover when or how the two young princes died – if die indeed they both had. As I left the White Tower I paused to gaze up at the windows of the adjacent Royal Palace where the princes had been accommodated and in which soldiers and other Tower residents had reported catching occasional glimpses of their small, pale faces – until all sightings mysteriously ceased.

Although his victory in battle against the usurper Richard had brought King Henry to the throne, I was aware that it must also have left him with an urgent need to feel secure on it and a strong sense that he was not. Several leading Yorkist knights and nobles, captured after the battle, were now incarcerated in towers around the fortress and might expect to lose their heads as traitors to the new crown. However, peering through the open gate in the wall, which led onto the green beside the castle's Church of St Nicholas, I could see that no scaffold had yet been erected there. Instead, bowmen had set up butts and were using them to hone their archery skills.

Remembering Sir Richard Guildford's vehement comment that all soldiers detested ravens, I became anxious when one of them landed on the gateway arch. Within moments I heard the threatening zing of an arrow and intuitively ducked, as it seemed almost to skim my headdress. My heart skipped several beats but relief flooded my veins when I saw the raven fly off and the arrow drop harmlessly over the outer curtain wall, presumably into the moat.

'Devilish bird!' I heard an archer shout. 'I'll get you next time.'

ENJOY MORE RICH AND COMPELLING NOVELS FROM JOANNA HICKSON

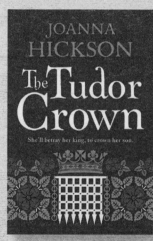

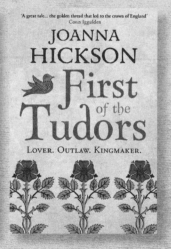

ALL AVAILABLE NOW